FIRESIDE SEDUCTION

Kent slid down to sit in front of the fire, resting his back against the rock. He winked and patted the ground next to him. "Come here, Miss Charly."

Charly didn't allow herself time to think. She just rose and hesitantly stepped over to stand in front of him. He reached out, running his hand up the calf of her bare leg. She quivered like a flighty filly. An intense longing immediately filled her, yet she stood ready to bolt. What was wrong? She'd dreamt of being in his arms again. This was what she wanted. Wasn't it?

Taking hold of her hands, Kent tugged gently. She swallowed, then stiffly sank down on the hard ground. She didn't resist when he pulled her over and settled her next to his solid frame.

If she was smart, Charly thought, she'd bound quicker'n a leapfrog ta the other side of the fire. 'Cause if'n she stayed . . .

As if sensing her sudden indecision, Kent lowered his head and took her lips in a deep, searing kiss. The moment his lips touched hers, Charly's resolve weakened. Conscious thought of wriggling from his molten embrace evaporated like morning fog in the heat of his delicious assault. Lordy, it felt good . . .

JUDITH STEEL

ARIZONA HEAT

ZEBRA BOOKS
KENSINGTON PUBLISHING CORP.

To my husband,
Curtis,
my real-life cowboy.

ZEBRA BOOKS

are published by

Kensington Publishing Corp.
475 Park Avenue South
New York, NY 10016

First printing: November, 1992

Printed in the United States of America

Chapter One

January, 1861

"Hold up there, you son of a belly-crawlin' horned toad!"

Charly McAllister squinted her eyes as she peered at the two-legged sidewinder through the lone cracked window of the Tucson stage station. The man hesitated, his head moving like a wind vane in a dust devil. When his face turned directly toward her, she sucked in her breath. It *was* him! That stage-robbing polecat. The varmint had a lot of gall to show himself so brazenly in town.

Her scuffed boots clomped across the packed dirt floor as she grabbed her flop-brimmed hat from the peg by the door and jammed it on her head. Her eyes were still trained out the small window, watching the progress of the owlhoot, when she barreled into a tall, broad figure that suddenly filled the doorway.

Careening off the hard-as-iron body, she spun in a circle. She was about to apologize, but she caught sight of her prey scurrying back toward the stables. With a tremendous push, she shoved the big form out of her way. Rushing into the street, she bellowed, "Stop, you lily-livered varmint!"

The son of a horned toad stopped, all right, but

when he saw her charging after him like a long-horned bull chasing a slinking coyote, she reckoned it must've scared him. He whirled in his high-heeled boots and made for the nearest horse quicker than an old maid could crawl under a bed.

The horse shied, but the man had the reins untied and vaulted into the saddle before the animal could roll its eyes. Both horse and rider were soon swallowed in a cloud of dust, leaving Charly fuming and sputtering and spitting sand.

She shook her fist in the air. "Dang nab it! You ain't gonna get away this time." Then, dejectedly, she dropped her arm to her side. She might as well be threatening the puffy white clouds in the sky. Her darned horse was clear down at the stables 'n' . . . Hold it! Hadn't there been . . .

She slanted a hopeful glance back toward a big black stallion she thought she'd glimpsed hitched to one of the station's posts when she'd made her hasty stampede from the station. Yeah! Exhilaration replaced feelings of defeat and propelled her feet as she ran back the way she'd come.

But she was wise enough to slow her steps as she neared the beautiful animal, not to spook it. The stallion snorted, but stood quietly while she untied it, almost as if it was used to someone making quick departures. Well-oiled reins felt thick and smooth in her hand and she was preparing to swing into the fancy tooled saddle when she noticed a movement from the corner of her eye.

The man whom she'd run into earlier was peeling his long, lean length from the adobe wall. Fleeting images of a black broadcloth suit, sparkling clean white linen shirt, and black string tie registered in her brain as she went ahead and grabbed the saddle horn, swinging into the hard leather seat without bothering to use the stirrups.

She was about to turn her head when her gaze

6

locked with a pair of eyes that reminded her quite suddenly of thick brown velvet. A mustache and long sideburns accentuated one of the most ruggedly handsome faces she'd seen in a long time.

But then he raised his hand. His thin lips parted and with a horrified expression he ran toward her, hurling curses and shouting at her to return his horse.

The spell was broken and she kicked the stallion into a gallup, quickly forgetting the good-looking stranger as she choked on dust stirred by the escaping *bandito*. Panic scorched through her when she saw he had almost a quarter of a mile lead.

Kent Ashford stood in the center of the small, mostly Mexican town of Tucson. Consumed with anger, he watched his horse—and, more importantly, his saddlebags—hightailing it into the rough desert countryside.

His index finger traced the snake-like scar at the corner of his left eye while he uttered a string of ungentlemanly curses. No one stole Kent Leland Ashford's belongings and got away with it. Especially some bully of a snot-nosed brat.

Nervous stamping drew his attention to a long-legged sorrel gelding hitched in front of a single-story adobe building a few hundred yards west of the Butterfield Overland Mail station. A quick glance around the street revealed that most of the bystanders who'd been drawn by the commotion were whispering amongst themselves and gradually seeking shade beneath the overhangs in front of several businesses.

What the hell! He'd have the sorrel back before its owner knew it was missing. How long could it take to catch the damned kid? And when he did, that youngster would get a well-deserved butt-kicking.

* * *

Charly reveled in the feel of a half-ton of powerful, straining muscles surging between her legs as she guided the horse over the rolling yucca- and cactus-studded plain. She loved horses and loved to ride them, but lately all she'd seen were the tail ends on teams of scrawny mules.

But this . . . this wonderful stallion . . . Oh, he was something. He responded easily to every nudge of her knees or the slightest pressure on the bit. What she wouldn't give just to have the money to breed and raise such an animal.

All the while she enjoyed the ride, her eyes never left the puffs of dust rising steadily in front of her. With each tremendous stride, the stallion was gaining. He ran effortlessly, his short, pointed ears pricked forward. He seemed to think of the chase as no more than a game, as if the hot sun and physical exertion weren't even lathering his gorgeous black hide.

Suddenly, the other rider yanked his horse to a bouncing, clod-throwing halt and turned in the saddle. A bullet whined over her head and Charly ducked low in the saddle. But she refused to stop. The *bandito* fired again. She felt a tug on the top of her shoulder, but never flinched.

Clumps of tall grass, snakeweed, and saguaro cactus flashed by the wayside. Suddenly, a tangle of fallen soap tree yucca trunks loomed ahead, blocking the way. Excitement throbbed through her body as she leaned forward, tightening the reins. The horse's muscles bunched beneath her as he gathered his huge body to make the jump. Charly felt as if she were soaring into the heavens as they cleared the landfall by a good foot.

The stallion landed with only the slightest jar and Charly reached down to pat his neck. Suddenly,

8

ground squirrel dens crumbled beneath the animal's heavy weight. The stallion stumbled, then scrambled for footing. With her body arched over the animal's front shoulder, Charly couldn't keep her balance and fell forward, into the path of the struggling horse.

She looked up. Sun glinted off iron shoes as wild brown eyes surrounded by glistening white frantically searched downward. Intense pain stabbed into her temple when a thrashing hoof glanced off the side of her head. Stars exploded behind her eyes a second before a black cloud descended.

Kent was only a few hundred yards behind the kid when he, too, saw the other rider stop and pull a gun. He shouted for the kid to watch out, but the damned hardhead continued his full-speed charge. As Kent watched, he felt an undeniable, if reluctant, twinge of admiration.

The lad was determined, hell-bent on finding trouble. And he could ride. The kid's leather leggings hugged the saddle as if he were a part of the rigging. He guided the big horse with a natural ease and ability.

But then the fool had the temerity to take the stallion over a deadfall of yucca. For a couple of heart-stopping seconds, Kent held his breath, only releasing it when they'd cleared the obstacle. But . . . the horse stumbled. The pair floundered, then the boy pitched over the horse's left shoulder.

Kent saw the flailing hoof descending, but was too far away to do anything to stop it. The stallion's front hoof struck the kid, felling him like a poleaxed steer. Kent's gut churned as he rode alongside the criss-crossed tangle of long, gray yucca trunks covered with dead, grass-like leaves. Dead. Like the lad? Yet he cast one longing look after the escaping stallion and the flapping saddlebags.

Indecision continued to war within his breast until he grudgingly glanced down and saw the blood splotching the kid's head and shoulder. "Damn it to hell!" The sorrel, plunging beneath him while he made up his mind, was finally pulled under control as he dismounted.

"If you're not dead, I'll wring your neck," he grumbled.

The kid lay on his side and Kent knelt at his back. No matter his words, his touch was gentle when he felt for a pulse. There! Beneath the soft, smooth flesh he found a steady throb.

Kent's hand jerked back as if he'd suddenly been scalded. Soft, smooth flesh? Good God!

Disconcerted, he reached down again, this time intent on removing the kid's hat—without touching any part of his body—to see the extent of the damage done to that hard noggin. He tugged and the brim bent in his hand. His lips compressed into a thin line. No wonder the boy acted like a half-wit. The hat was so damned tight it cut off circulation to the brain.

Kent tugged again, more determined than ever.

The sudden jolt to her pounding head caused Charly to groan. Her hand fluttered weakly upward to find someone yanking at her hat. "No-o-o." Her throaty voice trembled slightly and she winced at the smallest vibration.

Gritting his teeth at the upstairs-maid-quality of the lad's voice, Kent decided he'd been too long without a woman, a fact he'd rectify immediately upon his return to Tucson. Meanwhile, he had started something here, and would damn well finish it. "Come on, kid. I need to take a look at that bump on your head."

"No-o-o," Charly protested. The deep, masculine voice was unfamiliar, yet she sensed the man's concern and wasn't afraid. She just didn't want him touching her again. The cool feel of his fingers

10

against the side of her neck still left a faint tingle that bothered her something fierce.

Rocking back on his heels, Kent frowned. A small amount of blood stained the kid's shirt and there was a long gouge in the leather where a bullet had torn its path. But the fool moved awkwardly out of reach before Kent could see if the wound was serious.

"Told ya. Leave me be."

Kent's good intentions fizzled. Damned smart ass. If he couldn't appreciate a little help, Kent would leave him all right and go after the horse, like he'd been tempted to do in the first place.

He rose to his feet, but before he took even one step to remount the sorrel gelding, thundering hooves showered dust and sand over them both. Kent spun, his left hand reaching for his pistol. Embarrassed, he curled his fingers over the butt. He'd been so intent on the kid that he'd failed to hear the riders approaching. His concentration had slipped. He couldn't afford to become so lax. Not now.

"You may pull that gun, señor, but drop eet to thee side. Reel eesy. You are een my custody for thief of the *caballo*." A dark, slender man sporting a handlebar mustache and pointed beard held his long-barreled pistol on Kent.

Hearing the kid whisper "Constable Ortega," Kent experienced a peculiar itch and constriction at the base of his throat. That term, the one he understood all too well as *horse thief*, could be fatal. Anger at his predicament, and at the kid for causing the complicated situation, boiled to the surface. His short-fused temper had been tamped down longer than usual, anyway.

"Then, by damn, you better arrest this . . . this . . ." He didn't want to look at the skinny excuse for a kid, but he did. And the blood and the dirt-smudged cheeks and the soulful green eyes pricked him in a place that hadn't felt compassion or tenderness in a

11

long, long time. He didn't realize the volume of his voice had lowered significantly as he continued, ". . . kid, too." He might feel sorry for the lad, but Kent Ashford wasn't going to hang alone, or at all, if he could help it. "I wouldn't have needed this horse if he hadn't bor . . . stolen . . . mine."

The green eyes darted away and Kent felt as if he could breathe again. Damned brat!

The constable took the sorrel's reins. "Your first beeg error, señor, was to thief a *caballo*. Thee second was to thief thee *constable's caballo*." Then he looked down at the leather-clad youngster. "You be all right, Charly?"

Charly sniffed and struggled to her feet, swallowing her pain. There wasn't a muscle or joint in her body that didn't ache, yet she nodded and slapped what dust she could from her britches and the front of her shirt—until she noted the stranger's rapt gaze following every brush of her palms.

Her chin came up and she straightened her spine. It had just dawned on her that the big galloot had ratted on her for taking his horse. Then she ducked her head and dug a hole in the sand with the toe of her scuffed boot before darting a wistful glance in the direction the scalawag she'd been chasing had taken.

No sign of the *bandito*. No horse. Her shoulders hunched. She hadn't really *stolen* the horse. Yet, she knew she had.

"Charly? Did you thief thees hombre's *caballo?*" The constable rubbed the end of his beard as his eyes studied every detail concerning Charly and the stranger.

"Well . . . I reckon . . ." Beneath lowered lashes, she shot a glare to both the constable and the tall, angry man standing with his hands on his hips, his brown eyes spearing her like daggers. She looked away, and with studied fascination watched a lizard crawl across a flat rock. "Reckon I must've."

12

"Damn right!" Kent heaved a great sigh, but he wasn't necessarily relieved. What would happen to the kid?

"And *you*, señor? Did you thief thees *caballo?*"

Kent rubbed the scar near his eye. "I had no choice. I *had* to get my horse back and my saddle . . ." He cleared his throat. It wouldn't be wise to mention the saddlebags.

His chest caved against his spine. Hell, for all he knew, whoever that other rider was, probably had himself a new black stallion and was on his way to San Francisco, itching to live it up in style. Still, he couldn't reveal any information about the bags or their contents.

"Thee time she ees leetle, señor. What ees your reply?"

With exaggerated insolence, Kent hooked his thumbs under his belt and answered, "Reckon I must've."

Frowning, the constable turned to the two men quietly sitting their horses behind him. "Ethan, get hees peestol. Manuel, he weel ride *mi caballo* back to town, but you eye heem like thee hawk."

Kent looked in the direction he'd last seen his horse. Shedding his surly attitude, he asked, "Could we look for my horse before we go back? The stallion is very . . . valuable . . . and I wouldn't want to lose him."

Roberto Ortega shook his head sadly. "I am very sorry, señor, but we have been too long away from our posts as eet ees. Perhaps mañana, sí?"

The constable held out his hand to Charly, and ordered, "Climb up behind me, Charly. When we get to town, I weel request thee doctor to look at your wounds."

Charly reluctantly grasped Ortega's arm and crawled up to ride behind his saddle. She lowered her lashes and cast surreptitious glances toward the

13

stranger, who seemed to be studiously ignoring her. Guilt warmed her body in the form of a red flush.

It was her fault he was in trouble with the constable. All her fault. And she felt awful about losing his stallion. Somehow, when all of this mess was straightened out, *if* it was ever straightened out, she would find the horse and return it.

Determination toughened her jaw. Her confidence began to return as she planned what she had to do.

The cell door clanged shut. Kent stood with his fingers wrapped around the iron bars and felt a sense of grim satisfaction when the second clang signaled that the kid was also incarcerated. In a way, though, it turned his stomach to realize he'd become so vindictive all of a sudden. It wasn't like him at all. Yet, he could feel his lips curling into a feral smile when the boy gingerly eased himself onto the hard, stained cot.

If Kent Leland Ashford was going to spend time behind bars for horse stealing, at least the kid would get a taste of justice, too. It was only right. Wasn't it? Of course it was!

He took a seat on his own narrow bed, hooded eyes watching the kid. The boy's baby-smooth cheeks were pale—too pale. In spite of himself, he asked, "Are you all right?"

Charly's head throbbed. The top of her shoulder burned. Every part of her body that had hit the hard-packed earth when she fell screamed with aching bruises. Acid coated her tongue and she snapped, "Wish you'd quit askin' dumb questions. I'm up an' kickin', ain't I?"

"Yeah. But not too high, from what I can see." Something about the kid's husky voice caused shivers to race up and down his spine. If he didn't know better, he'd describe it as . . . seductive. He scrubbed

14

at the back of his neck, bitterly wondering where his good sense had gone.

Arguing with the unsettling stranger would serve no purpose, so Charly brushed her hand over her forehead and discovered a thin trail of dried blood. Her gaze shot to her handsome neighbor. Thankfully, his eyes were closed, the back of his head resting against the hard adobe wall. His hat was hooked over his knee and for the first time she noticed his light brown hair.

It looked fine and thick and the sun, filtering in through the tiny west window, glinted off a mixture of lighter, sun-streaked strands. In a land of dark-haired people, he was a man apart—different, intriguing, and captivating.

What must he think of her? She'd stolen his horse. Then she'd endangered the beautiful animal's life. And now here she sat, probably adding to his anger, living proof of her tomfoolery.

She grabbed the brim of her hat and with the ease of long practice, flicked it off her head. A long braided coil of hair fell from beneath the band and hung over her shoulder. She was just reaching up to test the size of the lump on the side of her head when she heard a gasp. Then a voice as deep and vibrating as thunder rolled over her senses.

"Good God! A woman! You're a woman!" Kent stared, incredulous. Thick, sable-colored hair had been fashioned into a long braid. Without the hat to control them, loose tendrils curled around her delicate ears and down her long, graceful neck.

His eyes widened at the way her pale face flushed beneath his surprised outburst. Lush dark lashes hid the expression in her eyes, but contrasted beautifully against her ivory skin and rose-tinted cheeks. And on closer inspection, freckles dotted the bridge of her nose. Hell, the kid, the woman, was . . . ravishing.

Then he scanned her baggy man's clothes. Gentle

15

roundness filled out the trousers' hips. What had to be a tiny waist was hidden beneath two layers of leather. And when she leaned back on her arm, he definitely saw the outline of breasts. "I'll be damned."

Charly bristled under the intense scrutiny. Arrogant stranger. Surely he hadn't mistaken her for a . . . Her brows drew together in an unfeminine scowl. He had! The skunk had thought she was a boy, man, whatever. Unfamiliar moisture stung the backs of her eyes. What did she care? She wasn't out to impress that fancy man. She'd been doing her job and would continue to do it long after the stranger was nothing but a speck of dust on the horizon. So why couldn't she swallow all of a sudden? What was causing the burning sensation in her chest?

Her head snapped up and she glowered at Kent. "'Course I'm a woman. What's all your blamed ruckus 'bout? An' quit eyein' me like I was some heifer up fer sale."

Kent leaned forward, as if she couldn't hear him well enough from where he was sitting. "I'll tell you what the 'ruckus' is about. What's a damn-fool woman doin' runnin' around in men's britches, stealin' a man's horse, and chasin' after someone dangerous enough to take pot shots at her?"

Wincing, Charly managed to get to her feet and indignantly stalk over to the bars separating the only two cells in the building. She wagged a finger at him. "I kin wear whatever I goldurned want, an' I needed that jack-assed animal you call a horse to wrangle in a no-good skunk of a stage robber. That's what this *wo-man* . . ." The word came out sounding like a four-syllable word but she was in no mood to worry about what *he* thought anyway. "Yes, what this *wo-man* was a-doin'. What're ya gonna do 'bout it? Huh?"

Kent leapt to his feet. He stormed over to the bars

16

and sneered when she backed up a step. "I guess it's up to me to point out how childishly and foolishly you behaved." He puffed out his chest. "That's what!"

Awed by the amount of muscle visible even through so many layers of clothing, Charly courageously moved forward until the tip of her nose nearly touched a thin, round bar. "An' how do ya reckon you'll do that, greenhorn?"

He brushed off the distraction of a glob of dirt dangling from his coat sleeve. "I'll keep you behind bars 'til you learn better sense, that's how." His jaws snapped together and he was the one who backed off when it dawned on him how childish *he* sounded. Dear God, what had reduced a thirty-year-old man to arguing like a wet-behind-the-ears teenager?

A smug smile tilted the corners of Charly's mouth. "Reckon we'll be neighborin' fer a spell then, eh?"

A jangle of keys alerted them that the constable was returning. From the sound of the voices drifting beneath the large space under the door, he wasn't alone.

Slender Constable Ortega and rotund Doctor Hornsby presented quite an incongruous sight as they bustled inside the jail. The doctor took one look at Charly and immediately clucked his tongue as if he were used to seeing her in dire predicaments.

While the constable unlocked her cell, the doctor scolded, "Charleen McAllister! What would your poor mother be a-thinkin' if she could but see you now?"

Charly ducked her head, but the doctor chucked her under the chin, tilting her head up again to get a better view of the swelling knot. When he wiped at the crusted blood, she winced. "Ouch!"

"Ummm-hmmmm." He rummaged in his bag and then swabbed the lump with a wad of cotton soaked in something that stung fiercely. But she

17

refused to utter another sound after seeing the amused glint in the handsome stranger's dark, beguiling eyes. From the suspicious twitching of his mustache, the varmint was enjoying her discomfort, and she couldn't rightly say she blamed him. She'd given him plenty of reason.

When the doctor tugged at her leather shirt, intent on pulling it off her shoulder, she squirmed uneasily. Doc Hornsby noted the direction of her gaze and placed his great bulk between Charly and the other prisoner. "Hold still, Charleen. I'm not going to undress you. I just want to clean up this scratch."

She bit her tongue and leaned her head forward enough to peek around Doc Hornsby's large middle. Her expression died in her eyes when she discovered the stranger wasn't interested in seeing her exposed flesh.

Finally finished with his ministrations, the doctor began replacing items into his bag, then looked sternly at his patient. "You were a mighty lucky girl, Charleen. *This* time."

She reached up and adjusted the heavy shirt more comfortably on her shoulder. "Thanks fer comin', Doc. I owe ya."

"Yes, well, uh . . . we'll talk about that later. Right now you just rest and give your body a chance to heal."

Constable Ortega and the doctor left the building together. Charly watched quietly through the grimy piece of glass called a window as the two men entered the newly constructed saloon across the street.

Stretched out on his bunk, Kent wondered about the pleased feeling that unknotted his gut when the doctor's words indicated that *her* wounds were not all that serious. Charleen. Charleen McAllister. Grudgingly, he let her name roll through his mind. He liked it—the soft sound of her name.

"Sorry 'bout yore horse."

He flinched and grunted when she unexpectedly broke the silence. Her throaty, rich-timbred voice put him in mind of the second floor of a whorehouse. Shifting his head, he scanned her buckskin-clad form. Her name and her voice were the only soft things about the woman. She was some tough customer—as he'd regrettably found out firsthand.

Charly's brows drew together. She wasn't used to making apologies to anyone. The least he could've done was appear to appreciate her gesture. "He's shore a handsome animal." Realizing her words could apply to either the horse or its owner, she clamped her lips together before she dug herself into a situation she couldn't escape.

She received another noncommittal grunt for her trouble, and her face puckered like she'd tasted sour milk. The arrogant snob. "Look, I wasn't aimin' fer any of my troubles to rub off onta any'un else." His eyes flashed across the small space. She suddenly welcomed the row of sturdy bars separating them.

"I should hope not." Although he believed she meant everything she said *right now*, he also sensed that she'd probably repeat her actions if she was faced with the same choices again.

Charly couldn't explain her need for this man to understand why she'd taken his horse. It was a feeling that seemed to come from her soul. "It's just . . . I had ta catch that rotten buzzard."

"Why?" Why would she, a *woman*, feel it necessary to do a man's job, he wondered.

She limped slowly back and forth in the small confines of her cell. "Why? 'Cause he robbed the stage a couple days back."

"So why'n hell didn't you let the constable go after him?"

Charly plunked down on the edge of her bunk. "Why not? 'Cause . . ." Because she had never counted on anyone's help before. Why start now? She

19

had learned long ago that if anything was going to get done in her life, she'd have to do it herself. She'd lived with that knowledge for a long time, and had pretty much buried her anger and resentment over things she couldn't change.

But what could she say to make this stranger understand? "What if'n Ortega warn't here? That hombre was skedaddlin' quicker'n a greased lizard." *After* she'd shouted and tipped her hand, that was. Next time, she'd play her cards more carefully.

Kent heard the conviction and determination in her voice, but couldn't fathom her reasoning. She was still a *woman*. Women didn't do rowdy things like chasing after highwaymen. They cooked and sewed and did . . . womanly . . . things. This person, Charleen McAllister, was beyond his understanding.

He closed his eyes and pinched the bridge of his nose. This one damnable . . . Charly . . . had been his undoing. And he still found it hard to believe, even locked inside a moldy, filthy jail cell. All he'd done was ride quietly into town, trying to attract as little attention as possible—and look what had happened. He'd lost his horse and his precious saddlebags. Now his mission was most likely doomed to failure.

Grinding his teeth, he glared at the cause of his misfortune. In one fleeting afternoon, she'd accomplished what a company of Confederate cavalry had not managed to do in two months.

A gunshot pierced the tension in the small, one-room building. Then an explosion of shots sounded from up the street. Charly and Kent both ran to the small barred spaces in the back wall of their cells, but all either could see was blue sky and the top of the blacksmith shop next door.

Charly turned and stared out the hazy front window. As the gunfire continued, townspeople scrambled for shelter in open doorways and hunkered down behind barrels of goods that had recently been unloaded in front of the emporium.

The shooting stopped as suddenly as it had begun. Charly blinked at the unexpected drone of a bee as it lazily investigated the corner of her cell.

She sighed and cast a covert glance toward the stranger and found his features grim with concern. Suspicion narrowed her eyes. Who was this man, anyway? What was his interest in Tucson? He seemed no more than a stranger just passing through. But was that *all* he was?

Before she had time to ponder the question of why he'd arrived at the stage station earlier, the door to the jail slammed open. Constable Ortega and the blacksmith herded in a scruffy-looking gang of five hombres who looked and smelled like they hadn't seen a soapy cloth or a pitcher of water in several months. One was American, two appeared to be half-breeds, and the others were Mexican. Two were wounded and one was so drunk he could hardly stand up, even with his friends' support.

The constable continued to hold his gun on the ruffians while he studied the cell situation. He'd purposely put Charleen in the largest, but it wouldn't hold six people. He rubbed the tip of his beard, thinking.

Finally, he nodded to himself and took the keys from his back pocket. The lone stranger appeared the least surly of the lot. Opening Charleen's cell, he motioned her out before he and Herman Waterman, the big, burly blacksmith whom Ortega had recruited to help round up the troublemakers, pushed the grumbling men inside and locked the door.

Then he opened Kent's cell and tilted his head, indicating that Charleen should enter the small enclosure. "I beg your apology, señorita. But you weel no be here long."

21

Chapter Two

Charly stared uncertainly into the small cell. To her mind, the intimidating aura of the stranger already filled every available space. "Y-ya cain't put me in there."

Worried over the rising number of occupants in his newly constructed jail, and the threat of more arriving soon, Roberto Ortega did not have the time to cajole the girl into accepting his decision. He snapped, "Sí, señorita, I can and I must. Now, enter. *Por favor.*"

She had nearly chewed the inside of her bottom lip raw. Hesitantly, Charly took one step, then another. Suddenly, the iron door shoved against her back and she was unceremoniously pushed the rest of the way forward. The lock clicked with the finality of dirt thudding on the lid of a coffin.

Instantly, she spun and grasped the cold metal rungs in her sweaty palms. "Constable . . . I-I . . ."

But Ortega presented his back to her as he busily instructed the blacksmith to fetch the doctor and ask Señora Salazar to cook something—anything—for the evening meals.

Kent smugly observed her hesitancy. "Might as well sit down before you fall down."

"Ain't necessary," she lied. O-o-ohhh! Charly

swallowed, hard. She gripped the bars so hard the skin stretched across her knuckles turned white. It would've been asking too much for the durned man not to notice her weakness. Though she tried her best to hide her attraction to him, her body began to tremble, starting with her traitorous knees. If she let go of the bars she would surely collapse to the floor.

The back of her neck felt the sudden sensation of a hundred needles pricking her sensitive flesh. She didn't have to turn around to know he was looking at her. A nervous warmth slithered down her spine under the heat of his eyes.

Before she knew what was happening, arms as hard as iron slid around her shoulders and beneath her knees. All five feet and eight inches of her was lifted into the air as if she were no heavier or bigger than a bedraggled kitten. She immediately let go of the bars for fear her flesh would've been left dangling there.

She'd never been picked up by a man before, other than maybe wrestling with her brothers, which didn't count for much in comparison. As tall as she was, especially in a town and family of shorter Mexican men, she'd always been looked upon as gangly and awkward. And in the face of those unqualified opinions, she now made sure nobody thought of *her* as a helpless and sensitive *lady*, like the other women of Tucson.

Something about the way the stranger so easily held her, and longer than necessary as far as she was concerned, spattered chill bumps over her flesh and set off a liquid glow.

She was plunked upon the straw-filled mattress and shivered when he stepped back, as much from the unfamiliar emotions filling her head as from the loss of warmth from his muscular body.

With her lashes lowered, she stole a glance at his handsome face and stealthily sucked in her breath.

He stared back at *her*, an odd expression on his features. What had she done?

Kent stood transfixed. He'd never thought that her gentle curves, barely hinted at beneath the layers of leather, would be so . . . soft. So . . . intriguing. And he'd never expected his body to react so . . . instantaneously.

Hell, she was too tall, too slender. Definitely not the type of woman that usually attracted his favors. Who would've thought just picking her up and carrying her two steps would cause his gut to contract and his loins to quicken until he was almost embarrassed to be seen?

In what he hoped was a casual movement, he sank onto the other end of the bed. "How're you feeling now?"

Charly closed her eyes and leaned her head against the wall. She answered honestly, "Tired." Excited and confused also came to mind, but she durned sure wasn't going to admit such things to *him*.

The plank door to the jail swung out as Doctor Hornsby paid his second call of the day. Constable Ortega unlocked the other cell so the doctor could examine the two injured men who were moaning their complaints about how long it took him to get here.

Doc Hornsby set down his bag and looked over at Charleen. "Saw your pa a while ago. Said he'd be over later to get you out of here."

Kent looked at her, too, expecting to see her all smiles. Instead, he found her full lips set in a grim line and her green eyes darkened with . . . what? Only the sparkling gold flecks swimming in their depths hinted at her buried emotions.

What was wrong? Was she that afraid of her father finding her in jail? Kent frowned. The man wouldn't beat her, or anything, would he?

Suddenly, as if it were the most important thing on

her mind, as if the doctor hadn't made a point o
mentioning her father, she surprised Kent by lookin;
directly into his eyes and asking—no, demanding
"What're ya called?"

He blinked. "Pardon me?"

"Yore moniker. Ya know, yore name? Whatta folk
call ya?"

Kent grimaced at her slaughter of the Englisl
language, but replied, "Kent. Kent Ashford. An
yours?" Of course, he already knew *her* name, but h
didn't want her to know that he'd been paying he
that much attention.

"Most folks call me Charly."

He snorted. "Charly? That's a man's—"

Her chin tilted upward and her eyes flashed
"That's short fer Charleen."

"Oh, I see." He turned his head, hiding the smil
that hovered near his lips. Teasing Miss Charly coul
be an entertaining pastime. Might even allow him t
exact a subtle revenge. Only from the constan
serious set to her features, she wouldn't be aware o
the enjoyment he was deriving at her expense. Tha
wouldn't do at all.

Charly mulled over his name. Kent Ashford. Sh
eyed his broadcloth suit and string tie. She should'v
guessed he wouldn't be a Mack or a Billy. No, he ha
a *dignified* name to fit his dignified style.

She ran her hand down the thigh of her leathe
pants and pursed her lips. Dignified. *Cultured*, he
mother would've said. Charly's eyes burned and sh
blinked rapidly. Anna Maria Consuelo Alvarez
Gutierrez. Highly educated. From a wealthy family
Her mother. And she'd struggled to teach he
daughter to be a lady—until the day she'd died.

Charly had been ten years old and the only girl lef
in a house full of men. And when her grandparent
had offered to take Charly and her two older brother
to live with them on their large rancho south o

Sonora, Jedidiah McAllister had drawn a gun and, staggering drunkenly, blustering loudly, ordered them from his house. He had told them in no uncertain terms never to come back.

From that moment she had learned to take care of herself. Now, at twenty years of age, she wasn't the least bit ashamed of the person she'd become—even if she was quite different from the well-behaved little lady her mother had taken such pains to train.

She darted a glance to the opposite end of the bed. So, why now, all of a sudden, was she feeling grimy and awkward and recalling all of those ladylike manners?

Charly caught Kent Ashford staring again and she squirmed on the hard cot. He was certainly a dandified city fella. And he was probably behind this outbreak of self-consciousness.

"Well, *Charly*, what do you suppose we'll do in here until your pa comes to get you?"

Her heartbeat accelerated, pumping blood through her veins so fast that it heated her skin—all over. Propping her heels on the edge of the bed, she rested her elbows on her knees so she could cup her burning cheeks in her cool palms. Shame on the wicked thoughts his innocent comment had sparked!

Kent's thoughts were anything but innocent. His comment had been harmless. Until he looked over and saw her fine, delicate profile and the thick braid of dark hair lying on her shoulder. If she was beautiful now, what would she look like with that long hair tumbling loose, sifting between his fingers?

But he quickly shook his head to clear it of such nonsense. Look at the creature, for God's sake. She wouldn't know the first thing about being a . . . woman. Judging by her costume and attitude and the well-toned muscles he'd felt, there were probably a few things she could teach him about the rough-and-tumble life of Tucson.

"Let me put it another way. What do you usually do when you're in jail?"

Charly's eyes snapped fire. The arrogant bastard! "Why, last time I shot the sheriff an' escaped."

Kent ground his teeth. Cheeky bitch. "Since this is my first experience at being incarcerated, I just thought you could offer a few pointers."

Incarcerated? Oh, he was a dandy, wasn't he? "So happens, this's my first time, too. Cain't say as how it's my favorite 'sperience, neither."

"Glad to hear that, since if it weren't for you, we wouldn't be in this snake pit." He couldn't help laying the blame on her. The anger and resentment he'd kept at bay for the past several hours burned a hole in his throat. That, and thinking of his lost saddlebags.

Charly narrowed her eyes to mere slits. "You ain't such a prize, Mr. Kent Ashford. Tucson don't have no law worth speakin' of. Ortega only catches them what falls in 'is lap. Yore the mule brain what had ta go an' swipe the constable's cayuse." Crawling stiffly off the bed, she limped back and forth in the confined space. "Of all the durned fool things—"

Already irritable, Kent was on the verge of losing his temper, but good. Was the brat laying the blame on *him* now? "How was I supposed to know the damned animal belonged to a constable? There wasn't a sign on its butt."

She stopped pacing and looked him directly in the eye. "You'll get yore horse back. That's a goldurned promise."

"Yeah?" His eyes raked her up and down. "And once you're out of here, who's to say you won' disappear, too?"

Her chin tilted a notch higher. "I told ya a'fore, ain't no thief, an' I ain't got no reason ta run."

Kent couldn't think of a rejoinder. She'd spoken

28

quietly and so sincerely that . . . Damned if he didn't almost believe her.

They stared silently at each other until Charly couldn't stand the sweltering heat building beneath her heavy leather clothing. Even the cool, late-January evening couldn't allay her strange feelings. Disgusted with herself, she sank back onto her end of the bunk.

Rubbing his weary eyes, Kent shifted his legs, grateful for the break in tension. His lower anatomy had to be reacting on pure instinct, because he certainly couldn't be attracted to this beanpole of a woman.

An hour or so later, Charly looked out the small window. The sun had gone down. The moonless night shrouded the little jail. She sighed and rolled her head on the hard adobe wall. Then the impossible happened—she actually dozed.

"Thought your father would have been here by now," he stated quietly. While she'd had the gall to fall asleep, Kent had been waiting, wondering when she'd be released. Indignation over that inevitable event roiled through his insides along with disturbing thoughts of all that had gone wrong that day.

Naturally, she'd go home while he moldered in jail. And where was the constable? Even condemned men were allowed a last supper. His stomach growled at the thought of food. Surely someone would bring them something to eat. Maybe he'd even get *her* portion if she were gone by then.

But he was sadly disappointed. At least another hour passed with no sign of the constable. Kent looked toward the girl, who was curled into such a tight ball he was sure that she believed that if she dared to spread out and land even one toe on his half of the small bunk, he might cut it off.

Strange, but as he watched the even rise and fall of her slender shoulders, he thought she didn't act like someone expecting to leave soon. "Charleen?" Her muscles grew taut, but other than that, she didn't move. "Charl . . . ly?"

Charly groaned when she shifted her body. The uncomfortable position had only intensified the soreness of her muscles. Rubbing the back of her neck, she winced as her fingers brushed the area close to her wound. To mask her pain, she snapped, "What?"

Regardless of Kent's feelings about the woman, he didn't enjoy seeing her hurting. He actually found himself hoping her father would hurry and get her out of there. "What do you suppose is keeping your . . . pa?"

She didn't turn to look at him. "He ain't gonna 'member me, or nothin' else, til tomorry—an' then only if'n some'un says somethin' ta remind 'im."

"What do you mean he won't remember you? How could a father forget his daughter's in jail?"

"'Cause knowin' my pa, he passed out drunk two hours ago."

Kent cursed under his breath at the same time the jail door opened and a bulky shadow entered. Soon, two candles and a coal-oil lantern cast flickering shadows on the walls.

Doctor Hornsby turned and nearly dropped the lantern when he saw Charleen still locked inside with the stranger. His fleshy lips curled down. "Your pa didn't come, did he?"

Charly shook her head. "Don't matter none. Ortega's been gone all evenin' an' I couldn't a got out noways."

Doctor Hornsby wagged his head back and forth. "I should've brought Jed right over when I first saw him. I'm really sorry, Charleen."

So was Charly, but she was used to it by now. Actually, the time spent in jail hadn't been too bad, except . . . She desperately needed to relieve herself.

Her legs were crossed so tightly that they cramped, but she steadfastly refused to use the pot in the corner in front of all those men.

The doctor didn't have a key to the cells, but motioned the injured men in the next cell over to the bars where he could see to reexamine their wounds. Suddenly, he glanced toward Kent. "Young man, do me a favor and take a look at Charleen's wound."

Charly shot her cell-mate a wary look. He cocked a roguish brow at her. She prayed he would refuse, and felt a tremor down her spine when he rubbed his stubbly chin and gave her a wicked grin.

"Tell you what, Doc," Kent said as his gaze bored into Charly. "I'll make you a deal."

Doc Hornsby grunted and tilted his head until he was able to peer over the top of his wire-rimmed spectacles.

Kent sauntered over to the near corner of the cell. "You hand me that extra blanket over on the shelf, and see about gettin' us some food brought in, and I'd even go so far as to kiss the young woman's shoulder and make it all better. What do you say? Do we have a deal?"

The doctor laughed at Charleen's outraged gasp. "That might be as good a treatment as anything I've got. It's a deal, young—"

"Kent. My friends call me Kent."

The wounded American groaned when the doctor yanked off a piece of scab with the bandage covering his wound, but the doc never wavered in his ministrations.

Charly fidgeted on the edge of the bed and would've jumped to her feet as Kent approached but he hurried his steps and closed the distance between them.

"You ain't gonna kiss my—"

"No, I sure *ain't*. But I *am* going to take a look at that wound."

31

"T'ain't neither." She curled the fingers of one hand into a fist and brandished it under his contrary nose.

"Come on, Charleen. Act like a grownup for a change."

The exasperated admonition stopped her short of returning a verbal threat. Maybe her reactions did seem a little childish, but she wasn't at all sure it was proper for some stranger to see or touch her bare skin—even under doctor's orders.

Huffing indignantly, she shrugged her shirt off her shoulder just far enough so he could glimpse the bandage.

Kent slouched down beside her. He took a deep breath and grasped her collar. His eyes blinked closed at the faint scent of roses and leather and woman filling his nostrils. As his fingers closed around the neckline, his knuckles brushed soft, silken flesh. He cursed to himself. Damn the bratty woman for having *any* kind of an effect on him.

The shirt tugged against his hand. She was struggling to escape his grasp and he mentally put aside the sensual sensations teasing his body. "Hold still, woman. I can't see what I'm doing."

"An' I s'pose ya don't *know* what yore doin' neither, huh?"

He wadded several inches of leather in his fist. "Why, you little . . . I know more—"

The doctor unwittingly interrupted. "What does it look like, Kent? Do I need to treat it again?"

"Yeah, you might," Kent muttered. Even in the dim light, he could see an angry flush to the skin around the bandage.

"All right, then. I'll be over in a minute or two. If you would, though, go ahead and get it ready."

"What?" the cell-mates echoed simultaneously.

"Take the bandage off if you haven't already."

Kent swallowed and flexed his knuckles.

Charly steeled herself for the next jolt. Every time his fingers caressed her flesh, sizzling currents radiated from her shoulder to the arches of her feet. Nothing like that had ever happened before, not even when Emilio Gonzales had touched her breast one night when he swore his passion had overwhelmed his good intentions. He had ended up on his knees begging her not to tell her older brother, and she had chalked the evening up as one of the most humiliating she'd ever spent.

Her older brother did that to people—inspired fear. He had been her protector, watching over the boys trying to court her like an eagle patiently awaiting unsuspecting prey. Five years her senior, Ned was her favorite brother, yet he had deserted her three years ago to go to California. Three years. She hadn't heard from him since.

Abruptly shaken from her memories when the soiled pad was yanked from her tender flesh, she gritted her teeth and swallowed back a whining moan. Instead, she released her emotions in a fit of temper. "You gol-durned, mangy son of a—"

Kent suddenly wound the fingers of his free hand into her braid, holding her head still while he leaned forward and closed her mouth in the most effective manner at his disposal.

As his soft but firm lips melded against her own, a dozen thoughts warred in Charly's mind. He shouldn't be kissing her. The sensation of his mouth on hers was wonderful. Her fingers dug into the hard muscles on his arms. He felt good, solid, secure. His lips were warm and moved with tantalizing sureness. Her body felt as limp as day-old porridge.

Through the buzzing in her ears she heard Doctor Hornsby murmuring to someone. What if the man who'd befriended both her mother and herself for so many years happened to look over and see Kent Ashford kissing her? With hardly a blink of her blazing eyes, she landed a fist in Kent's rock-hard stomach. Air burst from his mouth, puffing out his cheeks. But he stopped the kiss.

Before either of them could utter another syllable, the doctor tossed the requested blanket to a pale Kent and ordered, "Move over here, Charleen, close to the bars, so I can take a gander at that wound. That's a good girl."

Finally able to stand up straight and take a breath, Kent harumphed and thought, "Good girl, be damned." She'd probably never been *good* in her life. But like it or not, he soon found himself mesmerized by the sight of more of her pearly skin. He shook his head, astounded by the sudden niggle of . . . surely it wasn't jealousy? . . . that he experienced upon seeing the doctor's fingers roaming over her body.

He turned and leaned against the bars, touching a finger to his lips. His mustache twitched, still tingling. Never had a woman had such an unsettling effect on him, and he was damned sure tired of it. There was no logic or justification for his reactions. He had to keep reminding himself that if it weren't for *her*, he'd have his horse and his saddlebags and be sleeping in a comfortable bed, maybe with a warm, willing partner, instead of residing in the local lockup with an unstable brat.

"Come over here, son, and hold her shirt away from the wound while I clean it out." The doctor busily searched through vials and small bottles, never thinking his request might be refused.

Kent hesitated briefly, but then decided to do as the doctor bade. A shudder ricocheted through his body when her flesh quivered beneath his fingers. His eyes narrowed. Could it be that *his* touch had a similar effect on *her*? What a laugh! How could such a rough and rowdy, foul-mouthed termagant harbor soft or feminine feelings?

It was only his imagination. Her skin was tender

and overly sensitive because of the wound, that was all.

Charly could hardly sit still beneath the shocking sensations his fingers created. The rough edges of his callouses rubbing over a thousand sensitive nerve endings sent disquieting messages screaming through her body. Sure his hands were coarse, but no more so than her father's, or her brother's, or even her own. So his touch couldn't be the cause of the unfamiliar fluttering sensations deep in her belly. Could it?

She was hardly aware of the doctor finishing with the dressing, barely heard him say, "Sorry you're still in here, Charleen, my girl. Surely Jed'll come for you tomorrow."

A slight shrug was the only communication she could muster as her eyes locked on Kent's muscular thighs. One of his legs nestled between her knees and she quickly scooted backward, instinctively spreading her legs to keep from touching him.

Slow realization widened her eyes. She and Kent Ashford were locked together—for who-knew-how-long. And it had been a mistake to open her legs. She really needed to use the facilities. "Doc?"

"Yes, Charleen?" Hornsby was almost to the door, but turned back at her call.

"You can't get me out? Even fer a minute?"

The doctor spread his free arm. "I don't . . ." Then he read the near-panic in her eyes, her strained features, and taut muscles. His face flushed red when he surmised her problem. "I'll look again, but the keys weren't here earlier."

He was truly distraught when he turned back, empty-handed. "Sorry, Charleen, but I'm afraid I can't help you."

Charly blinked rapidly as the doctor backed out of the doorway. Kent Ashford suddenly stepped away from the cot and she sighed with some relief. But even that breathing space did little to ease her problem.

The blanket Doctor Hornsby had passed in to Kent was suddenly shaken and spread before her. Through the dust motes she warily watched as her cell-mate walked over to the corner and held the blanket in front of the smelly pot. His strong hands anchored the woolen material to the adobe bricks.

When he tilted his head and looked at her, cocking that aggravating brow, Charly thought she'd never been more mortified in her entire life. She sat in stony silence and glared through the bars toward the front window. A candle sputtered and gutted out, leaving only the dim illumination from the one taper remaining on the constable's desk.

Slowly Kent lowered the blanket to stare at her profile. The hollow of her deep-set eyes. The straight line of her delicate nose, which he remembered as being sprinkled with freckles in the sunlight. High cheekbones. Rounded chin.

And then she turned to look at him. Even in the near-darkness he imagined he could see the golden flecks in her eyes dancing with anger. He raised and lowered his brows, then held the blanket up again.

Charly tore her eyes from his and gazed up at the beamed ceiling with a long-suffering expression. Using the pot would be far less embarrassing than the alternative.

Darting a glance toward the next cell, she held her breath. But if any of the hombres were aware of the dramatic scene about to take place next to them, they hid their knowledge well. The two wounded men shared the small cot, their eyes closed. The other three were sprawled on the floor in various uncomfortable-looking positions. The one who'd been so drunk earlier snorted and scratched, causing her to flush and guiltily look away.

If it were possible to hurry and drag her feet at the same time, Charly managed to do it. Heat spread from the innermost core of her being and suffused her face when she drew even with Kent. Through the thickness of her lashes, she looked up at him. "Ya ain't gonna look?"

He rolled his eyes. Females! "Now why would I want to do that?"

Yet as she moved by him with all the enthusiasm of a prisoner on her way to the gallows, and he heard the soft swishing of her clothing, his imagination provided more than he could ever hope to *see.*

Even Charly's bottom felt flushed as she squatted amidst the folds of blanket. Why couldn't women be built as conveniently as men when it came to relieving themselves? This was all so embarrassing.

Then the drunkard let loose a loud, nasal snort which increased in crescendo as he exhaled. She sighed with relief. Taking advantage of the distraction, she had no more than finished and begun pulling up her britches when the snoring abruptly halted.

"Damn you, Jose. If I had my knife, I'd put an end to that racket once and for all." The cot creaked as the American attempted to ease into a more comfortable position.

Charly grinned. She owed ole Jose. And, grudgingly, her cell-mate. Kent Ashford'd done a kind, gentlemanly thing.

"Everything all right, Miss . . . Charly?"

She cringed at the barely suppressed amusement in his voice. Drawing herself up to her full height, Charly speared him with a sharp glance. "Should'a known a snake jest cain't change its colors."

Kent blinked. He hadn't meant to sound like he was making fun of her. He guessed he just couldn't control the resentment still smoldering in his gut. But . . . since they were to remain cooped up together for at least another twelve to fifteen hours, maybe they could settle on a truce—of sorts.

So, he held the blanket out to her. "Would you mind?"

"Mind what?" She didn't trust his sudden conciliatory tone.

"Would you hold the blanket for me?"

Her eyes widened. He wanted her to make a curtain for him? Surely men didn't . . . A sound came from the other cell and Charly glanced over to see one of the desperados taking care of the same chore, without benefit of a curtain. She closed her eyes as, once again, her cheeks flamed scarlet.

When she opened her eyes, they locked with Kent's. Maybe it wouldn't be so bad, holding the blanket for him. City dandy or not, he was trying to shield her sensibilities. Sensibilities? How long had it been since anyone had treated her as if she had any?

When he was finished, Kent took the blanket from Charly and gave her a tentative smile. She nodded and went back to what she now considered her end of the bunk. When she dared cast a surreptitious glance back toward Kent, she was surprised to find him hanging the blanket so that it partitioned off a portion of their cell from the five men next door.

Warmth filled her chest and another pang of guilt pricked her conscience. What a thoughtful man. She didn't deserve his kindness, not after everything she'd done.

When he turned and sat down on his end of the bed, she forced herself to mutter, "Thanks." His responsive grin even prompted the corners of her lips to curve up slightly.

Two identical dimples appeared in her peach and ivory cheeks. Kent sucked in his breath. A smile? Miss Charly had actually smiled. The motion transformed her face, giving her natural beauty an impish quality that tugged at his chest.

Needing to switch the direction of his wayward thoughts, he muttered the first inane thing that popped into his head. "Maybe someone will remember to feed us before long."

She merely nodded and leaned her head back against the wall. As hungry as she was, she was even more tired.

Kent, too, began to feel his eyelids grow heavy, though he tried his damnedest to stay awake.

A short while later, the opening of the door and the aroma of spicy food awakened Kent. An unfamiliar warmth against his left side drew his blurry gaze and he found Charleen slumped on his shoulder.

The feminine softness of her features, the trusting in her gesture of turning to him in her sleep, so unlike the woman he'd encountered during her waking hours, unbiddingly coaxed a deep surge of tenderness into his chest. His fist clenched. No!

With a grim set to his mouth, he shook her awake. "Food's here. Wake up."

He had to do something—either get her away from him, or him away from her. Tomorrow, first thing, he knew what he had to do.

Chapter Three

Charly blinked, then jerked away from the firm wall of Kent Ashford's shoulder. In the coolness of the night and the darkened cell, and suffering extreme exhaustion, she must've drifted toward his warmth. And he was definitely warm. Her flesh still tingled from the sudden separation of their bodies.

She sniffed. Her nose twitched. "Grub?"

"No." Kent grimaced and watched the doctor help a plump, middle-aged woman distribute dinner trays. "Grub is what pigs root for. This is food. You know, something served on a plate and eaten with a fork."

"Beg yore dang-nab-pardon, Mister City Man." She tilted her chin and glared at the dandy who dared to make fun of her. "Guess we ain't never heard o' such way out here." Quickly averting her gaze from his rugged features, she realized she found it easier to think of him as overbearing and arrogant if she wasn't looking at him.

His eyes narrowed as he walked over and pulled two trays beneath the bars, scraping them across the floor. Looking morosely at the watery beans and thin tortillas, he handed Charly a plate. "Turns out they *are* pigs. Here's your grub."

41

Though her stomach recoiled, she flashed a sickeningly sweet smile and readily accepted the plate. "Thanks."

He looked on in disbelief while she rolled a tortilla, dunked it into the bean juice and took a big bite.

Hungry, and unwilling to appear cowardly, Kent sat back on the cot and cast wary glances toward Charly as he folded the flat, floppy piece of flour and lard. Tentatively, he dipped the tip end into the beans. The food was halfway to his mouth when he felt a prickly sensation along the back of his neck. He allowed the sloppy tortilla to drip as he swung his gaze toward Charleen. She was staring at him.

Oh, it was subtle. He could just see the slight movement of her eye, the barely noticeable twitch in the side of her cheek. With a studied air of nonchalance, he refocused his attention on the food.

He raised the tortilla in a mock salute and opened his mouth, bracing himself before his teeth sank into the rubbery substance. After several tries, he finally managed to tear off a chunk. It settled in his mouth like lead. His senses acutely attuned to the annoying Miss Charly, he casually cocked his head to the left, listening intently. He could have sworn he detected a muffled giggle.

He swiveled toward the woman. She gazed back, all innocence, with just a hint of question in her emerald eyes. He frowned and began to chew. It was a marathon affair—chewing, swallowing, chewing, swallowing.

"Hey, Doc, when's the constable coming back?" he called in an effort to distract her attention.

Doctor Hornsby scratched his chin. Amusement flickered briefly in his tired eyes. "Why? You in a hurry for something?"

Kent sighed. "Yes."

"Anything I can do?" The doctor strolled over to

42

the cell door and looked inside. "You all right, Charleen?"

She nodded despite a mouthful of beans.

"Anything I can get you?" The doctor's gaze returned to Kent.

Kent replaced his plate on the tray. "Just the constable."

"You're not sick, or anything? You look a little pale."

"No. No . . ." At least not in any way he wanted to talk about. He'd been exposed to the exasperating Charleen McAllister for hardly any time at all and his emotions were shifting uncharacteristically from anger to ardor. He doubted the doc had anything in his black bag to cure those symptoms.

Ardor? He still couldn't believe *he,* a grown, intelligent, fairly sensible man, could feel such an emotion for the scruffy urchin. Yet the anger she stirred was certainly real enough.

Doctor Hornsby watched the changing expressions on the young man's face and the sparks that flared in those brown eyes whenever Kent glanced toward Charleen. "Well, let me know if there's anything else I can do."

"Sure." Kent disgustedly waved the doctor back to his other patients. A long, slow breath hissed through his teeth. Though he dreaded even the thought of it, he and the "wo-man" would be forced to spend the night together.

Charly sighed at the doctor's retreating back and realized she was truly stuck with her cell-mate 'til morning. She casually scooted to the very end of the cot, determined to do her darnedest to stay awake and not repeat what had happened before. If only she weren't so tired. "Where ya from, city . . . er, uhmm—"

"Kent," he snapped.

"Oh, yeah, Kent." As if she could've forgotten. But

she didn't want him to suspect she was the least little bit interested in remembering anything about him. Unable to force down another bite of the tasteless food, she set her plate aside and avoided his eyes.

"I'm from Pennsylvania," Kent told her. Rubbing the back of his neck, he slouched against the cold wall. Tired and sleepy himself, he was grateful she'd initiated a conversation. He daren't risk falling asleep and waking up next to her again, or Heaven forbid, find himself in an even more compromising position. "What about you? Were you raised here in Tucson?"

"Off 'n' on." She yawned and curled her legs beneath her. "I was born here, 'n' then we moved 'roun' some. Spent time back in Virginny 'fore comin' back here."

"Oh, yeah?" He perked up, wondering if her family might be some of the people he'd been sent here to observe. "Your folks live here now, too, do they?"

"My pa, 'n' one brother."

"What about your ma and—" He frowned slightly as he sensed every muscle in her body tensing.

"My *mother's* dead." Her pa was her pa. But the woman who bore her and worked so hard to raise her was *mother*.

"Sorry." Kent knew he'd summarily been put in his place. "Didn't mean . . . Should've known . . ."

She'd made him uncomfortable, though he had no way of knowing her feelings. And why was she so riled, anyway? Her mother had, after all, been dead for many years. "Don't matter none."

Something in the strained tone of her voice told him it did matter, quite a lot. He wished the light were brighter so he could see her expression.

Charly's eyes blinked closed. She snapped them open. She wished he'd say something else—anything. Finally she asked, "Ya got family out here?"

44

"No."

No? That was all? Close-mouthed devil, wasn't he? "Whatcha doin' in Tucson?"

He winced. "Just looking for . . . work. I need a . . . grubstake."

She shook her head. Just as she'd expected, a drifter. Granted, a well-dressed drifter, but a drifter just the same. Too bad. "Mebbe ya should mosey out ta the mines. Might be some'uns lookin' ta hire."

He tried to tamp down the excitement in his voice. "Mines? There are mines around Tucson?"

"A few." A disgusted sigh escaped her lips. Everyone knew of the silver and copper mines around the area. No stranger could ride within a hundred miles and not be vaguely aware of that.

Kent cleared his throat. "Have you heard if any of those mines are producing? Or making a . . . profit?"

She shrugged. "Some."

He gnashed his teeth. Damn, but he wanted to pump her for information, like—How many mines were there? How much profit did they expect? Were any for sale? Then he remembered. If he didn't find his horse and saddlebags, what good would the answers do him?

Maybe later he could question her—or better yet, someone else who didn't look at him quite so intently. He shifted, aware that she had somehow probed his soul and he came up wanting.

So why should that bother him? What did *her* opinion matter?

Charly stared outright at his profile. One of the few times she'd been able to look at him that he wasn't scowling at her with his own dark, fierce gaze.

She couldn't deny he was nice to look at—the chiseled line of his square jaw and the tip end of his blunt nose. The thick mass of hair curling at his collar, though without his hat she noticed it was shorter and neater on the top and sides, as if he could

45

see to trim it there himself, but couldn't reach the back.

Though she took a measure of pleasure in what she saw, she was disturbed by his questions. Just what did he *really* want to know?

Lost in their wandering thoughts, the conversation dwindled. Charly's eyes blinked once, twice. Lifting her eyelids felt like lifting anvils. Kent also nodded, then he scooted down and stretched out with his hips and legs angled toward the edge of the cot, his feet planted firmly on the floor. There was plenty of room for Charleen to do the same, if she wanted.

Sometime later the sound of a creaking door aroused him. A comfortable warmth was blown away instantly by the cold night noises of the jail, and though he was alert to his surroundings, his attention became focused on the dark head resting on his thigh. The vixen had stretched out to take advantage of the space—and the cushion he provided.

The sight of her and the slight pressure of her cheekbone nestling into the inside of his upper leg caused certain parts of him to respond spontaneously, with painful intensity.

His clothing had a damp and sticky feel as perspiration beaded his body. In desperation, he looked up to see the constable stumbling wearily into the jail. Ortega sank into his chair with a huge sigh and bent over to pull off his boots as Kent tried to sit up. He couldn't move, though, without rousing the sleeping woman, which he didn't want to do until *after* he'd had a chance to talk with the constable.

Kent waved his arm. One of Ortega's boots clattered to the floor. Kent lifted his shoulders from the bed and called softly, "Constable . . . Constable Ortega."

Roberto Ortega glanced into the near cell and found the group of silent, surly characters staring back at him. He shrugged and tugged at the remaining boot.

"Over here."

Ortega's eyes snapped wide open when his gaze swept into the next cell and he saw a hanging blanket and a man's arm waving in the air—signaling like a flag of surrender. Groaning with relief as the last sweaty boot bounced off the packed dirt floor, he wriggled his toes before lumbering to his feet and hobbling barefoot to the far cell.

His eyes really rounded when he peered inside and saw Kent's predicament. "Bless the Virgin! I forget thee señorita."

A stifled "Yeah" drifted through the bars. The constable's lips twitched. He scratched the dark stubble on his chin. "What ees eet you wanted, señor? What do you weesh me to do?"

"Get her out of here."

Roberto's arms spread wide as he gazed innocently around the room. "But what would I do weeth her?"

Kent nearly moaned out loud when her cheek snuggled higher on his thigh. He ground out, "Just do *something*. Quick!"

"I am sorry. Eet ees you who weesh the señorita arrested. The judge, he weel be here in two months. Until then . . ." He glanced at the sleeping woman, shrugged, and turned to leave.

"Wait."

"Sí?" Ortega stopped and looked over his shoulder.

"What if I drop the charges? When could you release her?"

"There ees mucho work weeth thee paper."

Kent exhaled sharply in frustration.

"But I deed no write down yesterday's happenings."

A ray of hope cocked Kent's brow.

"Perhaps I could set her free and no have thee

47

work. But, no, that would no be proper way of doing business. Would eet?"

"Proper?" Kent grimaced as Charleen's left hand curled under his leg, as if she thought he was some damned pillow. Shafts of fire splintered in his lower belly. Good God! "Just what would it take to make everything . . . proper?"

Roberto smiled and curled the tip of his mustache. "Ten pesos should wipe the incident from thees poor, humble mind."

Kent muttered under his breath. Poor and humble? He doubted the man had ever seen a humble day. At least the constable's demands weren't too outrageous. Making a show of slowly and carefully emptying his pockets, Kent gave the "lawman" the impression he was scrounging for his last dollar. Finally he shrugged and held out the money. "'Fraid nine's all I've got. That be enough to properly cleanse your memory?"

Roberto licked his lips. Nine pesos that he wouldn't have to share with his wife and large family. Three months pay in one beautiful morning. "Sí. I am no a cruel man. Wake thee señorita. She may leave now."

Kent sighed. His teeth flashed in a wide smile as he put his fingers on Charleen's shoulder. She flinched and moaned. He jerked his hand back. She squirmed and dug her nails high into his inner thigh. He smothered a gasp and sat up quickly, dislodging her from the dangerous vicinity of his lap.

Charly blinked awake, confused by the sudden disappearance of her pillow. Her muscles screamed a protest at every twitch of movement, and she couldn't suppress a loud groan. Scrubbing the back of one hand across her eyes, she blinked again and with squinted eyes peered around the dim, musty cell. Her breath caught in her throat when she saw Kent Ashford, his back against the wall, staring at her as if she'd just poked him with a hot iron.

"Wh-what? What'sa matter?"

"No-nothing. You were sleeping so soundly that I must've startled you when I shook your shoulder. Th-that's all." His own voice sounded none too steady. He coughed. Damn it! Now he was behaving like a wet-behind-the-ears plow boy.

Charly didn't notice his discomfort. She shivered as his deep, rumbling voice vibrated across her senses. "Wake me?" He nodded and she mumbled, "Why?" The first sound sleep she'd had in months, and he had to go and disturb her so early in the morning.

She stared blurrily out the window. The sun was barely up and though it was already an hour past her usual rising time, she kept her guilt at bay. After all, she was in jail. What was there to do when you were locked behind bars?

Constable Ortega rattled the keys and unlocked the cell door. "Because, señorita McAllister, you are free to go."

Surprise and shock widened her eyes. She looked suspiciously from the constable to Kent Ashford. "Free?"

"Sí."

"Yeah."

Her gaze narrowed on Kent. "Why? Yore horse's still gone. Nuthun's changed."

He couldn't meet her eyes. "I . . . made a mistake." And that was no lie. The biggest mistake he'd ever made was getting involved with Miss "Charly" McAllister.

Ortega impatiently shook the door. "You must go now. I have work to feeneesh."

She moved stiffly to the opening, afraid to question her good fortune. But she turned to look at Kent, then swung around to impale Ortega with her glare. "What 'bout him?"

49

Kent answered defensively, "What about me?"

"If my bein' here's a *mistake*, ya shouldn't be here neither."

Roberto rolled his dark eyes and shrugged, casting Kent a conspiratorial wink. "The day, who knows what she weel breeng, no?"

"Whaddaya mean?"

"Just get out of here, will you? Before the nice constable changes his mind."

Since that same thought had been festering in the back of her mind anyway, Charly edged on through the door. There were too many things she needed to do to be stupid enough to argue. Besides, with Kent Ashford's surly attitude this morning, he could durned sure take care of himself. She wouldn't bother to put herself out for him again.

So, with a jaunty wave, she hurried from the jail amidst grumbling complaints from the other five desperados. The last sound she heard from inside, though, was something that sounded like clinking coins, and then the resounding click of the door as it closed.

That ominous sound followed her, echoing through her soul as guilt plagued her. As soon as she set things straight at the station, if that were at all possible knowing her father, maybe she'd have time to look for the missing stallion.

Her steps quickened as she neared the Overland office. The empty feeling in the pit of her stomach had more to do with the fear of what she would find inside than the small amount of food she'd eaten in the past twenty-four hours.

But when she approached the long building with the tower guarding the entrance and darted a peek inside, she stared in open-mouthed wonder. There stood her pa, all right, behind the counter, deftly taking money from ticket-buying passengers as if he'd been doing it for years.

She blinked, but the image of Jed McAllister, wearing a dirty undershirt and baggy trousers, refused to go away. At least his suspenders spanned his stooped shoulders and his reddish-brown hair was slicked away from his face instead of hanging in its usual greasy, scraggly strands. The stubble on his chin had even grown until it almost resembled a beard.

Charly cautiously stepped inside, half-afraid that any sudden movement would cause the scene burning her eyes to vanish in a puff of smoke. But then she heard his raspy chuckle and knew that what she saw was real, though her pa hadn't looked so respectable since a few months after he'd been lucky enough to stumble into this job—just after John Butterfield lost the mail line to Wells, Fargo & Company.

Leaning back against the wall, she propped one booted heel against the boards and crossed her arms over her chest, seeing in her pa's face the same jubilation he'd shown that day when he discovered that most of Butterfield's employees had followed after their boss and that the new employers were desperate for operators.

She sniffed. Few supervisors had since bothered to take the long, dangerous, roundabout trip to check up on the stations. That was all he needed to know. Her pa saw there wouldn't be anyone to watch over his shoulder and he'd started drinking, slacking off on his responsibilities 'til Charly herself had to handle the chores and keep the office open.

Levering away from the wall, she bit her lower lip, warding off the smidgeon of resentment trying to work its way into her breast.

"Where ya been, gal?"

She sighed. By jiggers, until he'd opened his mouth, she'd almost gotten her hopes up. But a man couldn't up and shed a lifetime of laziness and indifference overnight, she reckoned. He'd been drunk again, all right. Hadn't recollected talkin' ta the doc. Otherwise, he'd of larruped her good for bein' tossed in the calaboose.

Delaying her approach until they were alone, she walked over to stand across the counter from Jed. "I been in jail, Pa. Waitin' fer ya ta come an' get me." The expression of guilt darkening her father's already ruddy features did little to appease her. It wasn't his guilt she wanted.

"Damn it all, daughter, I knew there be somethin' . . . But we been busy. Lots o' folks wantin' ta travel an' all. Couldn't up an' leave the place untended now, could I?"

Sadness ached through her chest and chilled her heart. "No, pa. Ya shore couldn't do that."

Jed grumped around, sliding papers back and forth on the desk. "Yeah, knew ya'd figure it that way. Ed's down at the stable. Reckon ya'd best go see if'n he's doin' ever'thin' ta suit ya."

Her head snapped up at her father's caustic tone. His back was turned, giving her no chance to question what he meant before an elderly couple entered the office and she had to step back.

With her father occupied, she had time to think—and worry. Ed? At the stable? No matter how hard she'd tried to teach her brother, he'd never learned the correct amount to feed the livestock. It was almost an everyday ritual, her following along behind him, adding more grain or forking out hay when he'd fed too much. A deep scowl furrowed her brow as she quickly exited the building.

A short, dark-skinned, bright-eyed youth bumped into her legs, nearly toppling them both. He giggled and shook his index finger at her. "You no look where you go, Missy. You no more careful, fall in beeg puddle."

Charly laughed and ruffled the boy's shaggy hair.

52

"Diego, ain't nuthin' ta fret about. We ain't seen nary a sprinkle in two months."

The youngster looked to the South and West. "It rain. Mebbe tonight. Mebbe mañana. But eet weel rain."

"Whatever ya say, amigo. Hey, wanna go ta the stable an' help curry the mules?"

"Already done that, Missy."

"Huh?"

"Sí." He reached inside the pocket of his white cotton pants and proudly showed Charly two pennies. "Señor Ed, he pay Diego *dos centavos.*"

Charly spun around and ran the half block to the huge stables. She stopped beside a new pile of manure and soiled straw heaped outside the double door. Her mouth gaped as she hurried down the wide center aisle, peering left and right into freshly laid stalls, shaking her head at the bathed and curried stock.

"Hey, Charly girl, there ya be. C'mon an' set a spell. We wanna chance ta win back some of last week's wages."

In spite of the conflicting emotions rolling inside her head, she smiled when she spied Uncle John and several of the other stage drivers sitting on bales of straw scattered in a haphazard circle with another bale in the center serving as their table.

She waved and walked toward the big ox of a man. He'd been one of the faithful, staying on to work for Wells, Fargo. If it hadn't a been for him, she'd never have become a driver, would've gotten lost more times than she could count, and been stuck along the routes with broken-down stages.

He grinned lop-sidedly and Charly found herself wondering for the thousandth time just who Uncle John was. She doubted he had one relative to call him "uncle," and often wondered if his real moniker was "John." Sometimes, he got such a faraway look in

53

his eyes when she called him by name. Other times, he didn't even respond. And if the man had a last name, no one knew it.

Cards shuffled. Charly took a deep breath. Cheap cigars. Leather. Horses. And sweet-smelling hay. It felt good to be home again with the drivers, the livestock, her pa and Ed—her family.

She looked around what had for months now been her first steady home. They'd actually been in Tucson long enough that people called her name when she walked down the street. The man who owned the emporium knew what she needed before she ever showed him her list.

"Heard you was in the calaboose, gal. How'd ya git out?"

Oh, how she wished she could give Uncle John a simple answer to his simple question. Nagging doubt still haunted her steps. Why *had* Kent Ashford decided to set her free? He'd been goldurned mad when he'd made the constable arrest her—and had seemed even more annoyed when he'd roused her that morning. What'd changed his mind all of a sudden?

But she grinned at Uncle John, Enrique Morales, and Herman Olivas. "Don't'cha know? Ain't no jail kin hold Charly McAllister fer long."

"Yeah, she's the toughest desperado I ever did see," Uncle John teased.

The drivers guffawed.

She glanced around the circle of men and into the darkened corners of the barn. "Where's Ed?" Usually he was the first one to pull up a bale at the mere suggestion of a game of poker.

John spat and tilted his head toward the rear door. "Mare threw a shoe yestidy. He's tackin' it back on."

Charly begged off sitting in on the game right away and went in search of her brother. She shook her head. Ed McAllister? Voluntarily working? It didn't sound like him at all.

A side door led into a large corral. To her right, a blaze-faced sorrel mare stood tied to the top rail. A man was bent over with the horse's foreleg tucked between his knees, hammering a short nail through a hole in a rounded iron shoe and into the animal's hoof.

Stuffing her hands into her pockets, she waited until he let the shod hoof drop and stood to arch and stretch his back. He was shorter than she by a good two inches and more swarthy in coloring. His features were fine and handsomely arranged on his narrow face. In fact, if he wasn't playing cards at this time of day, she usually found him at the cantina with a woman, or maybe several, "entertaining" him.

Now he turned his too-charming smile on her. "If it ain't the 'Boss Lady'."

She stiffened. "Come ta see how my 'younger' brother's doin'."

"I'm older'n you."

"Yeah, but yore the 'youngest' brother I got."

He shrugged and squinted. "Where were ya last night? Ever'one's been askin' for ya."

She doubted that. More'n likely, they were glad she hadn't been around to ride them about doing their chores. She scratched the end of her nose. However, from the looks of things, they'd gotten along fine without her.

Ignoring his question and the leer in his eyes, she said, "Looks like ya got everythin' done already."

"Yep. Surprised?"

The question caught her off guard. What had gotten into her pa and Ed to put them both on the prod today? "Well . . . yes . . . no . . . I mean . . ."

Ed shoved his fingers through his thick, dark hair. "Never mind, I know what ya mean." His eyes traveled over her wrinkled, unkempt clothing and began to sparkle with a knowing gleam. "Never said

55

where ya been."

She felt the flood of heat in her cheeks. How'd a person explain that she'd been locked up like some common . . . "I been in jail. So what's it to ya?"

Ed laughed.

Charly sucked in her breath and stiffened her spine. She didn't know why, but in the back of her mind, she'd hoped that maybe her own brother would've shown just a little compassion, or even outrage, that someone'd had the nerve to treat his sister so callously.

"M-my . . . Bossy Britches . . . The self-righteous Charleen McAllister . . . locked behind bars. By damn, I wish I'd been th-there to see . . ." He couldn't finish as a round of laughter choked his words.

Draping her hurt about her like a well-worn serape, Charly glanced at the mare and asked, "Is the horse ready to ride?" Her voice was brittle, but she had no fear Ed would even notice.

Her brother wiped his eyes. "Yep. Why?"

"'Cause I got business ta look after. I need a horse, if'n ya think ya kin spare one, bein' as yore busy an' all." Of course there were spare horses. Extra stock was always kept on hand in case of emergencies.

He sighed and started back inside the barn. "Take what ya need, Sis. I shore ain't gonna argue with a criminal what's as dangerous as you."

She gritted her teeth as the door closed on another burst of barely muffled chuckles. "Goldurned smart aleck pup." She cursed and muttered unrepeatable descriptions of her brother and every other male within twenty miles of Tucson while saddling the sorrel mare.

Urging the mare into a gallop, she rode away from the corrals in a cloud of dust.

Kent Ashford walked through the barn door. He

56

sauntered over to the grinning card players, who seemed to be chuckling at some private joke, and pushed his hat to the back of his head.

Ed glanced up and asked, "What can we do ya for, mister?"

"I need a horse for a couple of days. Heard I might be able to hire one here."

Chapter Four

Kent Ashford retraced the trail he'd taken the day before in pursuit of the black stallion and the *thief* who'd stolen the animal. Mile upon mile rocked beneath the ground-covering lope of the gelding he'd hired from the young upstart of a man at the stage depot. As he rode, he rehashed the unlikely, onerous events of the previous day.

The most confounding happening, besides that of watching helplessly as his stallion disappeared over the boundless horizon, was the discovery that the sharp-tongued, bratty thief was a *woman*.

Definitely a woman. His left hand effortlessly guided and controlled the powerful, long-legged beast beneath him while his right index finger traced the curve of his lips. The imprint of Charleen McAllister's soft mouth was an almost tangible sensation, even now.

The hard muscles on his belly contracted as he also recalled the strength and determination behind the fist that had painfully ended his unexpected surge of desire. What a woman.

The hard set to his mouth softened as he wondered what her reaction would've been if he'd ... He snapped his shoulders erect and forced his concentration back to the trail ahead. Damn it, just as soon as he retrieved his horse and saddlebags, he would have nothing more to do with the aggravating ruffian.

A deep groove formed between his eyes. He wanted nothing more than to have her out of his life for good. Yet he couldn't escape the nagging possibility that he could make use of his acquaintance with her to learn more about those residents of Tucson who'd openly cast their lots with the South.

It was already rumored that one of the first goals of the Confederate Army would be to disable the mail route to California. His duty was to see that it remained open. The North needed the stage line to remain in contact with the western coast and to encourage California to declare fidelity to the Union.

He nudged the gelding to a faster gait as tension coiled like an angry snake in his gut. There would be time enough to decide his strategy *after* he found the damned stallion.

Charly scanned the countryside until her eyes burned. She'd bitten the insides of her cheeks until they were raw. This was the place where she'd fallen from the horse, but wariness caused her to fidget like a cat on a red ant hill. The ground was trampled by hoofprints. Unshod hoofprints. Many more than they had left yesterday.

Apaches! And from the particles of dust still crumbling into the tracks, they had passed through the area recently. Very recently.

The sorrel mare sensed Charly's unease and stamped impatiently at the flies taunting its soft underbelly. "Whoa, girl," Charly soothed. "At least they're riding in the opposite direction from where we need to go."

Amidst the jumbled tracks, it was more than she could handle to sort out the stallion's prints. Charly sighed, cast a long, considering glance over her shoulder, then urged the mare in the direction where she'd last glimpsed Kent Ashford's horse running like a horned jackrabbit.

She'd traveled almost half a mile, keeping a sharp eye on her back trail, before she came upon a slow, crisscrossing pattern over the rugged ground. Suddenly she slid the mare to a stop and all but fell out of the saddle. There. Two sets of tracks. One surely belonged to the dadburned stage robber, and the other, lighter set, had to be the riderless stallion's.

Her lips twisted into the semblance of a smile as she cast a grateful eye toward the sky and then back to the area ahead. She had found the tracks just in time. While the first set continued in a straight westward direction, the second weaved and wandered around before finally breaking off toward the south. The darned animal seemed to be having a heck of a time deciding where it wanted to go.

Climbing stiffly back into the saddle, favoring her tender shoulder, Charly followed that second trail. She leaned over, pitching her weight into one stirrup, and scanned the ground. The tracks were even more difficult to follow as the horse ambled up and down brush-covered ridges and through deep ravines. Finally, her hand tightened around the reins when she lost the trail completely. Just like an ignorant cayuse to walk into solid rock! She rode ahead, circled back, scoured either side of the crumbling shelf of stone. Nothing. Tired and defeated, she drew the mare into the shade of a three-armed saguaro cactus.

But she only rested a couple of minutes. After her boast about finding and returning the horse to the arrogant city dandy, she wasn't about to let an aching head and a few sore muscles stop her now. Flexing her shoulder, she studied the broken landscape.

If she were a pampered city-bred stallion, lost in

the desert, where would she go? The more she thought about it, the more she figured the horse would head for the foothills—toward trees, scrub though they were, and shade. The four-legged critter would be thirsty. And once it found the trees, it might smell the creek a couple of miles back into the mountains.

Well, most of the year it was just a wash, but there was usually water during late summer and fall, after the monsoons. It was the best hope she had.

By late afternoon, Charly had just about given up hope of finding the horse *anywhere*. It was as if it had sprouted wings and soared into thin air. Water flowed through the wash all right, but that was all she'd seen. Water. Rocks. Cactus. Salt cedar. Cottonwoods. No horse.

Desperation spurred her weary body as she urged the tired mare to keep moving. From the sun's position in the hazy blue sky, she had two more hours of daylight. Luckily she'd come prepared to stay out overnight. But day after tomorrow she had to be in Tucson, with or without Mr. Kent Ashford's precious horse.

The thought of facing him empty-handed galled her something fierce. She'd given her word. Even bragged she could do it.

Up one rocky incline she rode, only to slide down the other side as the mare's new shoes slipped on the loose rocks. The shadows grew deeper. Up and down. Up and down. A sense of urgency nagged at her. By tomorrow, the horse could be anywhere—maybe sizzling over some hungry Apache's campfire.

The mare stumbled as it reached the top of the rise. Charly gasped in surprise as she looked into the next depression. She blinked. She'd never been this far up the wash.

There were tall trees—cottonwoods and sycamores. Water gurgled down a gradual slope of smooth rocks and collected into a small pool before continuing to wind down the narrow wash. Grass covered a small meadow-like area. Green grass, though it was late January.

And there, knee-deep in the forage, stood the black stallion.

Charly laughed out loud. The big horse tried to lift its head at the sudden sound, but the reins appeared to be tangled around its foreleg. The saddle girth had loosened, and the bulky chunk of leather hung clumsily beneath the animal's belly. The horse rolled its eyes, as if complaining about all of the contraptions humans invented to make an animal's life miserable.

The mare started toward the oasis even before Charly nudged its sides. As far as Charly was concerned, she couldn't have found a better spot to camp if she'd looked all day—which she *had*, come to think of it.

Kent was as surprised, and wary, as Charly had been when he reached the location of "the accident." His scalp prickled when he recognized moccasin prints and tracks made by unshod ponies.

Every muscle taut, his well-honed instincts working with the power of a steam engine, he skirted the area and also spurred his horse in the direction he'd last seen the stallion heading. The further south he rode, the more unruly and fidgety the gelding acted. It pranced and snorted, made nervous from Kent's taut control.

Someone else was either on the stallion's trail, or was coincidentally riding the same direction. Somehow, Kent doubted the latter explanation was the answer. What if that someone had discovered his true identity? Knew what was in the saddlebags? Was this one set of tracks all he would find, or were others laying a trap somewhere ahead?

He slid his Colt Navy pistol out of its holster, checked the cylinder, then replaced it slowly, gently sliding it in and out of the oiled leather.

He gave the gun the tender care he would reserve for a mistress—caressed it with loving hands and kept it continually by his side. It had meant the difference between his life and death. No woman would ever be that trustworthy.

But he hoped he'd never need the weapon again. He was out here now to see if some little something he could do might help prevent a war. A shudder racked his spine at the thought. War loomed so close on the horizon that he could almost reach out and touch it, taste it. Oh yes, there would be a war. Already he'd seen families on the verge of being ripped apart—fathers arguing with sons—brothers fighting brothers. There would be no greater tragedy. But it was coming.

Kent shifted in the saddle, forcing his thoughts to the present. At least the conflict was still in the future. Right now he needed his wits about him. One mistake could be costly.

Charly unsaddled and hobbled her mare, tossed her gear in the shade of a brown-leafed cottonwood, and strode into the small meadow after the big stallion. It raised its head as high as it could and waited, snorting and nickering like she was a long lost pal when she finally stood next to it.

"What'sa matter, boy? Lonely out here, huh?" The horse whickered and nosed her rear end while she untangled the reins. "Lucky ya didn't fall an' break one o' them purty legs, eh, big fella?"

Once freed, the stallion arched its neck and shook its head. Coarse strands of mane whipped across Charly's face, but she just laughed and patted the sleek neck. When she started toward her makeshift camp, it trailed behind her like an ungainly puppy dog, lifting its hind legs awkwardly to avoid tangling with the saddle rocking beneath its belly and flank.

"Hang on, fella. We'll get that off'n ya quicker'n a bull frog kin croak." Not about to lug the heavy saddle any farther than she had to, Charly walked on, talking to the animal as if it were human. The stallion flicked its ears and placed its nose level with her hip pocket, daring her to try to get away now that she'd found him.

Stopping where she'd left her own saddle and gear, she edged around the horse, trying to figure the easiest way to unload the saddle without having to cut the cinch. The latigo was drawn so tight that she cursed a blue streak trying to work it loose.

Finally, she spit in her palm, rubbed her hands together and kneeled down to find a better angle to approach the stretched strips of leather. Ten minutes and a sprained finger later, the saddle thudded to the ground. Her chest collapsed on a long sigh.

She hobbled the horse a short distance from the mare and went back to straighten out the fancy saddle. It wouldn't do for Mr. Ashford to think she hadn't taken good care of his belongings. Suddenly a smile curved her lips. She could hardly wait to see his face when she rode into Tucson with his precious horse.

As she bent to turn the heavy saddle, a flap on one of the saddlebags flopped open. Reaching down to thread the thin leather thong back through the loop, she hoped nothing had been lost out of the bag. The city dandy acted pricklier than spiny cactus. A person'd think he'd stashed his weight in gold inside, or something.

"Hey! Get away from that saddle! Just what in holy hell do you think you're doing?" Kent Ashford spurred the gelding down the rocky incline toward the camp—and the snoopy woman.

He'd never been so surprised in his life as when he'd crested the top of the ridge and looked down to find his black horse and the indomitable Charleen McAllister. Who would have thought the tracks he'd been following could belong to *her?* And she was messing with his saddlebags. If the money was still there . . . If she had seen . . .

Once again the brat had stepped in where she wasn't wanted and held the success of his mission in her sticky little hands. Hell, if she were a man, he'd have no compunction about what should be done. But a woman? Damn right. Especially *that* woman.

At Kent's roared challenge, Charly started and stepped away from the saddle so fast that her heel caught on a hidden root and she fell backward, landing with an embarrassingly hard "thunk" on the ground.

"Of all the ungrateful sidewinders I've ever run onta, yore belly scrapes lowest of 'em all." A mask of outrage settled over her features as she scrambled to her feet, shaking her fist. "Yore the dang nabbedest piece a buzzard bait west o' the Missy'sip. Who found yore goldurned horse? Who's takin' keer o' yore possibles? Who—"

"Who asked you to in the first place?" Kent dismounted nearly on top of her and turned to stand so close that he could almost feel the heat from the sparks igniting her deep emerald eyes.

The power and anger radiating from him backed Charly up a step. He filled the small space with his body, placing himself between her and his bags.

"Shore t'weren't you, were it, Mr. dang nabbed city man? Ya wouldn't have the sense ta do sump'thin' so intel . . . intel . . . smart."

Kent's flexed fingers itched to snake around the contrary woman's slender throat. What was *her* problem? *He* was the one who had the right to be incensed. "What were you doing with my saddle-bags?"

Charly took another step back. The deep growl rumbling from his throat was frightening. City dandy, or not, there was something dangerous and threatening about Kent Ashford today that she'd never noticed before. Maybe she'd best give him more consideration or she might just bite off more'n she could chew.

"The ties'd come loose. All's I was doin' was cinchin' it closed agin. Why? Ya afeerd I might up an' git dirty fingerprints on yore fancy outfit?"

"You damned little . . . I'm gonna put more than a few fingerprints on your tough little hide if you don't tell me the truth." His fingers clamped onto her shoulders, a safer target right now than her throat.

She gasped and looked up, and up, into his glinting brown eyes. "Truth? Ya think I done *lied*? 'Bout what?" She was stunned. Never having told a fib in her life, or even been accused of such, she couldn't figure out what the man thought there was to lie about.

When he saw the pain in her expressive eyes—whether from his words or his hurtful grasp, he couldn't be sure—Kent's grip loosened. What he did know, though, was that he had never intentionally hurt any woman in his life, and he would not be goaded into it now.

He took a deep breath to control his raging emotions. What if she was telling the truth? Perhaps she had just been retying the flap. Sometimes he had trouble with that right side himself. Maybe she hadn't seen the contents. If she had, surely she would have already questioned him about the money. Rough and tough she might be, but she was still a *woman*.

Calm down. Act reasonably. His actions so far had probably only served to make her suspicious and

67

curious as to what he was trying to hide. And from what he'd witnessed, she wouldn't have had time to do anything with the money even if she had searched the bags.

Charly stiffened her shoulders, regaining some of her pride and composure while he seemed lost in a private inner battle. Her chin tilted up as she watched him.

It occurred to Kent that he needed to see if the money was even there. If the flap had been open like she said, currency could be scattered clear to El Paso by now.

"Damn!"

"Ya curse too much. Ya know that?"

Kent didn't realize he'd spoken aloud. But talk about a pot calling the kettle black. "And you, young la . . . woman, have the foulest mouth I've ever heard on a female."

Charly tried to duck from under the large, too-warm hands still trapping her shoulders, but his fingers automatically tightened. So she doubled up her fist and socked him in the stomach.

"Ooooff!"

A grin spread clear to her narrowed eyes when his hands jerked away from her to tenderly probe his belly. "I ain't neither got a f-fowl mouth, dang nab ya. Ain't never said a goldurn bad word my en-tire life."

He gasped several exploratory breaths before scowling and muttering, "Just what the hell do you think "dangnab" and "goldurn" are?"

"T'ain't curse words."

"Might just as well be."

"Ain't so."

"Whenever you *say* those words, you're *thinking* curses."

"Warn't doin' no such thin'." She felt a faint flush spread across her cheeks.

"Same thing." Kent blinked. Good God. How had he regressed to such a stupid argument? Yet . . . He rubbed his chin. Perhaps it was a good thing her concentration had been diverted from the saddlebags. He'd check and see if anything was missing. Only if it proved necessary would he mention them again.

Charly jerked her hat off and shook her head. A cascade of shiny, dark hair tumbled over her shoulders and down her back to hang in thick waves. Kent sucked in his breath. "Damn!" She posed a pretty sight—eyes spitting fire, her delicate nose tilted enough at the end to give her an endearingly impish quality. And those freckles—so vivid on her flushed cheeks.

"There ya go agin. Cursin' fer no good reason a'tall. Why, if'n ya warn't—"

One giant step put Kent upon her. Once again his fingers bit into her shoulders. His head dipped and his mouth silenced her open lips. She was too stunned for an immediate response, but he slid his hands down her arms and clasped her elbows just in case she should take a notion to hit him again.

Caught unaware, Charly had been warming up to give the dandy an earful—but the feel of his warm, firm lips on hers left her speechless. She clasped the only part of him his constrictive hold allowed—his forearms. His tendons rippled beneath her fingers like the supple muscles of the blooded stallion. The sensation warmed her all over.

Kent felt her fingers clutching at him, but ignored them. The rest of her body was liquid heat against his own. When her lips parted, he pushed his tongue between her teeth, teasingly exploring the soft, moist cavern of her mouth.

Charly's heart pounded in her ears until she could hear nothing over the roar. Dark spots danced beneath her eyelids. Feebly she began to struggle, then more forcibly as panic overwhelmed her.

Kent felt the pain of sharp nails gouging his arms. Charleen's soft, pliant body gradually stiffened. Reluctantly he broke the kiss.

She gasped for air, clawing at her shirt with each ragged breath.

He watched her struggle for oxygen in stunned silence. Each gulping pant drove home the fact that he had practically suffocated her. Suddenly he smiled and shook his head. Laughter vibrated through his body. In his arms, he held an honest-to-God innocent. How long had it been since he had, or had he ever, experienced anyone so naive and untried? An amazing rush of tenderness overpowered him.

His first woman had been the seducer. For as long as he could remember, women had made the passes and he had "succumbed" like the gentleman he'd been raised to be. He didn't feel vain or conceited, but he was relatively good-looking and blessed with a fair-to-middling body. Women liked him, he liked women, and that was the way of things.

No fuss, no muss, no trouble. No clinging when he had to leave. And that was the way he wanted it—would have it no other way.

Charly knew she was a babe in the woods of romance, but she was woman enough to recognize the hooded expression in Kent Ashford's eyes. She flushed and lowered her eyes, then raised them again just to make sure she really was the reason the fancy dandy had softened so.

His white teeth flashed in a dazzling smile. She shivered. His eyes roamed over her with a ferocity that put her in mind of a hungry man eyeing his last meal. Yep, she'd ruffled the rooster, all right.

But it was her own feathers that were fluttering like a hen in a whirlwind when she stepped back, clenched her fists, and demanded, "What'd ya go an' do a thing like that fer?"

He cocked a questioning brow. "A thing like . . . what?"

She blinked and gulped, suddenly unable to look him in the eye. "Ya know, k-kiss . . . me like . . . that?"

"You didn't like it?" He spread his hands across his lean hips, drawing her attention to the tight fit of his broadcloth suit pants. She struggled to catch her breath, wondering what was wrong with her. She'd never had these breathing problems before. And *like it?* Like the way his warm lips fit so perfectly to hers? Wasn't no way she was gonna answer *that* stupid question.

Kent stifled the urge to tease her further when he noticed the uncharacteristic ruddiness of her features. He didn't need a hysterical female on his hands during the trip back to town. He nodded toward her neatly stacked gear. "Looks like you were setting up camp for the night."

She looked at the ground and became absorbed by the unwieldy progress of a black beetle. "Yep, reckon so. But—"

"If we hurry, we could make it back to Tucson." Worse than the thought of traveling with an uncontrollable woman, was the notion of spending the night in the middle of nowhere with one.

"Ya some kinda idjit, city man? Ride back over that rough country, an' it gettin' dark? That's a darned good way to cripple a horse."

He glared into the waning afternoon sunlight. "Well, maybe you're right. But—"

"'Course I'm right." She started toward her saddle and possibles with the intention of carrying on with her chores. But she stopped abruptly. Hold on jest a dadburned minute, she scolded herself. The dandy had an awful peculiar look to his eye. Jest what was on his mind? Did he think she *wanted* to stay out here—alone—with him? After that kiss, did he think

71

she might be inclined to take advantage of his . . . body . . . or something? He durned sure had another think comin' if'n that was his . . .

"If we're goin' to camp here, we have a lot to do to make it comfortable before dark." He rubbed his hands together impatiently. Damn, but he wished he was back in town. Spending the night with a cocklebur like Charleen McAllister was going to be torture—even if she did have an awfully sweet, tender mouth.

Charly gulped. Just how *comfortable* was he talkin' 'bout? All she needed was enough space to throw down a bedroll and a small fire to heat water for her tea. 'Course, *he* was a city dandy. No telling what comforts he was accustomed to. "M-maybe we oughtta—"

"What? I can't hear you."

She spraddled her legs, suddenly wearing her temper on her shirt sleeve, and shouted, "All right. *You* set up camp. I'll scout fer wood."

"You don't need to yell, Miss . . ." For a moment, he just stared thoughtfully at the woman. Miss McAllister was much too formal. And somehow, the feminine, Charleen, didn't suit the leather-clad hoyden. What was it he'd called her that time in the jail cell? "Miss . . . Charly." Yes, he liked that even better than "brat." His brow arched quizzically, stretching the skin around his scar. Then again . . .

When Miss Charly snorted and stomped toward the creek, he nodded and hid a triumphant smirk by spinning on his heel to unsaddle the hired gelding. After picketing the animal with the other horses, he pulled a handful of sweet-smelling grass and rubbed down all three. By the time he returned to camp, Charly had a small, smokeless fire going and a battered pot of water sitting on a rock beside the flames.

"Uhmm, I haven't had good trail coffee in days."

"An' ya ain't gonna start now."

"Pardon me?"

"This here water's fer my tea." It tickled her to watch the grimace of disgust wrinkle his handsome face.

"Tea! That's a damned inconsiderate way to end a lousy day."

"It's alls I brung. 'Course, if'n ya got yore own makin's—"

"Tea's fine," he snapped. Of course he hadn't thought to bring supplies. He felt the hint of a flush prickle his cheeks. Damned obstinate woman. He'd been too concerned about his saddlebags to think rationally. And that wasn't like him. He'd never gone into unfamiliar country so ill prepared. She should know that.

Charly blinked at the hangdog expression on the pedigreed pup.

Kent turned away so he wouldn't have to look at the dimples denting her perfect, peaches and cream-tinted cheeks—at his expense.

From her small store of goods, Charly miraculously created a meal of bacon, beans, and tortillas. Kent had never tasted anything so good. And while he ate, he continually watched her, amazed at the contradictions she presented. Seasoned tracker. Wonderful cook. Rough garb. Soft to touch. Mouth like a mule drover. Yet those same lips . . . So sweet. So kissable.

Her eyes downcast, Charly managed to do a little studying of her own as the flickering flames cast Kent in sharp relief. He might be city-bred, but his face and neck and the backs of his hands were tanned a rich mahogany shade, something she must've noticed before. May-be, the dandy wasn't such a dandy after all. But then who, and what, was he?

He wasn't like any other man she'd ever known. None of the Tucson natives, or any of the stage drivers, had his looks, charm, easy grace—and that . . . something . . . that said he was all man. And she'd sure never been attracted to anyone like she was to him. She was acting like a kid who couldn't resist a piece of candy.

It was that clammy feeling in the palms of her hands when he looked at her—the queasy sensation in the pit of her stomach whenever he touched her— that set him apart from the rest of the men in her life. No one else'd had the power to set her body aquiver with just one lazy smile.

"Reckon I'll clean up." Charly shot to her feet, desperately needing to put more distance between herself and the durned attractive man. She gathered up the few utensils they'd used, then stomped off toward the creek, leaving an astonished Kent Ashford staring after her.

"What'd I do?" he muttered to himself as he bent to the task of spreading out the extra blanket Miss Charly had thrown in his direction earlier in the evening.

He puttered around the fire, doing everything he could to keep his mind off the woman, and the fact that they were alone, beneath a blanket of stars, the moonlight shimmering . . . A flicker of light interrupted his daydreaming. He glanced into the sky. The vision had only been in his imagination. There were no stars. No moonlight. Just an occasional spear of lightning and the distant rumble of thunder.

In a way he was relieved to think it might storm. It would provide the perfect damper to the romantic scenario he'd been picturing in his mind. He chuckled. Romantic? With Miss Charly? That was rich. Just because she had a pretty face . . . and round, swaying hips . . . and breasts that bobbed enticingly beneath that baggy shirt . . .

Lightning cut a jagged path to the ground, much closer than it had been. He glanced toward the creek.

74

Where was the woman? She'd been gone a lot longer than it should take to rinse off a couple of plates and spoons. His brow knit with worry. No matter how tough and indestructible she tried to act, she was still a woman—still needed a man's protection.

Quickly he set off after her. His steps became even more hurried as he approached the creek. Images of rattlesnakes, rabid coyotes, and haunting memories of her lying unconscious on the hard ground ripped through his mind. Not realizing the water was so close to the thick growth of salt cedars, he literally burst through the tangled branches.

Charly was bending over a natural pool formed by smooth stones and driftwood, patting the cool liquid on her throbbing temple and rinsing her aching shoulder. Kent's unexpected charge caught her off guard. She jumped to her feet and grabbed the knife from a leather scabbard looped over her belt.

The quick movement caused her to slip on a moss-covered rock. She fell, twisting and clawing frantically at branches that were too far away. Cold water surged over her head. Gasping and sputtering, she fought to sit up in the shallow stream. Tendrils of soggy, tangled hair clung to her face and eyes.

She expected to open her eyes and find a band of vicious Apache warriors, but when she finally focused her gaze, only Kent Ashford stood on the bank. She raised a dripping fist and shook it in his direction. "If'n ya ain't the clumsiest goldurned dandy. God must git right tired o' lookin' after yore mangy, flea-bitten hide."

Awkwardly clambering to her feet, stumbling farther into the stream amidst muttered oaths, she wailed, "Jes' look what ya gone an' done now."

Chapter Five

Kent stood transfixed by the wondrous sight of the bedraggled woman. Her dark hair hung in a heavy, dripping braid down her back. Loose strands curled enticingly around her ears and coiled in little ringlets on her long, slender neck.

Hardly able to tear his gaze away, he caught another movement from the corner of his eye and turned to find her hat, spread flat on the water, washing against a large boulder. His lips quirked upward. Her fall had done the impossible—separated Charleen McAllister from her hat. With a satisfied tilt of his brow, he stooped to retrieve it and gallantly held it out. "I believe this belongs to you, ma'am."

"Ooohhh! You son of a billy goat!" She reached for her hat, but he held it too far away. She knew he wouldn't wade any closer and risk soaking his own precious hide.

Gritting her teeth, and with her arms spread out for balance, she dragged first one water-filled boot forward and then the other. Slowly, with the cotton shirt she'd changed into earlier and her leather britches clinging to her body like a second skin, she inched her way over the slippery rocks to the dry bank.

Her angry glower sliced into Kent as she snatched her hat and slung it on. "Ooohh!" she shrieked, as the crown emptied more water over her head. "Damnation! Damn! Damn!"

Kent shook his head. "Tsk, tsk. What'd I tell you? Mouth like a muleskinner. Yes, ma'am."

"Shut up. Ya hear? Jest shut yore trap." Charly slogged through mud and weeds, grimacing as water squished between her toes and through the soles of her boots with each ungainly step.

"Oh, yes, ma'am. My pleasure, ma'am."

She scooped up the plates and spoons and with one last cutting glare at the sidewinder, made her way slowly back to camp, the wet clothing chafing her tender flesh.

Kent silently watched her awkward progress, knowing full well the cause of her spraddle-legged gait. There was nothing more uncomfortable than heavy, wet leather. He'd worn plenty of it when, as a youth, he'd gone through a rebellious streak and run away to the Rocky Mountains. For two winters he'd lived with an old mountain man, run trap lines, and grown into a man.

He traced the scar near his left eye. If his father hadn't passed away suddenly and left his mother ailing and in need of his care, he might have stayed in the rugged wilderness forever. He had really loved his freedom, with no one to answer to but himself. And for a long time he'd blamed his father for purposely ruining his life, for up and dying and forcing him home to take over the reins of the family business.

But now, at the ripe old age of thirty, he realized that times were changing quickly and he enjoyed being at the forefront of new challenges and discoveries. If Kent Ashford had anything to say about it, one day soon the Ashford & Company Railroad would be a contender in transcontinental travel.

Lost in his thoughts, Kent had fallen behind Charleen on the way back to camp. He tensed as he neared the area. Scouring the surroundings for the cause of the indistinct rattling noise, he began to realize that it became louder as he approached the woman. Then he frowned when he saw her hunkered over the fire, shoulders shaking, teeth . . . rattling.

In an instant, he had snatched up his blanket and stood by her side. "Get out of those wet clothes, woman. For God's sake, do you want to catch your death of pneumonia?"

"I-I'll b-be . . . f-fine, soon's I dr-dry out . . . s-some."

"You bet you will, but you're not going to do it that way. It'll take days for that leather to dry, and you know it."

She swallowed the urge to fling back a cutting retort. He was right. She *did* know better. But she wasn't about to take her clothes off right here in front of Mr. Kent all-mighty Ashford. And she couldn't seem to pry herself away from what heat the small fire offered.

Kent followed her gaze as it darted from him to the fire and into the dark foliage near the creek. He took the hint that she needed privacy. A deep growl rumbled in his throat as he threw her the blanket and stalked toward the trees. "Hurry up. If you're not out of those clothes in five minutes, I'll peel them off you myself."

Walking swiftly away, putting as much distance between them as possible, he concentrated on tamping down the urge to remain behind and help her get naked. She was amazing. How had the ruffian managed to look so adorable, sitting there with puffy eyes and a red nose, her clothing outlining every rounded curve? She had a tempting body, no doubt about it. And he could just imagine her skin

79

feeling all soft and dewy after her unexpected *bath*.

His gut contracted at the thought of bare, satiny, female flesh. Damn it, why'd she have to go and flaunt herself at him like that? Her type of woman wasn't at all appealing to him—usually. She was probably as hard as iron springs and tough as a rope. Probably.

He shook his head as he unwittingly recalled the coiled heat that had seeped from those velvety lips. Hell, if her response to his kiss was any indication, her woman's flesh sheathed a veritable volcano. So what? So why was he, after just listing reasons as to why he shouldn't, suddenly itching to be the one to unleash her passion?

He was a man. That was the only answer. Hidden beneath those unkempt men's clothes beat the heart of a woman. Her innocence was a challenge, that was all. Those big green eyes that touched him to his very soul had nothing to do with his lust. The vulnerability peering from her pixie features had no effect on his desire.

Finally reaching the river, Kent knelt and scooped handfuls of cold water over his head. He gazed longingly into the stream and contemplated a quick dunking just as lightning lit up the sky like a Fourth of July fireworks celebration. Close on its heels followed a rolling boom of thunder that literally shook the ground. He sniffed the air and detected the telltale smell of rain.

A frightened cry rode on the wind from the direction of the camp. Kent spun in a heartbeat and ran back to find Charly cowering in the voluminous blanket, shaking like a leaf in a blue norther. Her arms were thrown over her head as if warding off the Devil himself.

"What's happened? Charly? What's wrong?"

She just shook her head until he reached inside the

blanket and cupped her face. Frantic that some wild animal might have harmed her while he'd stupidly left her alone, he lifted her chin until she had no choice but to look into his eyes. "Tell me. Are you all right?"

She gulped and nodded, then blinked, trying to hide her shame beneath her lashes. "I-I . . . the storm. I'm afeered of . . . storms."

Lightning crisscrossed the sky. She flinched. Twisting, she sought to escape his hands long enough to cover her head. Thunder rocked the earth and she trembled so violently that she almost lost her grip on the blanket altogether.

Large drops of rain spattered on the dry ground and disappeared immediately, leaving only puckered blobs of dust as proof of their existence. Then the heavens opened in a heavy deluge.

For a moment, he was stunned by her confession of any kind of fear. Then he glanced quickly around the camp, but the only shelter he saw was in the trees. He had learned better than to hide there during a lightning storm.

All at once he became aware of a frantic tugging on his shirt. He looked down. Charly stared up at him, wild-eyed, her mouth working convulsively.

"What? What is it?"

"C-cave."

"Where?"

She glanced toward the stream. "B-by w-water . . . fall."

That was all he needed to know. In one lithe movement, he gathered her into his arms and began to run, sheltering her as best he could with the width of his shoulders. He had to lean almost double to fight the dragging, gusting wind.

Keeping his footing on the rounded stones near the creekbed proved to be a feat in itself. But when he lifted his head to get his bearings, another bolt of lightning illuminated the area around the pool.

"Th-there." A bare arm snaked out of the blanket long enough to point at a black, shadowy space just to the left of the falls. Seconds later, with water dripping from his hat brim down the back of his neck, he discovered the yawning opening. Setting Charly on her feet, he slopped through puddles of water to the nearest salt cedar and broke off a long branch.

Above the roar of the storm, he shouted, "Wait here." Holding the branch in front of him, he knelt and shook it inside the cave and swept the feathery leaves over the rocks. Crawling in as far as he could go, he repeated the movements until he was certain no other creatures had taken refuge there.

Thunder ripped overhead.

The cave was shallow, providing barely enough shelter for the two of them. If they cuddled close, they could both stay out of most of the wind and water, but nothing would block out the thunder and lightning. "Come on."

Charly felt like a skittish filly as she stood at the opening of the cave. Cave? Why it was nuthin' more'n a hollow in the rock, she realized. Surely they couldn't *both* fit into that small space.

Suddenly a bolt of lightning struck a nearby tree. Terror seized her as the air sizzled and the hair on the back of her neck stood on end. Instantly a resounding crack thundered through her as the tree split, adding the sound of toppling limbs and the smell of singed wood to the ever-increasing storm.

Kent had barely turned to see what was happening when his arms were filled with damp, scratchy wool and hard-breathing woman. His brow furrowed. She was dangerously close to losing the protective shield of the blanket.

Charly chewed the inside of her lower lip and tried to stifle her mewling sounds.

Kent's back hugged the wall of the cave, and Miss Charly was tucked into the curve of his body. There was nowhere to put his left arm and leg but on top of her chest and thigh, respectfully. His chin rested in her damp, fresh-smelling hair as he faced the raging storm while sheltering the she-cat who'd become a scared kitten.

Before too long Charly started to fidget. Kent's wet clothing was soaking her blanket and his body had begun to tremble so violently that she couldn't find a place for her head. For the first time since the storm had begun, her fear was eclipsed by concern for the man who'd gone out of his way to shelter her.

One hand crept out of the blanket to touch his cold, wet cheek. His skin was taut and she shivered along with him as a stray blast of air chilled flesh exposed by the slipping cover.

Durn it, why'd she have ta go'n strip down nekkid as a jay bird? If'n she hadn't been so dratted cold, and the fire and the dry blanket hadn't felt so good, and her long johns hadn't stuck to her like snow to a grizzly bear . . . Well, she'd just gone and done it, that's all. She'd stripped off *everythin'*. And now look at the predicament she was in.

As much as she hated to think of the consequences of what she was about to suggest, she knew there was no other choice. "I-If'n ya don't shed them duds, you'll catch that there new . . . new-mon-ya, shore as a fish'll catch a worm."

Kent tried to keep his teeth from chattering as he grinned at the wary trace of amusement in her voice. He'd never heard her tease him—or anyone, for that matter. It suited her so much better than stark terror.

"So, you're turnin' the tables, are you?" His body tensed when he felt the rise and fall of her round little chin on his chest as she nodded.

There was barely room enough to lift his shoulders

in a shrug. "Wish I could oblige you, but I'm afraid we're packed in here too tight to do a thing about it. And I'm damned sure not crawlin' back outside just to shuck my clothes."

Charly had wondered just how he would manage to undress, and found that she wasn't a bit disappointed when it turned out he couldn't. Being so close together, at least *one* of them should keep their clothes on.

Then the darned man started shaking again, hard enough that her teeth rattled, too. Oh, hell, no one had ever accused Charleen McAllister of being a lady. Besides, what would she do if the citified dandy took sick? She lifted her head and looked into what she hoped were his eyes—it was so blasted dark when there was no lightning.

"Listen up, mister. If'n yore not out o' them there clothes in five minutes, I'll have ta peel 'em off'n ya my own self."

Kent's lips were too numb to feel his own smile. He hadn't realized just how soaked he'd gotten on the way to the cave. And now, with the cold rock biting into his wet skin . . . He couldn't seem to get warm, no matter how close he cuddled to Miss Charly.

But he wasn't too cold to accept her challenge. She'd asked for it, and it was the sensible thing to do. "You're on my right arm, and I can hardly get out of wet clothes with just one hand, so . . . you're goin' to have to help me. Start peelin'. And hurry, please. I'm freezin'."

Charly was dumbfounded. He had taken her up on her threat to peel off his wet clothing, dang nab the luck. And although she'd believed every word he'd said about undressing *her*, surely he didn't expect . . . couldn't possibly . . . "Oh, no." She tried to free his arm to no avail.

He lowered his head next to her ear. "Oh, yes. You can't let me get sick and maybe die, can you?"

Another chill shook him from the roots of his hair to the soles of his wet boots.

Hell, he probably shouldn't have asked, he mused. What did she care what happened to him? Sick or dead, at the least, it would get him off her back. He hadn't even thanked her for leading him to his horse and saddlebags.

Saddlebags! His head bounced off the wall of the rock enclosure. Good Lord, the bags were out there . . . with no one to guard them.

Suddenly the top button on his shirt popped free. A hissed breath became trapped in his throat as the second sprang loose. By the time she'd reached the button above his belt, thoughts of going out and checking his precious bags, or even disentangling himself long enough to jump up and quickly disrobe, were replaced by a burning heat coiling inside him which did a pretty effective job of chasing away the cold.

Charly's fingers hesitated over the buckle. So far she'd managed his shirt with little qualm, but his pants? Did she dare?

"I-I think I can get my belt." Kent flipped the buckle. But the heavy trouser material was wet and stiff. Though he'd thought to save her, and himself, the embarrassment, he couldn't unfasten his pants alone. Humiliated by his weakness, he said, "Sorry, honey. I'm all thumbs."

His husky voice filled Charly's overactive senses with a force almost as powerful as the raging storm. *Honey.* He'd actually called her by a pet name. No one had ever done that before. Did he mean it as an endearment?

Well, no matter. She had to get him out of his clothes, or he really might get sick. Unaware of the fact that it was her gentle handling, even more than the cold, that caused his infirmity, she swallowed and took hold of his waistband. Her fingers trembled when the muscles beneath the backs of her hands jerked and rippled at her barest touch.

She closed her eyes when his breath passed her cheek, only to be indrawn sharply again when she finally pressed the brass button through the damp opening. "D-did I h-hurt ya?"

God, Kent thought. What could he say? One minute he ached to the chilled marrow of his bones. The next minute, his body threatened to burst into a thousand white-hot sparks. Yes, he hurt. No, her touch sent ripples of pleasure radiating through his limbs. "I'm all right. You about done?" Please! But he couldn't bring himself to put an end to the tormenting pleasure.

Something warm and hard pulsed next to her fingers when she reached the last button. Her face flamed and she silently blessed the darkness for hiding her reaction. She wasn't ignorant about the male body. Her only family and close companions for the last ten years were men. But she'd never . . . touched, or felt . . .

Then his hand covered hers, ending her increasingly clumsy attempts to finish. Goose bumps puckered her flesh when he literally growled, "I can take over from here."

"Ya sure?"

He took several deep breaths. "Yeah."

"Good," she gulped.

But as he struggled to ease around and slip out of his clothing, their bodies brushed and collided until every nerve ending on Charly's skin screamed out. "I-I'll slide out an' give ya more room," she generously, but selfishly, offered.

"No. The blanket'll get wet and it's all we have to . . . We just need to trade places, is all. Can you kind of scoot down and let me crawl over?"

She tried, but if she slid her upper body down, she had to raise her knees.

"Damn."

She hadn't realized his mouth was so close to hers until the exhalation from his whispered curse teased her lips. And then his chest was over hers, sliding the woolen blanket back and forth against her sensitive nipples. Her stomach contracted. The blood in her veins boiled and surged like molten lava.

A moan must've slipped past her clenched teeth, for he immediately hesitated, suspending his body directly above her. Charly's flesh tingled. Charged air filled the space between them.

He asked, "Are you all right?"

She felt the concern in his voice deep in her breast. "Y-yeah. C-cain't ya git over?"

Kent smiled at the tension cracking her words. It was gratifying to know that he was as disconcerting to her as she was to him. He closed his eyes and stifled a groan when she licked her lips and unavoidably stroked the tiny tip of her tongue over his lower lip. He followed her movement with his own. She tasted like heaven.

Realizing he had to move fast or stay where he was for the rest of the night, he gave a mighty lunge and rolled past her to lie prone in the opening, one arm thrown over his eyes, the other over his belly. Rain splattered against his shoulder and he welcomed the return to reality. It felt almost as if he was instinctively protecting himself from her womanly aura.

Charly immediately scooted into the space he'd vacated and hugged the blanket tightly about her. Without his hard, encircling warmth, damp chill had begun to seep through every small pin hole and split in the worn material. "H-hurry. It's c-cold."

Kent flinched as if he'd been suddenly raked by two-inch rowels. How could a gentleman refuse such a request? He tried to pull off his boots, but they might as well have grown to his feet. By the time he

87

finally wriggled out of them, it felt like he'd left most of his skin attached to the soaked leather. As he shed his clothes, he tried to spread them out over the rocks protruding into the shallow depression, irrationally hoping they'd somehow have a chance to dry.

Frigid air gusted into the hollow and prickled like icy fingers over his flesh. Neatness was quickly forgotten when he shivered, hunched his shoulders, and picked up a corner of the blanket.

Charly felt the tug and clenched her fingers. "Wh-what're ya doin'?"

His brow cocked comically. "I'm going to dry off and get warm. What did you think I'd do?"

She scowled. Actually, she guessed she hadn't thought that far ahead. "Ya ain't gonna shinny in here, with me?" But there was only the one blanket. And she *had* insisted.

"You know any place else I can go?" She shook her head, which he felt when her hair slid over his arm. The soft texture of it sent a spiral of heat through his belly.

"B-but—"

"That's right. Move your butt over. It's freezin' out here." Giving her no chance to argue, he lifted the blanket and slipped and wriggled until he covered every exposed inch of his body.

"B-but . . . yore nekkid!" she squealed as he plastered his frozen flesh against her.

"So're you," he said, surprised and delighted, as he pulled her close.

She squirmed to get away from the icy fingers inching their way around her waist, but her backside already scraped the rocks. "Get them hands of'n me, ya—"

"Here now, Miss Charly. All we're going to do is keep each other warm. This *is* the best way, you know."

88

She snorted at the amusement in his voice. Cozying up nekkid might be all in a day's work for the city dandy, but it was a brand new experience for her. Sure she'd heard about people warming their bodies after being caught in blizzards—flesh to flesh—for the sake of survival. But could two nekkid folks really lie together and not . . . well . . .

Kent could almost hear the cogs churning in her mind. He had to admit their predicament was a little unconventional. All right, a *lot* unconventional, but he hadn't honestly thought she'd be buck naked. Lord, his hands couldn't feel enough of her fast enough.

Her body was lithe and well-toned. Supple muscles sheathed by skin as soft and smooth as satin. And the parts of her that were all woman were . . . all woman. Firm, yet cushiony. Round and curvaceous.

He groaned, the sound reverberating through the small enclosure. Charly stopped struggling, and one of her palms cupped the bristly cheek nestled just above her breast. "Yore hurtin', ain't ya?" Unseemly as it might be, she couldn't turn away from him. He'd put her comfort and well-being above his own earlier—she could hardly do less now.

She felt strange, unfamiliar yearnings when she was around this man. And although she hated losing control of any situation, she sensed something happening between the two of them—something impossible to describe and completely unexplainable—a kind of *bond*. She'd felt it the moment the cell door clanged shut, enclosing them—together.

His breath fanned the sensitive flesh at the base of her neck. She shivered and instinctively clutched at him as her body melted to liquid heat.

Kent had been battling to rid his mind of the pain he was suffering. He had no intention of telling her the truth, or she'd never allow him to remain snuggled up next to her, so warm and cozy. Then he

89

felt her tremble and guilt flushed his cheeks. He really was an insensitive bastard.

"I'm all right. Just startin' to warm up some. What about you?"

Finally, she nodded.

Kent released the breath he'd been holding. He couldn't believe it. Here he was snuggled up against the beautiful body of a woman who only hours ago he'd have described as a brash and bold brat. He'd survived worse weather than this when he'd been wet and cold and come out unscathed. She just didn't need to know that, did she?

Somehow he managed to slip an arm beneath her and turn her so they lay like two neatly stacked spoons. His chin rested on her shoulder as he soothed, "We'll just lie real still and let our bodies warm to each other. All right?"

Charly was afraid to say a word for fear her voice would betray the turmoil raging inside her. She longed to rant and rave and snap, "That goldurned better be all ya warm." Yet she was also tempted to whine, "That's all?"

No doubt he wasn't even tempted to amuse himself with her. She knew darned well her faults and shortcomings. She was too tall. Too skinny. Too strong. Her breasts were small. Her nose tilted at the tip. Her lower lip was too big. Most women had wide, generously rounded hips, but hers were slender with just a hint of a curve at the sides of her thighs. She could cook, but spent little of her valuable time doing other feminine chores. Naw, there was nuthin' about her that would appeal to a man like Kent Ashford.

So, knowing all of that, why was she disappointed?

"Are you comfortable?"

His warm breath filled her ear and wafted teasingly down her neck. She tilted her head against her shoulder in an effort to block a strange, warm shiver.

"Uh-huh," she murmured truthfully.

A large hand spread flat against her belly. The flesh beneath his fingers crawled with sensations that were foreign and pleasurable.

She'd never felt the sensation of her bare flesh pressed so closely to a man's. His muscled body was hard and unyielding, yet his skin was smooth and the hair covering portions of his torso was soft and springy and tickled her back and bottom.

The closer he snuggled, the more pronounced became the warm, pulsating length of his manhood. Beads of perspiration formed wherever their flesh came into contact. Durned if'n flesh didn't heat flesh quicker'n beans'd boil over a hot fire, she thought.

She swallowed what felt like a mouthful of sand and asked, "Are . . . are ya warm enough, yet?"

"Hmmm?"

Charly had to bite back a moan as his deep rumble snaked down her spine with the potent sensuality of a tender caress. With a corner of the blanket, she fanned her face. "Ain't ya warmed up?"

"I'm workin' on it." His chin nestled in the hollow between her neck and shoulder. His thighs curled up to meet the backs of her legs. Suddenly he liked the way this tall woman fit his length—the way her soft places filled his flat, hollow spaces.

Like a female cougar he'd stalked once, she was sleek and supple, graceful in motion yet intense in her concentration on survival. Miss Charly—so busy going about life that she had no time to smile or laugh.

Perhaps, during his time in Tucson, he could do something to change that. Sure as hell, she'd provide a pleasant diversion. He smoothed his hand up and down her silken belly. As he'd known she would, she wriggled and he hardened against the sensual friction of her dérrière.

Charly gulped and instantly stilled when she felt

his body's response to her motion. She also stifled a purr of pure female satisfaction. Why, she'd aroused a spark or two of desire from the city dandy!

"Reckon if'n we turned 'round, ya'd heat up quicker? Lord only knows it's plumb fried me better'n a trout in a pan o' hot lard."

Chapter Six

Kent blinked rapidly. "You think that will warm me up, huh?"

"Yep."

He wasn't all that certain about that prospect. "Anything's worth a try, I guess." And truth be told, his back was still chilled where he couldn't reach to tuck in the blanket and ward off the swirling wind.

Another few minutes were spent sorting and bending limbs as they shifted onto opposite sides. Kent pulled the blanket beneath his chin. He already missed holding her and was tempted to renege on her offer when he felt her tentative movements against his back.

Charly rested her cheek on the back of his shoulder and slid her arms around his waist. Two pairs of shins, knees, and thighs molded together. Shy efforts to keep a distance between her upper body and his flexing muscles went for naught when he suddenly shifted and settled back against her.

A tiny gasp was proof of how deeply she was affected by the contact.

Kent had doubted his body would receive a reprieve in this turnabout position. All it took was one warm puff of breath over his shoulder blade and the gentle nudges of taut little nipples to strike a match to his already smoldering desires.

Every nerve ending, every hair on his body instantly attuned to her subtle movements. Long fingers sifting through the wiry hair on his chest incited a riot in his groin. His breath rasped through gritted teeth. "Damn, honey, you were right. This seems to be workin'."

Charly smiled against the corded tendons on his back. "Reckon'd it might."

He hunched up and threaded his fingers through hers to keep them from roving to more dangerous locations. When she didn't immediately try to jerk free, he knew she was feeling more relaxed with their situation. Now, if only *he* could ease the tension coursing through his body.

He ached to take the woman with every fiber in his being. The last time he'd suffered with such a tremendous need was . . . Well, he wasn't sure he'd *ever* been this consumed by a woman. But he couldn't do it. Not now. Not when she was susceptible because of her fear of the storm and the circumstances that had brought them together—naked.

Although she was definitely aroused, and it would only take a few well-placed touches and tender caresses to make her his, he didn't want her *that* way, not knowing if she was giving herself because she felt beholden to him for keeping her safe. For some damned reason, he wanted more from her—more for her.

Kent sighed and stared into the night. Rain continued to pelt the ground outside their cozy cave, though the thunder and lightning seemed to be gradually diminishing.

Charly yawned and rubbed her soft cheek into his back and he groaned. Looking into the black clouds, he prayed for the strength to survive the next few minutes, let alone the rest of the night.

As her eyes drifted closed, Charly languished in a

feeling of peacefulness she hadn't experienced since her mother used to tuck her into bed at night and listen to her prayers. For the first time in a long time, she felt safe and protected, in a cold little cave in a forgotten little valley.

She inhaled and reveled in the scent that she would always recognize as belonging only to Kent Ashford—a hint of spice, oiled leather, and virile male. Her nose wrinkled with pleasure as her arms tightened about his massive chest. She yawned and blinked her eyes. Tired. So tired.

Kent exhaled a sigh of extreme relief when he at last felt the even rise and fall of her breasts. Hell, if she'd squeezed him one more time, branding him with those hard, hot nipples, he'd have flipped over and given the little minx exactly what she was asking for.

His teeth flashed white in the darkness. He had a gut feeling that she'd give back as good as she got. From the quickness and intensity of her responses, she would more than likely prove to be a passionate bed partner. And he promised himself, one day soon, he would damn well find out if his instincts were correct.

Charly wriggled her nose. It didn't relieve the itch. She was either going to have to scratch it or sneeze, and she wasn't sure she could summon the energy for the former.

Durn it, something tickled her every time she breathed. Slowly, she cracked one bleary eye at a time. As soon as she was able to focus, they popped wide open. Dark, curly hair teased her cheek and nose. Chest hair. Her pillow was a warm, uncommonly comfortable, very masculine chest.

Then she remembered. The stream. Falling in. Changing out of her wet clothing. The storm. Her

95

terror. Kent Ashford carrying her like a two-year-old baby to a cave. The cold. His naked body pressed to hers. The warmth.

She shifted uneasily at the restless feeling suddenly pervading her body. And there was a persistent . . . ache . . . in that private place at the juncture of her thighs. How could just *thinking* about a man's bare body cause her to feel so . . . strange? His flesh had been so smooth and pliant when she ran her hands . . . A shudder slithered down her spine.

"You're awake." Thank God, he thought. Deep and hoarse, Kent's voice grated in his ears. He felt as raw and ragged as he sounded, too. Not only from a night spent with his long body crammed into such a small space, but also because of Miss Charly's lush curves curled so trustingly in his arms. His hands clenched into fists as he exercised supreme control to keep from fondling the enticing round orbs burning little holes in his rib cage. Somehow, during the *long* night, she'd managed to snuggle around and switch positions without waking him.

"Uhmm hmm." She arched her back, as contented as a milk-fed cat. Suddenly she found herself being lifted from her cozy resting place to be unpolitely dumped on her backside. She stammered, "Wh-what?"

"Sorry. I gotta go . . . out."

Through lowered lids, she watched Kent crawl from the cave and reach for his clothes. His beautifully proportioned body was mesmerizing. Muscles rippled over his lean form as he struggled into his damp trousers, hopping first on one foot, then the other, coming dangerously close to losing his balance.

When he finally stepped out of her range of vision, she stretched and draped the blanket around her. Sliding from the cave, she blinked at the brilliant blue sky and warm sunshine. The air smelled fresh and clean. Except for the pooled water in the rock depressions, rimmed by a thin layer of slush, no one would guess there'd ever been a storm, or that the night had turned frigid.

She caught sight again of Kent's tall figure as he disappeared into a thicket of greasewood. Her brow furrowed. The man was more prickly than a porcupine this morning. What burr had gotten under his skin? If she didn't know better, she'd almost think he was running from something. But what? Surely not *her*.

A few minutes later, he stalked back to the cave with her dripping leather britches and muddy shirt. He could hardly look her in the eye. Why? What had she done?

Kent had been dismayed to find her clothes in such an unusable state. What in the hell was he going to do? Somehow he had to cover the gorgeous flesh she seemed intent on flaunting. If she were purposely testing his will power, she would soon discover just how little he possessed.

Finally, he dropped her soggy clothes and reached over for his shirt. Thrusting it in her direction, he ordered, "Put this on."

Charly snapped her jaws closed, suppressing an angry retort as she snatched the shirt. All right, she could see that it would take a long time for her clothing to dry, but he didn't need to act grouchy as an old bear about it. Still, she refused to allow him to ruin her morning and replied with a stiffly sweet, "Thank you." When he continued to hover, staring, she narrowed her eyes and added, "Do ya mind? I cain't dress with ya standin' there."

Kent scoffed, "Woman, I've seen and felt everything you've got. Can't figure why you're so modest all of a sudden." Even as he voiced the words, though, he turned, hoping she hadn't noticed the evidence of what just thinking about her nude body had done to him.

Charly's eyes grew round with embarrassment. Heat flushed her body all the way down to her toes. Durn his arrogant hide. A gentleman wouldn't have mentioned her lack of propriety, especially when the circumstances had been out of her control. He, better than anyone, knew that.

But as soon as he turned his back, she dropped the blanket and hurriedly shrugged into the huge shirt. Even as tall as she was, the hem fell to mid-thigh and the sleeves fell well below the tips of her fingers. She rolled the cuffs to her elbows. At least the scanty covering was better than parading around in the bulky blanket or wet clothing that concealed nothing.

"Shore 'tis a pleasure ta know there's such a gallant gentleman around ta watch after poor little ole me." Indignantly, she yanked her filthy pants and shirt from the ground and stormed toward the ruined camp.

From his stance near the creek, Kent watched her carefully pick her barefoot way over the sharp rocks and through thorny weeds, trying to protect her ankles and legs. Damn, but she was a fetching sight. Every time she spread her arms, the shirt slid higher up her long, perfectly shaped thighs and he remembered just how smooth and soft her skin there was.

Cursing under his breath, he jammed his hands in his pockets and followed her. Perhaps giving her his shirt hadn't been the best idea he'd ever had. The voluminous material covered too much and yet not nearly enough. He could tell already—it was going to be a long day.

Several hours later, Charly shifted uncomfortably in the saddle. Though she'd secured the blanket over the hard leather seat, the prickly wool irritated the tender flesh of her inner thighs. And just to add to her discomfort, every time she looked ahead, the sight of Kent's bare back and the rippling contours of his muscles caused a disturbing heat to coil in her lower belly, arousing that aching sensation again.

Lord, but he was some kind of a man. He had a danged fine body 'n' was smart 'n' kind, too. An' she found herself drawn to Kent Ashford in ways no other man had ever attracted her.

How come *he* had to be the one? Why a citified dandy? Why couldn't some young man from Tucson have swept her off her feet? Someone who'd be around a while, who had the grit ta make somethin' of himself, rather than just bein' a good-lookin' drifter down on 'is luck.

He turned and looked at her. Anyway, she *thought* he looked at her. Charly sighed as a fluttering sensation tickled low in her stomach. For a moment, she'd glimpsed a fire blazing in his potent brown eyes as he yanked the gelding's lead rope in an effort to keep the horse in pace with the stallion's long stride.

He hadn't spoken a word since they'd broken camp and headed toward Tucson. Whenever it appeared he might, a shadow fell over his face and he'd keep any expression from his eyes. He was such a darned contrary man, and he was beginnin' to wear on her nerves.

So he'd treated her like a lady—had allowed the perfect opportunity to take advantage of her to pass. She sniffed and peered down the front of the baggy shirt. So what if she wasn't beautiful? So what if she'd never be considered attractive to a man?

There were more important things to keep her life full and meaningful. The stage station. Looking after her family. And so what if she'd never be soft-spoken and demure, would never be genteel or cultured. She didn't need a man or a family of her own. Diego and his friends visited her and kept her entertained with their childish antics. She wouldn't miss having a husband or children . . .

Life was good. Wasn't it?

Abruptly, Kent swung around in his saddle. Charly was startled from her reverie as he shouted and waved, but she couldn't hear a word he said.

Squinting, she tried to make sense of his gestures, but was almost blinded by a reflection off to one side.

Crack!

She jerked at the sound of the rifle report. Apaches? Bending low over the mare's back, she spurred it to catch up with Kent. Her heart leaped to her throat when he urged his stallion toward a nearby arroyo and the gelding was thrown off stride.

Yanked backward, Kent hung suspended between the two horses. She held her breath and offered a silent prayer until the gelding moved forward and Kent righted himself. Her own horse nearly ran over the gelding as the mare slid up behind Kent's stallion.

Off to her left, she spotted a gang of Mexican bandits riding toward them, their wide-brimmed sombreros flapping in the wind. Gun belts crisscrossed their chests. Goldurn it, she didn't know which was more vicious and dangerous—Apaches or the bandits.

Kent spurred the stallion down a steep incline, trusting to his horse's surefootedness as he chanced a glance over his shoulder. Thank God, Charly was following close behind. When he'd first sensed something wasn't right and then saw the reflection off a rifle barrel, he'd tried to warn her. But she'd been staring into space, lost in some private daydream. Fear had gripped him, knowing she was in danger.

But then she'd looked up just as the bandits charged into the open. With amazing agility, she'd kicked her mare into a dead run. Her skimpy clothing had to make clinging to the horse rough. Damn, but she could ride.

Ping!

Bullets whined by, too close for comfort.

Two of the outlaws left the main band and rode parallel to the arroyo, following the flatter surface on the rim. Cursing his inability to draw his pistol and still keep control of the gelding, Kent urged the stallion forward and hoped they didn't end up trapped in a box canyon.

The sound of rifle fire directly behind him drew a hasty glance from Kent. He looked just in time to see one of the banditos sprawl sideways from his deep-seated saddle. Surprise and admiration shone from Kent's widened eyes when he saw Charly sighting her Sharps, riding as hard as he, gripping and controlling the mare with only her knees.

Her hat brim flopped crazily in the wind. The shirt had ridden up almost to her waist. Determination and satisfaction were evident from the cocky tilt of her head as she nodded in his direction. Damn!

Turning his attention back to the trail, he spied a fork directly ahead. The route to the right was wider, but the banks on the left seemed less steep. In a split-second decision, he reined the stallion down the narrower, shallower cut. Sand churned beneath the horse's hooves. Dust clogged his throat. His eyes scanned the plateau in search of a place from which to defend themselves. The horses wouldn't be able to keep up the grueling pace much longer.

When he couldn't stand it, he risked another look back. Pride suffused him when he saw that Charly's marksmanship held the bandits at a respectful distance.

Minutes passed like hours as the depression narrowed. Stones grew to the size of boulders. The horses stumbled, nearly losing their footing time and

101

again. Kent's hand was raw from where the rope burned whenever the gelding balked. But close behind he heard the clicking of the mare's shoes and Charly muttering earthy curses. He grinned. Bless her heart. As long as she kept hitting her targets with such accuracy, she could curse like a sailor and he'd never say a word.

Sweat dripped down his back and soaked into the waistband of his trousers. Ahead, heat waves shimmered and disappeared. He straightened in the saddle, his eyes narrowed. Finally—the opening for which he'd been searching.

The arroyo continued on through another wide plateau, but just to his left a shallow ditch, probably cut by last night's runoff, branched off into a deeper gully. Several trees grew along the rim, and where their roots had been exposed, sand and dirt had collected to form a stairway of sorts. He shouted back to Charly, "Up here!"

The stallion needed little urging to escape the tight confines of the spooky arroyo. The gelding, too, seemed to sense they were finally leaving the narrow space and followed with barely a tug on the lead.

Charly was relieved to see that Kent had found a way out. The bandits were closing quickly and another had joined the one on the opposite rim. Before she could reach the spot where Kent had turned off, a bullet buzzed past her head. She raised her rifle. The mare struggled over the rough ground, spoiling Charly's aim.

Then, just as one dark-eyed, bearded bandit sighted down on her, she squeezed the trigger. The outlaw's gun dropped to the ground. He yelped and grabbed his injured shoulder. Charly grunted and reined the mare aside and out of the arroyo as another hail of bullets peppered the air.

She and the mare cleared the ridge as one of the stallion's front hooves caught on a hidden root.

Charly sucked in her breath as the animal went to its knees and she could only watch helplessly and pray it wouldn't go completely down.

Kent took a firmer grip on the reins and kept the stallion's head up until it regained its footing. For a moment, it seemed everything was all right, until he felt the horse's ungainly gait and realized it was lame.

In the next instant, Charly's pale face leaned close to his as she shouted, "Turn right. Used ta be a homestead t'other side o' them trees." He nodded and hoped the stallion could make it that far.

He followed Charly, gritting his teeth every time she turned to check his progress. Sometime very soon he was going to have to inform her that he wasn't a complete tenderfoot. He could take care of himself on occasion. His horse was limping badly, but if it was only a bit further . . .

Charly burst through the line of trees like an Apache on the warpath. The first thing she saw was the tumble-down barn. Her heart skipped several beats. Goldurn it, the buildings had still been standing the last time she was here. But then her gaze shot to the house and her hope soared anew.

Most of the old building was gone, but the end wall and two corners remained in fairly good condition and would give them a good barricade from which to defend the clearing. She rode inside the meager protection, dismounted, and was there to catch the gelding's lead rope when Kent tossed it down.

They had barely secured the horses when four outlaws charged through the trees, yelling blood-curdling threats and promises.

Charly ran to the nearest corner and rested her Sharps on the flattest rock she could find. She sighted carefully, but when she fired she squeezed the trigger too fast, jerked, and grazed a horse's hip. The animal squealed, put its head between its forelegs and bucked out of sight. At least one of the bandits had his hands full for a while.

Kent drew his Colt and slid into place a few yards from Charly. He fired just as one of the Mexicans neared the wall. The man fell and the horse wheeled and ran off.

The remaining outlaws rode out of gun range, stopped, and looked back as if reconsidering the importance of stealing from these particular hombres. A moment later, the one whose horse Charly had grazed rejoined them. After a brief discussion and a few shouted curses, the bandits disappeared back the way they'd come.

Kent looked at Charly. "What'd they say?"

She shrugged and checked the loads remaining in her rifle. "Didn't catch it all, but it don't appear they got much respect fer our ancestors."

He watched their departing dust until he could no longer see it. "Think they'll be back?"

She polished the rifle barrel with the tail of Kent's shirt. "Naw. They figured we'uns was easy pickin's. Prob'ly would've quit sooner if'n they hadn't reckoned I jest got off a lucky shot 'r two."

He cocked one brow and grudgingly admitted, "That was some mighty fine shooting, Miss Charly."

She grimaced at the name he'd taken to calling her. She wasn't anybody's *Miss* anything.

Actually Kent had also wondered if she hadn't "gotten lucky," until he'd looked back and seen her take out another bandit before following him out of the arroyo. Personally, he was glad she'd been on his side. "Who taught you to shoot? Your father?"

She shook her head. "My older brother, Rigo." Or Ned, to her pa. Jed, Ned, Ed, and Charly. Her pa liked things simple. But in her mind's eye, she pictured her brother, Rodrigo. She'd always preferred to call him by the name her mother had given him. He was as tall as she—dark, handsome, always smiling. In a lot of ways, her two brothers were quite

104

alike. But Rigo had always been the one to look after his little sister, to protect her, and see that she knew how to handle herself if the need arose.

The backs of her eyes began to burn. It was almost as if he'd known he wouldn't be around much—that she'd need to be able to handle herself. Rigo. Why had he disappeared? Was he still alive?

Kent watched the expression on her face change from one of proud assurance to sadness. Come to think of it, she'd mentioned she had another brother once when she spoke of her mother. She must've lost him, too, poor kid.

But when he reached out to comfort her, she had already turned and was heading toward the stallion. Annoyance written across his features, he trailed after her.

"Prob'ly hurt 'is leg that time he fell with me, but it'd had a spell ta heal."

"Probably," he said distractedly, looking at the expanse of bare *human* leg revealed when she bent over.

She ran her hands gently down the big black's shin to its ankle. "There's some heat in the joint." Straightening, she gazed toward Tucson, still some ten miles away. "Be best ta rest it tonight, too."

He nodded, wondering how he could survive the agony of another night on the trail with Miss Charleen McAllister.

"Least ways we'uns got shelter," she said, reaching up to scratch the stallion's ears, causing the shirt to ride up and expose the ivory flesh of her upper thigh.

His features went taut as sun-baked leather. In that instant, he realized just how near they'd both come to losing their lives. He'd almost lost her before he'd ever had her. And just look at her now, all that silken flesh exposed for anyone to see.

Completely ignoring the fact that the contents of his saddlebags would have been cause enough for the

105

attack, he shouted, "Damn it, woman, no wonder the bandits came after us. They thought they'd found easy pickings, all right, and a whore for the night. What do you mean by ridin' around almost naked?" Nope. He was taking her under his protection. For her own good.

"Why, you dadburned idjit. Of all the danged foolish . . . Why, yore the one what gave me this . . . shirt . . . 'cause ya said yore own self I couldn't wear mine. Ya . . . ya . . ." She couldn't think of anything bad enough to call him. What a bastard! Saying it was *her* fault they'd been attacked. "If'n they was after anythin', they wanted yore dumb ole stallion." Mr. Ashford himself should know they couldn't of wanted *her*.

When it appeared he had nothing more to say, she stormed over to her saddle.

Kent was astounded by the way she'd flown off the handle. And she'd had every right. He hadn't meant the words to come out the way they had. He'd just been frightened. What if something had happened to her? She'd only been out in this godforsaken wilderness in the first place because of him and the fit he'd thrown over losing his horse. If those men had gotten hold of her . . . It would have been on *his* conscience.

"Where are you going?" Damn it, couldn't she stand still for one minute?

"I'm gonna fetch us up some supper."

He thrust out his chin. "You can start a fire, just a small one, mind you, if you want. But *I'll* be the one to hunt the food."

Her eyes rounded at his declaration. She didn't quite know how to take this angry, irrational Kent Ashford. "Wal, if'n ya want—"

"I want."

"S'right."

"You damn well betcha."

106

Finally, rather than waste time glaring at each other, Charly shrugged and began to scrounge up small twigs and dry leaves for kindling. By the time she had the smokeless fire blazing, Kent stomped back carrying two rabbits and a handful of wild onions.

She unsheathed her knife and reached for the rabbits. Kent jerked them back. "Huh-uh. Where I come from, a man kills and cleans his meat. The woman does the cookin'."

How wonderful, she thought. All her pa'd ever done was the killin'. 'Course, he'd cleaned some of the game once, but he'd always cut off too much fat or left some skin, until finally she'd told him she'd best do it herself.

The sun had set by the time the stew was cooked. Kent had unsaddled and picketed the horses just outside the rock wall, and was now sitting on a rounded stone, staring at her. Self-consciously, she handed him a plate and spoon, then held her breath.

He licked his lips before tasting the aromatic stew. Swallowing appreciatively, he admitted, "Uhmm, this's good."

She lowered her lashes. "Thanks." But she raised them again when his attention was focused on the food. Her mouth went suddenly dry and she licked her lips as she watched the firelight dance across his broad, muscled chest. Her breath caught in her throat as the tendons on his upper arms flexed hypnotically every time he lifted the spoon. When he chewed, the hollows in his cheeks filled and the muscles in his chiseled jaw contracted, giving him a stern, even dangerous, appearance. Lord, but he was a fine figure of a man.

Kent surreptitiously made a few appraisals of his own. She had unbraided her hair to allow it to dry and he could hardly take his eyes off the long, wavy mass. The luxurious brown color burnished with

107

glowing red sparks was highlighted by the flickering flames.

Besides her glorious mane, his fingers ached to touch her vibrant, silken flesh, of which more was exposed to his sight than was comfortable for his burgeoning manhood. And when her head came up and her eyes locked with his, damn, but he thought he might be sucked whole into their deep green depths. He had the strangest sensation that if she wanted, she could look right into his soul.

Charly was sure Kent Ashford could read her thoughts right to her heart. And if that were so, he knew that she admired his beautiful body, that she remembered how his skin had come alive beneath her inexperienced hands and that her own body had glowed like hot coals as she'd learned the shape and feel of him.

Kent's gut felt as if a snake slithered through it when she suddenly ran her tongue over her full, pouting lower lip. Last night that pink tip had tasted his mouth, too, albeit accidentally.

Charly gulped in her breath as she watched Kent trace his index finger down the length of his scar. That same finger had chucked her under the chin and caressed the line of her jaw with a softness reminiscent of the flutter of a butterfly's wings.

Kent slid down to sit in front of the fire, resting his back against the rock. He winked and patted the ground next to him. "Come here, Miss Charly."

Chapter Seven

Charly didn't allow herself time to think about Kent's request. She just rose and hesitantly stepped over to stand in front of him. He reached out to her, running his hand up the calf of her bare leg. She quivered like a flighty filly. An intense longing immediately flooded her senses, yet she stood ready to bolt at any minute. What was wrong with her? She'd dreamt of being in his arms again. This was what she wanted. Wasn't it?

Kent thought her skin was softer and more fragile than silk. He could never get enough of running his hands over her graceful body. Yet, a frown creased his forehead. Only twenty-four hours ago he'd have bet good money that the last thing in the world he'd be doing right now was seducing Charleen McAllister. A typical woman she was *not*. Hell, at one time, he hadn't even known she *was* a woman. It had taken an irate constable and the raging forces of Mother Nature to bring them together.

Taking hold of her hands, he tugged gently, urging her with his eyes and a tender expression to sit willingly by his side. She swallowed, then sank stiffly down on the hard ground. The coiled muscles in his stomach slowly unwound. She had come willingly— even if she was still almost a foot away. But her right hand remained clasped in his left one and he twined their fingers together.

He shifted so that he faced her and reached with his free hand to smooth the hair from her damp forehead. His fingers squeezed the delicate hand he held until they ached. She flinched and started to pull away. "It's all right. I just want to check that bump," he soothed.

Gently, he probed the purple bruise. Her eyes drifted shut. "The swelling has gone down. Does it still hurt?" She shook her head and his fingers sifted through the dark mass of hair, finding and capturing several strands. He rubbed them sensuously between his thumb and forefinger. "It's so soft."

Charly gulped. "It's too thick, an' too long. If'n I don't tie it back, I cain't keep the stuff outta my way."

"I like it hanging loose like this, like a dark sable cape."

Pleasure snaked through her. No one had ever said anything nice about her unruly hair before. Tentatively, like a coyote pup sniffing a cactus blossom, she touched his fingers and heard his faint, indrawn breath. Frowning, pulling his hand down to where she could see, Charly gasped at the sight of his torn, raw flesh where the lead rope had burned into his palm.

"It's nothing," he told her, and tried to pull away. She refused to let him. "'Tis too. Might git infected."

Finally, he wrested his hand from her strong grip. "It'll be all right until we get back to Tucson."

Without thinking, she raised his palm to her lips and kissed the puckered flesh. Then flustered by her rash action, stammered, "I-I usually tote a salve . . . fer the horses . . . an' all. B-but—"

"Thanks. It already feels better."

His husky voice wrapped around her senses like a woolen cloak. She blinked, breaking the spell his nearness seemed to weave around her. He'd moved

110

closer—a lot closer. His heat seeped into her chilled body. A moment ago she'd been too warm. How could she have cooled off so fast? Trying hard to ward off a telltale shiver, she failed when she looked into the soft brown velvet of his eyes.

Kent took advantage of her preoccupation to wrap his arm around her shoulder. "Are you cold?"

"Y-yes. No. I—"

"I know what you mean."

"Ya do?"

"Uhhmm-hmmm. Every time you look at me with those huge, green eyes, I get hot all over. And when you touch me, then start to turn away, an icy wind blows down my back."

Yep, he understood. She didn't resist when he pulled her over and settled her next to his solid frame. In fact, he felt so good, so secure and comfortable, that she snuggled as close as she could get. Reveling in the wonderful stirrings ignited by brushing against him from shoulder to hip, she wondered why she'd been so reluctant and shy to touch him.

Lowering her lashes, she darted glances toward the usually immaculate man. Tonight, he was disheveled, so much more approachable and real. He'd thrown his hat over the saddle horn and a wavy crease depressed his thick hair where the band had set. His rain-soaked trousers had dried on his body, fitting his lean hips and muscular thighs so tightly that she flushed and looked quickly away.

Her mouth went as dry as a desert windstorm when it dawned on her why he filled out the front of those pants. If she was smart, she'd bound quicker'n a leapfrog ta the other side of the fire right now. 'Cause if'n she stayed . . .

As if sensing her sudden indecision, Kent lowered his head and took her lips in a deep, searing kiss. Slowly, carefully, he slid his back down the rock and shifted her more firmly against him until she practically covered him like a blanket. His fingers moved with calculated precision over her shoulders and down her spine, massaging the muscles that held her upper body so rigid.

Gradually, she began to relax. He whispered, "You feel good, honey." And when her lips parted, he kissed her again, teasing his tongue over the ridges of her teeth. Like a spring flower she opened for him, allowing him to sip from the moist cavern of her mouth.

The moment his lips touched hers, Charly's resolve weakened. When he hugged her to his huge, warm body, any thought of wriggling from his molten embrace evaporated like morning fog in the heat of his delicious assault against her starving senses. Lordy, it felt good to be cuddled and kissed so thoroughly that she forgot her cares and worries.

And when his hand slid under the hem of the big shirt, smoothing her quivering flesh and cupping her breast, she was nearly in danger of falling prey to a light-headed, female swoon.

No man had ever touched her bare breasts. She'd never even imagined it happening. But for some strange reason, being held and caressed intimately by Kent Ashford seemed . . . right. Shore, she was a little skittish of the quickness with which things were happening. But for a woman who'd reckoned ta probably go through life never knowing . . . well, what . . . this . . . was all about . . . And if'n it came to it, she'd have ta fess up ta bein' attracted ta him— mighty attracted.

Her body tingled and throbbed, demanding that she experience . . . everything.

She shuddered when the shirt fell open and his mouth replaced his fingers on her breast. The sensations that roared through her were so intense that she clenched her fists and her nails bit into her palms before she rounded up her senses and tried to

112

push him away. He lifted his head. Cool air closed over her skin as her damp nipple puckered. Her breath rasped in her throat. Red-hot heat coursed through her veins. She was branding-iron hot inside and gooseflesh cold outside.

Kent's eyes were liquid brown pools half-veiled by sensuously drooping lids. Her stomach turned a flip-flop.

"What is it, baby? Did I hurt you?"

"N-no, no. It's jest . . . I ain't never . . ."

"I didn't think so. Are you afraid? Do you want me to stop?" Kent swallowed an agonized groan. Surely that hadn't been his voice asking such a generous question. His body was on fire. He ached to bury himself deep inside her feminine flesh.

Strange, after all the women he'd had, that it was this particular one who could set his soul aflame with just one look from her sultry green eyes. What was it about her that made her so special? That caused *him* to feel so . . . different?

Impatiently awaiting her answer, he sought to discover his own. His hands roamed over her flat belly and narrow hips. She was as soft as a fluff of cotton, smelled fresher than morning dew and tasted sweeter than clover honey.

While Charly fought her desires, she squirmed beneath his expert manipulations. Everywhere he touched left her yearning for another stroke of his fingers or a smoothing caress from his palm. Yet, gaining control of her senses, she suddenly wondered why he'd stopped kissing her. She liked the way he kissed.

Somewhere, deep in the back of her confused mind, she reckoned that she might've pushed him away. That searing sensation, when he'd suckled her breast, had frightened her. The feeling . . . somethin' she'd known of no word to describe . . . had shot clear through her body and lodged in her lower belly.

It was still there, wriggling, burning, until she could hardly hold still.

"What do you want, Miss Charly?"

His voice sounded hollow and reedy to her ears, like he'd run a long distance without taking a breath. Funny, she was breathless, too. "I-I . . . don't reckon I know . . . 'zactly."

"Tell me if you want me to stop. Say it now, before it's too late."

Feverish thoughts raced through her mind. Should she save herself for marriage? Shucks, she'd never be asked. What harm would it do ta make love with Kent Ashford? No one'd know—only herself—and Kent. No one'd scold her, or even care. "Reckon I'm jest a mite skittish, is all. Ya see . . . I don't know . . . I cain't . . ."

A chuckle vibrated in Kent's chest as he sent up a prayer of thanksgiving. He wasn't sure he'd have been able to exercise the kind of super-human control it would've taken to stop. "Don't worry. Do anything you want. Touch me. Kiss me. Do whatever comes natural."

"You'll help me, won'tcha?"

Kent smiled. "It'll be my pleasure." He guided her arms around him as he wrapped her in a bear hug that lowered her body to lie fully atop his. His hands ran up her rib cage, over her shoulders and down her arms to divest her of the shirt's meager covering. He groaned his satisfaction when she was completely naked and spread as an offering for his hands and eyes to devour.

Charly reckoned the feel of her breasts nestled against his chest was absolute heaven. The curly mat of hair made a perfect home for her sensitized nipples. Once again, that melting sensation prickled in her lower belly. And something else, a weird tightening in her chest prodded her arms to slide around his neck. Instinctively, she lowered her head,

114

hungry for another kiss.

But Kent's lips strayed lower. He nibbled greedily on first one rounded breast, then the other. His appetite was both sated and heightened each time he touched her. Though her breasts might have seemed small beneath her clothing, they filled his palms and his mouth to perfection.

His hands worked their way down her supple back to cup her buttocks. He positioned her in a most tantalizing manner over the pulsing bulge straining the confines of his trousers. When her back suddenly arched and her pelvis ground into him, he slipped a hand between her legs. She was wet and ready for him. A satisfied grin spread over his lips.

In a motion so smooth and fast that Charly barely realized they had moved, he rolled her onto her back. Rising to his knees, he unfastened his belt and the first three buttons of his pants. Then his shoulders stiffened with impatience as his conscience got the best of him. A blanket. Where had he put the damned blanket? He couldn't wallow her in the dirt. And his boots. He still wore his boots. Hell!

"Kent?"

He looked down into wary, questioning green eyes. "Two seconds. I'll be back in two seconds. Don't go away?"

She shook her head and reached for him, but he was walking away. Leaving? Now? Her eyes grew wide with fear. Why? Had he changed his mind? What'd she done?

But then, as promised, he came back. His large body loomed over her and she caught her breath as a blanket flicked out to land on a soft bed of sand. Quicker'n a heartbeat she was in his arms. Just as suddenly, she was placed gently on the pallet. He sat on one edge of the blanket to pull off his boots and she watched the muscles on his broad back stretch and ripple and knot as he struggled.

115

At last the boots clunked to the ground and he fell back, panting and grinning. "If those bandits had killed me, they'd of had a hell of a time stealing my boots."

Charly had just opened her mouth to tell him it wasn't funny to even *think* such a thing, when he rolled to his feet and finished unbuttoning his trousers. But she couldn't speak. As she watched him, her mouth turned to sandstone.

Heat suffused her cheeks and her eyes flew to his face. Gone was his mischievous grin. In its stead was an expression of taut expectation. His dark eyes gleamed like a predatory wolf's after it'd trapped its prey and the intended meal was unable, probably even unwilling, to flee.

She tried to hold his hypnotic gaze, but her eyes seemed irresistibly drawn back to his fingers, which were slowly but surely freeing himself. Her lips parted. Her breath quickened.

As Kent peeled the trousers down his hips and they fell in a crumpled heap around his ankles, her eyes grew round. He was magnificent. Just as she could appreciate a well-made stallion, she knew she was looking at a male form of splendid perfection.

Not a spare ounce of flesh marred the wide shoulders, flat belly, narrow hips, and muscular thighs. And that portion of his body that was all male jutted out from a nest of dark curls—long, strong, and powerful.

She whimpered, whether with fear or from anticipation, she wasn't sure. He knelt beside her. Taking one of her trembling hands, he placed it . . . there. The flesh was hot and smooth as satin. Her fingers clenched, then relaxed, then stroked him. A gasp escaped her lips when he pulsed and hardened in her hand. Confidence surged from his body to hers as he threw back his head and groaned his delight.

Her slightest movement elicited a response. His

116

body was hers to command and she sensed that their coming together was right. It wasn't like a stallion mounting a mare. They were sharing pleasure, each of them unselfishly giving to the other.

As she met his eyes, she felt her cheeks flush. Kent thought he'd never beheld a more beautiful woman. The flecks swimming in her green eyes shone like gold. But it was her dimples that almost unmanned him. "When you smile like that, honey, do you know what you do to me?"

She laughed. He must've forgotten that she still held him in her hand. No, she hadn't known before. Yep, she knew now, very well.

Kent cupped her cheeks in his palms and nuzzled his nose to hers. "You need to do that more often, Miss Charly."

"Wh-what?"

He nibbled at her chin and finally returned to her delectable lips. "Laugh. I could listen to you laugh forever."

Forever. That sounded nice. Must be one of those sweet nothings men s'posedly said just a'fore . . . His mouth covered hers. He gently unwound her fingers, then shifted and sank down to enfold her in his arms. She gasped for air as his hands cradled her like a piece of delicate china. Surging beneath him, her ability to think rationally was consumed by a deep, aching need.

Kent marveled at the fluttering motions of her hands as they glided over his body. It felt good to have a woman touch and tease him. Her fingers grew bold—exploring, tantalizing, arousing him beyond his wildest expectations.

Wedging his knee between her legs, his left hand slid down her rib cage and over her hip, coming to rest at the downy thatch of dark brown curls. She gasped into his mouth and shuddered when he touched her there. "Easy, honey. I wouldn't hurt you.

117

It'll feel good. I promise."

His own pulse rampaged out of control when his finger delved into her moist inner heat. She was more than ready, but he wanted to prolong this first time, to assure her the greatest pleasure.

Charly inhaled deeply when she felt him fondling her most private place. She wasn't afraid. She was on fire, throbbing with unfamiliar sensations—with need. Her jagged nails scored his back as her body arched. "Please."

His hand stilled. "Please what, honey?" It was all Kent could do to keep from plunging into her.

She wasn't sure what to say. Somehow, though, she trusted him to put out the fire. "Please . . . don't . . . stop." Her voice was a husky whisper.

Kent had already shifted his body between her legs. He poised above her. The tip of his manhood penetrated her feminine lips and nudged inside until he was stopped by a silken barrier.

Hell, she was a virgin!

Her body screamed for release and she instinctively bucked against him before he could withdraw. It was as if some primitive savage had taken over and she was powerless to control her actions. But as he suckled at one pulsating nipple, she determined not to worry over it now.

Her slender legs clamped around his lean hips. Blunt nails dug into solid muscle. Her lips tasted every inch of his flesh she could reach from his chin to his taut nipples. When she felt a slight burning and tearing sensation, there was no time for regret. She opened to his plunging body. His hard length filled her. Every pulse from his shaft sent waves of heat spiralling clear to the tips of her fingers and toes.

The intensity of the feelings that shook her was like nothing she'd felt before. Was it always like this? Her senses were keenly aware of his every movement. His special scent and the slightly salty taste of his

118

skin were forever locked in her memory.

He groaned when her breath cooled the perspiration at the base of his neck. Now that the deed was done, that her virginity was taken, he found himself holding back—filled with unfamiliar feelings of doubt and uncertainty.

"Oh, God." His buttocks clenched when her hands grasped them. He arched forward, burying himself inside her molten depths. Rhythmically he rose and fell. She met his every thrust, bringing him to the threshold of exquisite, tormenting release.

A keening wail escaped Charly's kiss-swollen lips. The pagan forces that had been driving them both burst into a million blinding, aching, joyful particles.

"Damn."

A strange, melancholy lethargy settled over Charly. She'd chosen the right man to show her the wonders of "making love." She blinked. Until that moment, she hadn't put a name to their . . . Love? She doubted any such feeling was involved, yet, what else could you call an act so intimate and soul-wrenching?

Kent Ashford. Why had he been the one? Only him. Yep, he had definitely carved a notch in her heart for being so kind and tender, for treatin' her like he cared. Shore, she'd listened ta other women. She knew a lot of men weren't so thoughtful.

A slight grin curved her lips. Maybe all those other women just needed a man like Kent Ashford in their beds fer one night.

Her grin turned into a frown. Pain wrenched through her chest. Other women knowing her Kent? To see his beautiful nekkid body or feel his hands on their . . . No!

"You all right, honey?"

"Hmmm?"

"You had a strange look on your face. I didn't hurt

119

you, did I?" In reality, he thought, she had looked like a thoroughly contented kitten that had devoured a particularly tasty meal. But he didn't quite know how to phrase a question to get an answer to fit that analogy.

His gut contracted when she looked him in the eye and smiled, displaying those adorable dimples. He had a weakness for dimples—he'd just found out. Who would've guessed a tomboy like Miss Charly would possess such feminine attributes? Who could've known she would turn out to be more woman than any woman he'd ever bedded? He smiled, too.

"That there was some kinda fun."

"Huh?" Had he heard her correctly? Of course, he'd known she was far from being a typical female, but he'd truly expected her first words to be more on the order of, "Oh, we shouldn't have!" Or, "What am I gonna tell my papa?" But to hear, "That was fun?" He chuckled. The chuckle deepened into full-throated laughter. "I enjoyed it, too, honey."

Chill bumps prickled her flesh every time he called her "honey." She was awed that as handsome a man as Kent seemed attracted to her. Surely there wasn't nuthin' 'bout *her* that would appeal . . .

She slowly stiffened. What had gotten into her? Worryin' 'bout if'n this man found her attractive was plumb foolishness. He were a drifter. 'Fore long, he'd head out an' she'd be right back where she'd been afore—frettin' 'bout her pa an' the Overland mail.

And she didn't want the city dandy thinkin' she'd be hurt'r nuthin' when he *did* leave. Which she wouldn't be, of course. Nope. Not plain, Bossy Britches, Charly McAllister.

"Jest want ya ta know, ya ain't got ta worry none."

Kent's brow raised and lowered. He nestled his nose against a soft, round breast. "Worry? About what?"

120

"Ain't gonna be nuthin' said 'bout this. Yore gonna be goin' yore way, an' I'll be a-goin' mine. Got that?"

He blinked and shook his head. Wait just a damned minute! Everything she'd just said, he'd said before. Too many times. So why'd he feel this unaccountable anger constricting his chest? Why'd he feel his pride had just taken a swift kick to the backside? Was this the way a woman felt whenever he thought he'd been so suave and forthright, avoiding complications and what he figured might later turn into hurt feelings?

"Damn right I got it. I'm just glad you understand the way it is, hon. You know, you aren't one of those clinging females. But you and me, we really set off sparks, didn't we?" He slapped her bare bottom and rolled away, afraid she might detect the niggle of doubt that he couldn't chase from his voice or wipe from his features.

He stood and looked down at her huddled form. She was different, all right. Too different. Hell, he ought to feel relieved and lucky that she had such an independent attitude. Life was difficult enough without someone like Charleen McAllister intruding into it.

Charly jerked back the hand she'd extended in apology. For just a moment, she thought maybe she'd been mistaken, that maybe she'd misjudged the situation. But then she'd glimpsed the chiseled set to his jaw and the hard glitter in his eyes.

Naw, she'd done the right thing by takin' the responsibility on her own shoulders. She'd not cause him the embarrassment of tryin' ta figure out how to get rid of her once they returned to Tucson.

"Miss Charly?"

No more "honey." She sniffed and pulled the blanket up over her chilled body. "Yeah?"

"You never answered my question."

121

She could just make out his shadow standing next to the wall. His back was toward her. A terrible sense of loss and loneliness knotted her insides. "Wh-what question?"

"It was good, wasn't it?"

Good? Her body gave off sparks every time she moved. She'd never felt anythin' like it afore and reckoned she never would agin. Nope, she *knew* she never would agin. 'Cause she'd never let another dad-blamed man open her up fer the kind o' pain she was feelin' now.

"Yeah. It were . . . fun."

Chapter Eight

Later that night, Kent was still awake, staring into a black backdrop of a sky filled with twinkling stars and the silver arc of a new moon. Naturally, his thoughts returned over and over to Miss Charly, and his fingers curled into tight fists.

Fun! She'd thought the most incredible experience of his life had been *fun*. So that was the thanks he got for taking special pains to please the woman. Damn it, his arms ached even now to hold her. He had a questionable desire to soothe and comfort her, to praise her for the glorious love-making they had shared. Yes, this desire was questionable because he'd never felt it before.

But she hadn't given him the chance to enjoy a little quiet time with her. Like the barbs on a cactus, she'd immediately lanced into him, driving him to lose his temper—again. No other woman in his memory'd had the ability to both anger and please him to distraction in such a short space of time.

He sighed and tried for the millionth time to find a comfortable spot for his head on the hard seat of his saddle before pulling his hat down over his eyes. Damn the woman. As soon as they returned to Tucson, she'd get her wish—he'd go on about his business and she . . . Hell, she could do whatever she

123

damned well pleased.

By the time dawn peeked over the top of the farthest mountain, Charly and Kent were up and making preparations to leave the old homestead. Neither had slept well, and whenever they had an occasion to speak, they growled like surly bears.

"If'n ya want any o' this tea, better git it now 'fore I toss it out."

Kent ground his teeth. Obstinate hard-head. Who'd she think she was talking to? Some ignorant hick? And he wasn't blind, either. The tea had just boiled. "You do, and your backside will be redder than that saddle blanket."

"Oh, yeah?" Charly stood with her legs braced apart, her hands splayed across her slender hips. "I ain't been spanked since I's a babe, an' ain't nobody gonna do it now."

He smirked. "Where I come from, we're raised to believe that it's never too late, or a person's never too old, to learn good manners."

He'd unwittingly scored a hit to one of Charly's sore spots. Some of the steam left her bluster. "I got manners." She might not be sophisticated and citified, but her mother had taught her manners. She just hadn't had much occasion to use them.

"Where? They must be well hidden."

She stuck her nose in the air, deciding against dignifying his accusation with a curse. That wouldn't be *mannerly*. Besides, she was well aware that he was every bit as irritable this morning as she. His eyelid twitched and he kept rubbing at his scar, which was more prominent and noticeable today than usual.

Then she sniffed and stiffened her spine, fighting off a twinge of sympathy for the man. If he was tired . . . Good.

She hefted her saddle and started carrying it to where the mare was tethered. Every once in a while

124

she stopped and pulled at her stiffened leather britches. They kept irritating her tender flesh. Between riding barelegged yesterday, and then . . . what happened last night . . . she was sore from her knees to her . . . To keep the pants from rubbing, she tried walking spraddle-legged, but could hardly move at all that way.

Once she stopped, thinking she'd heard a snicker, but when she spun to face the ornery dandy, his back was to her. It was a good thing. He was partially . . . a lot . . . totally . . . to blame for her discomfort, and it would've done her soul proud to give him a good tongue-lashing.

In fact, she was disappointed that when he did turn to look at her, his expression was all surprised confusion to find her staring at *him*. Oooohhh! Drat the man.

Charly only *thought* she'd been uncomfortable. She learned what real pain was after mounting the mare and riding a couple of hundred yards. The insides of her knees and thighs felt as if she straddled a cholla cactus rather than smooth leather. And . . . there . . . the sensitive flesh ached and burned with every movement.

Kent suffered her antics of standing in the stirrups and painfully squirming as long as he could. He rode the gelding up beside her. "You can't ride all the way to Tucson like that."

She glared and puffed up like a horned toad. "I can. An' I shore 'nuff will."

He threw her off guard when he just sighed and shook his head. But the next thing she knew, his right arm snaked out and hooked her around the middle. She was dragged, kicking and swearing, from her saddle and deposited roughly across his lap. His saddle horn pressed the outside of one thigh, his hard belly trapped the other. One steel band of an arm supported her back, the other pressed just beneath her breasts, daring her to breathe and risk touching him. She was as firmly locked in place as if she'd been shut into Constable Ortega's jail cell.

With fire spitting from her eyes and her hands curled into claws, she turned to face the loathsome creature. However, all it took was one fierce threat from his uncompromising eyes to stifle her sputtering and fuming. She snapped her jaws closed with a click of her teeth and rode in silence.

"That's a good girl. Sit real still and we'll be there before you know it."

Oh, but she was tempted to wriggle her hips and make him squirm some himself. The evidence that he wasn't as immune to her presence on his lap as he'd like to pretend was long and hard beneath her hip. However, she had to admit to being much more comfortable now, and that she even enjoyed the close fit of her body to his.

Every once in a while, the undersides of her breasts brushed his forearm and they would both jerk away from the contact. Soon, though, moving with the rhythm of the horse's gait, they'd relax, touch again, and the whole reaction would start anew.

By the time they reached the outskirts of Tucson, they were both so stiff from trying to hold their bodies erect and apart that a good strong wind could have disintegrated them and blown their dust clear to Texas.

Humiliation burned Charly's face and neck as they had to ride through the center of town to reach the stables. She nibbled her lower lip, worrying about what the townspeople would say to see her perched on a man's lap, as useless as warts on a witch's nose, while he also led her horse and the stallion.

She hunched her neck and pulled her hat over her eyes as they rode past the stage depot. Maybe if she didn't look in that direction, her pa, or Ed, or any of the other workers, wouldn't see her.

126

The muscles on Kent's chest contracted and she turned her head just in time to catch him smiling and nodding to two of the . . . *ladies* . . . who worked at the saloon. Dark and sultry, they flashed wide smiles and sashayed their hips in wanton invitation.

Charly was unprepared for the painful clutching sensation that ripped through her chest. She jerked her head back around and stared between the gelding's flicking ears. It wasn't until she felt a pressure on her foot that she realized they had stopped and looked down to see her brother staring up at her, speculation rampant in his dark eyes.

How long had they been standing in the stable doorway? Why had she let her attention stray away from the troubles she would soon be facing? Who the dandy smiled at was of little concern to her. Confound the dratted man, anyway. She had to get away from him—before she made a horse's rear of herself, and in front of an audience, to boot. Mortified at the questions that would be directed her way, she began to slide from his lap.

But his arm suddenly grasped her, restricting her flight and her breathing. Then, very slowly, he lowered her to the ground. His breath fanned her ear as he whispered, "I ran into you a few miles out. Your head wound acted up and you were dizzy."

Her narrowed eyes popped open. Heat suffused her body. Dadburn it, did he think these people, people who knew her, would believe such a silly lie? She'd never been dizzy, or sick, a day in her life. Well, she'd just have to tell them . . . But by the time her feet touched the ground, she hadn't thought of any excuse that might be more believable.

Ed eyed the stranger with wary suspicion as he questioned, "What happened, Sis? What're ya doin' with this here fella?"

"I . . . was . . . I . . ."

Kent slapped the gelding's and the mare's reins

into the younger man's hands. "So, she's your sister. What luck. I just happened on to her a few miles out. Said she wasn't feelin' well. Only helped her out a mite."

Ed looked to Charly for confirmation. She quickly glanced at the water trough, the open door, the piled manure. She'd never been able to lie well, and it was painful to look at her brother and admit to a weakness. And dangnab it, here came her pa and Uncle John.

"Yore just in time, Pa. Charly's fixin' ta tell us why she come in with this here stranger." Excitement was plain on Ed's face, as if he expected trouble and welcomed it.

Embarrassed tears burned the back of her throat. "T'weren't nuthin', Pa. It's just . . . my blamed head . . . Damn it!" And damn Kent Ashford for causing her to look like a snivelin' *woman*. She broke and ran to the tiny living quarters connected to the stage station. Slamming the door closed behind her, she wrapped her arms around her waist and stared up at the viga ceiling, muttering every curse that came to mind and then some. What would Ed an' her pa an' Uncle John think? What would they really think?

Kent, standing amidst the group of open-mouthed men, shook his head. "Tsk, tsk. Poor little lady. She just isn't as strong as she'd like to pretend."

Jed McAllister ran a shaky hand over his red cheeks, then looked from his house back to Kent, giving the younger man a thorough inspection. "Don't never remember seein' my gal in such a state." When the other men began to shift their feet and look uncomfortable, he waved his uncertainty aside. Whatever was bothering his daughter, she'd handle soon enough. To the stranger, he said, "Ya new in Tucson? Ain't seen ya around."

Kent quickly held out his hand. "Kent Ashford. Just rode in the other day. Met Miss Ch . . . McAllis-

128

ter then, too. We, uh, spent some time together, in jail."

Suddenly, as if a summer breeze had melted a glacier, the McAllister men looked at each other and smiled. In turn, they shook Kent's hand and pumped it up and down until he thought he'd never bend that elbow again.

Only the huge man, who introduced himself as John, continued to remain aloof and Kent vowed to keep a wary eye on the fellow. Those pale eyes looked to be a hundred years old and sharper than a Missouri pig-sticker. The way the man was looking at Kent almost prompted him to check if his fly was unbuttoned, supplying blatant evidence of what had really transpired in the hills.

"So, my little Charly's hurtin', is she?"

Kent cleared his throat. Only a man the size of John would call Charly "little." "Yes. Reckon she is." And he made the statement with a clear conscience. When she'd run off, she'd looked like Apaches had forced splinters beneath her nails.

God, his heart had gone out to her then. He didn't doubt most of the men believed the story he'd concocted, but why had she acted as if she'd been humiliated, or was ashamed to admit that she was only human? If he thought taking back the little lie and telling the truth would help matters, he would do it, just to spare her feelings. But all it took was one look at her family and friends, and admitting to just a bit of selfishness in wanting to keep his good health, to help him decide that confessing wouldn't work. Not at all.

"So, you just decided to help her back to town, did you?" Uncle John glared down at the stranger.

Kent rolled his eyes. He'd almost forgotten the big man. Almost. "I did what I thought was best." He held his breath while John eyed him up and down and then gave him an easily read, I'll-be-watching-you look.

The breath hissed silently from Kent's lungs. He clenched his fists and studied the backs of his knuckles, wondering how many "protectors" Miss Charly had to back her up if she decided to take a disliking to a man.

Later that afternoon, Kent stretched out as far as he could on the short cot in his rented room. He'd been lucky that one of the stage drivers had a widowed sister with spare accommodations. Tucson may have been the only organized settlement between Mesilla and Los Angeles, but that still wasn't saying much about its capacity to accommodate travelers, other than those using the Butterfield facilities.

The calico curtain hanging in his only window wafted in the breeze and Kent glanced into the tree-lined courtyard. Though dry leaves littered the ground, Mrs. Mendoza was lucky to have several tall trees and bushes to block the sun's heat during the summer months.

From what he'd understood from listening to the drivers, until the Americans settled in Tucson and Butterfield brought his mail route through the city, there had been little outside influence. Travelers had slept in deserted adobe houses, camped on the plaza or in corrals until Butterfield had purchased a large hacienda and turned it into a decent station.

There hadn't even been a jail until recently. A whipping post on the plaza had served the town's needs. The only place to purchase "medicinal" whiskey had been the emporium. At least now there was a cantina. Thank God. He licked his dry lips. In fact, that sounded like just the place he ought to be.

Lumbering to his feet, he changed into fresh clothes. With his string tie knotted at his throat, he donned his hat and started jauntily from the small room. But a pile of leather in the corner caught his eye. The saddlebags. Hell! He couldn't just go off and leave a hundred thousand dollars lying in his room.

In a twinkling of an eye, he remembered his reason for entering the stage station the fateful day he'd run into Miss Charly. To be truthful, he hadn't seen her coming because he'd been too intent on the safe located just to the left of the counter.

With the cheerful notion that perhaps he'd be able to make it into and out of the depot without encountering the "whirlwind in leather," he slung the bags over his shoulder and left through the side door. Mrs. Mendoza had said he could use that entrance during his stay so he wouldn't have to worry about disturbing the rest of the household with his comings and goings.

Though Tucson had also received some of the rain from the night before, dust rose in small puffs with each step he took. The alkaline creek that ran through town was muddier than usual, and he noticed several Mexican women, balancing *ollas* on their heads, walking toward an *acequia* outside of town for their drinking water. They all wore *rebozos* or *mantillas*, and veils covered their faces except for one eye left open so they could see.

The closer he got to the station, the more he noticed another sign of the city's prosperity. Vagrants and ne'er-do-wells of every description lounged in whatever shade they could find. Some looked to be Americans, probably fugitives from California's vigilante committee, on the dodge but not yet ready to commit to crossing the border and leaving the states completely. A few were half-breeds, who more than likely found it difficult to fit in anywhere. But most looked like the Mexican bandits who'd chased Charly and Kent the day before. They were all hard cases and he let his left hand drop

131

closer to his pistol butt as his grip automatically tightened on the saddlebags.

A slight tremor of relief traveled through his muscles when he finally stepped inside the stage depot. The sensation was fleeting, however, as he stopped abruptly to listen to Charleen McAllister arguing with her father.

"But, Pa, ya cain't take off'n leave now. I gotta take the three A.M. stage, an' I ain't had no . . . much . . . but jest a little nap." She tried to keep from flushing a guilty red as she thought about the reason *why* she'd been awake most of the night.

Jed McAllister set his bristly jaw. A stubborn gleam drifted through his pale green eyes. "Sorry, gal. I done made plans ta see Josie. I broke 'em last week 'cause ya needed me fer somethin' else, but I ain't a-gonna do it agin. Git Ed ta work fer ya."

Charly's shoulders sagged as she rubbed her scratchy eyes. Sometimes she just wanted to give up and let her pa face the consequences of his laziness. This was *his* job. If *he* wasn't worried about losing it, why should she?

Because, goldurn it, for just once she wanted the McAllisters to stay in one place for more than a few months. She wanted their name to stand for something, wanted to keep the respect the people of Tucson had shown them when they first arrived to take on the job of stationmaster.

So far, no one suspected how close they'd come to shutting down a time or two when her father had forgotten to bag the mail, or request supplies, or had been too drunk to make sure there were enough fresh horses or mules on hand for the next relay teams.

But *she* knew. She'd been the one to scramble like mad to get things done before the stages rolled up. Yet she'd managed. And everyone had complimented her pa on what a fine job he was doing.

She sighed, "Go on, Pa. Don't worry 'bout nuthin'

132

here." As if he would. Wearily, she moved behind the counter and used its sturdy support to hold herself upright.

"Evenin', folks. Mind if I put my saddlebags in your safe for a few days?" Kent thought he'd better make his presence known before they caught him eavesdropping. Besides, he hoped Jed would stick around and help him so he could avoid Miss Charly.

Jed McAllister looked around and shrugged.

Charly's head snapped up as she recognized the voice. Suspicion stiffened her spine. What was *he* doin' here? Had he come back to gloat over her earlier embarrassment? Well, she'd make sure she'd have to have as little to do with the man as possible.

"No!"

"Sure."

Both Charly and Jed spoke at once. Jed glowered at his usually polite and solicitous daughter. "What's gotten inta ya, gal? That's what the safe be fer. Take the man's bags an' put 'em up fer 'im. Now."

Their continued arguing gave Kent a few extra minutes to digest the notion that he thought he'd heard Miss Charly say that *she*'d be taking the early morning stage out. Surely he'd misunderstood.

The station door suddenly opened and a young, good-looking man with dark hair and sparkling black eyes sauntered forward.

Kent bristled when Charly took the opportunity to ignore him as she flipped her braid over her shoulder and joined the newcomer. "Howdy, Orlando. Reckon I kin count on ya ta be here 'bout two this mornin', jest in case I need ya ta help sack up the late mail?"

Kent grimaced when the young pup took Charly's hand and flashed her a beguiling grin before kissing the backs of her knuckles. Kent'd give him knuckles. Nice hard knuckles. Right in the middle of those flawless white teeth.

As if sensing Kent's hostility, Orlando glanced in his direction, frowned, and fingered the bandana circling his neck, but then turned back to his employer. "I am most pleesed to have been given theese new job, an' weel come to your service gladly, Mees Charleen. We weel go all thee way to Dragoon Springs, no?"

"Sí, Orlando. Then we'uns'll meet the next stage West an' bring it back."

Jed had taken the saddlebags to the safe, but all the while they were being secured inside, Kent's attention was focused on the other two people in the room and their conversation. By God, it was true. *She* drove the damned stage. What in the hell were the Butterfield people thinking, anyway, to let a *woman* handle such a dangerous job?"

"Well, son, there ya be. Them bags is as safe as a widder woman at a prayer meetin'." Jed hooked his thumbs in his suspenders and grinned proudly at the preoccupied young man.

Kent put his hand on Jed's shoulder and pulled him aside. "I'm not hearing correctly, am I? That *lady* doesn't drive a stage."

"What lady?"

Kent scowled at the older man. "That lady right out there. Charleen McAllister." Damn the man. Didn't he have any regard at all for his daughter?

Jed shot Kent a funny look. "Yep, she do."

"Why?"

Thick brows almost hid the bewilderment in Jed's eyes. "Why not?"

"She's . . . She's a *woman*, that's why."

Jed leaned close and rolled his eyes. "Don't go an' be a-tellin' *her* that, son. Ya might up an' rile 'er." Laughing uproariously, he slapped Kent on the shoulder, handed him a receipt for the bags, and lifted a hand to Charly in a mock wave as he departed.

Orlando was leaving, too. "Sí, Mees Charleen. I

have everytheen you said I would need. I weel return in a few hours."

Kent waited until the office was empty before turning to Charly. However, at the mutinous expression on her face, he lost the will to do battle. What good would it do, anyway? She was the most stubborn, pig-headed female person he'd ever had the misfortune to come across.

So, he politely inclined his head, hurried out the door and grinned when he heard her muttering a string of expletives worthy of a sailor. He stepped into the street and happened to notice the boy, Orlando, walking a short distance ahead.

"Hey! Orlando, hold up." Kent hustled forward when the Mexican hesitated and directed a questioning glance over his shoulder. "I need to speak with you, please." Since most genteel Mexicans were nothing if not polite, Kent figured the word *please* would get the fellow to stop. And it did.

"Señor? What do you want?"

Kent held out his hand. "Name's Ashford. Kent Ashford. Just wanted to congratulate you on your new job. I imagine it's . . . Say, just what is it you're gonna be doin'?"

Orlando continued to warily eye the strange, suddenly friendly man, but he puffed his chest out proudly and explained, "I weel be a conductor of thee mail, Señor. *Muy importante.*"

Far from being enlightened, Kent clasped a narrow shoulder in his powerful hand and turned the kid toward the cantina. "That sounds downright interestin'. Why don't I buy you a drink? You know, to celebrate your good luck."

"No, señor. I must not. The stage, she weel leave in just a few hours. There ees much I must do."

"Then we'll have just *one* drink. I've never known a real mail conductor before."

Orlando hefted his shoulders and preened with

135

pride. "Well, perhaps just one."

Kent cocked a brow and smiled. "Sure. Whatever you say, kid."

Charly stood in a small room just off the main office, separating letters into sacks to be delivered to the stations along the route as well as back East. They used the smaller sacks instead of one or two larger ones in case anything happened to the stage. If necessary, it was easier to load several small sacks onto the team and continue on to the next rendezvous.

A satisfied smile played about her lips as she thought about the many miles she'd covered during the past few months. An' she had the cleanest record of all the drivers, havin' had only a couple of lame mules and no breakdowns. But then, she had Uncle John to thank for that honor. Whenever he finished 'is chores an' had some spare time, he puttered aroun' the coaches. 'Cause o' him, their section of the route had the fewest delays.

Oh, there were delays, of course. An' plenty of 'em. Mostly from Apaches or road agents. She put down the mail and went over to check her pack, which was neatly bundled and ready to load onto the stage. Her Sharps rifle rested against the wall, and inside the canvas were one hundred spare cartridges. She'd strapped a Colt Navy revolver around her narrow hips, similar to the one Kent Ashford wore, only hers wasn't nearly as well used. And she was takin' another two pounds of balls. Then there was her knife. Always her knife, secure in the scabbard attached to her belt.

A sense of well being settled over her. She had all of the necessary weapons. Then, mentally, she counted off the remainder of the items she'd packed. Besides the tunic and breeches and heavy leather boots she wore, she'd included an extra pair of woolen pants; six pairs of woolen socks; three undershirts and, on a whim, a lacy camisole. Two pair of blankets were stuffed inside since it was winter and who knew what the unpredictable weather would decide to do; an Indian rubber cloth to keep the blankets dry; a pair of gauntlets; a small bag of needles and pins; sponge; brush; comb; and soap, in an oiled silk bag. Two pair of thick drawers and three or four towels completed her outfit.

A whip and a pair of thin gloves neatly stacked on top of the strapped bundle were her driving tools.

Yep, she was ready. Though the length of her trip wouldn't be nearly as long as that of some of the travelers, she still carried the same items the Company suggested the passengers bring along. One thing fer shore, surprises could, and did, happen along any given stretch of the road.

Yawning, she rubbed the aching muscles in the small of her back. A noise drew her gaze to the door, and she was shocked to see Kent Ashford sauntering inside. Her mouth dropped open. Gone was the citified dandy and in his place stood a rugged man dressed in denim pants and a wool plaid shirt. A bright bandana was knotted around his throat and his blasted hat was tilted forward, the wide brim shadowing his face. She only hoped her surprise hadn't been too obvious.

If Charly's expression had conveyed her shock at finding him in the stage office at that ungodly hour, dressed and ready to tackle the wilds of the unknown, Kent wouldn't have noticed. He was too busy taking in her appearance. Hell, Charly carried off her job so well that if a man didn't already know there was a woman hidden beneath all those layers of leather and artillery, she'd look just like a young, but rough and seasoned, driver. "You don't chew, do you?"

Charly blinked. "Huh?"

"Chew. Do you carry a plug?"

"I always tote a chaw. Don't always use it, though. Why?"

He sighed. "Just wondered, is all."

She put her hands on her hips and glared at him. "What're ya doin' here?"

He was mightily tempted to yank the saucy brat over his knee and give her a good paddling for having the nerve to be so different from any other woman he'd known. But that would only make her angrier and defeat his purpose. "I'm looking for a job."

"At this hour of the night?"

He spread his hands, palms up, and shrugged. "Anytime's a good time when a man needs work and something to fill his belly."

Hungry? He was hungry? Surely he . . . Then she hardened her heart. He was goin' his own way. His worries weren't hers. "Wal, we're full up. Don't need no help."

The door opened and Jed McAllister rushed inside. "Damned wind's gettin' up. Looks like a storm blowin' . . ." When he saw Charly squared off against the stranger, he stopped and stared, then spat and set a nearby spittoon to rocking haphazardly on its bent, rounded bottom. "Where's Orlando? He shoulda been here by now."

Charly tore her gaze from Kent to scowl at her pa. She'd thought he wasn't coming back to the office tonight. Why'd he have to show up now?

"Well, gal, do ya know where'bouts Orlando got off to?"

She shook her head.

Kent grinned. "Then maybe I'm in luck. You remember me, sir? Kent Ashford? I need work awful bad."

"Pa, I done told 'im we's full up an' don't need no city fella botherin'—"

"Hush up, gal. Tell ya what, son. If'n this Orlando

138

don't show up in another half hour, ya got yoreself a job."

Charly threw up her hands. No matter what she said or did, her pa was bound and determined to sabotage her at every turn.

Kent reached for Jed's hand and pumped it enthusiastically. "Thank you, sir. You won't regret it. Guess all those good things I heard about you were true. You're a fair shooter, yessiree."

Jed straightened his shoulders and swaggered into the room where Charly'd been readying the mail. "C'mon, son, an' I'll show ya just what the mail conductor's s'posed ta do. That was Orlando's job, ya know. Mail conductor."

Charly fumed. Dadburned men. Why, they were talkin' like Orlando'd already lost his job. Well, the feller had a few minutes left. He'd show up.

Chapter Nine

It was almost three A.M. Charly fumed silently
while Kent set down the mail sacks beneath the
overhead tower that had once been part of a
protective wall built around the *presidio* of Tucson,
housing mostly Mexican soldiers and their families.

When she glanced over and saw his neat pack
resting next to her own, an unreasonable rage
bubbled up inside her. Blamed stubborn hardhead.
He was more contrary and determined than a
quarrelsome team of mules. But she wasn't 'bout ta
let him get 'er all stirred up. Nope. He warn't nuthin'
ta her. So there!

A flush heated her neck and cheeks. Or so she'd like
herself an' ever'un else ta believe. He was jest the man
she'd allowed ta take her virginity. She clasped her
trembling hands together. If only he didn't rile her
so—she'd be honest with herself an' admit that the
notion of Kent Ashford, rather than the young'un,
Orlando, ridin' beside her in the box was actually
pretty pleasin'.

That disturbing thought drove her to the door
where she scanned the street for the hundredth time.
Dang it, what could've happened to the boy? He'd
really wanted the job. Even the early time schedule
hadn't daunted his enthusiasm. Finally she shrugged

and turned back inside, only to grit her teeth at the sight of her pa still hangin' around. And he had the gall ta smile at her.

"Yep, Charly, we was right lucky Mr. Ashford showed up like he done. Stage might've been late if'n we'd had to hunt us up a replacement fer that Orlando fella."

Kent had followed Charly inside. He tilted his hat at a rakish angle and ran his fingers through his hair as he glanced out at the deserted street. "You all talk as though the stage is goin' to be here any minute. I've never seen a stage that was on time yet."

Charly shook her head. The fool man didn't know nuthin'. "Tucson's a time-table station. Driver's'll do their darnedest ta get here on schedule."

"And do they, usually?"

She nodded, proud of the record established by the Butterfield Overland Mail. "Shore do."

Seconds after she'd made her brag, they all heard the sound of a bugle. A few minutes later, pounding hooves vibrated and echoed through the eerie streets. Kent pulled out his watch. The stage had arrived early. "I'll be damned."

Charly flashed him a smug I-told-you-so grin and hurried over to record the time of arrival. She pursed her lips, wondering if her pa'd remember ta write down the time when she pulled her stage out if'n she warn't there ta look over his shoulder. The pen nearly slipped from her fingers when his raspy voice spoke from directly behind her.

"Don't'cha fret none, gal. I reckon I kin handle them books."

She blushed and nodded. When'd her pa learned ta read minds? Surely he hadn't been around Mr. Ashford long enough fer Kent's disgustin' habits to rub off on 'im. Or had he?

Jangling harnesses and weary voices drew her attention outside. Ed and several of his Mexican helpers were unhitching the tired, lathered horses, all of which were sturdy, long-legged beauties. A twinge of envy tingled in her lower lip as she bested the urge to pout and watched the high-strung animals prance and jerk their leads, still full of heart and the desire to run, as they were led toward the barn.

"Hey, Charly. What's happenin' further east?"

She was nearly knocked off her feet when the burly driver slapped her affectionately on the shoulder. "Far's I've heard, there ain't been no trouble. Cochise'n 'is people musta moved on ta their winter camp."

Kent listened to the exchange with keen interest. It hadn't dawned on him just *where* and through what kind of country the road to Dragoon Springs would take them. As soon as the opportunity presented itself, he grabbed little Miss Charly's arm and literally dragged her into the small mail room. His breath was a hissed whisper. "What do you think you're doin', driving a stagecoach over some of the most dangerous sections of road in five states?"

She struggled to free herself from fingers as solid as steel bands, but was standing on her tiptoes as it was and couldn't get a good grip on the obnoxious oaf. "Let me go, durn ya."

"Answer me, woman. Why are *you* driving the eastbound stage?"

"'Cause," she spat, "too many drivers've been killed. Cain't hire no one ta take it on."

"What about your pa, or brother?"

"They got their jobs. This'uns mine." Her eyes were green sparks of fire. "I ain't skeerd, if'n that's what's botherin' ya. An' I'm a damned good driver. Ain't lost a stage." With a slight lifting of her brows she added, "Or a mail conductor . . . yet." Her tense body proclaimed her angry challenge.

Kent swallowed a mouthful of bitter frustration. No wonder the men around Tucson showed her so

143

much respect, and his admiration grew considerably for the young man he'd drunk under the table earlier in the evening.

Charly jerked her imprisoned arm. Kent abruptly let her go, the impetus nearly careening her across the room. Staring intently, she demanded, "So?"

He rubbed the throbbing muscles in the back of his neck. "What do you mean? So . . . what?"

"Ya still gonna go?"

"Why wouldn't I?"

Her eyes narrowed. "Even knowin' ya might not make it back?"

He thought of the saddlebags and the job he'd been sent to Tucson to do. Maybe he was taking a stupid risk, but his pride was at stake, and he couldn't . . . wouldn't . . . allow this contrary woman to go without him. Damn it, where were the *men* in Tucson? Why did it seem *he'd* been elected to be her keeper?

He stared her in the eye and promised, "We'll make it back."

His confidence took the steam out of Charly's defiance. She nodded and stalked from the room.

Soon Kent heard the jingle and clink of harness as the fresh team was brought out. Charly's voice rose above the others as she shouted instructions on how she wanted everything packed and then her tone mellowed as she introduced herself to the new passengers and those who'd gotten out to stretch their legs and use the facilities.

He took a deep breath and entered the office, only to be stopped short when Jed McAllister stepped in front of him, holding out a cup of hot coffee. "Y'all have a safe trip, hear?"

Kent nodded and studied the older man's face. Jed's nose and cheeks were puffy and suffused with tiny red lines. The narrow lips were slack, and pale green eyes rheumy, but there was a certain alertness

144

that years of hard drinking hadn't dissipated. There might be more to this man than first impressions warranted. "I certainly intend to."

Taking a sip of the scalding brew, he walked to the door to watch the commotion. He stopped the cup midway back to his mouth. Damn! Mules? What had happened to the racy-looking horses? He and mules had butted heads too many times.

And the stage. Where was the roomy, comfortable coach he had always pictured at the mention of a stage line? This . . . thing . . . was definitely neither roomy nor comfortable.

Charly passed by at that moment and he stepped in front of her. Forgetting he held the cup of coffee, he pointed, almost spilling the steaming liquid all over her.

He brushed off the drop or two that had managed to escape the cup and nearly managed to lose his train of thought when his palm smoothed over the ripe swell of a tantalizing breast. Memories of the silken flesh with the coffee-brown areola and pert little nipple glazed his eyes. His breath caught as her hands pressed against his own chest—and shoved.

"Get out'n the goldurned way, dadblast ya. Cain't ya see we're fixin' ta hightail it out of here?"

He blinked and then recalled the reason he'd stopped her in the first place. Taking hold of a thin but well-muscled arm, he turned her around to face the "stage." "What is that contraption?" His jaw clenched when he thought her lips twitched, but discarded the notion immediately. Miss Charly? Smile? Naw.

"That there is one o' them "Celerity" things. Kinda like a stage, an' kinda like a wagon. It's lighter an' faster an' made ta use in rough mountain and desert country." She pulled him over for a closer look. Several passengers were waiting to board, and she quickly pointed at the empty seats. "The backs o'

145

them three seats kin be laid down ta make a bed, an' the passengers kin take turns sleepin' if'n they've a mind ta."

Kent glanced at one of the men who rolled his eyes at her informative statement and proceeded to meaningfully rub his aching back. Kent grinned, well able to imagine how comfortable the hard wooden planks would be, especially in a coach bouncing over rough roads.

Charly slipped out of his reach. He watched the gentle sway of her hips as she walked away—until one of the men coughed and Kent quickly turned to see if they'd noticed his preoccupation. They hadn't. The man had just coughed up some of the dust he'd probably swallowed. Kent had no doubts but what he'd be doing the same thing soon.

Then he turned his attention back to the coach, marveling at its truly lightweight construction. The wheels were smaller than a regular coach. The top was a frame structure covered with heavy canvas and the doors and sides had curtains of the same material that could be raised and lowered. The body had a low center of gravity and was suspended on leather straps, or thoroughbraces, hung between the wheel supports in front and back.

He shook his head and commiserated with the passengers who had to ride in the thing for such a long distance.

The next thing he knew, Charly was taking the coffee cup from his hand and giving it to her father. He eyed the narrow bench seat that would be his and Miss Charly's home for the next few days, took a deep breath, and then smiled wickedly.

Charly caught his evil grin from the corner of her eye as she took the tickets from the passengers boarding at Tucson. An uneasy feeling settled between her shoulder blades. She hoped that by the time they reached Dragoon Springs he'd still have

146

something to smile about. She doubted *she* would. Blamed obstinate man. Why'd he have to appear from out of nowhere and ruin her life?

For the last time, she scanned the street for Orlando. What had happened to keep him from showing up for work?

Once they had climbed into the box and settled in, she pulled on a pair of thin buckskin gloves and expertly threaded the reins, or *ribbons* as she liked to call them, into her left hand. With her right hand, she picked up a whip and threw the long coils onto the ground.

A quick glance over her shoulder assured her everyone was loaded. She checked up and down the street to be sure no one was in danger of being run down, then deftly bent her wrist and flicked the tip of the whip past the lead mule's ears.

"Let's go," she shouted. The mules lunged into their traces and the stage jolted forward. The wheels began to spin. The tip of the whip popped and cracked. The mules plunged into a canter, shaking their heads and ringing their tails.

Kent had nearly been thrown backwards from the seat and was just righting himself when she shouted, "Blow the blamed bugle, conductor. Let the folks know we're a leavin'."

He fumbled under the rough-hewn seat until he grasped a piece of cold metal. Hefting it into sight, he was pleased to see that it was, indeed, the brass bugle. But now that he had it, what did he do with it?

"Get to it, city man."

He was tempted to silence her—but he'd wait until he had the witch alone . . . on a stable surface. Gritting his teeth, he put the bugle to his mouth and blew. The damned thing hardly squeaked.

"Blow harder, dang it."

He gleefully imagined the brass instrument was her beautiful, slender neck as his fingers clamped it

147

tight. He blew until his cheeks puffed out and he was red in the face. One good toot was all he got for his effort.

"Ya best practice afore the next stop, Windy, else we'll be there an' gone 'fore ya ever git the hang of it."

Her expression was stony, but inside Charly was chuckling like she held a straight flush, ace high, with a hundred dollar pot ripe for the taking. Lordy, it was almost worth having to spend the next few days cooped up beside the aggravating man just to see his eyes bulge when he blew the little bugle. Darn, but she could hardly wait 'til the station at Cienega de los Piños to watch him do it again.

Kent fumed. Oh, it wasn't apparent by looking at her, but he sensed her laughter. Let her have her fun. He'd find a way to get even. And then she'd be sorry. Very sorry.

Charly had expected it to happen, but was disconcerted to hardly be able to keep her eyes open as the stage rocked doggedly along. But she had to stay alert. She'd seen and heard of too many wrecks where the driver had lost his concentration and the animals had tangled, or fallen, and the coach had crashed into them, overturning and . . .

She blinked and looked at the shadowy countryside. Even in the darkness she could make out the almost-human shapes of the saguaro cactus and the plentiful Spanish dagger, a yucca with a short trunk and spine-tipped leaves. Her mouth spread open in a wide yawn.

Kent, too, was suffering from fatigue and an irritating hangover. Though he hadn't gotten drunk like the young Orlando, he'd had plenty on top of being so damned tired he could hardly hold his head up. The short rest he'd taken that afternoon had only tempted him to want more—say, a nice *long* forty-eight hour nap.

Well, it was hardly a wonder. He wasn't a young stud any more, able to handle the long hours, liquor, *and love-making*, like he used to.

Thinking of love-making and feeling the tightness in his groin from the prolonged contact with Miss Charly reminded him of the fact that he'd completely forgotten his determination to let the whores in Tucson take their pleasure with his abused body. He'd been too intent on his purpose—and again one Charleen McAllister was the root of his problem—to pay the ladies in the cantina any attention. Now *that* was a scary thought.

When Miss Charly slumped against him and then quickly righted herself, nodding and yawning all the while, he realized he had to keep her awake or face the consequences. The damned woman's stubborn pride had probably kept her from taking even a short rest.

His brows lifted as he decided upon a course of action that wouldn't be entirely disagreeable—to him. Very subtly, he shifted on the hard seat until his body joined hers from shoulder to knee. Glancing from the corner of his eye, he saw and felt her jerk and turn to look at him with a puzzled expression on her gorgeous face.

Charly tried to edge away, but was already perched as far over as she could slide without sittin' on air. She blinked and shook her head. The last she remembered, she'd been tryin' her darnedest to keep from touchin' him—anywhere. Her whole durned body ached from holdin' herself so stiff and erect.

Kent stretched and let out a noisy yawn. When his right arm came down, he rested it behind her back atop the coach frame. The burning sensation of her quick gaze raked him, but he kept his lids lowered, pretending innocent unconcern. He almost laughed out loud, though, when she muttered a long stream of oaths, colorful even for *her*. The woman really had

149

to do something about that!

He settled more comfortably, if one could call it that, by sliding down and spreading his legs. Naturally his hip and thigh ground intimately into hers and, once again, he found himself recalling the feel of those particular portions of her anatomy in vivid detail. He ran his index finger under the tight bandana.

Even through the thick layers of clothing, Charly tingled wherever their bodies made contact. The fingers on her left hand felt every nuance of the ribbons' give and take, and she heartily welcomed the opportunity to stand up and encourage the right lead mule when it became sluggish. She snapped the whip and shouted, "Get up here, Sunshine. Pull."

Kent looked up and arched his brows. "Sunshine?"

She squirmed as telltale heat suffused her neck and cheeks. Nobody had the temerity to make her blush like Mr. Kent Ashford. "Yep, Sunshine. An' they all know their names, an' when I'm a-talkin' to 'em."

"Do they now?"

She nodded. It was physically impossible, but he had to have moved closer. If she sat back down, she'd have to sit on his lap. "Look, yore gonna have ta move over. I gotta sit down an' have room ta handle the ribbons."

"Sure. Sorry."

"Ya didn't move."

"Did, too."

She wouldn't argue with the hard-headed jackass. Didn't want him to think his nearness had *that* much of an effect on her. But he couldn't have moved. Finally, she squeezed down almost sideways and scrunched and wriggled her hip until she carved a small space for herself. But even as she did so, her body became acutely aware of every aspect of Kent Ashford. The hardness of his big body. His alluring scent. And how his nekkid skin had felt beneath her

150

exploring fingers.

Her palms grew suddenly damp inside the gloves. She licked her dry lips and shivered when the cold air chilled them. With a quick glance in his direction, she saw his strained features. The revelation was quite unsettling. What was he thinking? Was he remembering, too?

She couldn't help but relive their night together. It continued to amaze her that things had gone so far. Other men had made advances, but none had tempted her. Yet along comes Kent Ashford. City dandy. Why? What was there about *this* man . . .

Kent's body was reacting more painfully than he'd intended with his playful attempt to keep her alert. Damn, but he'd never been around a woman who only had to cast a wary glance at him to have him hard and aching . . . "How far 'til the next stop, Miss Charly?"

She bit her tongue. See there? He was the most irritating person she'd ever had the misfortune to be around. Why couldn't he just call her Charly, like everyone else? Why'd everything he did have to be *different?*

She looked up at the stars. From their position in relation to the moon, she figured they'd traveled a good two hours. "Reckon we'll be there in 'bout five hours."

He sighed. Five hours. A lifetime. "How many miles do you usually make an hour?"

She flicked the whip to straighten one of the wheel team. "We'uns average 'bout five miles an hour."

"Not bad." Actually, he was impressed. No wonder the Butterfield line had such a good record. But he couldn't help comparing the stage unfavorably to the faster trains. And with that thought, he cast a covert glance to Miss Charly. If, or when, a track was ever laid this far south, it would decimate the stagecoach business. Surprisingly, he found

151

himself thinking it would be a little sad.

A lock of Charly's deep brown hair straggled from beneath her hat and curled around the index finger of the hand he'd draped across the back of her seat. It felt like a silken band. His chest felt heavy. Dragging air into his lungs became a chore, even though the force of the wind was so strong that it whipped his eyebrows.

Amazing, Charly thought, as she shifted on the rough plank. The conversation had wiped the sleep from her eyes. The weariness had drained from her tired body and, much to her consternation, was replaced by a too-acute awareness of the man beside her.

Every movement of her arm drew the leather tunic she wore into contact with her breasts. Her nipples contracted, causing her to shiver. Her thigh rubbed constantly against Kent's. The friction generated that intriguing heat in her lower belly, a heat that seemed to be spreading.

Suddenly the wagon lurched, yanking her attention away from Kent. The mules had hit a stretch of deep sand. Instantly she hopped up, keeping the ribbons taut as she cracked the whip. "Get up, mules," she hollered, assuring the animals that she was there and in control.

As the mules found solid footing and strained to pull the loaded wagon free of the sand, Charly glanced at Kent. He'd wisely moved to give her room. Keeping a firm hand on the reins, she plopped down and tucked the whip handle beneath her hip. "Brace yourself," she warned and grabbed the friction brake with her free hand.

He looked at her questioningly, but put his right boot up against the front of the box.

Suddenly, the stage dipped precariously and they sped down a rutted incline. The vehicle shuddered and rocked back and forth with the deep bumps, jarring the occupants and creaking ominously.

He leaned over, trying not to hinder her use of the reins. "How in the hell did you know that was coming?" She shrugged and grinned, but he knew then just how well she'd learned the route and how adept she was at handling the mule team.

He experienced another suffocating sensation as his chest swelled with pride. No, this lady was definitely not a *typical* woman, and was probably better than most men at doing her job. Though he still couldn't say he was comfortable with, or even that he understood, the idea of a woman taking on a man's risks and responsibilities, he had to admit that he admired her pluck and courage.

The coach leveled out again as the ground flattened. Kent had just taken a deep breath when the coach's right front wheel hit a hole. Charly bounced out of her seat and landed again with a dull thud. A pained "Ooomphh!" escaped her lips and he quickly scooted back to her side. Grabbing her firmly around the waist, he pressed her against the solid strength of his own body.

Capable and spirited she might be, but she still needed a man to protect her every now and then.

At first, Charly was unnerved by Kent's arm wrapping so securely about her waist. But the longer he held her, the more she welcomed the warmth emanating from his big body.

Dawn began a gradual ascent between intermittent layers of dark clouds. The wind blew constantly from the southwest, chilling them to the bone when the sun was covered, keeping them miserable even when it shone brightly in their eyes.

As the landscape changed with every passing mile, towering saguaro cactus appeared again, some standing as high as ten to twelve feet, with trunks two feet in diameter. Soon the road entered a white sandy riverbed. The team strained into their harness in an effort to keep the coach rolling. Salt grass and dry sunflower stalks lined the bed on either side.

Charly turned to inform Kent that they would soon reach the Cienega River station and found herself cheek to windburned cheek and nose to dust-covered nose with the man. His eyes were dark and fathomless, drawing her into their murky, unreadable depths. Her lips parted as she started to tell him to get ready to blow the bugle, but his mouth settled firmly and insistently over hers.

He ravaged her honeyed moistness until she urgently pushed her free hand against his chest. When he finally released her, he gasped in a deep lungful of air. Then he rested his forehead against hers, and her toes tingled as he chuckled and admitted, "I've been wanting to do that since you cracked that damned whip and nearly left me in the dust in Tucson."

Charly grinned. Yup, she'd been pretty pleased with herself. He was entirely too cocky and deserved to be taken by surprise every now and then.

Someone tapped on the wooden frame from below. "Driver? What is the delay?"

"Yeah, what's goin' on? I don't see no station."

Charly blinked. Uh-oh. They weren't moving.

Kent smothered a curse, but grinned when she made a face and a very unladylike gesture.

She wriggled her hips and scooted him over enough that she could stand. Cracking the whip, she called to the team. "Get up, Sunshine. Let's go, Crackers."

Kent leaned over the side and hollered, "Sorry about that, folks. The sand's so deep we just gave the mules a short rest."

There were a few muttered grumbles from inside the coach, but no one seemed to question the hasty explanation.

Once the wheels began to roll, though it seemed

154

only an inch at a time, she grasped Kent's arm. "The bugle. Hurry and blow the dangburned bugle."

He frowned at her impatience. "Why? What's the rush? We can't even see the buildings yet."

"That's the point, dern ya. When they hear the bugle, the folks at the station go ta gettin' the new team and the grub . . . food . . . ready." She nervously slapped the ribbons. She was embarrassed and angry at herself for letting him catch her with a kiss at such a stupid time. She was so blamed weak-willed, so susceptible to his charm.

Kent picked up the cold piece of brass and ran his tongue over his dry, cracked lips. If only he'd remembered to practice. But he puckered up and deflated his chest with all the force he could muster.

The bugle blared. The mules jumped and lunged in their traces. Charly, who'd just started to rise with one hand holding the whip, nearly tumbled from her precarious perch.

Pleased with his success, Kent inhaled deeply and blasted the horn again.

When he announced their imminent arrival for the third time, Charly sat down and unconsciously imitated Kent by cocking her brow. "Musical, you ain't. But I reckon they oughtta know we're a comin'."

He patted the instrument triumphantly, then tenderly rubbed his lips where the mouthpiece had almost frozen his flesh. The burning sensation was quickly forgotten, though, when he looked ahead and saw a small clearing containing a fair-sized adobe building, a barn, and corrals.

As the stage lumbered near, two men scurried around the corrals. They already had three mules harnessed and ready to buckle into the traces. Smoke rose from the chimney, scenting the air with burning mesquite. Kent sniffed greedily. The wonderful aroma of bacon on the gusting winds teased him as they entered the station from the north.

"Gus Hatfield's one o' the dangedest cooks along the line. Enjoy it 'cause this here'll be the only meal we'll git fer awhile."

Kent frowned, not sure that he liked the sound of that dire prediction.

She stopped the stage close to the station's front door. As the passengers stumbled out, rumpled and bleary-eyed, she told them, "We got twenty minutes ta eat an' stretch whatever needs stretchin'. Agent here charges fifty cents fer breakfast if'n ya want it. If'n yore late when we load up, we go withoutcha."

The numbed passengers seemed immune to understanding anything but the word "breakfast," and started filing inside. By the time Kent had washed up, almost everyone was sitting at a long table with crude benches pulled up on either side. He slid into a space on the end and stared at a plate filled with slabs of thick, greasy bacon, browned biscuits, and lumpy gravy. Coffee poured from the tin pot almost as thick as molasses, but he ate like it was his last meal. Which, he thought dourly, it could very well be if Miss Charly knew what she was talking about. If this was the only food they were going to get . . .

Fifteen minutes later, he looked out the door and saw Charly walking around the fresh team, inspecting the harness and the braces supporting the coach. One of the station helpers was bent over greasing the axles and Kent bristled when the man said something and she smiled sweetly in return. Just who was that fellow? And what was he to her?

He quickly rose and walked outside. "Excuse me, Miss Charly." He drawled out her name and was gratified to see the long-suffering expression settle on her face. At least she wasn't indifferent to him. "Is there anything I need to be doing?"

She clamped her teeth down hard and grimaced. Oh, how she'd love to tell him exactly what she'd like to see him do, but there were other ears around.

Yanking her watch out of her pocket, she snapped open the lid. "Yeah, give a toot on that there bugle. We'll be a pullin' out o' here in two minutes."

Kent crawled up in the box and did as ordered. The new team of mules started. The helper grabbed the harness. Charly yelled when the near wheel stopped just an inch from her toes and when the young helper had the nerve to send Charly a sly wink right in front of Kent, he didn't feel a bit bad. He might have been just a little disappointed the team stopped before running the boy down, though.

Charly stormed around to glare up at him. "Ya ain't gotta blow that blamed thing clear ta Kingdom Come. We ain't deef."

He shrugged and gave her a sheepish grin. Practice. He definitely needed to practice.

All but one of the passengers had returned to the coach by the time their twenty minutes expired. Charly stood in the box and hefted the whip. Kent stilled the hand gripping the reins. "Wait. That salesman hasn't gotten on."

She scowled and freed her arm so she could wield the ribbons. "Ya heerd what I done told 'em. We be leavin', *now*. The schedule don't make room fer no lollygaggin'."

"But . . ."

She cracked the whip over the mules' ears and hollered, "Let's go, mules."

The fresh team was eager to be off. They quickly lunged into their harnesses and, this time, Kent was ready and had braced himself. At the same time, the salesman ran out of the station, stuffing one last biscuit into his fleshy jowls. "Wait up! Wait! I'm coming."

Kent glanced expectantly toward Charly, but she didn't stop. He looked over his shoulder and held his breath as the portly gentleman held onto his hat with

157

one hand and ran to catch up. Another passenger opened the coach door and another held out his hand. At last the salesman gave a skip and a jump and launched himself through the door.

Breathing a sigh of relief, Kent glowered at Charly. "You've got a lot of heart, woman. You know that?"

She urged the mules into an easy, rocking lope and sat down stiffly beside him. "I kept 'em goin' slow. An' rules'r rules."

"You'd deliberately go off and leave a paying customer?"

"He'd catch the next stage. No problem."

Several miles sped by before he finally said, "You take your job too seriously, Miss Charly."

"Thunk!" A bullet cracked the wood beneath Kent's seat.

With a baleful glance over her shoulder toward Kent, she yelled, "Some'un has ta."

Charly ducked as another bullet whizzed past her ear. She shouted at the mules and whipped the team into a run.

Chapter Ten

With bullets flying left and right, Charly was grateful that they'd finally left the sandy riverbed behind. The mules' hooves were cutting into firmer soil and they were able to travel faster, but she scolded herself over and over for not paying more attention to the broken hills and tall mesquite. The ambush had been perfectly timed, because in another few miles, they would've entered a flat plain devoid of shrubs or trees tall enough to hide a horse and rider.

A bullet buzzed overhead and she yelled and cracked her whip. When she would've stood in the box to urge the team on, Kent's arm, planted firmly around her waist, held her in place.

"Stay down, you little idiot. Do you have a death wish?" As soon as she shook her head, he released her and turned to brace his knee against the bench and his right elbow on the coach frame. Sighting on a rider closing in on the left, he squeezed the trigger just as the stage jolted over a deep rut. He cursed when his bullet went high and wide.

Dust swirled in the air from the churning mules' hooves. Kent swiped at his eyes with the sleeve of his coat.

Another outlaw was gaining on them, firing a steady barrage. Kent aimed and fired, and was rewarded with a cry of pain as the rider jerked and fell from the saddle.

A pistol report sounded from below as one of the passengers joined the fray. Kent nodded approval when another outlaw clutched at his leg and pulled his plunging horse to a stop.

The remaining riders seemed undaunted. They continued coming hard and fast. Kent sighted, squeezed the trigger, and cursed the rough-riding stage when he missed. Lifting his arm from the coach, he held the rifle firmly against his shoulder and fired, and fired again. An outlaw's hat flew from his head and the man slumped to the ground like a sack of potatoes. That one wouldn't attack another stage, Kent thought, as he quickly reloaded.

Charly's jubilant shout rang in his ears. "They're lightin' a shuck. By golly, ya done it, Windy." She pulled the frightened team down to a trot, then to a walk to let them cool and to ease their labored breathing. The coach jerked and rocked and then steadied.

She called to the passengers, "Ever'one all right down there?"

"Yeah. No one got a scratch."

"Sure are. Good drivin', little lady."

Charly smiled and glanced toward Kent. She was one to give credit where credit was due. "Danged good shootin'. If'n ya hadn't a-been along, we'uns might not've got away."

The praise was like a balm to Kent after all the other times his pride had been wounded, thanks to Miss Charly. And now here she went, calling him "Windy," for God's sake. Damned brat.

Yes, it had been a good decision to ride shotgun, so to speak. Maybe, just maybe, she might realize that she was only a woman after all, and needed a man to handle these situations. Like it or not, it seemed to be his duty to protect her.

But he had to say, "They're right, you know. You're a hell of a driver."

She blushed and clucked to the team. "Thanky."

He scratched at his twitching scar. "Are we carryin' a payroll or something?"

"Nope. Jest mail."

"Why do you suppose they tried to stop us?"

She sat very still as she surveyed the rolling hills ahead. "Ain't got no idea. But they's stoppin' us real reg'lar nowadays. Some o' the other drivers've had their mail sacks searched an' then been let go."

"No one knows what they're lookin' for?"

"Nope."

"And these holdups have just started recently?"

"Yep."

Kent removed his hat and combed his fingers through his damp hair. A thoughtful expression stole over his features. He wondered if the attacks on the stages had anything to do with the impending war. Were the rumors true? Were the Confederates already trying to stop the Overland mail? Had they found him out? No. Impossible. But it could be that they'd learned a spy had been sent to Tucson.

Damn it, he hadn't been in Tucson long enough to set up his base of operations, but when he did, he'd have to send his reports by mail. Somehow, he had to see to it they made it past these so-called "outlaws."

About an hour later, the road had leveled out and the stage rocked peacefully along. The late afternoon sun poked through the clouds and the wind died down to a pleasant breeze. Warmth began to seep into their chilled flesh. Kent was startled when Charly suddenly slumped against him, eyes closed, her breath coming in deep, even rasps.

Gently, he eased the reins from her fingers and took over the driving while she slept. He shifted

161

around almost sideways on the bench so his free hand held her nestled comfortably to his chest. He'd wondered how far her determination and strength of will would get her, and had expected her to collapse long before now.

Hours passed and she settled more firmly into him. Her soft curves molded to his hardness and his lower body responded with a throbbing ache. He was paying a high price for the teasing he'd initiated throughout the long night and day. And though her words were sharper than a razor's edge in her effort to hold him at bay, her body sent a different message entirely. She wanted him. He knew it. And she knew he knew. The situation was becoming very interesting.

His arm tightened around her as he looked down at her pixie-like features. She looked even younger and almost carefree with the corners of her mouth tilted slightly upward. Her cheeks were dusty and a smudge of dirt darkened her chin. It was quite a different pose for the woman who was always so intense and stern. Although he knew it wasn't prudent to continue, or rather to start, a relationship, he'd really like to get to know the Miss Charly hidden beneath her tough exterior.

He mentally shook himself. No! Every minute they were together—except for a few very special moments—she'd been nothing but trouble. All he'd be doing, if he persisted, would be causing himself more inconvenience.

No. He definitely didn't need a woman of Miss Charly's caliber to stir up a hornet's nest. He was quite capable of disturbing it himself if he didn't watch every move carefully. Of course he'd maintain a certain friendship with the woman, just to keep tabs on her comings and goings, and those of her family and friends. And to learn any pertinent information concerning the mail line. But that was all.

Any physical desire on his part could be satisfactorily handled at the cantina. In fact, if he'd just taken the time the other night . . . Well, he wouldn't be in such an *aroused* and painful state right now — probably.

So, now that he had everything settled in his mind, all he had to do was to convince his body. "Damn it, man, let it go."

At the sound of his voice, Charly stirred, snuggling her nose into his soft shirt. Her breath warmed the flannel material covering his right nipple. His body shook with the pleasurable sensation.

"Hmmm? Didya say somethin'?" Charly's voice was low and husky from sleep. She slowly opened her eyes. "Oh. Oh!" She sat up so quickly that a wave of dizziness swayed her. If Kent's arm hadn't still been wrapped securely around her shoulder, she might've tumbled from the bench.

She glanced at the walls of dirt on either side of the stage as Kent guided the team through a deep gully. "Ya shouldn't a done it."

He looked confused. "Done what?"

"Let me sleep fer so long."

He shifted to face straight ahead and groaned at the added pressure the movement and the tight fit of his trousers exerted upon a certain distended portion of his anatomy. In a gruffer tone than he'd intended, he bit out, "You needed the rest. Besides, it would've been more dangerous for you to have continued, being only half-awake."

She couldn't argue. Still, she felt as if she'd let him down in some way, as well as herself. In the months that she'd been driving, she'd never drifted off before. Or more importantly, had never imposed upon the mail conductor to hold her or take over her job.

Charly's cheeks burned as she recalled their heated words the night they'd made love. For someone who'd vowed to stay away from the man, she was

163

doing a mighty poor job of sticking to her convictions. Of course, she'd been angry and hurt then, never taking into consideration the fact that her body might possess a will of its own, one that she would have a difficult time controlling.

With a disgusted shake of her head, she drew herself together and took back the reins. Keeping her lashes lowered, refusing to look in his direction, she muttered, "Thanky. Think I kin handle 'em now."

Kent pulled the brim of his hat down over his face and slid down as far as possible on the bench without breaking his tail bone. "Then I may grab a little shuteye myself. Wake me if you see anything unusual or suspicious."

She nodded, grateful that she would have some time to herself to regain command of her rampaging thoughts and throbbing body.

Kent was certain he'd just closed his eyes when he felt a gentle touch on his arm. Always a light sleeper, he jerked instantly awake and sat upright, grabbing hold of the seat as the Celerity dipped down a steep embankment and into a dry creekbed.

"Sorry ta wake ya. Blow that there bugle, Windy. We's almost ta Dragoon Springs."

Dragoon Springs. Relief at last. Kent picked up the brass instrument and eyed it warily before he pursed his lips against the mouthpiece. This time he exerted a steady pressure as he blew. The sound was shrill and loud, but milder than his first efforts. The mules merely flicked their ears.

After a second toot, he grinned. Charly looked him directly in the eye and winked. "'Bout got the hang o' it now, Windy."

Kent was amazed by the feelings that jolted through him with her innocent comment. On the one hand, he felt like a kid who'd been given an unexpected treat for doing something not-so-special. And on the other hand, an unfamiliar warmth spread

164

through his chest cavity, awfully close to his heart, as her eyes radiated a sparkling glow when she called him "Windy."

He realized then that she wasn't taunting him. It was kind of an endearment, in a way. A name that only *she* called him. He'd never had a nickname before. The strait-laced and stern Ashfords never stooped so low as to call their only child anything other than Kent, or Kent Leland if he'd done something unforgivable.

Thinking of his family brought back the old hurt. His mother and father, though strait-laced, had loved him, almost as much as they loved each other. And he still missed them. One day, he hoped to find a woman who would be as selflessly devoted to him as his mother had been to his father.

He'd learned his lesson the hard way, in Richmond before his father, and then his mother, had died; and again in Savannah, when he'd gone to stay with his Uncle, James Jefferson Ashford. Women wanted two things from him—his wealth and the prestige of his name. Maybe, some day, he'd find a woman more interested in love and commitment.

The mules struggled up and out of the creekbed, jolting Kent back into the present. They had ridden out of the broken country and ahead, as far as the eye could see, lay a flat plain, skirted on either side by high hills.

As Charly pulled up in front of the stone station at Dragoon Springs, Kent sagged tiredly on the seat, glad that their stretch of the journey was over.

A thin, white-haired man stepped outside the station. "Supper's ready, folks. Come on in and get beef, bacon, and shortcake while it's hot. Only a dollar."

The passengers began to alight and Charly called out to remind them, "Be ready ta pull out in twenty minutes. The fella takin' over don't cotton ta

165

dawdlin' none, either."

The salesman stopped as he was about to enter the station. "I'll be there. You can count on it."

One man patted him on the back while another made crude remarks about making hard-to-keep promises as they hurried in to eat.

Kent looked over at Charly. She was grinning as she set the brake and laid the coiled whip on the bench. "Evidently he's not one to hold a grudge."

"Nope. I've seen 'im afore." She yanked off her hat and let the long braid fall down her back as she rubbed the red crease in her forehead. "Fact is, seems I rec'lect that he's been left a'hind a time er two. But I cain't be shore."

Ten minutes later, Charly was licking the last crumbs of sweet shortcake from her fingers when the attendant tapped her on the shoulder. "Howdy, Tim. Ya serve a right fine meal."

Tim Lowry cleared his throat.

Charly frowned when the man wouldn't meet her eyes to acknowledge her compliment. "All right, Tim. Out with it. What ya got stuck in yore craw today?"

Tim shuffled uncomfortably beneath Kent's hard, unwavering gaze. "Well, er, I, uh, got some, uh, got some bad, uh, news."

The hair on the nape of Charly's neck prickled. "What kinda bad news? Somethin' happen back to Tucson? My pa, is he—"

"No! Nuthin' like that, Charly," he assured her, his Adam's apple bobbing conspicuously as he tried to swallow. "It's old Friday. He up an' quit yesterday. There ain't nobody here what can drive the stage on to Stein's." He wrung his hands and ducked his head to one side as if expecting a particularly violent response.

Kent's brows drew together as he looked askance at Charly. She just took a long sip of strong, thick coffee.

The only disturbance to the heavy silence was the smacking of the passengers' lips as they continued to eat, oblivious to the turn of events.

Finally, Charly set the mug down and stretched. She took out her watch and flipped open the lid. "Reckon we's burnin' daylight, folks. Y'all git the pleasure of this here conductor an' myself fer the rest o' the trip to Stein's Station, like it 'r not."

Kent glanced at Tim Lowry and shrugged, indicating that he didn't know any more about the unpredictability of women than the old man. He only knew that if someone had gone off and left him in Charly's fix, he'd be damned mad.

His eyes settled on her back as she left the room. Even knowing her as little as he did, he couldn't believe she hadn't thrown a rip-roaring tantrum or, at the least, offered a few choice curses.

Charly had her own and Kent's packs reloaded and the passengers settled in five minutes. She collected the fresh team's ribbons and leaned down to inform the passengers, "We'uns should make 'Pache Pass afore first light. Don't reckon on any trouble."

The last pronouncement brought a cheer from the otherwise stoic men. She sat back up, ready to direct the team straight east. She glanced at Kent. "Ya ready, Windy?"

Kent gazed out over the sprawling desert panorama ahead and thanked the Lord that they'd be traveling under the cover of darkness. He gave the bugle a toot, to another resounding cheer, and they were off. One of the lead mules was a tad fractious as they started, and Charly had to take extra caution to avoid tangling the team in the ribbons. Finally, after the freshness had worn off and the mule tired of acting up, Charly relaxed.

"How're you going to do it, Miss Charly?"

"Huh?"

"How're you going to drive the stage all the way to

167

Stein's, or wherever, without a change of drivers?"

She puckered her lips and grabbed hold of the friction brake as the team began a gradual descent onto the plain. "Don't reckon I ever thought 'bout it."

He laid his arm companionably across her narrow shoulders. "You're one hell of a woman, Miss Charly. Shore 'nuf."

Charly frowned, not quite sure what to think of this different side of Kent Ashford. It was almost easier to deal with the intimate suggestions and roving hands than this unaccountable *friendliness*. He had ta be up ta somethin'.

"If you get tired again, I'd be happy to spell you a while." He stretched and settled down in the seat, barely touching Charly. "It would be a welcome change, anyway. This has to be the most boring job I've ever had."

Her eyes narrowed. He was talking about the *job*, wasn't he? Or was he remarkin' on *her* company? She couldn't resist asking, "What's the matter with ya?"

"I beg your pardon?"

"Why're ya . . . Why . . ." She couldn't do it. Couldn't come right out and ask why he was sittin' way over there, and what had prodded him into acting so *friendly* of a sudden. He'd know fer shore she was some kinda idjit. And he might be right.

"Yes?" Kent could sense her unease and was puzzled. For his sake as well as hers, he'd come to the conclusion that the trip would be much more pleasant if he quit tormenting her. But instead of relaxing, she seemed even more tense and distressed. Women. Who could figure them?

"Nuthin'," she grumbled. Why was she complainin'? She'd wanted more room. She'd wanted him to stop actin' so . . . so . . . forward. He had. She'd gotten her wish.

Damn!

* * *

The journey to the Apache Pass station seemed to drag on interminably. Though they'd tried to converse civilly, just to pass the time, both Charly and Kent had resorted to sniping at each other like two coyotes fighting over a carcass.

They had five minutes to take care of business of a personal nature at the station and then they were on their way again. Charly was determined to keep her promise of making it through the pass before sunup, so that they would be less likely to run into Apaches bent on starting trouble.

And it was just about an hour before dawn when they approached a line of hills and the road began to narrow.

"I suppose this is the famous Apache Pass?" Kent asked.

Charly nodded. "Some folks call it Doubtful Pass." Just as she spoke, the mules began a steep descent and the right-hand side of the coach scraped a boulder.

One of the passengers, who'd had his hand resting on the window frame, yelped when the rock smashed his fingers.

Kent surveyed what he could see of the narrow, twisting road and recalled the horrors he'd heard of Apache attacks through this canyon. The term "doubtful" was very appropriate.

But they made it through the pass with no further incident. It wasn't until just after dawn that Kent's gaze traveled up the side of a hill and suddenly focused on the crest. There he noticed either an odd-shaped cactus, or an Indian sitting on his pony watching the stage. The hair on the back of his neck prickled. He blinked and the shape disappeared.

He nudged Charly. "I think I just saw an Apache."

She shook her head and shot him an indulgent

169

glance. "If'n ya seen 'im, he weren't 'Pache."

"But . . ." What the hell, there wasn't any sense in arguing the point. He wasn't that sure he'd seen anything, either.

Stein's Station was located in a small hollow beneath a mountain. Though Kent had blown the bugle and was watching for it, he didn't see the adobe headquarters until they were only a few hundred yards away.

As he watched the men leading out the new team, he narrowed his eyes. A sense of foreboding wedged beneath his shoulder blades. His sixth sense told him something was wrong.

Sure enough, when the handlers came closer, one had a white pad secured to his forehead. The station agent, who stepped out to greet them, carried his right arm in a sling. But before Kent could question the men, Charly cut in. "Burt, who beat the tarnation out'n y'all?"

The agent sheepishly scuffed his toe in the dirt. "Weren't our doin', Miss McAllister. Some card-sharp 'n' his pals stopped by a few days ago an' asked us ta sit in on a game. Bigelow caught 'em cheatin', an' 'fore ya knowed it, all hell busted loose."

Charly's already strained features went ashen. She swayed slightly, but felt Kent's hand under her elbow and took a deep breath, gathering her wits as she looked past Burt into the shadowed gathering room. "An' Bigelow? What hap'ned ta him?"

Burt's fingers fiddled with the wooden button on his vest. "The card-sharp plugged 'im right 'tween the eyes, he did. Bigelow never knew what hit 'im."

"Oh."

Kent supported her over to a shaded bench. "Who was this Bigelow? What's he to you?"

She smiled wanly as she slumped onto the hard seat. "Jest the relief driver."

"Oh," Kent parroted. Poor Charly. "Does this

170

kind of thing happen often? Here I thought Indians and bandits were your main worry."

Both Charly and Burt spoke together. "Of'en enough."

His eyes on Charly's slumped shoulders, Kent straightened to his own full six feet and four inches. "Well, someone else is going to have to drive the next stretch. You, my dear Miss Charly, are not going to even think about continuing on."

Yet before he even began his attack, a sensation of defeat spread throughout his aching muscles. He looked from Charly's suddenly splotched face and spitting green eyes to the injured manager and then to the three helpers who'd just come up to the station. As he'd noticed earlier, one of them had a head injury and the other two were hardly in their teens. Both of the youngsters had blank looks on their dark faces, which gradually changed to expressions of fear and suspicion when they realized they'd become the focus of his attention.

For just a second, Charly let herself bask in the feeling that someone cared enough to look out for her. It was nice. She appreciated the thought, but she hadn't asked for and didn't need his help.

"I durned shore will drive that there stage." Poking Kent's solid chest, she punctuated each thought. "If'n I see fit. An' there ain't nuthin' ya kin do'r say ta change my mind." Ornery, no 'count man. Who'd he think he was, bossin' her around like that? An' what'd he think she was? Some soft, milquetoast of a woman who couldn't do her job when things got a little tough?

Kent grimaced. "Fine. Do what you damned well please. You will, anyway." Talking sense to Miss Charleen McAllister was like trying to talk to one of her stubborn mules.

Breathing a noisy sigh of relief that everything had been settled, Burt gestured toward the dim interior of the station. "Come on in an' eat up, folks, 'fore the chow gets cold."

The passengers, who'd been waiting and listening to the heated conversation, pushed eagerly inside.

Kent dragged his feet, but the smell of bacon and biscuits helped take the sting from his defeat.

Once his belly was full, he remembered to tell Burt about the Apache scout he thought he'd seen. The stationmaster nodded. "Thanks, mister. We'll keep our eyes open. This used ta be one of their campin' grounds. Still show up here every now and then. Mostly, though, we mind our business an' they mind theirs. Ain't had too much trouble."

Back on the trail, Charly's show of defiance at Stein's seemed to give her added energy. She shifted between standing up and sitting to help keep alert, and her running conversation with the mules drove Kent to the point of gritting his teeth and taking a stranglehold on the butt of his rifle.

When they reached the Picacho Pass station, she allowed to Kent that they would be in for a treat. Sure enough, when the new team was brought around, the handlers hitched up racy California-bred horses. However, not even the pleasure of watching their rippling, elegant lines allayed the tiredness that seeped into the marrow of his bones. And if *he* was weary, Charly had to be *exhausted* after almost forty hours on the road.

He shucked out of his heavy coat, hoping the chill air would revive him. Even the blast of cold couldn't stifle another yawn.

Charly glanced over and understood what he was trying to do. She lifted and lowered her shoulders, easing some of the tension settled there, then fished into her pocket. The plug of tobacco was hard and stiff when she bit into it, but she finally tore off a chaw.

172

"Want some?" She held the tobacco out to Kent.

"Sure." He grimaced, but took her offering. He was willing to do just about anything to stay awake. And besides, he wasn't about to let the brat best him, even with chewing tobacco.

Charly worked and worked to moisten her chaw. She'd forgotten it had been in her pocket for a long, long time. Once, she accidentally swallowed a bit of the foul stuff and almost gagged. Quickly she looked toward Kent. She didn't think he'd noticed, but his mustache was tilted at a suspicious angle.

Kent turned and said, "Good stuff, huh?"

"Yep." She choked and almost swallowed more juice before she managed to spit. But she didn't hold her head far enough over the side. Brown spots stained her jacket and she muttered curses beneath her breath.

Kent glanced away, afraid that if she looked him in the eye he'd start laughing and really put a bee in her britches. It was nice to know, though, that she really didn't make chewing a habit.

But as they pulled into the outskirts of Mesilla, and he looked around at the squalid little community of adobe and stick houses, his good humor quickly dissipated. Even in the city, the housing was little better. He continued to be appalled that a town of over three thousand inhabitants could exist with such horrid conditions. It seemed the fertile land and rich agriculture they'd driven through was the only redeeming feature of the area.

Climbing down from the coach, Charly was so exhausted that she stumbled and had to rely on Kent's quick reflexes to hold her upright. She blinked and swayed and gratefully allowed him to guide her inside the station.

Hardy Anderson, the driver relieving her, stopped and cuffed her shoulder on his way out. "Hey, Charly, gal, what's a matter? Ya gettin' too old fer

173

this job?''

Kent had to chuckle. The man looked to be seventy if he was a day, and seemed as spry as a yearling colt.

Hardy stopped his teasing and nodded toward the back room. "There's a couple pallets already spread out. Gotta admit, they sleep pretty damned good."

Charly smiled and caught Hardy's arm. "You be careful, old man. Didn't have no trouble from the 'Paches, but them durned bandits hit us agin. Woulda stopped us fer shore if'n Kent . . . Mr. Ashford, here, hadn't been along."

Hardy bit into a twist of tobacco. Ignoring her warning, he winked at Kent. "Hear that? Called me an old man. Cheeky squirt, ain't she?"

She squeezed his arm. "Go on an' get outta here 'fore they leave without ya. Jest mind what I said."

He patted her hand and gave her an affectionate grin. "See you next trip."

As he walked through the door, she called, "Only if'n yore lucky an' I'm careless." She waved when he stopped, spat, and smiled back at her.

Kent had stood in the background watching the exchange. He was amazed how all of the drivers accepted Miss Charly as one of their own. They all treated her like a favorite sister or daughter, yet also as an equal.

When he glanced over and saw that Charly's attention was on the stationmaster, he rushed outside after the old driver. "Excuse me, sir."

Hardy Anderson tugged on a buckskin glove similar to Charly's and turned to regard the stranger. "What ya need, son? Better hurry, we're about ta pull out."

"Just answer one question."

The old man spat. "Go ahead."

"Why do all of you drivers make that woman drive this eastern route?"

Hardy's eyes narrowed. "You ask her about that?"

174

"Yes."

"What'd she say?"

"She implied that no one else would take the route because it was too dangerous."

Hardy snorted. "Figures. The part she left out was that *she* won't let no one else drive it. Big John went so far as to hog-tie the gal one time, but she ran him down before he reached the first change station. She's taken it in her head she's the mother hen an' we're all her chicks. Says no one can do the job any better'n her. An' mebbe she's right. She's a damned fine driver, no doubt 'bout it. Anyways, we finally gave in an' let her do as she pleased, since she was gonna do it nohow. But we make sure she has a good, dependable man ridin' conductor."

Kent cocked an eyebrow. "I don't know about that. You should have seen the boy who was going to ride with her if I hadn't stepped in."

The old man's gaze settled sternly over Kent. "What was this 'boy's' name?"

"I don't know. Orlando something-or-other, I think."

Hardy spat and sprinkled dust over Kent's boots. "Orlando Ruiz was his name, if I'm guessin' right."

"You know him?"

"Know of him. He's only the fastest draw in Tucson. His daddy was the head honcho of the Mexican army when Tucson was still a *presidio*. Boy's trained military through and through."

"Oh."

The old man's laugh was like a leather sole grating over loose gravel. "Well, if you bested the boy, then you was the better man for the job. Glad you cared enough about our squirt to keep an eye out. Godspeed, son."

Kent stepped back as Hardy and his mail conductor mounted the box. Behind another team of mules, the conductor tooted the bugle as Hardy spat and wielded the whip. "Let's go."

Staring after the departing stage with a bemused expression on his face, Kent wished he'd had a chance to explain to the old man that he'd had it all wrong. Kent didn't *care* for Miss Charly—not in *that* sense, anyway. He just hadn't wanted her to get hurt, or worse. That was all. He just . . . Hell, he was too tired to rationalize his reasons. Besides, the old man was gone and it was too late to try to explain it.

As Kent entered the station and found Charly watching him with bloodshot eyes, his ire at her overbearing behavior evaporated. Miss Charly was Miss Charly. Take away her hardheaded independence and she wouldn't be the woman he'd come to respect and admire.

But by damn, one day she was going to have to admit that beneath the layers of leather and that floppy hat brim, beat the heart of a woman.

At that very moment, he set a goal for himself. Before he rode away from Tucson, she would know she was a woman, in every sense of the word, or his name wasn't Kent Leland Ashford.

Kent rolled over, and over again. He stretched and tried to settle more comfortably on the thin pallet, but once he was awake, he couldn't go back to sleep. Gradually he opened one eye, then the other. The room was in total darkness. He arched his back and stretched again. He must've slept a good ten or twelve hours.

As his eyes became adjusted to the darkened room, he wondered how Miss Charly was faring. She was probably still passed out, as exhausted as she'd been. He turned his head to the side and looked toward her pallet. Wrong again, damn her. Even in the dark, he could tell the pallet was empty.

He sat up and flipped each boot upside down

176

before pulling them on, just in case some crawling creature had decided to take up residence while he'd slept.

When he entered the small kitchen, he found the stationmaster eating a bowl of steaming beans. The fellow nodded toward a pot over the fire and a stack of tortillas. "Help yourself, mister."

"Thanks. Believe I will." Kent's empty stomach grumbled in anticipation as he filled a bowl and picked up a handful of the thin, flaky tortillas.

"There's bacon if ya want I should fry ya up some," the other man offered.

"No, thanks. This'll be plenty." He'd eaten enough greasy bacon to last a lifetime, and there was still the return trip to Tucson to look forward to. "You seen Miss . . . Charly around this evening?"

"Yeah. She ate 'bout an hour ago, then left with a couple o' the boys."

Kent's eyes narrowed. His teeth clicked as he chomped through a tortilla. Left with the *boys?* "Any idea where they might've gone?"

"Heard the fellas talkin' 'bout gettin' up a game o' poker. Probably be at the cantina by now."

Kent's gut knotted as he swallowed a mouthful of beans and nearly choked. "Think Charly'd be with them? At the cantina, I mean?"

The other man nodded as he rinsed out his empty bowl. "Shore. She always sets in on a game when she's waitin' 'round town."

Damn her. What was she thinking, going into a cantina, of all things? Gulping the rest of his food, not tasting a bite, Kent hurriedly used the last of the tortilla to wipe his bowl clean. "Where abouts is this cantina? I might find a game myself." Or break one up, he determined.

"Go left two blocks an' it's across the street. Can't miss it."

Kent was on his way before the stationmaster

177

finished giving directions. "Thanks," he called, as he stepped outside.

The constriction in his belly refused to abate as he walked down the rutted street. The haunting strains of a flamenco guitar, drifting out of a dimly lit adobe and stick hut, halted in mid-strum, and the hair on the back of his neck stood on end.

Kent began to run. Hell fire and damnation! He had a sickening feeling that a certain hot-headed female needed help—again.

Chapter Eleven

Charly placed her cards on the table, face up. "Make mine a full house, fellas." She reached out and raked in her third pot in a row.

One of the players, a middle-aged, redheaded man with colorless eyes and a perpetually downturned mouth, threw in his hand with a sharp glance in her direction. "You're damned lucky tonight."

"Ain't no luck to it," she lied. Picking up the deck, she shuffled three times and passed the cards to her right for the redhead to cut. The man pushed his hat to the back of his head and for the hundredth time that evening, Charly darted sly peeks at his face. There was somethin' about the man . . . Those eyes . . . Somethin' real familiar . . .

Antonio Farraday, one of the helpers from the stage station, hiccupped and spouted, "Cut 'em deep 'n' weep."

The older man snorted, watching Charly's deft fingers as she dealt the hand of five-card draw. "Men don't go in for that superstitious claptrap, boy."

Tony's face darkened as he picked up his hand. His brown eyes glittered with malevolence, but he didn't acknowledge the slur.

Charly studied her cards and discarded two. As the

other players followed suit, she dealt them replacements.

The mustachioed player to her left folded. "Thee luck, she no good for me tonight, no?"

"Cain't afford ta lose more'n my ante on this mess," another player said and threw in his hand.

Tony Farraday opened with fifty cents. The redhead called and upped the pot another fifty cents. "Dollar to you, little lady," he sneered.

Charly eyed the man over the top of her cards. She held two pairs—aces and tens. Heck, why not? Lady Luck seemed to be squattin' on her shoulder. She paid the pot and called.

Tony folded. "No sense throwin' my money away. Guess it's up to you two."

The older man smiled smugly and casually tossed in two more dollars. "Still feelin' lucky, little lady?"

Charly bristled. The toad'd called her *little lady* all evenin' an' she hadn't raised a fuss. But he'd said it then, like an *insult* . . . Well, she was dang near riled.

But she smiled and flipped in four dollars. "Reckon it'll cost ya ta find out." By durn, if'n she only held a pair o' deuces she'd of stayed in an' bluffed the lizard.

Red's lips thinned. He counted his money. Only five dollars left. Damn. He'd wanted Conchita tonight, but she cost four dollars. If he lost the pot, he'd also lose the best lay in town. His eyes narrowed to dangerous slits as he called the pot. "There's your friggin' two dollars. Let's see you beat kings and queens, bitch. Two pair to you."

Charly's knuckles whitened. The cards bent in her hand. "Reckon aces'll always bump kings 'n' queens." She lay down her two pair.

"Goddamn you. You bet five dollars on two stinkin' pair?"

She grinned and reminded him, "So'd you."

"It ain't natural. No way you could be that *lucky.*"

Charly tensed, but her face remained expression-

180

less. Suddenly she recalled the battered men at Stein's Station and the death of her friend, Bigelow. Hadn't Burt said the driver'd been killed by a card sharp? It was unlikely, she knew, but if this galoot was the same slinkin' coward . . . More determined than ever, she demanded, "You sayin' I cheated?"

"Is a pecker hard?"

The vibrating cadence of the guitar in the background fell silent. Buzzing voices dwindled to mere whispers. The atmosphere in the cantina turned dark and hazy. Odors of unwashed bodies, stale liquor, and cheap tobacco became stifling.

Tony gulped and spread his arms. "C'mon, mister. Ya know the lady won fair and square."

"Don't know no such thing. She handles them cards a mite too fancy to suit me."

Tony scooted his chair away from the table. The two other players quickly scooped in their money and left.

Charly's right hand had fallen to her lap. Her gaze was glued to Red's as his pale eyes shifted around the room and back to her, as if he'd sized up his opposition and was satisfied to have found none. The faint flicker of his lids warned her that he was going to draw.

Desperation clawed at her chest. She leaped to her feet and her chair scudded out behind her. His fingers curled around his pistol butt. Charly instantly slipped her knife from its scabbard.

The bat-wing doors slammed open. Two pistol shots reverberated through the small room. A bullet ripped into the tabletop in front of Charly. The other tore through flesh. Red dropped his gun and fell to the floor, gripping his bloody hand.

"Goddamn. Goddamn, lookit my hand. You bastards've ruint me." The injured man squirmed on the floor as Kent strode forward and placed the toe of his boot on the gunman's arm so he could see the wound for himself. Holstering the smoking Colt, Kent's eyes widened.

Besides his own bullet hole, which completely passed through the man's hand, there was a bone-handled knife protruding just below the fellow's thick wrist. He turned to stare at a calm, seemingly unaffected Charleen McAllister.

He silently cursed as a prolonged shudder rippled through his body. Hell, he'd been sure she was going to die. And the pain that had clutched his gut had yet to release its icy grip. In a blink of an eye he could've lost her. Lost her . . .

Finally, he bent to yank out the blade.

"Yeow! Goddamn sonofabitch. I'll get ya for this. I'll get the both of you." Red's pale eyes fell maliciously on Charly. "You 'specially, bitch. You're gonna regret this night. See if ya don't."

Two men, who'd been standing quietly at the bar, came forward to haul the raving man to his feet. Without a word, they removed him from the cantina. Kent's eyes narrowed as he wondered if the two men knew the bully, or if they were just doing a good deed. Somehow, he didn't picture the pair as the "kind" type.

But he barely had time to file their faces in the back of his mind when he felt the bloody knife being tugged, none too gently, from his grasp. He glanced down to find Charly coolly wiping the blade in the loose dirt covering the floor. All of a sudden, he felt like an enraged bull taunted by a waving red blanket.

She straightened. He hunkered down and grabbed the backs of her knees while thrusting his shoulder into her middle. He slung her over his shoulder as effortlessly as if she were no more than a lumpy sack of grain, rather than five feet, eight inches of kicking, squirming, female flesh and muscle.

"Put me down, dang ya. Ya hear? Put me down!"

They brushed past an astonished Tony Farraday,

who grinned and yelled, "Don't worry none, Charly. I got your winnin's."

Kent strode past the rest of the gaping patrons and through the door. More infuriated than he'd ever been, he scanned the dirty street searching for a spot where Charly would have no friends to intercede. Swatting her bottom for good measure, he ignored her squeal of protest and rounded the side of the cantina, walked past the back door and into the greasewood and mesquite-dotted countryside.

By the time he reached the top of a fair-sized hill, she had finally tired of pounding her fists against his aching back.

Her shouts of outrage switched to moans of pain as his hard shoulder gouged her tender middle. "Please. Ya gotta let me down. I'm gonna be sick."

He dumped her, a heap of floundering limbs, into the sand and weeds at his feet.

She scrambled up and stood unsteadily, one arm held protectively across her stomach. "Ya . . . ya overbearin' bast—"

He reached over and pinched her cheek between his thumb and forefinger. "Don't call me that, woman. Don't let me hear you say that again. You savvy?"

She nodded, and as his grip eased, jerked away. He was threatening her. Just who did he think he was? With the sizzling speed of a freshly struck match, she stepped forward and teased the tip of her knife against the pulse point beneath his jaw. A droplet of blood formed and trickled down the thin blade. "An' don't ya never haul me 'round thataway agin. *You* hear?"

With a brief flicker of amusement, he nodded carefully, feeling the increased pressure from the knife as he did so.

Slowly, ever so slowly, she pulled the knife away. They stood in the darkness, glowering at one

183

another. Crickets chirped and leaves rustled to the accompaniment of their hard breathing. Tension hung about them as thick and heavy as Spanish moss.

Kent was the first to collect himself. "Damn you, woman! Don't you have a lick of sense?" He yanked off his hat and scraped his fingers through his rumpled hair. "I can't believe you had the gall to enter a filthy cantina. Let alone sit in on a poker game—to fight over the cards like some hot-headed . . . And . . . and then, by damn, to pull a knife against a gunman? Good God, not even a *man* is that crazy. Not even a woman who *thinks* she's a man could be that stupid."

Charly's fingers curled into fists so tight her knuckles throbbed. "What's bein' a man or a woman got ta do with anythin'? An' if'n I recollect, there be a night not so long ago when even *you* didn't think of me as a *man*, Mr. City Dandy."

"That's right, *Miss* Charly. And I imagine that's the first time you've ever been made to act like a woman in your life."

She cocked her head. "What is it that makes ya so angry, Windy?" she asked very quietly. "That I dress like a man, or that I've got a man's job? Or maybe that I handle myself as good as a man?"

He blinked. She'd hit a sore spot, but he couldn't *admit* to it.

Hell, just look at her—with her flushed cheeks and sparkling eyes and dewy lips. And the soft swells of her breasts were outlined to perfection by her soft leather shirt. His gaze dropped to her rounded hips and the firm little bottom that stretched her britches until nothing was left to his imagination. Or any other man's?

Suddenly all he could think of was taking off every stitch of her man's garb. He thought her ivory flesh should be glimpsed beneath a gown of delicate lace

184

and satin. Her long hair should be freed from the confines of that battered old hat so that it could hang down her back in silken waves. And those clod-hopper boots should be replaced by a pair of kid slippers that molded her slender feet like soft gloves.

She deserved better than to have to take on a man's world. She needed someone to show her how a lady should be treated. Someone to take care of her, shower her with gifts. She needed . . . him?

Kent could no longer ignore the erection straining against his trousers. She was too desirable for her own good. His gut knotted as if he'd been punched with an iron fist. God, if she could attract him looking as she did right now, coming directly from a barroom brawl, what would she do to him if she looked like a real lady?

Charly crossed her arms over her chest, impatiently tapping her foot, waiting for his answer. "Well, be ya jealous that there's some things I kin do better than a man? Mebbe even better'n you?" she bravely taunted.

She backed up a step as the strange expression burning in his eyes turned dangerous. He advanced toward her. She gasped, afraid that she'd pushed him too far. He was, after all, just a man. No tellin' what he was capable of when he was *really* angry.

Charly dodged around a thorny mesquite and then ducked behind a soap tree yucca. She stood silently, holding her breath, listening. If he'd intended to intimidate her, he'd done a heck of a good job.

Then she stiffened her stance and squared her chin. Maybe she should show the city dandy just how able she was to take care of herself. But that'd mean she'd have to *touch* him. A shiver quaked down her spine. No, she didn't wanna go an' do *that!* Danger might be a constant in her life, but she warn't foolish enough ta go searchin' fer it.

Without wasting another minute, she spun quickly and ran straight into the circle of his arms.

185

Her heart thundered. She was certain he'd overhear and guess just how frightened she was. Frozen in place, the last thing she expected was to feel his tongue licking the lobe of her ear, or to hear him whisper, "I know what you can do as a 'man.' Now show me how much of a 'woman' you are."

Her throat closed. Her lungs felt as if they would burst. Was he challenging her? "Ya already know I'm a woman. Ya *made* me a woman. 'Member?" Her voice cracked and came out whiny. She stiffened, determined not to appear weak in his eyes.

"Did I really, Miss Charly? Or was that one time just a little girl making a new discovery? Did you learn anything that night? Do *you* think of yourself as a woman? Or do you prefer to hide behind your man's disguise?"

Distressed, her eyes grew wide. Dang him! Who'd he think he was to say such a thing? But . . . Was he right? Was she hidin' from the truth? From herself? She inhaled a deep breath and resisted the urge to bolt from his disquieting embrace. "I ain't afeerd to be a woman. I ain't. Why should I be?"

He nuzzled her neck and laved the pounding pulse in the hollow of her shoulder. "I don't know. Why?"

His deep, husky voice caressed her senses. Doubt and fear diffused like smoke in the wind when his hands cupped her bottom and pulled her to the long, hard shape of his manhood. Delicious tremors rioted down her spine. For days he'd tormented and teased her until her flesh felt as soft as clay, willing to be molded to any shape he desired.

"Are you a woman, Charly? Really a woman? Do you have a woman's wants and needs? A woman's desires?" He unlaced her tunic and discovered the lacy edge of a delicate camisole. A wide grin curved his lips. The woman was an exciting package of contradictions that only served to make her even more enticing. He palmed the warm mounds of her

186

breasts and fire sizzled to the throbbing core of his being. Her nipples seared into his skin like twin branding irons.

When he squeezed her distended nipples, Charly whimpered. How could he question the fact that she was a woman? How could *she* have questioned it?

For the past week, she'd felt more feminine than at any time in her twenty years of life. Here was the most handsome, virile man she'd ever seen. Not only was he intelligent and gallant, but he made her feel like she was *someone*. He made her aware of her woman's body and feelings.

She felt alive. Her body yearned for his touch. Heat radiated from the center of her being, warming every tingling part of her. And the way he held her breasts . . . The sensations he aroused in her nipples . . .

"Oh, yeah, I'm a woman." Her throat was so dry that she choked out the words.

Kent lowered his head and touched the tip of his tongue to one rosy nipple. When it instantly hardened, he groaned with satisfaction. Her silken flesh quivered beneath his hands. He raised his head. His eyelids felt heavy as he gazed into the liquid emerald pools. "Are you cold, honey? You aren't wearing a coat or—"

She put a trembling finger over his lips. "No, I'm 'bout ta burn up." Trying to grasp hold of her raging emotions, she looked into the clear sky and sighed, "Ain't it a beautiful night?"

Kent took a deep breath. Now that was just like a woman—dragging up nonsensical, romantic notions just when a man was in the heated throes of seduction. But to appease her, he raised his head and gazed around the shadowed countryside. "It's gorgeous. You're gorgeous."

Charly's entire body flushed beneath a new and different kind of heat, at heat that seemed to seep right into her heart. "That's right nice o' ya ta say, but t'ain't necessary."

"Oh, but it is. Because it's true." He couldn't believe she had no idea of what a beautiful woman she was.

She shook her head. "I ain't no such thing." She gathered her courage about her and stood on tiptoe to place a tentative kiss on his moist lips.

When he didn't move, she became bolder and pressed closer, slanting her mouth over his.

Stunned, Kent held himself in check until her tongue began tracing the outline of his lips. Then he crushed her to him, deepening the kiss, molding her body to his as if she were a second layer of his own flesh.

She'd shown once before what a truly passionate creature she could be, but he was just discovering his own hidden depths of ardor. She dragged emotions from the recess of his soul, emotions he'd thought were securely chained away.

Damn it, why couldn't he have met Miss Charly McAllister at another time, in another place, when their coming together might have had a chance to work into something deep and lasting.

Suddenly, he grasped her shoulders and pushed her straining body back to arm's length. Her fingers clutched at his sides. He thought he would die from the torture. Gazing into her glazed, dreamy eyes, he wondered if what he was going to do would recommend him for sainthood, or relegate him to the bowels of hell.

"Honey . . . Charly . . . We better go back. Now. Your friend's probably lookin' for us. Might even be spendin' your money."

His hands shook. He could hardly take a breath. Damn it, when had he developed a conscience? She wanted him. He needed her. So why was he letting her go? No, *pushing* her away?

He swallowed and stared up at the stars. Why? Because of her sweet face. The innocence that peered from her cloudy green eyes. There was "that look," the look that told him he would break her heart. She'd had no complaints about her life before she met him, or so it had seemed. Then, who was he to come along and awaken her to a woman's passions, only to waltz away later without a care or worry?

When her eyes began to clear, then darken, and she looked at him with confusion and pain, a tearing sensation ripped through his chest. He had to wonder just which one of them would suffer the worst? Charly McAllister? Or Kent Ashford?

With an ungovernable strength of will, he released her shoulders and stuffed his hands in his pockets. He had no choice, he told himself. He had a job to do, a very important job. People depended on him. He could not involve Charly. She would be in the way, could even get hurt.

And he was frightened—yes, frightened—of the unfamiliar emotions that just looking at her caused to rampage through his body and soul.

"Go back to town, hon . . . Mi . . . Charly." He turned away, rubbing the throbbing crease near his eye. "I'll follow you in a few minutes."

When he turned back, she was gone—running as if a rabid wolf was foaming at her heels.

He cursed and stared into the dark heavens. He'd done the right thing for once in his life. Some day she would thank him. So why did he feel so damned rotten?

Charly ran to the bottom of the hill and collapsed into a trembling heap beneath a tall mesquite tree. She felt the leather thongs that laced her tunic dangling loosely and wrapped her arms protectively about her upper body, gulping back her sobs.

She willed herself not to cry. She would not feel sorry for herself. Hurt? Humiliated? Oh, yes. But not sorry. He'd given her one wonderful night and had awakened her to the notion that she was, indeed, a woman. A woman who felt comfortable with herself.

But why'd he have to be so cruel all of a sudden? Why'd he lead her on tonight, forcing her to realize how badly she wanted him and how much she needed him to love her?

She stiffened and went cold all over. Had he discovered she wasn't the woman he wanted her to be? Had she done something wrong? And then she remembered. *She'd* kissed him. Charly's cheeks burned. She'd been brazen and wanton, teasing him into kissing her back. Maybe he didn't like his women so forward.

She shivered. Forcing herself from the ground, she brushed the dirt from the seat of her pants, then lifted her chin and took a deep breath. By golly, she wasn't goin' ta wallow in self-pity. If the city dandy didn't want a strong woman—so be it.

She was Charleen McAllister. He'd made her face that. And never again would she . . . Now, how'd he put it? Never again would she hide behind her man's disguise. Whatever she wanted to do, she could do. Whether it be driving a stage or . . . seducing a man.

A determined mask settled over her features. Never again would she allow Mr. Kent Ashford close to her. He'd tromped her affection and feelings beneath his feet like so many horse droppings.

She turned her gaze toward the stage depot. Another day. A whole day to get through before the westbound stage headed back to Tucson and *home.* Home—where she could lick her wounds and start over again.

Her eyes closed as she dreamed of peace and security, until it suddenly dawned on her that the entire trip would be spent sitting next to Kent Ashford in that tiny, narrow box. She recalled the state she'd been in by the time they'd arrived in Mesilla—after the constant rubbing of their bodies—shoulder to shoulder, thigh to thigh.

She quickly relaced her tunic. The leather brushed her throbbing nipples. She gasped. Lord, if she thought she'd been in a state before, just look at her now.

Goldurn it, she'd never handled a woman's passions and desires afore. What if she attacked the next attractive man that passed by? That was possible, wasn't it? She'd heard of men doing it to women when they'd become too aroused. Oh, damn. She could handle a six-mule team better than her own emotions.

A stone skittered down the hillside. Quickly, Charly returned to the shadows. Another stone rolled to within inches of her hiding place. She held her breath. She wound her hand reassuringly around the bone knife handle.

Kent's familiar figure strolled into view. His hands were still jammed in his pockets. He kicked at every rock in his path. He cursed, and she winced as his handsome features twisted into hard, chiseled planes.

He passed without looking in her direction, and she set free the breath she'd been holding. It was only her imagination playing tricks on her. There was no way he could be hurting as much as she. He was a cruel man, and she would do well to remember that.

She waited a few more minutes before slowly following after him.

The next twenty-four hours seemed like two weeks as far as Charly was concerned. She surprised herself, though, by being able to sleep, even with Kent only a

191

few feet away. She was too exhausted to do anything else.

Although she refused to spend the winnings Tony had saved for her, she enjoyed walking through the two emporiums in Mesilla. The American owners were making a fortune, charging whatever prices they wanted, and getting them. But *she* didn't have to buy from them. A smile fleetingly crossed her lips. She was getting smarter every minute.

At last, the westbound stage pulled in. Charly stood off to one side, watching the passengers disembark. There were only three men aboard the coach and two more would be getting on here in Mesilla. Five altogether. None was immensely overweight or too tall, so at least they should be able to enjoy a fairly comfortable trip.

She inhaled, then nearly dropped her pack when Kent came noiselessly up behind her. "Mornin', Miss Charly. You all refreshed and ready for the trip back?"

A brief nod was all she could manage. Dadburn him. The man was goin' to pretend that nothin' had happened the other night, just as he had all day yesterday. How could he act so cool and composed? Her insides turned to cold mush every time she saw him, or heard his deep voice, or smelled his masculine scent.

But then, she guessed, it hadn't meant as much to him. After all, he'd sent her away. She scowled at a grasshopper climbing up her pant leg.

Her hands shook when she gave her pack to Tony to load. "See ya next trip, Tony. And . . . thanks fer standin' by me the other night."

Tony blushed. "Any time, Charly."

In a small voice, she said, "Charleen. My name's Charleen," and flushed a bright pink.

She took the passengers' tickets, concentrating on the paperwork. Her fingers were suddenly clasped in

192

a very firm, masculine grip. Her gaze darted up. A pair of cloud-gray eyes sparkled with . . . What exactly? She tilted her head. A love of life? Of adventure? A new conquest?

"Mawnin', lovely lady. Don't tell me we're goin' to be in *your* capable hands all the way to Tucson?" drawled a soft southern voice.

Chapter Twelve

Charly stared at one of the nicest looking men she'd ever seen.

Heat crept up her cheeks. She darted a quick look over her shoulder. All right, she admitted to herself, so the new fella didn't quite match up with the city dandy. He'd certainly do. Besides, Kent Ashford didn't count any more.

She smiled at the "nice-lookin'" man still holdin' her hand. His fingers were warm and slightly calloused. She enjoyed his gentle touch. But a little voice butted in, "Yore insides ain't meltin'. Yore heart ain't trippin' over itself. Where's that buzzin' sound that rings in yore ears whenever . . . the dandy . . . touches ya?" She gritted her teeth.

The dashing, soft-spoken gentleman doffed his wide-brimmed plantation hat. "Miles Cavanaugh at your service, lovely lady. I've always heard that Western ladies were quite extraordinary, but I must admit I never believed it . . . until now."

Charly blushed. She tugged her hand from his grasp and hid it behind her back. A singular burning sensation caused her to look over her shoulder. Kent Ashford was glowering at her fingers as if they'd just been caught stealing a fifty dollar gold piece.

She jerked her arm, and her gaze, back around and

nearly stumbled into the persistent passenger.

"An' to whom do I have the pleasure of addressin' myself, ma'am?"

She looked into amused gray eyes. "I-I'm . . . M-My name's . . . Charl . . . Charleen. Charleen McAllister. I'll be a-drivin' ya ta Tucson."

Suddenly, she felt extremely self-conscious—about her grubby looks, her masculine garb, and her crass manner of speech. What a bumpkin she was.

"My, my, Charleen. What a pretty name." The gentleman's eyes turned thoughtful. "McAllister. McAllister. Seems I've met someone by the name of McAllister."

"Say, mister. You gettin' on here, or what?" One of the passengers who'd stepped off to stretch his legs was impatient to return to his seat, but Charly and Miles blocked his way.

And when Kent then snapped his watch open directly beneath her nose, Charly jumped a foot.

"We're late, Miss *Charly*. You know the Overland Mail's reputation for being on time. Wouldn't want to upset the schedule, now, would we?"

Charly flushed and narrowed her eyes. Drat that man! Late? She hadn't noticed. Her fist clenched around the passenger list. And how like Kent Ashford to slyly get his licks in. She smiled her most gracious smile and quickly took the Southerner's ticket. "Ya have a good trip, Mr. Cavanaugh."

"Miles, my dear. My friends call me Miles. And I predict that you and I shall become *very good* friends, Charleen."

Kent cleared his throat, but before he could challenge the fellow's forward behavior, Miles Cavanaugh stepped into the stage. The remaining passengers crowded in behind, edging between himself and Charly. The scar twitched as the muscles in his jaw tensed.

When his eyes collided with her brilliant green

ones, his breath quickened. A wild, reckless sparkle danced in their depths. He'd never noticed it before. And he had a horrible premonition that he'd made a *big* mistake. The kitten with sharp claws had turned into a full grown tigress. Hell!

Climbing on top of the stage, muttering beneath his breath, he tried to convince himself that perhaps things would work out for the best. Perhaps now that she was more aware of herself as a woman, she'd be better prepared to meet some nice man and live a happy life.

But why was the thought of Miss Charly and another man—smiling and touching, making passionate love to one another, ripping his gut to shreds?

Especially disturbing was the image of Charly and that damned fawning idiot below. Sure, the fellow seemed a likely candidate for a woman like Miss Charly—handsome, well-mannered, and probably had money running out his ass. But there was something about the man . . . Too smooth. Too self-assured. Too . . . Southern—for his Union fidelity to trust.

Why was a *gentleman* like Miles Cavanaugh traveling all the way to a backward little burg like Tucson? And why did he pay such special attention to a rough-around-the-edges woman like Charly?

Kent sighed and shook his head. There he went again, thinking up reasons to protect the fool woman. From what? Or better yet, from whom? The *gentleman?* Herself? Or from Kent Ashford?

Why just look at him now. He hadn't been sitting next to the minx for more than two minutes and already his hands were trembling and his insides felt like the stage had jounced over a mile of rough road. Damn!

Charly stood in the box, carefully threading the lines from each of the six mules through her gloved fingers. She was achingly aware of the man seated so

197

pensively on the bench. Durn it, why couldn't that nice Mr. Cavanaugh take her mind off the dirty city rat for even a few minutes?

She glared over at Kent. He blinked and finally picked up the bugle.

A loud, blaring screech set the mules off to a jerky start. Charly was thrown sideways and lost her balance. She plunked ungracefully into his lap.

Hard thighs and flat belly surrounded her bottom and hip, and she didn't question *how* he'd managed to move quickly enough to catch her. His hand on her waist completely wiped rational thoughts from her mind.

But instead of holding her, or caressing her, he merely helped her to her feet. He held her steady until she regained her balance. Sensations of disappointment, anger, and bafflement coursed through her. When she hollered, "Let's go," her voice was a shrill squeak. The wheel team hesitated, bouncing the stage again. It took another shout and the cracking whip to get them lined out smoothly.

She suddenly thought of Miles Cavanaugh. How confident would he be in her abilities now? Her face burned as she plopped down on the bench.

Charly glared from the team to Kent. Catching his contrite expression, she looked back to the mules and narrowed her eyes. Had the blamed man blown the bugle so lousy on purpose? Or was the blast an accident?

Charly was nearly at the end of her limited store of patience by the time they'd reentered what she referred to as the Arizona side of New Mexico Territory, since the durned politicos back East were draggin' their heels over recognizin' Arizona as a separate Territory.

Oh, Kent Ashford hadn't done anythin' *real*

198

noticeable . . . It was the little things. The gestures, the little touch here, a light caress there. Her smoldering senses were ready to ignite.

If he dared to lean over one more time and whisper in that low, growly voice, she'd . . . she'd . . . give him a taste of her whip. By golly, she would. Her fingers clenched around the rawhide handle.

"Well, Miss Charly, I sure hope they've roasted a beef at Stein's. I'm hungry enough to eat a hind-quarter all by myself. How about you?"

Her eyes narrowed. Instead of low and gravelly, his voice was silky smooth. When his hand raised, and it appeared he might be tempted to explore her flank, she jumped to her feet. "I ain't got yore kinda appetite, city man."

Kent sadly shook his head and lowered his hand back to the bench. "Damned shame, too. Perhaps, someday, you'll develop a healthy taste for—"

Disbelief sharpened her wits. "Why, you . . ." Her eyes grew as big and round as the stage's wheels. The whip trembled in her hand. "Ya goldurned randy peacock."

She watched his brown eyes rake over her like she was a tempting, creamy piece of taffy and he was a starving little boy.

Trying to get a better hold on the lead mules' ribbons, she sat down. The animals sensed the approaching barn and the manger filled with oats and hay. "Easy, Bertha. Hold up, Mike."

God, Kent thought, he loved to tease his Miss Charly. Just because he'd declared her off limits didn't mean he couldn't torment her some. Especially when she made it so much fun. She still needed to loosen up, to laugh and enjoy life. And he was bound and determined to see it happen.

Once she had the mules under control, Charly glowered at him. Was the arrogant oaf purposely bein' thick-headed? "Yore jest aimin' ta get me

199

flustered, ain't ya?"

He frowned. "Me? Why would I want to do that?"

She sniffed. "Well . . . Don't reckon I know. But I meant what I said." Wagging the whip handle under his nose, she repeated, "Ya randy peacock."

He clicked his tongue. "That's a shame. But I guess you'd know."

Durned right! It was 'bout time he . . . She scowled. "Ooohhhh! Ya dangnabbed—"

"Watch your mouth, Miss Charly. There's a *gentleman* aboard. You know what I've told you about cursing."

Charly was speechless. The son of a jackass.

Kent blew the bugle and concentrated on the road ahead.

If her memory served her right, hadn't *he* rejected *her?* So why was he wastin' time tryin' ta turn her head agin? What made him think she'd want to . . . to . . . Dangnab it, she had to quit lookin' at him an' rememberin' how smooth an' hard he'd felt.

As the station came into view, she took a deep breath to clear her head. She studied the rocks and cactus, sniffed the aromas of beans and bread, anything to keep her mind off the exasperating man beside her.

After she pulled the team to a stop, Kent reached out in his usual manner to help her from the coach. She pretended to be busy folding her whip. Then she puttered underneath the bench, checking her shotgun and making sure everything was packed tightly enough that it wouldn't roll around under her feet later.

Finally, the Celerity rocked. She exhaled quietly, relieved that Kent had finally gone on without her.

She started to climb from the opposite side. Miles Cavanaugh stood there, holding up his arms expectantly. She looked down into his smiling gray eyes. "Allow me, miss."

Lordy, she sighed. The man's voice was as soft and smooth as churned butter. When she took his hand, she noticed that his fingernails were manicured. Once on the ground, she stuck her own fingers in her pockets, hoping he hadn't seen the dirt smudges and broken edges.

"Miss McAllister, I don't know how you manage to look so fresh and beautiful after that long, dusty ride. It's purely amazin' to me how a sweet, fragile lady such as yourself can handle such a difficult job."

She blinked. Sweet? She took a long look down her leather-clad length. Fragile? Wouldn't the folks in Tucson get a hoot out of hearin' that?

Suspicion narrowed her eyes, but when she lifted her gaze to his, she found only sincerity shining back. She gulped and pressed a hand over her chest, hoping the hummingbirds battling to get out would at least wait until he'd turned his back. "I-It's really not so har . . . diff-i-cult. Th-The job, that is. Once ya git the hang o' . . . of it."

Miles bowed, then took her elbow. "Do you mind if I escort you in to dine? I realize we're not well acquainted, but perhaps, under the circumstances, we can excuse some of the formalities."

She looked up at him through a veil of lashes, grateful she didn't have to crane her neck the way she did when she looked up at Kent Ashford. "I-I reckon we could do that . . . under the cir-cum-stan-ces. An' ya kin call me Char . . . Charleen, don't ya reck . . . think?"

"I just wanted to be sure it was all right . . . Charleen. And I'd be very pleased."

His perfectly straight teeth flashed, though not quite as brilliantly as Kent's. But then Miles Cavanaugh wasn't nearly as tanned or weathered. Blame it all, she scolded herself. Why'd she keep doin' that? Comparin' everthin' 'bout Miles ta Kent?

She tried to flutter her lashes, but gave up when he

201

bent down, all concerned to help her get out whatever was in her eye. Durn it, there warn't nuthin'. There was a lot more ta bein' a dadgum lady than she remembered.

The cook at Stein's Station hadn't had beef on hand, but he served up antelope steaks, mesquite beans, some rare and prized boiled potatoes, and corn cakes. The chicory coffee could even be sweetened with molasses if a person wanted. Everyone heaped their plates with seconds, including Charly.

Throughout the meal, Kent stared at the pushy passenger. But the only thing he could read from the other man's cool gray eyes and impeccable features was that the fellow had a fascination for his . . . for Miss . . . Charly.

Kent didn't trust the *gentleman* one bit. Sure, the man was soft-spoken and mannerly. And he was solicitous and treated Charly like a grand lady. Maybe *that* was what aroused Kent's suspicion. How could a man hold her calloused hands or look at her leather britches and not think of her as anything but a tomboy, a rough-and-tumble hoyden?

He scratched his chin. However . . . He recalled a time not so long ago, when her naked flesh pressed close to his. Then he'd thought of her as all woman—fully female. Even now, when he looked into her pixie face and was lanced by those huge emerald eyes . . .

Damn it! He couldn't afford to keep torturing himself. Why couldn't he just stand in the background and let the smooth-talkin' Southern gentleman solve all of his problems?

He couldn't understand the ax-sharp slash to his heart every time that Miles fellow leaned close to Charly and whispered something that only she could hear. And then, damn her, she'd bat those long lashes and smile that sweet, enchanting smile. The one he so rarely saw. Kent gulped down the last of his coffee and slammed from the station as Cavanaugh leaned toward her again.

Why'd he sign on for this job in the first place? He'd thought he'd do a good thing and look after the helpless little female, did he? Well, while he was protecting Miss I-don't-need-no-help Charly, she'd slipped up and grabbed him by the heart.

But he'd get it back. See if he didn't.

After the fellow called Kent had stormed from the room, Miles looked into Charly's eyes. "If I may be so bold, Charleen, are you and that . . . man," his eyes cut in the direction Kent had taken, ". . . together? I mean, are the two of you . . ."

Charly attempted to conceal the heat creeping into her cheeks by taking several sips of her cold coffee from the huge crock mug. Goldurn it, he wasn't askin' 'er ta confess that she'n Kent Ashford were cozyin' up together. So why'd she all of a sudden feel shameful and guilty?

"N-no. Mr. Ashford's just the mail conductor. That's all. There's certainly nuthin' a'tween us. Nuthin'." *Mr. Ashford* had gone ta a lot o' trouble ta pound that message inta her feeble female brain.

"Good." Miles ran his index finger over the back of her hand.

She ducked her head. Good? What'd that mean?

"I hope you won't think I'm too forward if I say that I'd like to get to know you better. After we arrive in Tucson, and I find suitable lodging, perhaps you'd allow me to call on you every now and then."

Her eyes widened. Call on her? Really? "Yore . . . you, ah, are gonna be a-stayin' on, then? In Tucson?"

"That's what I'm hoping. I've heard there might be a position open there. I'm a schoolteacher, you see."

"That's wonderful." Golly. She'd never met a

teacher who'd actually *chosen* to settle in Tucson. Most kept right on a-travelin' 'til they reached the bigger, more civilized cities in California.

Miles' face became more animated. "You've heard of the opening, then? Do you know if the position is still available?"

"Far's I know."

"Then we must celebrate when we get to Tucson. You will take pity on a poor lonely stranger and have dinner with me, won't you, Charleen?"

He picked up her hand. She let him hold it. When he smiled so graciously and ran his thumb so delightfully around her palm, she wondered how any self-respecting female could refuse? "Sho-ure. I reckon I could chow . . . eat gru . . . have dinner . . . with ya, Mister Cavanaugh."

"Ah, my dear, you granted me permission to call you by your given name. Can you not afford me the same honor?"

"Huh?"

"Call me Miles."

The freckles on her nose and cheeks darkened. "All right, M-Miles."

"That's much better, Charleen. Much better." While he studied her face intently, she squirmed under the serious observation. "You know, there is something so very familiar about you. I wish I could think of where I've heard the name McAllister before."

She slumped down in her chair, trying ta make herself smaller. She hoped he hadn't met her pa somewhere, drinkin'. But she reckoned there were lots o' McAllisters. Tucking a straggling lock of hair behind her ear, she was embarrassed to realize she still wore her hat.

Dismayed by the discovery, she searched his eyes, looking for signs that the attention he was paying her was just a joke. How could a gentleman like him

204

look at her, really look at her, and still be interested in celebrating anything with *her?* But he gazed right back at her without one blink.

The bugle blared. Charly jumped like a grasshopper. Pulling out her watch, she looked at the time. Late. Again. She thought she might die from mortification. Her head had been so turned by Miles Cavanaugh's compliments, she'd put the stage almost ten minutes behind schedule. She grabbed Miles and tugged. "C'mon. We'uns gotta hurry."

Outside, she was greeted by a loaded stage and a fiercely scowling Kent. After making sure Miles was safely seated and securing the door, she crawled up into the box. She was sheepishly reaching for the reins when Kent picked up the whip and shouted the team into motion.

"Hey! Jest a goldurned minute here. What'cha think yore a-doin'? Ain't supposed ta be no'un else a-drivin' this here coach but me."

Kent slid his hat back on his head and settled himself firmly on the bench. He cracked the whip and expertly placed the tip just to the right of the reluctant lead mule's ear. "Shut up, woman, and take a rest. It's a hell of a long way to Tucson." Since there hadn't been a driver waiting at Stein's, Kent didn't hold out much hope that there'd be one at Dragoon Springs, either. He sighed with pleasure. For once, she needed him.

Charly yawned in between glares. The filling meal *had* made her sleepy. Maybe jest a little nap, she thought. Then she'd take over again.

When she finally opened her eyes, it was almost dawn. She stretched and nearly fell off the narrow seat. She also realized her head was pillowed in Kent's lap. Trying to sit up too quickly, she plowed her forehead into his sharp elbow.

"Damn! Ouch!"

"It's about time you rejoined the living, sleepy-head."

She frowned. Sleepyhead? She was usually the most alert driver on the route. Why was everything goin' wrong with her life?

Instead of taking the reins, she closed her eyes and leaned back against the rocking Celerity. Within the space of a week, everything in her world had been turned topsy-turvy. Her pa and brother were actin' stranger'n ducks outta water. And she'd turned into a woman with a man she hardly knew.

Last week, she wouldn't have been able to name a man who'd a stopped ta give 'er the time o' day. And now two very handsome men, for some reason she couldn't explain in a thousand years, seemed to want ta win her favor.

She yawned and stretched, causing her back to pop, and she winced.

"I don't think we're going to make it this time."

"What?" She straightened, swiveling her head, looking for sign of bandits or Apaches. Though a light haze glowed behind them on the eastern horizon, it was still too dark to make out anything but shadows.

Kent cracked the whip. "Through Apache Pass. I don't think we'll make it before sunup."

"Nope. Don't reckon." She shifted and moved closer to him. "Give me the ribbons. I'll take over now."

He glanced at her sleep-heavy lids. They teased him with the barest glimpses of forest-green eyes. His stomach lurched. "Naw. I'll take it on in through the Pass. Use the extra time to wake up."

"Thanks."

"No trouble. Do you like him?" He bit hard on his tongue. Now what had caused him to voice the question that'd haunted him all night? She was bound to misunderstand. To think he was jealous, or

206

something. Which, of course, he wasn't. Not a bit.

"Like him? Like who?"

"Miles Cavanaugh." Hell, in for a penny, in for six bits.

Her eyes opened. Wide. Heck, she'd just met the man. But if she really thought about it . . . "Yeah, reckon I like 'im good 'nuf. He's a gentleman."

Kent grimaced. The way she said the word "gentleman," it sounded like she hadn't met many "gentlemen" before. One of the wheel team tossed its head and his fingers clenched around the reins. "Is that all you know about him? That he's a *gentleman?*"

She glared at Kent. "Why? What should I wantta know?"

He shrugged. "Just wondered why he was going to Tucson. If he was sellin' something."

At his words, she slanted him a smile. "Nope, he ain't sellin' nuthin'. He's a schoolteacher. He's gonna get a job in Tucson."

"And you believe that, do you?"

Her head snapped around, her eyes ablaze with inquiry. "An' why wouldn't I, city man?"

"No reason." Kent regretted ever opening his mouth. Yet there was something about the Southerner that didn't ring true.

Charly was reluctant to accept his answer. Surely he'd had a reason for askin' such a question. Suddenly her lips quirked. A strange lightness suffused her chest. Was Kent jealous?

She tilted her head, studying him while he was busy with the team and unaware of her scrutiny.

Something was wrong. If he didn't want her, as he'd said the other night, why'd he get so mad when Miles was flattering her, and showing her a lot of attention? Why were the grooves around his mouth so deep? Why'd the scar twitch every time he looked at her? *Somethin'* was sure botherin' 'im.

Her heart started an erratic pounding against her ribs. Could he *care* for her—more than he was willin' to admit?

She gnawed her lower lip. So what if he cared for her? When it came right down to it, he didn't seem to want her enough. And she'd just end up with a broken heart. 'Cause she *cared* for him—more than she'd ever thought she'd care for anyone.

She took a deep breath and trained her gaze on anything but Kent. Maybe that nice Mr. Cavanaugh was just what she needed. Maybe if'n he got the job of schoolteacher, he'd stay around Tucson. It was more'n she'd ever be able ta say 'bout the city dandy.

Besides, who needed smolderin' glances, or burnin' touches, or heart-stoppin' passion? And what was so goldurn excitin' 'bout pain an' turmoil?

Chapter Thirteen

Streaks of pink and orange and red colored the eastern horizon by the time the stage rolled through Apache Pass. No matter how closely he looked, the only living things Kent noticed were cholla cactus and slithering lizards as the mules strained up the steep grade.

Unused to driving a team for such a long period of time, his shoulders and upper arms ached and throbbed with every tug on the reins or lick of the long whip. Once in a while he'd sneak a glance at Charly, marveling at how the thin wisp of a woman managed the grueling job twice a week.

Dragoon Springs was a welcome sight to his tired, scratchy eyes. Charly picked up the bugle and gave the thing several perfect, melodious toots. He sighed and barely suppressed a grin. Wasn't there anything the hoyden couldn't do? And do well?

Kent drew the stage to a stop in front of the station and wrapped the reins around the brake handle. He straightened and coiled the whip, leaving it exactly as he'd found it. From the corner of his eye, he noticed Miles Cavanaugh stretching and relieving cramped muscles. Kent turned and nearly bumped Charly over the side of the Celerity in his haste to beat the Southerner in assisting her to the ground.

Charly had to grab Kent's shoulder to regain her balance. He grinned and made sure she was steady before he spun and jumped down, then held up his arms for her. She moved to the side of the box and stood staring down in bewilderment. Kent and Miles looked back at her, both pairs of eyes reminding her of hound pups expectantly awaiting a pat on the head.

When it dawned that they were both waiting for *her,* confusion rioted through her brain. A choice? She had ta pick a fav-or-ite? Jest ta get off'n the durned stage?

She splayed her fingers across her hips and gazed beseechingly into the hazy blue sky. Finally, she threw up her hands and lit a shuck down the opposite side.

Miles muttered an oath and drawled, "Now see what you've done, sir." A grin split Charly's lips.

"And just what is it you think *I've* done, mister Southern *gentleman?*" Kent pushed his hat to the back of his head and massaged his throbbing temples.

Miles glared at the uncouth ruffian. "Why, you frightened Charleen, that's what. I could tell right away that the young lady is far from desirous of your attentions, sir."

"Quit callin' me *sir.* The name's Kent Ashford. Mr. Ashford, to you." He grudgingly stuck out his hand. Anything to take Cavanaugh's mind off the fact that Miss Charly was doing her damnedest to avoid her prized conductor.

Taken aback by the unexpected introduction, Miles stared at the outstretched hand, then blinked and reluctantly offered his own. "Miles. Miles Cavanaugh."

"Yeah. I know." Kent had been keeping a wary eye on Charly and saw that she had busied herself by helping the handlers hitch the new team. A little obvious, wasn't she? Suddenly, he clapped Miles on the shoulder. "Come on inside. I'll buy you a cup of coffee."

"Well . . ." Miles looked over his shoulder, saw Charleen struggling with a buckle and being quickly aided by a young Mexican boy, and shrugged. "Ah, all right. I guess . . ." Although he was hesitant to be in the conductor's company, he couldn't think of a graceful way out of the situation.

The stationmaster gestured at Kent as the two men stepped into the room. "Tell Miss Charleen that Dave Turnbow's here. He'll be drivin' the stage on in to Tucson."

Kent sighed. Thank God! Charly'd borne enough of a load just on the trip to Mesilla. Her wan features and the dark smudges beneath her eyes had him worried. Maybe now she'd get a chance to recoup her strength.

He took a seat at the plank table and swung around to speak to the Southerner. Damn! The "gentleman" had gone back outside and was helping Miss Charly up the steps. And the fool woman actually seemed to be enjoying the fawning idiot's attention! All she'd ever given Kent for his efforts was a punch in the gut.

Kent filled a mug full of coffee from the pot that had been set on the table. The boiling brew scalded his tongue and he desperately searched from side to side for a place to spit it out. Miles escorted Charly inside at that moment, and Kent was tempted to ruin the fine polish on the Southerner's fancy boots. But, finally, he gulped it all down and glowered across the table.

"Charleen, my dear. Good news. That fellow," Miles pointed to the stationmaster, who'd just turned his back to refill a plate with corncakes, "says you're going to be relieved by another driver. Since you said you're going to Tucson, too . . . does that mean

211

you'll be riding the stage with me?"

Charly bit her lip to keep from shouting with joy. Dave was here. Thank the Lord! She would be delivered from Kent Ashford's presence—at last. One more hour of riding that close to his hard, muscular body, and she'd be darned tempted to drop the reins on her whirling emotions.

But when she looked up, it was into excited gray eyes. "Ah, yeah, I reck . . . I think I kin . . . could do that." She'd never ridden inside one o' those contraptions. The thought kinda tickled her fancy. Miles'd be good company, an' . . .

Suddenly the hair on the back of her neck prickled. She jerked her head up and her gaze locked with scintillating brown eyes. Oh, Lord! Just her luck. She would be trapped inside the tiny confines of the coach with both Miles and Kent breathin' down her neck like two coyotes hungerin' after a bone.

She cleared her throat and looked back to Miles. "But, then agin, I ain't so sho . . . sure—"

"Chow down, folks. Stage leaves in five minutes." Big Dave Turnbow, a taller man but slighter of build than Uncle John, stomped through the room. Charly nearly laughed out loud at the stunned faces around her as the driver glared at the passengers, making certain they understood he meant what he said. When he walked out the door, there was a collective sigh of relief and she had to turn her head. Big Dave was a mountain of a man, but his large, gruff exterior concealed the heart of a pussycat.

Miles excused himself, and Kent quickly filled the empty seat beside Charly. "Looks like we'll be travelin' to Tucson in style."

She sighed. "Reckon so."

"Aw, wipe that sickly grimace off your face, honey. It won't be so bad. I'll try to keep that pup Miles from botherin' you too much."

Charly inhaled sharply. It wasn't Miles she was

worried about. But before she could correct him or offer a verbal reprimand, he was helping her from the long bench and escorting her outside.

Kent was about to hand Charly into the stage. From out of nowhere a huge hand settled on his shoulder.

"Just where do ya think you're goin', mister?"

Kent spun. He came face to face with Dave Turnbow. The immense size and power of the driver gentled Kent's reply. "I'm going to Tucson. Why?"

"Ain't you the mail conductor?"

"I was, but—"

"Git yourself aboard, then. We got us a job to do."

"But—"

The big man's grip slackened and he slapped Kent's sore shoulder. "Sorry, pal. But the chap what gen'r'ly rides with me got hisself another job last week. Workin' in some damned bank. Kin you imagine that?"

Kent thought the poor stiff was probably the luckiest man alive, but he mimicked Charly's weak grin. "Yeah. How about that?" And as he reluctantly moved away from Charly and stepped up and into the box for what he prayed would be the last miserable time, his eyes met the amused gaze of Miles Cavanaugh.

Soon he heard Miles' soft drawl spouting nonsensical drivel and then Charly's answering giggle. Kent grumbled under his breath and took a death grip on the butt of his rifle. Damn Miles Cavanaugh! Damn Miss Charly for allowing herself to be taken in by all of that sweet-spoken hogwash.

Damn the whole Overland Mail Company!

Charly ground her teeth and hoped the curve she tried to paste on her lips resembled a smile. Tarnation, but she'd never been bounced on her

213

bottom so hard, or been poked by more sharp elbows, or eaten so much dirt in her entire twenty years. Even with the canvas side-panels pulled down, granules of sand sifted inside the Celerity and liberally coated her hair, her face, her clothing, even her teeth.

Kent Ashford had thought she'd be travelin' in style. Well, if'n *this* was style, she was a hoity-toity lady o' the mansion.

An' the durned passengers . . . Some of 'em was tryin' ta sleep. One was snorin' louder'n a puffer-bellied engine, only to strangle an' jerk awake when a wheel bounced in a hole. Two more were passin' a "sample" of rye whiskey back an' forth, an' Miles Cavanaugh was busy tellin' her *all* about the large family he'd left back in good ole Tennessee. As if she was dyin' ta know 'bout Uncle Lester's cotton crop, or Aunt Lulu's priceless porcelain collection.

She yawned and let her head drop back against a wooden brace. Right now she'd trade places with Kent Ashford in a heartbeat. Hellfire, she'd even sit next ta the arrogant son of a gun if'n she could jest escape this bone-jarrin' rattletrap.

The coach lurched and skidded into deep ruts. Kent rubbed at his tender backside and glared at the oblivious driver. The big man possessed the most extraordinary ability to guide the team, and therefore the stage, over the roughest section of the road.

Or maybe the point was, Kent observed, that Dave wasn't guiding the team at all. The driver was too busy flappin' 'is jaw an' snakin' out the whip, as Miss Charly would probably say, to watch the damned road.

"Hey, Windy," Charly poked her head through and shouted. "Whatcha doin' up there? Why ain'tcha blown the dadburned bugle?"

Dave grinned and slapped Kent's raw shoulder for the hundredth time. Kent gritted his teeth. One more time. Just one more. His index finger itched to sneak into the rifle's trigger guard, but he sighed and obediently reached for the bugle instead.

"You know, fer a little fella, you ain't half bad, Windy."

Kent winced. Damn Charly! The brat had been showing off in front of her new *gentleman* friend. How dare she think he needed to be reminded to blow the damned bugle! And now Dave was calling him by that stupid nickname. Windy, indeed. Kent shook his head. Coming from Miss Charly, he hadn't minded it so much. But from Big Dave?

"Dave, you know good and well that I'm nearly as tall as you," Kent defended. By damn, nobody had ever called him "little fella" and gotten away with it.

"Mebbe so, but ya cain't be more'n half my weight. To my way of thinkin', Windy, you're a mite scrawny."

Kent wasn't in the mood to argue the point. A long silence dragged out, for at least sixty seconds, until Dave changed the subject. "Shore were a shame 'bout ole Hardy Anderson, weren't it?"

"Hardy Anderson?" Kent vaguely recognized the name. Then he remembered. The nice old man who'd taken Charly's place in Mesilla. "What about him?"

"Reckon ole Hardy's settin' fire ta Hell right this minute." Dave clucked his tongue.

Suddenly a wheel jounced over a large rock and Kent grabbed hold of the bench to avoid being thrown across Dave's knees. All the while, he conjured up images of a vibrant old man joshing with Charly. "Maybe we're not talking about the same man. The Hardy Anderson I met was in Mesilla few days ago. He looked fine."

"He was the one, little fella. Old Hardy was a-drivin' the stage a mite east of El Paso. Hear tell a gang of bandits come chargin' from behind a pile o' boulders while the stage were a-movin' real slow up a steep grade. Hardy never knowed what hit 'im.''

"Damn!" Kent rubbed the back of his neck. Then he thought of Charly. She couldn't have heard about her friend yet. Double damn! The stage hadn't been carrying anything of value—that he knew of. And the bandits had to know that all the Overland carried was mail.

Dave cracked the whip. "Conductor told the stationmaster that them bandidos went through near ever mail sack. But they didn't take a single piece o' nuthin. Didn't even search the passengers fer their valuables.''

"Hmmm. That *is* strange.'' Kent gingerly tested the growth of beard stubbling his jaw. The hair on the back of his neck prickled. Had it started? Already? His superiors had been afraid the Overland Mail would bear the brunt of the coming conflict.

Soon, he'd be sending out his own important messages. What would happen if they fell into the wrong hands?

Dave Turnbow pulled the team to a stop at the San Pedro station. Kent and the driver exchanged knowing glances just before Kent swung to the ground. Charly needed to be told about Hardy Anderson, but Kent wished now that *he* hadn't been the one to take on the chore.

Below, bored to a frazzle, Charly was more than ready to flee the Celerity, but hesitated when she saw the determined expression on Kent's face as he stood beside the door—waiting. She stuck out her chin and decided that once and for all, she would prove just how oblivious she could be of his attentions.

Pasting a bright smile on her face, she turned and held out her hand to a startled, and pleased, Miles Cavanaugh. One look out the open door was all Miles needed to quickly descend ahead of her and adroitly

216

place his body between Charleen and the restless Kent Ashford.

As Charly was about to step out, instead of keeping hold of her hand, Miles reached up and encircled her slender waist. He lifted her out, holding her suspended longer than was really necessary in Charly's opinion, then landed her so close to his side that their bodies touched.

A nervous giggle escaped Charly's constricted throat. She nearly died of embarrassment. Miles had just taken her by surprise. Once they were well away from Kent and the passengers, she would make sure he didn't take such liberties again.

Yet, the thunderous expression darkening Kent's face made Miles' possessiveness almost worthwhile. Maybe she would thank Miles rather than scolding . . .

The next thing she knew, bands of steel shackled her wrist and yanked her away from Miles so quickly that even her long legs couldn't keep pace. She had to run to keep from falling and being dragged like a sharecropper's plow.

"Hey, hold up, ya lily-livered lizard." She looked back over her shoulder to see if Miles intended to come to her rescue. The Southerner had taken a few steps in her direction, but was looking at Kent's stiff shoulders and the left hand that dangled threateningly close to a Colt revolver. Charly sighed, disheartened by the expression on Miles' face, which had turned as pale and sickly as curdled cream. He only lifted his shoulders at her imploring call for help.

"Looks like your *gentleman* friend is smarter than I gave him credit for," Kent growled. His long strides ate up the ground until they were finally a good distance away from the station.

Jagged nails dug into Kent's forearm, but he refused to release his grip on the spitting she-cat.

Figuring they were out of earshot of the gaping men staring after them, he jerked her wrist and swung her around until she faced him.

Sensing a change in Kent's mood, Charly tilted her head and watched him intently. Somethin' was wrong. She nibbled on her lower lip, erasing her smile.

Kent scratched harshly at the burning scar. "I'm sorry, honey. I don't want to hurt you."

"C'mon, Ashford. Spit it out. What're ya tryin' ta say?" She shoved her hands in her front pockets. Whatever was botherin' him couldn't hurt worse'n his rejection in Mesilla. What was he gonna do? Order her ta stay the hell away from him? Demand she act like she didn't recognize 'im if'n they met on the street? She could do that. Durn shore could.

So why did the pain cut deeper an' deeper every time she looked at the dadblamed man? Why'd her heart feel like little pieces were being sliced off every time he glanced her way?

Kent reached out and cupped her narrow shoulders in his large palms. She flinched and he winced. "I just wanted to tell you in private that—"

She spun on her heel and turned her back to him, afraid for him to see the effect his words might have on her. "Don't worry none, city man. I know what ya wanna say—"

"Hardy Anderson was killed a couple of days ago."

Her chin snapped up. She took a deep breath. "Wh-what'd you say?"

"I'm sorry, honey. He seemed like a good man."

Suppressing an icy shudder, she stared at Kent. Hardy was gone? Her friend was dead?

Kent pulled Charly's unresisting body into his arms. He cupped her neck in one hand and coaxed her head into the hollow of his shoulder. His other hand soothed up and down her back as he softly whispered his condolences.

"H-how'd it happen?"

"Dave Turnbow said Hardy'd been attacked by bandits."

She stiffened.

"He went fast, so they say."

She sniffed.

"The outlaws were looking for . . . something . . . in the mail."

Charly inhaled deeply. "Yeah." How strange she felt. Numb with cold, yet warmed by Kent's touch.

"Honey?"

"Hmmmm?" Was he really talkin' to her? If'n he didn't want her, why was he callin' her *honey?*

"What's wrong?"

"Whadda ya mean?" If he didn't know the answer, how could she?

"Well, I thought . . . I mean, I thought you and Mr. Anderson were friends."

"We was."

Kent frowned. "Yes, well . . . I guess I thought you'd . . . maybe you'd cry . . . or something." Or that she'd need him? Why else would he have taken her so far from the others, except to spare her the embarrassment of showing her feelings in front of everyone? Why, indeed? And then he remembered his rage at seeing Miles Cavanaugh's hands on her.

Charly lifted her head and pulled away far enough to look into his eyes. "I liked Hardy—a lot. We was good friends. But I ain't never been a puddler, city man. Ain't gonna start now. Hardy wouldn't a wanted no female critters a-blubberin' o'er 'im, noways." She defiantly willed an unfamiliar scratchy feeling from the backs of her eyes.

He let her go. She stepped completely away from him. If he lived to be two hundred, he'd never understand the female mind. Just when he thought he knew Miss Charly well enough to anticipate her

219

reactions, she had to go and trample his crazy notion.

Tucking a persistent strand of flyaway hair behind her ear, Charly glanced toward the station. "Reckon we'd best be gittin' back. Dave'll be chompin' at the bit ta get started."

"I imagine he already is. But before we leave, I'd like to ask your friend, Mr. Cavanaugh, a question or two."

"Why? What'd Miles do?"

Kent tried to appear casual at her familiar use of the *gentleman's* first name. She hardly deigned to call him Kent, and they'd known each other a good while. Long enough to . . . But this Miles character comes along, and she seemed as comfortable around the man as a filly bedded on new straw. Hell!

All right, he thought. What could he tell her? Why did he really want to question the Southerner? "Since your *friend* came through El Paso, I thought maybe he might've heard something about the holdup. Or perhaps have heard something further back along the route about when the mail line would be severed." He spoke the last sentence softly. He was taking a chance, mentioning his suspicions, but he wanted to gauge her reaction.

Charly felt her brows pinch together. Just who was this so-called drifter? She'd heard rumors of the mail route being cut, too. They all had. But how would Kent Ashford know?

She chose to pretend like she hadn't heard what he said about the mail. She'd bide her time and keep an eye on the man. He was up to somethin', and she was bound to find out what.

Stepping closer again, she shook her fist beneath his nose. "You don't like Miles. I kin see it in yore eyes. You jest wanna make trouble for 'im." And that much she did believe. Men! They musta all had some kinda kink in their britches.

"All right, Miss Charly, do you want to explain

220

yourself, or will I have to report you to the main office?"

Kent gazed into Charly's astonished eyes for a long moment after the question left his lips. Dear God. That wasn't what he'd planned to say.

Charly's jaw worked, but it took several seconds for her to form a coherent sentence. "Ya . . . Ya wouldn't . . . Why? What've I . . . I don't understand."

He opened his mouth, closed it, then said the only thing he could think of to justify his outburst. "For running the stage late—twice. For fraternizing with the passengers. For letting a passenger run his goddamn hands over your goddamn body." He stared at her chest as her rapid breaths caused her breasts to pull her shirt tightly over them. "And those're just a few of my complaints. I could go on."

Oh, she bet he could. Charly grinned. For some unexplainable reason, she was suddenly happy. The durned city dandy was jealous. She stared at the green flecks dancing in his eyes, from his flushed cheeks to his twitching mustache. He was easier ta read than a trail in broad daylight and was durned sure as jealous as an old rooster in a hen house full o' young chicks. Hot damn!

And other than his accusation about her causing the stage ta be late, he might as well be spittin' in the wind.

"I mean it, Charleen McAllister, if you let that Southern pup touch you again, I'll damned sure report you." Instead of the hissing tirade he'd expected, the brat had the nerve to stand there and smile at him. Smile! Hadn't she listened to a word he'd said?

Charly shrugged. "Reckon you'll do what ya gotta do." She sighed dramatically. "'Cause if'n he wants ta touch me, I'm durn shore gonna let 'im." She rolled her eyes. "Ain't he just the purtiest, finest man ya ever saw?"

Kent's jaw closed so swiftly that he heard his teeth click. "Pretty? Fine? Him? Why . . ."

He took a deep breath, letting it out slowly as he removed his hat and raked a hand through his hair. Whatever notion had routed him on this self-destructive path would have to be put aside.

"Look, all I want is to ask the man a few questions. Where's the harm in that?"

The harm, he berated himself, was that she'd ignored, or maybe hadn't heard, his hint about the mail. Was it possible that the operators of the Overland Mail hadn't warned their people of the impending danger?

"Ain't none, don't reckon." Scuffing her toe in the dirt, Charly jerked her fist behind her back. Maybe she'd flown off the handle, just a tad. "But that there Miles, he be a 'gentleman'. 'Tain't right ya think he'd know anythin' about a holdup."

Kent threw up his hands. "Can you hear yourself, woman? You don't know anything about Miles Cavanaugh. He could be running two steps ahead of the law. Just because he wears fancy clothes and talks like an educated man doesn't make him a damned *gentleman*."

Her mouth turned down. Maybe the city dandy was right. She'd once thought Kent Ashford was a gentleman. And look how wrong she'd been. She slanted him a cocked eyebrow, you-should-know look.

At that moment, it dawned on Kent exactly what he'd said. If he truly believed that drivel, why was he still always running Charleen McAllister down?

Before he had a chance to ponder the intriguing question for any length of time, he heard her shout, "Hey, Miles. Reck . . . Think you could come talk to this galoot?" She jerked her thumb over her shoulder in Kent's direction. He scowled and cursed under his breath.

Now why'd she go and do that? But as the Southerner walked toward them, his expression questioning and wary before a wide smile for Charly wreathed his too-perfect features, Kent's determination grew. Jealousy was a mild term for the emotions the *gentleman* ignited inside Kent. He just plain didn't like the man.

"Here he be . . . is, city man. Fire away." Charly stood smugly beside her new friend, certain she'd taken a little of the smoke from Kent's fire.

"What's this all about, Charleen?" Miles came to a stop behind the beautiful woman. Though he wondered what Ashford wanted, Miles was pleased she'd called him over, since he'd been trying for the past few minutes to think up a good excuse to join the pair.

Kent hooked his thumbs in his belt. He had to admit, the man was damned good. Just look at that innocent expression. Why, one would think the Southerner drank nothing but milk and said his prayers every day.

"Miss Char . . . McAllister heard that I wanted to talk with you and was kind enough to get your attention. Isn't that right, honey?"

Charly's eyes narrowed. She sputtered, but wasn't quick enough to think up a good retort. Drat him!

"This pretty lady is really something. I've looked a long time for a woman like her." Miles glowered at Kent, but turned back to Charleen with a warm smile. He moved closer, and placed a proprietary arm around her waist.

Charly gulped, but managed to keep from bolting the scene entirely. Miles' touch wasn't all that unpleasant, and she did want Kent to believe he had no more effect on her. If Miles was willing to play into this hand, she'd let him ante up, for a while.

Kent clasped his hands behind his back, so hard

that his knuckles ached. He forced a smile and even choked out a chuckle. "Oh, my Charly, she certainly is a . . ."

Stomping her foot, Charly raised a small cloud of dust and dried grass. "C'mon an' get on with it. Ask Miles your blamed questions."

Miles blinked. He dropped both hands to his sides. "Questions? What questions?"

Kent studied the Southerner. "Dave Turnbow, the driver, just told me about a stage holdup near El Paso. Just wondered if you might've heard something about it, since you recently came from that direction."

Miles reached up and began to twist his watch chain between his thumb and forefinger. "Why are you askin' me, sir? Are you perhaps the law?"

"No. Hell, no. I'm only taking an interest because of Miss Charly . . . and because of my job with the Overland Mail, of course. Wanted to help out a little, is all."

"Of course." Miles shifted from foot to foot as he contemplated Kent's earnest expression and probing brown eyes. "Naturally, I want to help. But . . . you know, I boarded the stage in El Paso. I have no idea what could have happened to any stage coming or going before then."

Charly cocked her head. Funny, she'd thought from their conversation earlier that he'd ridden the stage all the way from Memphis. But then she remembered that he'd been lookin' for a job.

"So you never heard a thing about a stage robbery?" Kent tried not to appear as disappointed as he felt.

Miles shook his head. "Sorry. Didn't hear a thing. N-not a thing." He rubbed his palms down his thighs and looked at Charleen. "I wish I could be of more help." Belatedly, he asked, "Did they get anything? The outlaws?"

MORE PASSION AND ADVENTURE AWAIT... YOUR TRIP TO A BIG ADVENTUROUS WORLD BEGINS WHEN YOU ACCEPT YOUR FIRST 4 NOVELS ABSOLUTELY *FREE*
(AN $18.00 VALUE)

Accept your Free gift and start to experience more of the passion and adventure you like in a historical romance novel. Each Zebra novel is filled with proud men, spirited women and tempestuous love that you'll remember long after you turn the last page.

Zebra Historical Romances are the finest novels of their kind. They are written by authors who really know how to weave tales of romance and adventure in the historical settings you love. You'll feel like you've actually gone back in time with the thrilling stories that each Zebra novel offers.

GET YOUR FREE GIFT WITH THE START OF YOUR HOME SUBSCRIPTION

Our readers tell us that these books sell out very fast in book stores and often they miss the newest titles. So Zebra has made arrangements for you to receive the four newest novels published each month.

You'll be guaranteed that you'll never miss a title, and home delivery is so convenient. And to show you just how easy it is to get Zebra Historical Romances, we'll send you your first 4 books absolutely FREE! Our gift to you just for trying our home subscription service.

BIG SAVINGS AND FREE HOME DELIVERY

Each month, you'll receive the four newest titles as soon as they are published. You'll probably receive them even before the bookstores do. What's more, you may preview these exciting novels free for 10 days. If you like them as much as we think you will, just pay the low preferred subscriber's price of just $3.75 each. *You'll save $3.00 each month off the publisher's price.* AND, your savings are even greater because there are never any shipping, handling or other hidden charges—FREE Home Delivery. Of course you can return any shipment within 10 days for full credit, no questions asked. There is no minimum number of books you must buy.

4 FREE BOOKS

Charly shook her head.

Kent cocked his brow. "Only a life. See there? You knew somethin' after all. It wasn't just one outlaw, but several."

"Well, er, yes . . . I guess . . . I assumed it would take a group of men to stop a stage."

Charly felt that peculiar burning sensation in the backs of her eyes again. Poor Hardy. So many men had been lost on the line, but he'd been one of the best.

Kent sighed and insinuated his large body between Charly and Miles. He draped an arm over each one's shoulder, letting his left hand drop awfully near Charly's breast. She started to struggle, but he tightened his grip and grinned. "Isn't this nice? Three friends, working together to help solve a crime. Those outlaws won't stand a chance . . . Will they?"

Chapter Fourteen

Kent thought he'd never been so glad to see a place in his life as the dusty little town of Tucson. He tooted the bugle almost as expertly as Charly, and was doubly proud of himself when they pulled up in front of the station and he handed over the mail safe and sound.

Jumping from the box into the street, he found himself dodging a freight wagon and a pack train of mules before he reached the shade of an overhanging portal. Even there he had to elbow his way through a throng of people. At one-thirty in the afternoon, why wasn't everyone at home taking a siesta?

When he stopped to switch his pack from one shoulder to the other, he happened to overhear two men talking. One mentioned a *baile*, or a dance, Saturday night. The other commented on the people coming to town early since it was Friday. Kent realized then that Tucson probably doubled in size every weekend when farmers and ranchers came in to do their shopping. And with a celebration planned, no wonder the streets were so crowded.

A throaty giggle to his left caused him to clamp his teeth together and pinch the inside of his jaw. He hated the weakness that made him turn to look in the direction of the entreating sound. Sure enough, there was Miss Charly, being lifted from the stage by gallant and groping Cavanaugh.

The sight damn near made him throw up. Fool woman. How could she allow herself to be attracted to such a . . . such a . . . *gentleman?* The man wasn't her type at all. What kind of fun could she have with a fella who was afraid to get a spot of lint on his clothing?

At that moment, Miles pulled a handkerchief from his back pocket and bent to wipe dust from the toe of his boot. Kent chuckled. But when he lifted his gaze, his eyes collided with glaring green ones. Uh-oh, he thought.

Charly had enjoyed Miles' witty banter during their ride into Tucson. It'd been a long time since she'd laughed so hard. Yet she had to admit that the man's preening was beginning to wear on her nerves. Every few minutes he had to swat the sand off of his suit. Then his hair had to be just right beneath the gray bowler hat.

When he bent down to polish his boot while he was standing in the middle of a dusty street . . . It was the last piece of straw that brought down the stack. And then a deep, growling chuckle grated down her spine. She looked up and shot a damning glare toward Mr. Kent Ashford. Of all the people who had to see . . . Of all the people who would know . . .

"There ya be, gal. Me'n yore brother been plumb worried 'bout ya."

Charly's gaze shifted to her pa. "What?" Her eyes widened perceptively at the sight of Jed McAllister's clean-shaven features and neatly trimmed hair. "Pa?"

"What'sa matter? Ya got somethin' in yore eye? Ya ain't sick er nuthin', are ya?"

She blinked and blinked again, then realized that she was staring stupidly. "N-no, Pa. I'm all right. Ya just look . . . Well, ya look mighty fine."

Jed snorted, but straightened his back and lifted his chin. "Thanky, Charly. Didn't allow ya'd notice."

She opened her mouth to protest, to ask him why he'd think such a thing, but he'd already turned to Dave Turnbow.

"How's the trip, Big Dave?"

Dave nodded as he threw his pack to the ground. "Fair ta middlin', Jed." Then the driver pointed to where Kent was standing. "Better keep that little fella around. He's a good hand."

With everyone's attention suddenly centering on him, Kent tried to blend into the crowd. It was difficult since he towered a head above most of the bystanders.

Charly made a face at him and he flicked the brim of his hat in mock salute. The little she-cat. Damn, but he pitied the man reckless enough to tie in with her. The poor bastard would never have a moment's peace—running between saloon brawls and holdups and fightin' off advances from Southern *gentlemen*.

He hooked his thumbs in his belt and leaned nonchalantly against the baked adobe wall. Speaking of Southern gents, that Miles fella appeared once again at Charly's side and she was introducing him to her father.

Kent also observed the change in the stationmaster's appearance. He kept his eyes on Miss Charly, though, fascinated by the way her eyes darted often to her father, as if she couldn't believe what she was seeing. Ever since he'd met the McAllisters, he'd sensed a tenseness between the family members and wondered what had caused it.

Was Jed McAllister the main reason behind Charly's overprotective attitude regarding the Overland Mail and everything connected with the stage line?

Charly bristled beneath the prickling sensation of

someone staring at her back. She knew immediately who it was. That durned Kent Ashford. The dratted lobo just wouldn't leave her be. Yep, lobo was a right fittin' description of the hard-eyed, smooth glidin' loner. And he always had that predatory air about him, like he was just waitin' to pounce on some unsuspectin' victim.

She tilted her head and studied him intently. The notion that there was more to the man than just being some drifter down on his luck continued to plague her. At certain times, when things were said, he'd prick his ears just like a wolf who'd sensed danger.

Charly shook her head. Right now she didn't want to think about who or what he was. Looking into the cloudy sky, she decided that now was as good a time as any to air her lungs an' give him what for. But when she looked up and took a step forward, he was gone. Vanished. Two seconds ago, he'd been standing there. Now he was gone, just like a lobo faded into nothing.

Goldurn it, why wasn't she happy that he wasn't glarin' at her anymore? She'd been about to march over and demand that he leave. So, why did her belly have that empty little ache, and why did her throat feel like she'd swallowed a prickly pear?

"Charleen, you will say 'yes,' won't you?"

She blinked and turned to gaze distractedly into Miles Cavanaugh's pale eyes. "Huh? I mean, what?"

"I asked if you would do me the honor of accompanying me to dinner tomorrow evening. As I recall, we had discussed celebrating my arrival in Tucson."

"Ah, I thought ya . . . you had to see if you got that there job afore . . . first."

Miles smiled. "Ah, pretty lady. I see no reason to wait. I've met an intriguing, beautiful young woman. We arrived in Tucson safely. There's a festive glow in the air. We've a good deal to celebrate, wouldn't you say?"

She sighed. Her word had been given. "Reckon it'd be all right. Less'n . . . unless my pa—"

"Go on an' enjoy yourself, daughter. Ya ain't took a Saturday off since I kin remember when." Jed had been standing a few feet away, handing a woman traveling to Los Angeles into the departing stage. When the lady was seated, he turned and made a shooing motion to Charly. "Have some fun, gal."

Looking into Miles' soft eyes and handsome face, Charly wondered why she wasn't more anxious to step out with him. She'd certainly be the envy of every young, available woman in Tucson, and probably some that weren't so available. "Wh-what time do ya . . . you wanna go?"

Miles took her hand and squeezed it gently. "How about I come for you at six?"

She gulped and nodded.

"Where?"

"Uh, what?"

"Where shall I pick you up?"

"Oh, uh, we live right next door there." She pointed toward the north end of the station.

"Good. I'll look forward to seeing you tomorrow evening, lovely lady."

Charly watched as Miles picked up his bag and threaded his way through the busy street. Where was he goin'? There weren't any hotels in town. Most folks had to take a room at the station. But then she reckoned if he was planning to stay on a while, he was probably goin' to look for a more permanent room.

Thinking of rooms, she wondered where Kent was stayin'. His saddlebags were still in their safe, so she supposed he'd also rented a room somewhere.

Charly entered the small living quarters occupied by the McAllisters and stopped abruptly. Someone

231

had swept the place out recently. Marks from the broom still scratched the hard earthen floor. A shirt and suspenders draped the back of one chair, but the table and the top set of shelves were dusted and orderly. Wood was stacked beside the hearth and several logs had been laid in the fireplace, ready to be lit later that evening.

She turned around and around. Her mouth snapped shut on a pleased sigh. The good fairy must've come in and done her chores while she was away.

The door behind her banged open and Ed rushed inside. He slid to a stop at the sight of his sister. "So, ya finally made it back, huh, boss lady?"

"Yep." Charly groaned inwardly. Well, nothin' much had changed after all. Her brother was as surly as ever. At least some things in life remained constant. She sat down in her mother's oak rocking chair and stared into the quarried stone fireplace.

"Pa says ya got yerself a man now."

Her eyes popped wide open. "How'd he know that?" Durn it, she bet the city man had to go an' blab. Well, the fat was in the fire now. Purty soon the whole blamed town'd be talkin . . .

Ed snorted. "Whatta ya mean, how'd he know? You introduced 'em over at the office." He frowned. "You did tell the fella you'd step out with him, didn't ya?"

Air rushed into her lungs in one giant burst which she hid behind a fit of coughing. "Y-yeah. I fer . . . forgot."

"Forgot? You ain't stepped out with a man since we moved in here." His eyes scanned her almost contemptuously. "If he don't hold his fork just right, or sit up straight at the table, you gonna give him what for?"

That did it. Charly leaped to her feet! The chair rocked wildly and nearly toppled over backwards before righting itself. "Hush yore mouth, Ed McAllister. It ain't . . . isn't right that you sass me. I've done my durn . . . best ta take care o' you men folks since mother died, an' all I get for appreciation be a heap o' lip."

She wiped her palms down her coat. "So I'm no ravin' beauty, it don't mean a man cain't find me attrac . . . attrac . . . passable. At least I ain't gotta go to a saloon ta find my men."

"Meanin' what, bossy britches?"

She splayed her hands over her hips and thrust out her chin. "Meanin' . . . whatever you want it ta mean, little brother."

"I done told you afore, I ain't your—"

"Don't matter what ya said, I'm through listenin'." She spun and ran into her room, the only one with a wooden door to separate it from the rest of the quarters, and slammed it behind her. She stomped over and flopped onto the straw mattress.

It seemed that fighting with her family was all she ever did anymore. Her pa, 'n' Ed, they just didn't realize what all she did around here. One o' these days, she'd leave, an' they'd be on their own. Then they'd see . . .

Suddenly, visions of her pa today, 'n' the neat house, flashed before her eyes. She hugged her arms around her waist. She'd been gone—longer than she'd ever been before—an' they'd managed just fine without her. Maybe even better. Maybe her family didn't need her. Maybe she didn't have a home *anywhere*, anymore.

Charly stood in front of her armoire Saturday morning, wearing nothing but her chemise and pantaloons and a lost and lonely expression. Leather shirts and pants. Cotton shirts and pants. Flannel shirts. One dress that she'd worn to her mother's

233

funeral when she was ten years old.

She had nothing to wear, so that settled it. She couldn't go out with Miles tonight.

Sighing, she pulled out a drawer and picked up a stocking. Slowly, she walked back to the bed, eased down on the coverlet, and emptied the contents. The meager number of coins she'd collected over the years didn't take long to count. Two dollars. The money would hardly buy a bottle o' that fancy toilet water.

Dressing quickly, she scooped the coins into her pocket and determinedly left the house on her way to Pederson's Emporium. Two dollars. Maybe she'd buy a feminine blouse to go with her trousers. After all, Miles'd asked her out when she'd been wearing her leather britches. Surely he wouldn't have bothered if he'd found her *that* repulsive.

The minute she stepped into the emporium, she was tempted to turn around and flee. None other than Mr. Kent Ashford's tall frame filled the first aisle, his broad shoulders nearly spanning the space between the rows of shelves.

The blamed bell above the door merrily announced her arrival and she muttered a curse. Every pair of eyes in the store turned in her direction, including Kent's. Drat. Why'd she ever come here in the first place? She usually wasn't the impulsive type.

Sarge Pederson himself came to help her. "How do, Miss McAllister. What do you need today?"

Heat crept from the roots of her hair to the tips of her toes. She couldn't just come right out and ask for somethin' fancy an' frilly in front of all those folks. Especially Kent. "Well, uh, I-I . . . Maybe I'd best—"

"Daddy? Why don't you go and help one of the menfolks. I haven't seen Charleen for ages, and if *I* help her, we'll have a chance to chat and catch up on all of the gossip."

Charly thought it cute the way the older man smiled and patted his daughter's blond head. A tiny

234

place in her heart ached at the loving gesture.

"All right, sweetie. I thought by now you'd be all gossiped out, though."

As the balding proprietor moved on, Charly's lips curved into a genuine smile as she turned to her friend. "Thanks, Nelly. Reckon it has been a spell since we've run into each other." Charly liked the short, chunky girl with the bouncing blond curls and rosy cheeks. Though Charly, herself, rarely had news to exchange, Nelly more than made up for it. She knew enough about the comings and goings of the residents of Tucson for any ten gossipers.

Nelly waited until her father was busy with another customer before hooking arms with Charly and walking her down an aisle of yard goods and women's store-made undergarments. And across the next aisle . . . Charly had to concentrate hard to keep from staring at Kent's broad back. "What'd you say, Nelly?"

"I was just wondering what you'd been looking at in the window before you came inside. I've never seen you stand still that long."

Charly blushed. She didn't realize she'd been caught staring. "Th-that fancy outfit. It's purty."

Nelly clasped her hands together. "Oh, yes. Isn't it the most gorgeous shade of blue you ever saw? The beads on the ruffle came all the way from some foreign country, you know."

Charly shook her head. "No kid . . . Really?"

Nelly nodded and glanced secretly around, as if she'd just shared something clandestine and wicked. "Would you like to try it on? The skirt, too? Bet that color would be beautiful next to your dark skin."

"Oh, I cain't. I mean . . . I-I never—"

"Pshaw. It's been lying in the window for two weeks. I'd like to see what it looks like on someone as tall and slender as you." She leaned closer. "It won't cost you anything just to see if it fits."

"Well . . . Don't reckon it'd hurt."

Nelly left and was back in two shakes carrying a royal blue skirt and blouse, both of which were trimmed in gaily colored wooden beads. Charly hesitated, wiped her hands up and down the legs of her pants, then held out her arms. The material seemed to melt into her hands.

Her heart fluttered as if it had wings. She wanted to bury her face in the sweet-smelling folds. Never before had she felt anything so deliciously soft and feminine.

Nelly led her into a corner where two blankets hung from rods in the ceiling and came together to form a small, private place for changing clothes. "Here you are, Charleen. Take your time and I'll be right here when you're ready to come out. I can hardly wait."

Charly ducked behind the blankets and just stood staring at the beautiful clothing. Brand new. And she was holding the frilly things in her own two hands. Charleen McAllister, who'd owned nothing but hand-me-downs for ten years, and most of them from her brothers.

She peeled out of her shirt and pants and folded them neatly onto a footstool. The skirt she hung from a hook until she needed it, and the blouse . . . Well, she just kept running the clingy material through her fingers. It felt so heavenly that she was afraid to put it on. What if it tore? What if she got it dirty?

But finally, her woman's instinct took over. She couldn't resist. Nelly was right. It didn't cost anything to try somethin' on. Just once she could know what it felt like to wear fancy clothes. And the memory would last a long, long time.

The blouse felt like soft, weightless bubbles against her skin, as she knew it would. It was cut in a peasant style, like most of the women in Tucson wore, but had three-quarter length sleeves and a four

236

inch ruffle that dangled from the gathered neckline. And the beads, so many of them, were hollow and magnificently decorated with tiny painted flowers.

Then came the skirt, which had a gathered waistline that was hidden beneath a bright red and yellow sash. In a moment of pure delight, she spun and watched the voluminous skirt flare in a wide circle around her legs. Legs. If it weren't for her boots, her ankles would be showing. Golly.

Almost in a daze, she stepped out of the blankets.

There wasn't a sound in the room. Not even the soft buzz of customers' voices. Where'd everyone gone? She gradually took her eyes off the skirt to glance around the room. Several people who'd been looking in her direction suddenly turned back to their browsing.

But one person continued to stare at her for a long time. She flushed beneath the intent scrutiny. Then Kent, too, turned away.

Charly felt a little chilled as his searing gaze abruptly left her, but in the wink of an eye, Nelly was there, her arms spread wide. "Ooohhhh, Charleen. I've never seen anything like it. Why, I didn't recognize you for a minute, you're so beautiful."

If the compliment were a little backward, Charly chose to ignore it. "Aw, shucks, Nelly. I, uh, I mean it's pretty, but—"

"The color is perfect for you. You are beautiful. You *are*, Charleen."

Charly lowered her lashes. Poor Nelly. She was so obvious. 'Course she'd say somethin' like that to make a sale.

Ready to run and hide back in the little room, Charly happened to catch a glimpse of herself in a reflection from the window. She stopped. She stared. Then she blinked and looked again. No, that couldn't be her. Yet when she raised her hand to the beaded ruffle, the reflection aped her movement. It was. The colorful butterfly was her.

"Goldurn, Nelly. Isn't that the purtiest . . . prettiest outfit you ever did see?"

Nelly smiled. "That's what I've been trying to tell you, goose."

Charly gulped. "H-how much is it?"

"Just a minute and I'll go ask my father."

Charly watched Nelly waddle over to where Sarge and Kent stood conversing. All three sets of eyes turned at once to look at her and she timidly lowered her gaze to the cracked board flooring. She had to glance away. It was impossible to meet and hold the intensity in Kent's eyes.

She didn't realize Nelly had returned until she felt a light tap on her shoulder. "Father says the blouse is two dollars, and the skirt is five. But you can have the pair for six dollars."

Charly's shoulders slumped. "All's I have is two."

Nelly looked over Charly's shoulder. When the plump girl's head moved, albeit quite imperceptively, Charly started to turn and see what had caught her friend's interest.

"Charleen, I'll tell you what I can do. If you buy the blouse for two dollars, I'll throw in any two of these hair combs."

A hair comb? Thoroughly distracted, Charly allowed herself to be led over to a case containing a variety of pretty, feminine gadgets and jewelry. A hair comb. She hadn't had one since her mother . . .

"Look, Charleen. We've got tortoise shell combs. Brass combs."

But Charly couldn't take her eyes off a pair crafted of silver. Around the edge of each was a narrow scroll design and a carved butterfly. They perfectly reflected the way she felt at that moment. Fragile and delicate. Weightless.

"H-how much are them . . . those two?"

Nelly frowned. "Well, they're a little more expensive than the others . . ."

Nelly's voice trailed off and Charly glanced up to see the girl looking at something behind her again. This time Charly spun quickly and saw Miles Cavanaugh standing in the doorway. It didn't appear he'd seen her yet, and she was glad. She wanted to keep her purchase a surprise.

Hurriedly pointing to the silver combs, she whispered to Nelly, "I'll take 'em," and then ducked and darted behind tables and stacks of goods back to the partitioned room.

Changing into her britches and shirt took a long time because she hated having to remove the pretty skirt. She'd love to be able to purchase it, too, but felt lucky enough to be able to take the blouse.

Before she emerged from behind the blankets, she stuck her head through the opening and looked warily around. Relief washed over her when she saw the only two people left in the store were Nelly and her father.

She took the blouse and skirt up to the counter and laid the blouse beside the combs. Running her hands lovingly over the skirt one last time, she sighed dejectedly and handed it back to Nelly.

Her lips compressed as she looked at the combs. They were an expense she hadn't counted on, but she had the two dollars plus a few extra coins. Would it be enough? Maybe she should have Nelly put them back and take the ones that wouldn't cost extra. It would be embarrassing if she didn't have enough money.

Nelly was already wrapping the blouse in paper. Charly cleared her throat. "Uh, how much more are the silver combs?"

The shorter girl glanced at her father and then at Charleen. "Not a thing. They're yours."

Beneath the counter, Charly's hands clenched. "No. Don't reckon I'd better take 'em after all."

"Why?" Nelly looked stricken.

"You told me they's more expen . . . costly. Just give me a couple o' the shells." She dug in her pocket and put the two dollars on the counter. Suddenly, she grabbed up her package. "Better yet, just keep 'em. I ain't got no use fer such things, anyhow."

Before she reached the door, Nelly caught up with her. "Charleen, wait." She stuffed the silver combs into a fold of the paper. Forcefully she took hold of Charleen's shoulders and looked her directly in the eye. "If you think we're giving you charity, you're wrong. Those combs go with the blouse. Just ask Father if you don't believe me."

Charly glanced sheepishly over her shoulder. Sure enough, Sarge nodded his head.

"What's wrong, Charleen?" Nelly demanded. "We've been friends for a long time and I've never seen you act so strangely. One minute you're bubbling over with excitement. The next you look like a trapped animal. What is it? If you tell me, I promise I won't breathe a word to another soul. Not even Father."

Charly blinked. She gulped in a deep draught of air. She looked back to see Sarge Pederson enter the storeroom. Then she peeked out into the street. It didn't appear anyone was turning into the Emporium. Her free hand gripped Nelly's. "I'm scared, Nelly."

Nelly snorted. "You? Afraid? Of what?"

Charly lowered her voice. Nelly leaned closer to hear. "I'm steppin' out tonite. With a gent."

"But that's wonderful," Nelly gasped. Then a dreamy expression entered her round eyes. "It's that man who was in the store earlier, isn't it?"

Charly nodded. Nelly sighed. "Oooohhhh, I just knew it. He's the handsomest thing I've ever seen, Charleen. What a lucky goose you are."

At that moment, Charly didn't feel lucky. "I reckon."

"Well, of course you are." Nelly stepped back and surveyed her friend. "You said you're going out tonight?"

Charly scowled.

Clicking her tongue, Nelly grabbed Charleen's arm and propelled her toward the back of the store. "Then we've got a lot of work to do."

"N-no, Nelly. You cain't. I cain't. I gotta—" She dug in her heels.

"You gotta get ready to impress that wonderful man. Now quit your lollygagging and come with me."

"But—"

"Now!"

"Uh, yes ma'am."

Charly dragged through the storeroom and into the Pederson's living quarters, muttering, "There warn't a blamed man alive worth the trouble a gal had ta go through ta get ready to 'impress' 'em."

Chapter Fifteen

Charly walked stiffly home from the Pederson's, afraid to move her head lest her carefully brushed curls spring loose and ruin all of Nelly's hard work. As she passed the one glass window in the stage depot, she stopped and stared once more, amazed at the difference in her appearance.

She looked sophisticated and . . . regal, to her way of thinking. The silver combs swept her hair back, and the long, dark tresses were coiled into a neat roll and pinned on the nape of her neck. Charly remembered that her mother had worn her hair in such a fashion on special occasions. And now, looking at her reflection, Charly could almost *be* her mother, with her almond-shaped eyes and olive-hued skin.

To Charly's dismay, she felt that peculiar burning sensation in the backs of her eyes again. Since when had she become so emotional and sentimental? The soft female in her was cropping out way too often nowadays.

Yet, as she hugged the package to her breast, she couldn't help wishing she had that pretty skirt to go along with the blouse. What was the use of having a fancy hairdo and new blouse when all she had to wear with them was a pair of white cotton trousers?

Oh, well. She would hardly know how to act if she was all gussied up. This way, half of her would be the old Charly, and she'd feel like she was in control of at least part of her life. She patted at one of her curls and stopped abruptly when she saw her pa's face peering out at her from the station doorway. She dropped her hand, tried to grin, and then scurried on to their living quarters.

Once the solid oak door was closed behind her, she leaned against it and wondered for the hundredth time what had possessed her to accept Miles' invitation. She'd end up embarrassing herself *and* him. And if her pa's incredulous expression was any indication, everyone in Tucson would hear that she was trying to make a silk purse out of a sow's ear. Lordy!

Her feet dragged the floor as she walked into her room. She was about to toss the new blouse onto her cot when she noticed there was another package lying in the center of the bed. *Another* package? How did it get there? With the curiosity of a ten-year-old child, she stalked the long, narrow cot, looking, not touching. Large black letters spelled her name. No mistake. It was hers.

She picked it up. The paper bent. She shook it. Nothing rattled. Excitement weakened her knees and she collapsed onto the bed. Her fingers shook as she tore open the paper.

Air escaped her lungs in a long, soft breath. The royal blue skirt spilled into her hands. Her heart thundered in her ears as she quickly dispensed with the paper. The skirt! The beautiful skirt. Suddenly she snatched up the pieces of paper, searching, turning over each piece. All she found was her own name. There was no hint as to who could've sent it.

Her pulse quickened. Miles. He'd come into the Emporium. He must've seen her after all. She bet he'd gone back and talked to Mr. Pederson and found

244

out all she'd purchased was the blouse. That Nelly! The girl'd probably been in on the whole thing. Nelly had fixed her hair and given her a few pointers on good speech and manners just to distract her.

And, golly, had the plan worked. Charly'd been taken completely by surprise.

At five o'clock that evening, Charly stood in front of the small, cracked mirror above her wash basin. She couldn't see her whole reflection, but what she *did* see was startling. In the place of tomboy-Charly shone a stranger, a young feminine woman— *Charleen* McAllister.

The blouse and skirt clung to her slender form, causing her skin to tingle all over whenever the sensuous material brushed against her. She actually felt like a lady. A real lady.

And she felt attractive. Thoughts of Kent, and then Miles, flushed her with heat. One had made love to her with his body, the other made love with his eyes every time he looked at her. What would they say when they saw her now?

She shook her head in an effort to dispel the image of Kent Ashford. He had no place in her life now, and she wished she'd quit thinkin' about the creature.

Miles was the man she needed to concentrate on. Miles was the thoughtful one who'd gone to so much effort to give her the beautiful skirt and to start the evenin' off perfect. What would *Miles* think when he saw her? And how would she ever thank him, or repay him?

Yep, she'd repay him. It warn't proper for a man to buy a gal such a personal gift. He was bound to expect somethin' in return, somethin' she wasn't prepared to share with anyone, ever again. Not after Kent.

Sure, Miles was nice and attractive and pleasant to

245

be with. But enjoying his company was as far as she would go. Somehow, she'd explain that to him in a way that wouldn't cause him too much pain. Guilt still plagued her 'cause she'd considered using him to take her mind off Kent. She'd never been that conniving afore.

Looking into the mirror again, she decided to practice the diction Nelly had taught her. "Good eve . . . en . . . ing, Mr. Cavanaugh." She drew the words out, pronouncing every syllable slowly and succinctly. "Good evening. Thank you for the wonderful gr . . . sup . . . supper. Good eve—"

A muffled choke startled Charly. She spun and found her brother gaping. "Thunderation. Are you really bossy britches?"

Charly scowled.

"My gawd, you are." Ed walked around his sister, eyeing her from the hem of her skirt to the top of her coiffured hair. A low whistle was his next response.

Shuffling her feet, Charly hid her toes so he wouldn't notice that beneath the frippery, she wore her scuffed boots. She nibbled on her lower lip in hopes of quelling a nervous twitch she'd just noticed. Her fingers curled and uncurled as he continued his inspection. "Well?" she whispered.

Ed plopped on the end of her cot. "You're all grown up, bossy britches. I never realized . . . I mean, it seems like only yesterday . . . You can be a purty woman when you want to be." His voice was hoarse. The admission came grudgingly.

Charly grinned and twirled. "Thanks, little brother." Then she reminded herself. "I mean, thank you, Ed."

"So yore gonna eat at the restaurant?" He cocked his head and eyed her closely.

She nodded. At least she reckoned so. Ed had referred to the eating room and kitchen connected to the large hacienda that John Butterfield had pur-

246

chased to provide rooms and meals for passengers traveling on his stages, since there was nothing of its like in the small town of Tucson. It was all a part of the Overland station.

Ed stood up. "Well, have a good time." Then he winked. "Don't do anythin' I wouldn't."

Forgetting her determination to act like a lady, Charly stuck out her tongue.

Laughing, Ed sauntered from her room into the living area. At the door, he stopped. "Maybe I'd better hang around and check out this new beau."

At that moment, there was a rap on the door. Charly shuddered and shook her head.

Ed shrugged, and with a mischievous grin, opened the heavy portal. He stared at the dandy standing so incongruously in the dust. His jaw snapped closed as he invited, "C'mon in. Reckon yore here to see my sister."

Miles flicked a nonexistent piece of lint from his lapel as he entered the small quarters. He peeled a tan glove, which perfectly matched his fawn-colored jacket, from his hand and held it out. "Miles Cavanaugh, here."

Ed quickly offered his own hand and they shook. "Ed McAllister."

Miles looked over Ed's shoulder and saw her for the first time. Charly felt a telltale heat suffuse her body. His stunned expression brought a smile to her trembling lips.

Miles stumbled forward. "Pretty lady. It doesn't come close to doing you justice. "You . . . you're . . . breathtaking."

Behind Miles' back, Ed rolled his eyes. "I gotta get back to the stables. Nice to meet ya, Mr. Cavanaugh."

Miles reluctantly turned from Charleen. "You have to work so late? Surely there isn't a stage coming through this evening."

"Naw, not tonight. Just gotta clean some tack."

Charly lowered her lashes in hopes that Ed wouldn't see her surprise and shock. Ed? Doin' chores on Saturday night? Was the world turnin' upside down?

Miles kept his eyes on Ed. "I imagine you're always prepared for an unscheduled stage or wagon."

"Sure. But most a the time, we know when one's a-comin'." Ed waved cheerily and went out the door. A low whistle drifted inside just before it closed behind him.

Once they could no longer make out the sound of the lively tune, Miles edged closer to Charleen. She sniffed, wondering where that sweet smell came from. It became stronger as Miles neared. Inwardly she smiled, realizing that some men wore toilet water. But she preferred Kent's spicy, masculine scent over Miles' flower garden.

Quickly she admonished herself. Kent wasn't there. Miles had asked her to step out. It was Miles she would spend the evening with, and not that other two-legged polecat.

Miles took her hands and spread her arms, admiring her shapely form. "You're prettier than any thoroughbred filly on our plantation. I'm almost afraid to show you to the rest of the town."

She ducked her head. Enough was enough. She knew what she looked like, and it certainly wasn't *that* good. But maybe outrageous compliments were just somethin' a woman had to get used to.

He crooked his arm. She stared at his raised elbow. He looked like a rooster with a broken wing. Then, all of a sudden, she remembered Nelly doing something similar and recalled her saying, "Now, you wind your hand under my arm. Lightly place your fingers on my forearm."

Quickly, Charly followed the unspoken directions and was rewarded by Miles' approving smile. She grinned and attempted the small, mincing steps

Nelly'd said were the sure signs of a lady. The toe of her boot caught on the door jamb. She tripped, but managed to catch herself with Miles' graceful assistance.

She decided against taking a wrap since the eating room was just around the corner. Besides, she was too nervous and excited to be cold. And she was worried. Worried about when, or whether, she should mention Miles' gift. She'd thought sure he would've said something 'bout it by now.

But then he hadn't included a card. Evidently he didn't want her to know who'd sent it. Would it embarrass him if *she* mentioned it?

At the entrance to the restaurant, she removed her hand from his arm. She wound her fingers together, twisting them until the skin on her knuckles was raw. She glanced up at the viga ceiling, wishing her mother would miraculously send a sign as to what she should do.

The dining space was small, consisting of only five tables and a short counter with four stools. At the early hour of six, only one other table was occupied. Miles directed her toward a table in the far corner, next to the fireplace.

He pulled out one of the chairs and looked at her. She darted her eyes from his expectant expression to the seat and back to him. Shifting her weight from foot to foot, she waited. What was she supposed to do? There were three other chairs. They didn't have to fight over that one.

"My dear, I thought you might enjoy sitting here, close to the fire." He indicated that she should sit down.

She moved in front of the chair. He pushed it in. She nearly fell on the floor when it hit the backs of her knees. Finally, once he was seated opposite her, she began to relax. Just in case he dropped something and might have to lean down, she demurely folded her feet, and the ugly boots, beneath the chair.

The waitress came to their table and Charly stifled a groan when she glanced up at Prissy Jenkins. Lordy, she'd forgotten that Prissy worked here. The girl was a "friend" of Ed's, and had been around on more than one occasion when Charly'd had to tell Ed off at the stables.

Charly sighed when the pert little redhead swung her hips provocatively and bent low over the table to place Miles' tableware just so. Charly's, she slapped upside down.

"Never thought to see the straw boss lowerin' herself to eat with the peons 'round here."

Charly slumped in her seat. She glared at Prissy and motioned the girl away, but could only sit and seethe as Prissy smiled smugly and launched into a short recitation of the evening specials.

Miles looked indulgently at Charleen. "What do you prefer, my dear?"

What she'd really like would be to crawl in a hole, or scamper like a jackbunny back home, Charly thought. But she took a deep breath, straightened her spine, and looked Prissy right in the vee of her plump bosom. Slowly, her gaze raised to the other girl's sour face. "I rec . . . believe I'd pre . . . fur to allow my . . . friend to order for me."

Miles beamed and Charly knew she'd made the correct decision. He chose ham, corn, yams with butter, tea, and fresh apple pie. Her mouth watered as she compared the meal to the beans and meat she'd been living on lately.

The restaurant door opened and closed. Charly was glad Miles had placed her close to the fire as the evening air had chilled considerably.

She looked up through her lashes to offer her companion a smile, but frowned when she saw his attention had been diverted across the room. Darting a discreet glance, she almost knocked over the cup of tea Prissy had just set before her. Goldurn it! Of all the luck. Him!

She fiddled with the cup handle, then rolled the hem of the checkered gingham tablecloth. No, he wasn't goin' to come over. Yes, he was. Damn . . . Oops, she'd meant to watch that.

"Miss Charly. Mr. Cavanaugh. What a surprise! You two enjoyin' this fine evening, are you?"

Unable to voice out loud the way *she'd* describe it, Charly muttered, *"Fine."*

Miles scowled and nodded.

Charly wondered if she'd turned into a horned toad when Prissy suddenly arrived and hovered between the two handsome men, asking if there was "anything at all" she could do for them.

And then to Charly's dismay, while Miles attempted to deal with Prissy, Kent leaned down, with his amused gaze intent on Miles, and whispered in her ear. "You're the prettiest woman here tonight, honey. Nobody else could've done that dress justice."

Charly blinked back her confusion. She'd expected some derisive comment, and instead he'd paid her a high compliment.

"And your *friend* is sure stylishly attired. For a minute there, I thought some deck was shy a joker."

Charly's lips twitched. This was the Kent Ashford she'd been afraid of meeting up with. Though it took a great deal of effort, she managed to dredge up a degree of anger over his slight to Miles. Her eyes bored into him as she turned to face him, then tilted her head back to avoid landing her nose in the left brush of his mustache.

"Ya . . . ahem, you . . ."

"And might I add that the color of your dress matches the highlights in your hair with every flicker of the fire?"

Charly gulped back the remainder of her tirade. His voice was thick and rich as whipped cream. He

251

stood so close that she could feel the heat from his body and it warmed her much faster than the flames from the fire.

One of his hands brushed the top of her bare shoulder. Suddenly she remembered another time when he'd touched her—all over. Her blood surged through her veins like liquid lava. She squirmed on the chair.

"Well, my good man, it's been nice, but as you can see, the lady and I are enjoying our *privacy*."

Charly glanced guiltily toward her escort. Prissy was nowhere to be seen, and Charly wondered how much of Kent's conversation Miles had heard.

Kent's hand brushed hers as he raised his large frame. Whether it was accidental or on purpose, she couldn't be sure, but her nerve endings jerked and quivered uncontrollably. Finally she drew in a long-denied breath. "Y-yes, it was g-good to see you."

Kent's teeth flashed in a broad smile. His eyes raked over her elegantly clad form with a thoroughness that couldn't be lost on anyone in the room. Her toes curled in her boots. She looked down at the tablecloth, and began to trace the outline of a red square. Why had this evening ever happened? She couldn't handle the . . . games . . . these men seemed so adept at playing.

A soft hand tilted her head up. Miles' gray eyes held nothing but concern. "Please, Charleen. Don't let that barbarian spoil our supper. The man has no manners or breeding."

She swallowed a moan. The man had oodles more manners and breeding than *she'd* ever have. What did Miles see in her? And just why was he goin' to such trouble to befriend a plain-Jane tomboy like Charleen McAllister?

Prissy must've read her mind, because the blasted woman dared to buck the daggers shooting from

252

Charly's eyes and continuously pampered *both* men. Charly was certain the woman was on the prowl, and became more and more upset as the hussy fawned more and more over Kent. It was disgusting. And it was awkward for Charly to keep turning around to see what was happening at Kent's table.

"Charleen?"

"Huh? Ah, what?"

Miles shook his head. "I just repeated my comments on how beautiful you look tonight. But you seem distracted. Is something wrong? Is the tea cold?"

"Oh, no. Nuthin's wrong. Everythin' is . . . very well." She ducked her head and forked a chunk of ham into her mouth. Chewing madly, she decided that maybe if she concentrated on what she was eatin', she wouldn't think of that city dandy.

But Miles had also reminded her of another problem. Maybe this would be a good time to thank him for the skirt, since he'd brought up how nice she looked. "Ah, Miles?"

"Yes, my dear." He leaned across the table.

"I've . . . been wantin' to thank you . . . for . . ."

Something touched her shoulder. Charly jerked around, ready to give the interfering scoundrel, Mr. Kent Ashford, what for. But when she raised her eyes, she found her friend from the emporium.

"Nelly. What're you doin' here?"

"Father brings mother and me over to eat almost every Saturday night."

Charly grimaced and figured she'd better introduce Nelly to Miles since the girl could hardly take her huge blue eyes off the man. And to show Nelly that her hours of hard work hadn't been in vain, Charly concentrated mightily on every word she spoke. "Nelly Pederson, this is Miles Cavanaugh. He's trying to get old Mr. Rogers' job."

Nelly smiled, but continued to look questioningly

253

between Miles and Charleen. "You want to teach school?"

Miles nodded. "Yes. I'm hoping to obtain the position, if it hasn't already been filled."

"Oh, I don't think it has, Mr. Cavanaugh. My father's on the city council. I can't recall him mentioning Mr. Rogers' replacement."

Miles glanced at Charleen and smiled.

She returned the smile, but narrowed her eyes at the funny looks Nelly kept giving her.

Prissy returned with hot water for Miles' tea, and Nelly took that opportunity to lean over and whisper to Charleen, "Charleen? What're you doing here with this man?"

Charly blinked. "Why, I thought you knew I was steppin' out tonight. You helped me—"

"But who is *he?*"

"The man who asked me out," Charly hissed, unable to hide her exasperation.

"*He* is?"

"Yesssss."

"Oh." Nelly glanced furtively toward the table where Kent sat, watching the goings-on intently. She turned back to Charleen and whispered again, "Then who's *that* man?"

Charly shrugged. "He talked my pa into giving him the job of mail conductor on my last trip. He's just a drifter. Don't know why he keeps hanging around."

Nelly frowned. "Then why'd he buy you the skirt and combs?"

"*What?*" Charly clasped her hand over her mouth too late. Every eye in the room was trained on her.

"My dear, is something amiss?" Miles asked with a slight frown.

"Ah, please excuse me fer just a minute." She grabbed Nelly's arm and yanked the young woman to the other side of the fireplace. In as low a roar as she

254

could manage, she demanded, "Now, what'd you say? Just who is it bought this skirt?"

The plump-cheeked girl darted another glance toward the lone man who grinned and nodded in her direction. She fussed with the top button of her blouse as if it were suddenly chokingly tight. She pointed to Kent. "Th-that man. He's the one wh-who wanted you to have that skirt, and especially the combs you thought so highly of."

Dread filled Charly as she also darted a look at Kent. But he was busy digging into a bowl of stew that Prissy had just set in front of him. She pushed her fists against her hips. The entire situation had turned upside-down and backwards. Lordy!

What would Miles have thought if she'd gone ahead and thanked *him* for the purchase she thought he'd made? And what would he have to say about another man buying the outfit she'd worn to please *him?* Naturally, he'd assume the worst. That Charleen McAllister was no better than some cheap floozy who could be bought for the price of . . .

"Pardon me, ladies. Is there anything I can do? You both seem a little upset over something." Kent had been watching the pair and couldn't resist butting in.

Charly glared daggers at Kent's innocent expression.

Nelly backed up and made a wild dash for her parents' table, mumbling that she didn't wish to be in the middle of the showdown about to erupt.

Kent also backed up, but only one step, before Charly's finger poked him in the chest. "Hey, just a damned minute. What'd I do?"

"Wh-what'd you do?" Charly sputtered. "What'd you do? You went and bought this skirt, that's what." Her fingers sifted through the soft folds and lovingly lingered as she held out one royal blue panel. Then she dropped the material like it had suddenly caught

255

on fire. She'd forgotten about her boots. And she'd exposed her feet for all to see. "Dad blame it."

Kent had known it would upset her if she found out who'd bought the skirt, but he hadn't expected this spitting, hissing wildcat. Hell, he'd just been trying to do something nice. "Calm down, Miss Charly. Why'n hell are you about to split your side-seams? That pretty blouse needed the skirt, and I wanted you to have it. What's so bad about that?"

She poked him again as she murmured, "It isn't right. You got no call to go buying . . ." Memories of their bodies joined and the possessive feel of his hands on her flesh abruptly cut her off. Maybe, in his eyes, he had every right. But not as far as she was concerned. He hadn't won the right to take over her life because of one wonderful night.

"Where'd you get the money? What about your grubstake?"

When Kent remained silent, she considered strangling the big ox. "I know my pa gave you some money to last until you get paid, but what'll folks say when they find out you've bought me gifts? Why, even Nelly thought we were . . . Well, she reckoned you had . . . we'd . . . Oh-h-h-h—damnation. I cain't take the skirt. But I cain't give it back right now, neither. I'll never be able ta repay you."

Kent's eyes gleamed as he thoughtfully scratched his chin. "I might know of a way."

Her eyes narrowed.

"I heard there was going to be a dance tonight."

She just watched him, her chin tilting belligerently.

"Has the joker asked you to go?"

Something big and dry clogged her throat. She reluctantly shook her head.

"Then how about . . . if after the *gentleman* takes you home, we go to the dance?"

She was about to shake her head when he added

quickly, "And we'll be even for the skirt."

"Charleen, my dear, you look upset. Is this man botherin' you?"

Kent smiled benignly as Miles joined them. "We were just discussing when we're going to get together—"

"On the next mail run," Charleen inserted. To Kent she scolded, "I thought you weren't gonna go out again. You don't *really* want to, do you?"

"Now why would you think a thing like that, Miss Charly? Of course I do."

"Oh." Pointedly staring at her skirt, she snapped, "Since you don't seem to . . . to be hurtin' none for money anymore, just reckoned . . ." She gulped and glanced at Miles. Damn Kent Ashford for completely ruining her wonderful evening, in more ways than she could count. "Figured you were fixing to move on." And for the first time, she wished he'd hurry an' get it over with.

Kent nonchalantly lifted his hand and became absorbed with his fingernails. "Guess I forgot to tell you. I plan to hang around Tucson for a while. Your father said I have a job with the Overland Company as long as I need it."

Charly sighed.

Miles took her arm and glared at Kent. "How nice for you. Now, please excuse me. Come along, my dear."

Kent gritted his teeth. One more drawled, "my dear," and he was going to puke.

A few minutes later, as she and Miles left the eating establishment, Charly began to feel quite pleased and relieved. Thanks to Miles' timely interruption, she'd never given Kent an answer about attending the dance. She could go home, sit in front of the fire and forget Kent, even Miles, and the whole regretful evening.

Walking out into the cold night air, Miles

graciously removed his coat and draped it over Charleen's shoulders, leaving his arm to weigh it in place and to hold her a little closer during the short walk to her quarters.

When they stopped in front of her door, Charly turned uncertainly. What did a lady do now? Thank him for a wonderful meal and send him packin'? Invite him inside? Uh-oh. He was leaning awfully close. There was a strange, almost determined, look in his dark gray eyes. And his arm tightened, trappin' her against his chest.

She'd bet two bits he was going to kiss her.

The clip-clop of a horse's hooves sounded behind them in the street. The horseman began to whistle. Miles suddenly stiffened and Charly was able to put some space between them. His lips still brushed the tip of her nose and she flinched.

"My dear, thank you for brightening an otherwise lonely evening, but I fear I must take my leave. Perhaps you will allow me to call again?"

Surprised, and maybe even a little disappointed that he hadn't tried harder to kiss her, she shrugged and fanned her lashes. "Mayb . . . Perhaps." She smiled, feeling much more secure and in charge now that he was leaving. Pulling it off her shoulders, she quickly handed back his coat.

"Wonderful." He grinned and tipped his hat. "Until the next time, then."

Before she realized his intent and could tuck her hand behind her back, he'd taken hold of it and brushed his soft lips over her knuckles. A surge of heat filled her cheeks. His fingers lingeringly squeezed hers before he stepped away.

Charly opened the door and rushed inside. Closing the portal, she leaned against it until her stomach quit flip-flopping. She held up the hand he'd kissed and wondered why his touch was just *pleasant*. Why irritating tingles didn't run up and down her spine.

Or why he didn't leave her feeling like she'd stuck her fingers into a hot campfire—the way Kent Ashford's touch, or even his nearness, affected her.

Suddenly there was a heavy knock on the door next to where her head had been resting. She jumped a foot, but she pulled open the door and smiled. "Did you forget . . . Damn." She couldn't help the one little curse. She'd been a lady all evening.

Kent scowled at the rosy flush staining Miss Charly's cheeks and the glazed look in her eyes. A fist clenched his guts and shook them. She'd let the damned Southerner kiss her. He'd bet money on it. And on their first time out together.

Irrational anger got the best of his wits as he wondered if maybe he'd been wrong about Charleen McAllister. Had she suddenly turned into a tease and a flirt? Maybe since she'd lost her virginity, she was out to hook *any* man.

His voice sounded like grating gravel when he demanded, "No, I didn't forget, honey. On the contrary. Now just how would *you* prefer to repay me? Want to go dancing? Or shall we stay in?"

Chapter Sixteen

Charly's mouth gaped open. Just stay in? Just stay in and do what? Then her eyes widened. Why, that belly-crawlin' varmint. The dirty polecat. And she wasn't packin' her pistol or her bullwhip.

She took a deep breath. There was the knife strapped to the calf of her leg inside her boot. Casually she began to bend down to reach for it.

"Hey, bossy britches. When did you get home?" Ed came out of the kitchen, wiping his hands on a dish towel. At the commanding sight of Kent Ashford looming angrily in the doorway, he stopped dead in his tracks. "Who's this? Ya trade the sissy in fer him? Well, well. You're growin' up fast."

Kent's thunderous expression darkened. He looked ready to erupt into a storm. Charly quickly forgot her impulse to gut the city dandy and barely had time to grab her old wool coat before she hustled him outside.

Once the door was closed behind them, Charly attempted to make a mad dash down the street. But Kent's firm hand on her upper arm brought her to an abrupt halt. "Whoa, there, Miss Charly." He needed a minute to settle his nerves and to question his own sudden reversal of emotions. He looked over his shoulder. "I should've thumped a little respect into that smart alec."

Damn it, when Charly had first opened her door and he'd noticed her flushed features, he'd been tempted to "thump" her. But then Ed had voiced the same accusations Kent had been thinking, shouting them out for all of Tucson to hear, and Kent had seen red.

Nobody talked to a woman that way, especially *his* woman.

"Why'd you let him talk to you like that?" Or worse, his conscience reminded him, why had *he* let the pup talk to her like that?

Charly sighed and didn't fight Kent when he helped her into her coat. But even the warm layer of wool couldn't forestall the shivers that began to shake her chilled body. "H-he's my b-brother."

"Yeah, and that makes it even worse." He turned back toward the door, set on doing what he should've done in the first place.

Charly threw herself in front of him. "N-no. Don't. There's been some hard feelin's lately. We'll . . . we'll work it out." Yet deep in her heart, she wondered if they'd ever be able to repair the damage that'd already been done. She sniffed and wrapped her arms around her upper body.

Kent couldn't stand the stricken expression on her face. He instinctively gathered her into his arms and held her. Soon, he vowed, he'd have a little talk with that brother—in private.

He rubbed his cheek against the softness of her hair, inhaling her fresh scent. His arms tightened about her. Like a lightning bolt from the sky, he realized how protective he'd become of her. How much he cared about her feelings. How much he enjoyed holding her in his arms. And how quickly she could arouse his jealousy. Yes, jealousy—an emotion he'd seldom experienced. Thank God.

Suddenly he shook his head and set her away from him. "C'mon, Miss Charly. The band's started without us." And as he clasped her cold little hand in his large, warm palm, he admonished himself to quit thinking like her protector. The possessive emotions that continued to crop up from out of nowhere were becoming disturbing. He didn't know how long he'd be in Tucson. She had her family. She wasn't his responsibility. She wasn't.

They reached the gaily lit barn where the baile was being held and waited for a large family in front of them to gather their many children into a tight group. Once inside, Charly managed to shed her cloak of sadness, determined that she would not let thoughts of Ed or anyone else make the evening any worse than it already was.

She took a deep breath and relaxed enough that she began to feel a little like a kid herself, with all sorts of barrels of different flavored candy to choose from, as she stared around the Alvarez's decorated barn.

Big red ribbons fashioned into huge bows hung from the rafters. Bales of straw had been stacked next to the walls to serve as seats. At the back of the building, a wooden platform had been erected for the band.

A handsome Mexican youth dressed in black, with a wide sombrero dangling down his back, plucked a guitar. Sarge Pederson tapped his foot and swung his elbow up and down, wielding his fiddle bow. An older Mexican man, with a long gray beard and mustache, picked the strings on a mandolin that had been polished until it gleamed even in the dim light.

Herman Waterman, the blacksmith, held an instrument she'd never seen the likes of before. It was some sort of folding contraption that he held in front of him by straps over his shoulders. His right hand worked up and down something similar to a piano keyboard, while the fingers of his left hand just covered a bunch of holes. But every time he squeezed the thing, music spurted out like it came from a fountain.

Kent was mesmerized, watching as her face would first crinkle into a frown, then brighten like a new dawn every time the blacksmith moved his hands. When she glanced questioningly up at Kent, he answered, "It's an accordion."

"Ac-cor-dion? You've seen one before?"

He nodded.

She stared in amazement, unaware that her body swayed in rhythm to the music. Kent was aware, though. Too aware. He cleared his throat. "Let me take your coat. There's a few empty pegs in the first stall."

When he came back, he placed his hand beneath her elbow and guided her to a table that literally groaned under the weight of a huge punch bowl. Kent dipped out a cup and handed it to Charly, then dipped himself one. Charly took a sip and made a face. At Kent's amused expression, she set her jaw and took another. The punch tasted unusual, but created a heady sensation of warmth once it reached her stomach. She licked her lips. She liked it.

Kent grinned. "They always have good 'punch' at these shindigs."

She smiled and took a deep draught. "Hmmmm." Since she hadn't been to a shindig, or a baile, she wouldn't know.

The band played a merry polka and she tapped her toe to the music, at least until she realized the noise her thick leather sole was making. Stopping abruptly, she moved her foot back, hiding her boot. She looked guiltily around to see if anyone had noticed. Her eyes collided with warm brown ones that smiled down at her. Just smiled. That was the only way she could describe that soft glitter. No mocking, deriding amusement. Just a smile.

"Would you care to dance, Miss Charly?"

Her grin disappeared. "M-me? Dance?"

He held out his hand. She hid hers behind her back.

He frowned. "Don't you want to dance with me?"

"I-It ain't that." She scanned the barn for the nearest means of escape.

"Then what is it?" He set both their cups aside and grabbed her hand.

"I never . . . I can't . . ."

His grip on her fingers tightened and he walked her to the edge of the throng of moving people. With one swift movement, he had her in his arms. "Hang on, honey. There's nothing to it."

The polka finished and the band struck up another tune. Kent started out slow, using exaggerated steps, pulling or pushing her shoulders and hips until she understood the body movements. Her natural grace soon took over and he grinned with pleasure as she followed his easy, swinging steps.

"See there? It's not so hard, is it?"

Charly laughed as he picked up the tempo and swung her round and round. For the first time in her life she felt elegant and feminine instead of big and clumsy. When Kent looked at her with those dark, velvety eyes, she thought that maybe she was as beautiful as he'd once claimed she was.

The music stopped. Regretfully, she tried to pull her hand from his to return to their place beside the punch bowl. Her throat was dry. Her knees trembled. Her palms itched where his fingers brushed her hand. Her heart pounded wildly and it was hard to catch her breath.

Kent felt the tug on his arm and saw her hasty glance toward the opposite side of the room, but he refused to release her. The band began to play a much slower song and he somberly took her into his embrace. He had his own problems catching his breath.

It felt as if their hearts throbbed as one and he held her as closely as propriety would allow.

Astounding. That was the only word that came close to describing the emotions she stirred every time he held her near. She fit so perfectly in his arms, against his body, as if her long, long legs had been created to allow their hips to meld together.

Frightening. His thoughts scared him silly—the *need* he felt to keep her in his arms, by his side—forever.

His mind shouted for him to release her—quickly. To run as fast as he could to *anyplace* else. But his body instinctively tightened and curled around her—to protect and possess.

He thought of her father and brother and the negligent way they treated her, almost as if they didn't care what became of her. But *he* cared. Too damned much. And right then he decided that as long as he was in Tucson, he'd make sure no one mistreated her or placed her in danger.

Charly knew it was dangerous, but she allowed herself to relax in the warmth and security of Kent's arms. For just that little space of time, she'd forget her worries and responsibilities. Everyone needed to just enjoy themselves once in a while, didn't they? Even to enjoy the sensation of being protected and cared for by a man with wonderfully strong hands and a firm, lithe body.

Several seconds later they realized that the music had stopped. Countless pairs of eyes were trained solely on them. Kent kept her hand nestled inside his. He winked and nodded to those closest to them, then quickly escorted her to the punch table.

She gratefully accepted a cup from Howard McKinney, the owner of the town's second general merchandise store, who seemed to be almost standing

266

guard over the bowl. She took a gulp of the cool liquid and nearly choked. That strange taste she'd noticed earlier seemed even stronger now.

Fanning her face, she looked at Kent. "Whew! This has a kick like . . ." Ooops, she'd almost said it had a kick like pa's home brew, but ladies weren't supposed to be familiar with moonshine.

While her thoughts were momentarily centered on her pa, she happened to glance around the room and spotted Sarge, Nelly, and Mrs. Pederson standing together talking and laughing while the band members took a few minutes rest. As she watched, Mr. Pederson casually gave his daughter a hug, as if it were something he did all the time, for no particular reason.

Charly's chest constricted. Why couldn't her relationship with her family be that friendly and loving?

She suddenly inhaled a shaky breath and handed Kent her cup for a refill. He cocked his brow, but graciously obliged. "You like this, do you?"

"Yep. Hic. Ooohhhh! 'Scuse me."

A heavy hand cupped Kent's shoulder. He frowned and turned to face the young Mexican he'd drunk under the table to land the job of conductor on the mail route. Orlando Ruiz. Hell!

Charly blearily spied the newcomer. "Orlando. Where have you been? Hic. 'Scuse . . ." She swayed until her hips touched Kent's. Rather than risk moving again, she stayed right where she was, using his strong body for support. For some reason, the floor seemed to be pitching beneath her feet. Stupid floor.

"*Buenas noches,* señorita McAllister." Orlando bent at the waist in a short, formal bow, but all the while his eyes burned into Kent. "An' you, señor? What happened to you after thee evening you so generously plied Orlando weeth thee wheeskey?"

267

Kent had the grace to blush, but he hid it by taking a drink of punch. "Well, I hated to think that I'd been responsible for causing the Overland to lose a conductor, so I talked Jed McAllister into letting me take your place. You'd have done the same for me, if the situation had been reversed."

Charly pointed her cup toward Orlando's chest, but almost smashed his nose. "You were drunk, Orlando?"

The Mexican glared at Kent, but nodded.

"Shame on you. You're too young—"

"Eet was not Orlando's fault, señorita. Orlando, he does not take thee spireets."

"Much," Kent helpfully inserted.

"But you just said . . . Hic."

"I said, Mees Charleen, that someone helped me to get een that condeetion."

"Aw—hic—who'd a done such a rotten thing?"

Orlando stared meaningfully at Kent. Charly blearily peered at the tall man who was again refilling her cup with the delicious punch. "You, Windy? Not very nice. Hic." Her upper body swayed backward as she wagged her finger at Kent. "What've you got to say for yourself?"

Kent handed her the cup. "I was just tryin' to be helpful, was all."

She poked at his chest, missed, and almost fell into him. "'Cause you needed the job. Riiiight?"

Kent put his arm around Charly's waist and, having second thoughts, pried the cup from her fingers. He had to bite his upper lip to keep from grinning too noticeably. Maybe it hadn't been such a good idea, using the spiked punch to "loosen" her up. She was so limber now that he could hardly handle her.

While she steadied herself against him, he held out his right hand to Orlando Ruiz. "I had reason, son. No hard feelings?"

Orlando hesitated, looking between Kent and Charleen McAllister. Then he took the proffered hand. *"Es bueno.* I found a good job, at a mine north of town. Thee pay, she ees *muy bueno."*

Kent stiffened. "Mine?"

"Si, señor."

"What're they minin' for? Lead? Copper? Silver?"

Orlando shrugged. "Mostly silver, an', I theenk, something else."

"Uh-hmmm. North, you say?" He steadied his hold on Charly when she reached for her cup. Orlando bowed and moved on, and Kent's gaze distractedly followed the young man's progress as he moved around the barn, eyeing the pretty ladies.

"Hic. I'm thirs . . . tee."

Kent began walking toward the door, keeping his body between Charly and most of the crowd. "I think you've had plenty to drink, honey. Right now, we'd better worry about getting you home."

It took all of his coordination to get her into her coat, keep her on her feet, and still make it appear as if everything were normal. Wagging tongues spreading the tale of Miss Charly's slightly inebriated state were the last thing she needed. And wag they would, he was afraid, because Nelly Pederson hadn't taken her eyes off them all evening.

Then he looked down at the woman hugging herself so close to his body. For God's sake, she wasn't a young child who needed a *duena,* or the town's permission to go out with the man of her choice. If her family didn't care, why should anyone else?

Yet he pulled her under the protection of his arm as they left the noisy barn.

Charly, taken off guard by the sudden weight of his shoulder, stubbed the toe of her boot on Kent's heel. "Ooops." Her skirt flew up as she struggled to keep her balance.

Kent bent to help, but the more his hands reached

269

for her, the further away she slipped. And then he was blinded by her skirt. Fighting to free his eyes, he saw the scuffed boots and froze.

Finally regaining her balance, Charly saw the direction of Kent's gaze and immediately rearranged the folds of blue material. But it was too late. This time she knew for sure he'd seen her boots. Her clodhopper, scruffy, manure-stompin' boots.

Kent choked. He coughed. He tried not to, but he chuckled.

His deep, belly-rolling laugh drew Charly up to her full height. She thrust out her chin. A wave of dizziness caused her to reach out for the nearest support, which happened to be Kent. "So you—hic—think something's funny?"

Her fists swung out sloppily, striking Kent in the lower belly. He winced. Then his eyes grew wide with wary caution. "Watch where you're swingin', honey. You unman me enough as it is."

She blinked. It felt like a river full of trout were swimmin' around her insides. An' he was a-lookin' at her like one of them fish'd eye a gnat—all hungry-like. "Whassa matter?"

He sighed. His arms crept around her waist and he hugged her to him. Something inside his chest burst and spread heat throughout his entire body. He buried his face in her hair and imagined a field of spring wildflowers.

What a woman! Who else could wear a brand new outfit, look like a princess, yet hide a pair of old boots beneath it all and carry it off?

At that precise moment, he understood that Miss Charly McAllister was something pretty special. She had to be to wriggle into his heart like a fuzzy baby kitten would burrow into the long hair on a mongrel hound.

Charly struggled to catch her breath. The man was smothering her. "Hey," she gasped. "Lemme go."

270

"Never." But he loosened his hold.

The chilly air refreshed her somewhat. She stared around them into the darkness. "Where'd the dance go? What're we doin' out here?"

"We're takin' you home to bed, that's what. You're not very good at handling spirits, are you?" Her eyes nearly crossed as she stared up at him. He chuckled again and unwound his arms from the squirming woman. Her jerky motions were tantalizing and teasing his lower anatomy until he felt like a tightly wound coil ready to spring free.

But he kept hold of her hand as he started walking, guiding her footsteps over the uneven, rutted path to her home.

Charly's numbed brain focused on one particular comment he'd let slip. "We're goin' home to bed." Her body heat soared to raging proportions as she pictured them in bed together. Her bed. Nekkid. Pressed against each other like two fleas on the same hair.

Approaching the McAllisters' living quarters, Kent could see a shadow moving between the only window and the coal oil lantern. Her brother, or father, or both were home—and waiting?

Unwilling to give Charly up quite so soon, he quickly pulled her into the darkened space between the blacksmith shop and the emporium. Before she could protest, he backed her against the thick adobe wall and held her in place with the weight of his body. From chest to hip they melded to fit one another and once again he was impressed with the fact that she must have been made just for him. No other woman had ever felt so perfect—so right.

Charly swallowed and peered into eyes so dark that they reminded her of a moonless night. And the bright flecks reflecting in their depths twinkled like a thousand stars. Lordy, but the man did crazy things to her body and mind. She felt out of control when he was near, lost and alone when he wasn't.

It was all so confusing. He didn't want her. She didn't want him. Yet they couldn't seem to stay away from each other. Something more powerful than their strength of will was drawing them together, forcing them to acknowledge that fate must have a plan for them.

As if thinking the exact thought, Kent groaned and lowered his head until his lips brushed hers. He'd intended his kiss to be sweet and innocent, a thank-you-for-a-memorable-evening kiss. But when his mouth settled over hers, a fierce hunger for more, a lot more, ignited in his gut. His hips arched forward, pressing the bulge of his throbbing manhood into the cleft between her thighs.

Through doubled layers of clothing, he felt her heat, the exciting essence of her being. His body responded with such force that he was on the verge of exploding.

Overwhelmed by her own desire to be held and ... loved ... Charly pressed into Kent, flattening her breasts against his chest and into cupped palms that had somehow found their way beneath her coat. The soft blouse was little protection from the flicking motions of his thumbs as they brought her nipples to taut, pulsing peaks.

She gasped in protest when his hands suddenly left her yearning for more. Just as quickly he wrapped his arms around her back, bringing her shoulders away from the rough exterior of the adobe building. She again felt the contours of their bodies melding and merging and was relieved.

He lifted his head, releasing her lips, but continued his assault by nibbling the tender flesh on the underside of her chin along her neck and behind her ear. Her head automatically tilted, giving him better access. Her breath came in rapid gasps. Her heart threatened to flutter from the confines of her heaving chest.

The clip-clop of approaching horses froze them like statues in the shadows. Only the frosty mists of their exhaled breaths gave proof that they weren't a natural part of the blackness.

Kent's back was to the street, but from the way he held her, Charly was able to see over his shoulder. Though it was some distance to the road, Charly thought there was something very familiar about the nearest rider when the trio rode into view. Her eyes narrowed as she stared intently, but his profile was blurred by the brim of his hat and the upturned collar on his coat.

She blinked and tried to clear the haze created by Kent's lovemaking and that damnable punch. It was probably just the long dusters and the dark clothing that put her in mind of outlaws and holdups.

Then, as if the mental scolding cleared more than just the fog in her brain, she opened her eyes wider and realized where she was, who she was with, and exactly what was happening. Drat it, she knew better than to let him touch her like that, but also knew she'd dreamed of this happening more times than she cared to recount.

Placing her hands on his shoulders, she gave a tentative push. He eased the pressure of his hold. She pushed again and felt the deep heave of his chest and the answering response from her nipples as he moved away.

Unable to look into his face and see his condemnation for her teasing behavior, she stared at the light in her window. Why, oh why, was Kent the one with the power to turn her mind and body to mush? She couldn't afford to rely on him. To fall in . . . love . . . with him. Soon he'd be gone. Soon, she'd be alone.

Yet the newly awakened womanly side of her argued that that was why she should fight for every minute they could spend together. She would need the memories later to recall the love of her life.

But the realistic, practical Charly asserted herself. Her life was bleak and lonely enough without torturing herself into thinking about what could've been. If only he were someone else. If only she were different.

"I've gotta go." She slipped from between the warm comfort of his body and the cold dampness of the adobe wall. For a moment she hesitated, swaying slightly toward him, before catching herself and pulling back again.

Kent caught her wrist. He didn't want to let her go. He didn't know what had happened, but it was simple enough to read the doubt and confusion in her eyes. "Wait, honey." She flinched at the endearment and he thought his heart would rip right through his chest.

"Don't. Don't call me that."

"Why? Why won't you let me call you *honey?*"

His deep voice rumbled seductively across her nerve endings. "'Cause . . . 'Cause we're no good for each other. You said as much yoreself, that night in Mesilla. Or have you forgotten?"

Kent sighed. "No. No, I could never forget that night. But—"

"Then leave me alone. Please. Just leave me be. I don't need you. I don't want you. Or anybody." She tore her arm free. Stumbling over her own feet, she gave him one last beseeching glance, then picked up the front hem of her skirt and ran across the street. She stopped in front of the door, breathing deeply, trying to catch her breath.

Kent watched her compose herself before entering the small living quarters. He felt as if the cold wooden door struck him smack in the face when it closed behind her. Oh, yes, he remembered every word he'd mistakenly uttered in Mesilla. How he wished he'd been able to hold himself to the vow he'd made so easily then.

But he was also aware that his feelings for Charly had escalated beyond his being able to reason with himself. He couldn't stay away from her any more than a bear could pass up a honey tree.

Damn. It was time he got started on the business that brought him to Tucson. But what was he going to do about Miss Charly?

Chapter Seventeen

Charly couldn't sleep. She tossed and turned and pressed cold fingers to her aching temples. The punch. It had to be the punch. She felt like a horse what'd been rode hard an' put up wet. Her mouth was drier an' grittier'n a desert in high summer.

And she couldn't quit thinkin' about Kent Ashford. Goldurn his hide anyway for sneakin' inside her defenses until there wasn't a day, or hardly even an hour, that his handsome self didn't crawl into her head or inch its way over her body. She'd turn hot an' cold almost at the same time.

When he came around, she wasn't able to think straight, couldn't seem ta handle anythin' in her usual competent manner. He was a threat to her hard-won independence, to her self-control. She could come to rely too easily on his warmth and strength. Let herself trust—too much.

Her thoughts became so disturbing that there was no hope for her ever going back to sleep. She sat up abruptly, throwing a double layer of quilts aside. The sudden movement caused her stomach to churn. She cradled her pounding head and cursed Kent for refilling her blamed cup with that devil's liquid so often.

"Ooh-h-h." She felt like a hundred miniature

277

miners were taking pick axes to her skull.

Deciding that food might not set too well in her stomach yet, she dressed and walked over to the stables to see after the horses. She opened one side of the heavy barn door and stepped inside. The first thing she saw was her brother at the far end mucking out a stall.

He hadn't noticed her. Picking her steps carefully and quietly until she reached the stall, Charly folded her arms across the top rail and watched him fork manure from the straw bedding. "What're ya . . . you . . . doin' up so early, little brother? Didn't think you'd ever seen the color of a sunrise."

Ed started and nearly stabbed his toe with the pitchfork. He spun to face his sister and scowled. "Mornin' to you, too, bossy britches." He stared into her red-streaked, puffy eyes and smirked, "Stay out too late last night or somethin'?"

"I reckon." She rested one foot on the bottom rail and lowered her gaze, noting how thoroughly the space had been cleaned. The manger had already been filled with hay and a bait of grain, ready for the horse to be turned back inside.

She cleared her throat. "I, uh, want ta thank you for lookin' after things around here lately. I've been . . . a little busy."

Ed stuck the prongs into the straw and leaned his palms on the fork handle. He looked at Charleen as if he couldn't believe what he'd just heard. He chose to ignore the compliment and went right for her jugular. "Busy? Is that what you call it nowadays?"

Charly reeled back into the center aisle as if she'd been slapped. "Look, Ed. I didn't come over to start no fight. Go on back to the house. I can take over from here."

"Ain't nuthin' left for you to do." He slung the pitchfork outside of the stall. "But then I forgot, I'm talkin' to the ramrod of this outfit. You'll find somethin' to bitch about. Cain't nobody please you."

Charly stood open-mouthed as Ed stalked from the barn. What had she said? She'd praised him for takin' good care of things, and he'd blown up. Here she'd thought he'd appreciate her noticing that he'd actually been working, and for quite a spell.

Pursing her lips, she gazed around the huge barn. It had been a long time since it had looked that good, even with her pushing everyone to keep things in their place.

Her eyes narrowed as she continued her perusal. Somethin' was different. Somethin' missing. Then she stopped in front of an empty stall, the one where Kent stabled his black stallion. It didn't take her long to figure out that if the horse was gone, so was Kent.

Her chest constricted. All of a sudden she felt like crying and screaming and ranting to the heavens. Instead, she leaned her back against the rails and slid down. At least when she was already sitting in a fresh pile of straw she didn't have to worry about her knees giving out.

She stared at the opposite wall, but might as well have closed her eyes for all she saw. She'd known he would leave. So why wasn't she feeling relieved instead of being doubled over with this belly-wrenching pain?

Last night they'd danced. He'd looked sincerely into her eyes. His hands had roamed her body and heated her soul. Today—nothin'. He was gone. Just like her innocence.

Her head fell back against a wooden rail and she closed her eyes. The blackness behind her lids foretold the dark bleakness of her future.

But she had a home, a roof over her head. Her family was near. People called her "friend." Nothin' else was important. Nothing.

*   *   *

An hour later, Charly sauntered into the stage office. She'd scrubbed her face, straightened her rumpled clothing, and felt halfway human again.

The door slammed closed behind her and Jed McAllister looked up from a telegram he'd been reading. His hand shook as he held it out for Charly to read.

She scanned the terse message. Her eyes widened with each word. Finally, she sighed and dropped the telegram on the desk. "So the rumors were true."

Jed, looking shaken and ten years older, collapsed into his chair. "Yep. Besides the stage that was stopped last night, no mail's gotten further'n Fort Stockton. Secessionists be crawlin' all over the Butterfield route. This could be the end, gal."

"No! Never!" Charly stormed to the window and glared out at the hazy winter day. Her fists clenched as John Butterfield's instructions to his drivers repeated themselves over and over in her mind, instructions that Uncle John'd taught her. Words that'd kept her goin' for many a mile when she'd thought she was too tired to go on. "Remember boys, nothing on God's earth must stop the United States Mail."

She spun to her pa. "By damn, I haven't lost no mail yet, an' I'm not gonna let a few ornery soldiers scare me off. The mail's goin' through if I have to carry it myself."

Kent rode north out of Tucson, heading for the Santa Rita mine. By accident last night, after he'd taken Charly home and gone into the cantina to try to drown the flames that had ignited his poor aching body to a fevered pitch, he'd learned that the owner of the mine had recently returned to the area.

So, in hopes of finding Mr. Tom Kelly at the mine, Kent had decided to leave early that morning. Since he hadn't been able to get even a wink of sleep, he'd been on the trail before daylight.

When he'd gone to get his horse, he'd been surprised to find Ed McAllister already in the barn. He'd been under the impression that Charly's brother was a n'er-do-well who'd rather play poker or chase women than work.

But the man had been civil enough, damn it. Kent would've given his good luck silver dollar for the man to mouth off about Miss Charly just once and give Kent an excuse to clean the barn with his butt.

A sinister smile curved Kent's lips. Perhaps another time.

The sun was directly overhead when Kent rode up to the Santa Rita mine. He noticed that the buildings were in good repair, and a new one was under construction. It was a good sign that the mine was making money.

He picked a one-story adobe to his right as the office, and rode over to hitch the stallion to an empty rail. Two saddle horses were tethered to a post and a wagon nearly blocked the door.

Rapping once, he pushed inside. A dark-haired man in a gray and white striped suit was the first to catch Kent's attention. Lounging behind a large mahogany desk, the fellow had bright, intelligent brown eyes and sported a neatly trimmed mustache and pointed goatee. An air of importance and command seemed to hover over the man.

A beautiful blond woman, dressed expensively in satin, perched on the edge of the desk. Two chairs had been drawn up and were filled by businessmen who appeared ill at ease and anxious to be on their way.

All four pairs of eyes turned to stare at Kent. "Excuse me, folks. I was just looking for a man named Kelly. Tom Kelly."

Kent watched the gent behind the desk slowly rise

281

from his chair. By the time he stood up straight, Kent could look him directly in the eye. The hand that took Kent's was large and calloused and the deep voice fairly boomed, "I'm Tomas Kelly. And who might you be, young man?"

"Kent Ashford, sir. I'd like to talk a little business with you." He nodded at the other people in the room. "When you can spare the time."

The two businessmen jumped at the opportunity to take their leave. The blond merely smiled and held out her fingers. "Mr. Ashford? I'm Christa Kelly. How nice to meet a gentleman in this godforsaken country."

Tom Kelly laughed. "You'll have to excuse my sister, Mr. Ashford. I'm afraid she's used to the finer things of life. According to her tastes, Arizona Territory's still a barbaric backwoods."

At Kent's raised eyebrow, Tom motioned him to sit down and then took his own chair. "Oh, I know Arizona's not a territory yet, but it will be—soon."

"Or your name's not Tomas Kelly, the best lobbyist in Washington. Isn't that right, brother, dear?"

"I try to be."

Kent decided they'd given him the perfect opportunity to voice his reason for riding out to the mine. "I was talking to a fella in Tucson last night who said that because of all the time you're having to spend in Washington, you might be interested in selling the mine. Is that true?"

Tom glanced at his sister. He smiled as her expression brightened. "It might be."

Kent slid forward in his chair. "I came prepared to make an offer."

At dawn the next morning, the black stallion was tied behind the buckboard and Kent was regaling

Christa Kelly about life in the West as he drove the team toward Tucson.

His saddlebags were considerably lighter, but he thought there might be enough money left to purchase yet another mine if he was lucky and found a bargain as good as the Santa Rita.

Tom Kelly had suggested he try an area south of Tucson where the mine owner was known to be sympathetic toward the Union. Kelly felt that tensions were going to escalate between people harboring loyalties for either the North or the South. And like it or not, it appeared Tucson would eventually favor and support the Confederates. Kent agreed totally, though he'd kept his opinions to himself.

But while Tom finished his business at Santa Rita and made arrangements with the miners to keep the work going according to previous schedules, or until Kent was able to return, his sister had begged to return to civilization. Even the rustic fare offered in Tucson sounded like paradise to Christa.

"Mr. Ashford, I want to thank you again for being so kind as to escort me to Tucson. Tom, bless his heart, gets so wrapped up in whatever he's doing that he forgets all about little ole me." She lowered her long lashes, then batted them open to gaze up at Kent with rapt attention.

Kent clicked to the team of matched bays and pretended to concentrate on the reins. "Well, now, it's beyond me how any man could ignore you, Miss Kelly, brother or no." And she *was* a beautiful woman. Maybe a bit too artificial, too made up, too over-dressed, and much too much of a flirt, but beautiful. Just his type, too.

Or *used* to be, he grumbled silently. However, today, when he looked at a woman like Christa Kelly, he mentally compared her to a dark-haired, green-eyed hoyden. And the sophisticated city lady came up lacking. Damn!

"Mr. Ashford?"

He shook his head. "Hmmm?"

"I was just saying that you don't look like someone that I would picture operating a silver mine."

Kent cleared his throat. "I'm . . . into investments. One day soon there'll be a lot of people moving West. Fortunes are going to be made."

"And one of those fortunes will be yours, I suppose?"

He nodded. It sounded good, but the profits would all be directed to a better cause.

Christa squared her shoulders. "You and Tom. Only he's made his money. Now he wants to become a part of the political expansion."

Since the lady didn't seem to expect him to respond to her revealing comment, he used the silence to mentally thank the Lord that her train of thought had been directed away from the mine. He wasn't prepared to answer questions about why he wanted the Santa Rita and what he intended to do with it.

"How much farther to Tucson, Mr. Ashford?"

He sighed. "Please, call me Kent. And I imagine it will be close to dusk before we reach town." Driving the buckboard forced him to keep to the main road, doubling his previous travel time. But how could he have gracefully refused her request?

Christa put her arm through Kent's and leaned into his side. "Oh, goody. Then there's plenty of time for you to tell me all about yourself, Kent. I think we could become very good friends, don't you?"

That same Monday afternoon, Charly was in the station sorting the mail that she'd collected from the post office for Tuesday's stage. She determinedly pretended that the Overland Mail would continue as usual.

The room's one small window opened toward the stable, and try as she might, she couldn't keep her gaze from straying across the street every time a rider stopped near the barn.

She wasn't lookin' for anyone in particular. She wasn't. It was just interesting to see who all came and went—to see the newcomers and be able to add a tidbit to Nelly's gossip when they got together.

So what if the black stallion was still gone. The sinkin' sensation in the pit of her stomach yesterday had predicted the inevitable. Kent Ashford was gone. Maybe a tad sooner than she'd expected, but he'd danged sure left town.

She swiped at her scratchy eyes with the back of her hand. No tears. She hadn't cried in years and she wasn't about to start now. Not over some no-good drifter. Sure she'd become attached to the man, just like she'd gotten attached to a stray dog that'd hung around one time, always underfoot and in the way until she'd just gotten used to havin' the cur around. That's what'd happened with Kent. That was all.

The door swung open suddenly and her heart began a frantic pounding. When Miles Cavanaugh peered around the jamb, her wide eyes blinked back to normal size.

"Afternoon, pretty lady."

"Howdy, Miles." She kept on sorting envelopes and packages, hoping he wouldn't notice her trembling hands. Lordy, but she'd been so caught up in her daydreamin' that he'd given her one heck of a scare.

"I stopped by to give you some good news."

She pushed a stray lock of hair off of her cheek. "Rec . . . I could use some of that."

Miles grinned from ear to ear. "Guess who was just hired to fill the vacant teacher's position?"

Charly looked up and returned his smile. "Why, that's real fine. Tucson's got a brand new citizen." At least *someone* was planning to hang around permanently, she thought.

Miles puffed out his chest and casually sauntered over to lean against the sorting table. His eyes left Charly's face and he concentrated on her hands as she deftly shuffled through the mail. "I never realized how much mail the Overland carried."

"It's amazin', isn't it? After the stage proved that it could safely carry mail from San Francisco to St. Louis, or Memphis, in as little as twenty-one days, more 'n' more folks have been takin' advantage of the route to get messages to friends 'n' family 'n' business pardners."

But as some of the letters slipped through her fingers, Charly thought silently that it was no wonder John Butterfield had gone broke and lost the line. Because of the expensive upkeep and repairs, each of those letters cost the company more than sixty dollars to transport. Sixty dollars. Lordy.

Miles eased around the table and reached out to touch a piece of mail. "Can I help you?"

She teasingly tapped his hand and shook a finger at him. "'Fraid not. 'Ginst . . . Uhmmm, it's against the rules for anyone but employees to handle the mail. Besides, you have enough to do, gittin' ready for that new job."

His upper lip curved crookedly. "That's certainly true." His hand slid along the top of the table as he backed away. "But perhaps we can both stop long enough to celebrate my good fortune. Will you have dinner with me tonight, pretty lady?"

"But we done celebrated Saturday."

He grinned and winked. "That was just a trick to get you to go out with me. Tonight will be the real celebration."

She wasn't upset that he'd used deception to get her to have dinner with him. In fact, she thought it was real nice he'd gone to such lengths. Someone *else* she

286

knew probably wouldn't've bothered.

But as she started to accept, her face paled. Once again, she was confronted with every woman's dreaded dilemma—what to wear. She couldn't very well use the same royal blue outfit she'd worn Saturday. "I don't know. Maybe I better not. I'll be workin' right up til supper time, 'n'—"

"Great. I'll come by here to pick you up. Don't worry about changing or dressing up. I just want to enjoy your company. All right?" He leaned across the table and ran his index finger along the rounded curve of her cheek. "All right?"

Heat skittered up Charly's spine and radiated to the tips of her fingers and toes. "A-all right."

"Good girl." He straightened and replaced a letter that he'd knocked askew. "I'll be by around dusk. That should give us both time to finish whatever we're doing."

She just nodded as he backed from the room, smiling like a schoolboy who'd been kept after class and was just released. He was a charmin' devil, he was.

But a frown settled between her brows. She still wanted to find somethin' besides a durned flannel shirt to wear. She snorted. When in blue blazes had clothing, or her lack of it, come to be so important as to turn her life inside out?

Charly left the stables early. She and her brother had worked together, silently, declaring a truce of sorts. Now she was on her way home to open the trunk at the foot of the bed. Her mother's trunk.

Before she'd left the station, she'd told her pa that she'd be goin' out with the new school teacher and asked him to tell Miles that she'd gone on home. Then Jed had just lifted his brows and listened quietly as she, for the first time in years, voiced her insecurities. He'd hooked his thumbs under his suspenders and stared at her for a long while. Finally, he'd been the one to suggest that she look inside her mother's trunk.

And now she felt *really* insecure.

It'd been ten years since she'd opened the trunk, though her mother would've been the first to insist that if there was something inside that Charly needed, she should use it. So . . . she believed she would. For her mother.

But once she was in her room, with the door closed, her body began to tremble. She knelt on the floor. Her hands hovered over the dusty lid. Should she? Could she?

Finally she took a deep breath and lifted the lid. The old leather hinge creaked from disuse. For moments, she just sat there, gazing at the top layer of neatly folded and stacked items. The backs of her eyes burned. She blinked rapidly.

For years she hadn't thought much about her mother, yet during the last month or so, she'd seemed closer to Charly than ever.

A white lace mantilla lay at the top of the chest. Charly carefully removed it and gasped at the beauty of the solid silver comb set with tiny red stones that sparkled with every movement or flicker from the lantern. How beautiful.

And from somewhere deep inside, Charly drew forth a memory of her mother dressed in a red velvet cloak, smiling and laughing and pinching a small girl's cheeks as a young, dapper Jed McAllister helped adjust the mantilla and then dashingly rushed her mother through the door.

Charly laid the mantilla lovingly aside and unerringly found the cloak beneath a white layer of cotton. The soft velvet tickled her palms as she lifted it from the chest. Standing, she draped it over her shoulders and tilted her head to rub her cheek against the smooth nap. She'd never felt anything so soft—so grand.

She hung the cloak from an empty peg to allow the wrinkles to fall out. Then she knelt back down to see what other treasures were waiting to be unveiled. Feeling inside the chest, her fingers brushed a small box. She picked it up and opened the lid. A gold locket peeked up at her.

The filigreed top felt hard, but warm, in her hands. As if uncovering forbidden secrets, she tentatively pried open the lid. The smooth gold was engraved. *To Maria. With All My Heart. Your Loving Husband. Jed.*

Charly really blinked hard. Her pa had loved her mother. Very much. Had she misjudged him all these years? Had his callous feelin's just been a shield to protect him from the unbearable hurt of losing the woman he loved? Had the loss of her mother been the start of his drinkin' an' his seemin' disregard for life?

Or was she a durned romantic wishin' it were so?

Gently, reverently, she replaced the locket, then continued to search through the trunk until she spotted a flash of intriguing green. Pulling the material from beneath more cotton, she unfolded a silk, peasant-style blouse that was so soft and slippery that it almost slid through her grasp.

Unable to resist the temptation, she unbuttoned her flannel shirt and pulled the blouse on over her cotton camisole. As the silk slithered against her skin, she shivered and plainly imagined a man's palms smoothing her flesh with the same kind of sensuous care.

And with the thought of a man's hands, came the vision of *one* man. Kent Ashford. Tall, broad, muscular, handsome Kent. Lordy, would she never be rid of him? And how could she have agreed to step out again with a nice person like Miles when the only man she could think about, dream about, was Kent?

But she *wanted* to think of Miles with more than just sisterly fondness. He represented permanence, stability. He was handsome, too. He seemed to like her. He was kind. He was a gentleman.

So, with pleasing and attracting Miles uppermost on her mind, she placed the lace mantilla atop her head. Before she had a chance to look into her mirror, a noise in the living room drew her forward. She opened her door and peeked through.

Her pa stared back at her, his face ashen. "My gawd, gal, fer a minute there I thought yore ma done come back to life. I ain't never realized how much ya look like her."

Charly inhaled deeply. Her pa couldn't of said a nicer thing. Shyly, she said, "Thanks, Pa."

He strode past her and into her little room. She followed and found him staring into the open trunk. He brushed at his cheeks. Charly gulped and remained silent.

"I'd plumb forgotten 'bout this here trunk, 'til ya was a-needin' somethin' ta wear." He bent and picked up a folded piece of black silk cloth. "Last time I went ta San Francisco, I bought this material fer yore ma. She was gonna make a scarf ta go with . . ." He turned to Charly. "Ta go with that blouse. It were her favorite."

He swiped at his cheek in pretended irritation. "She'd be right proud ta know ya was wearin' her things. I know fer a fact."

She blinked when her pa suddenly turned and left, absently taking the material with him. How guilty she felt for thinking him an unfeeling man. She just hadn't understood.

Charly was alone in the house when Miles knocked on the door. After one last look in the cracked mirror, she sighed and hesitantly let him in.

Miles' smile froze on his lips as he took in the vision before him. Her thick, dark hair hung loose down her back and was held away from her face with a pair of silver combs. A green silk blouse, gathered at the neckline, rode just off her creamy shoulders, displaying her full curves to perfection.

She also wore a pair of white cotton trousers and worn boots, but he wasn't a bit put out. He liked a woman with long, graceful legs, and the pants definitely fit her gorgeous limbs. "My dear, you'll be the envy of every woman in Tucson this evening."

Charly ducked her head, thinking he had to be the kindest man on earth to spout such nice lies. Every gal in Tucson would look the other direction when she passed by in her britches, but she'd long since ceased to care. It was their acceptance of Miles that she worried about.

His knuckles warmly brushed the exposed skin on her shoulders as he helped her into her coat. For a fleeting moment she wondered if she'd done the right thing, wearing such a revealing garment. But he liked it. She could see his pleasure in the darkening of his gleaming gray eyes.

Just as Miles pulled the door closed behind them, a covered buckboard passed. A black horse tied to the tailgate caught her gaze and her head jerked in the wagon's direction. "I'll be a horn-swoggled canary."

"What was that, my dear?"

"N-nothing." But she looked quickly away from the buckboard and started walking determinedly down the street.

Miles increased his stride to catch up. "Look. Isn't that your friend, Ashford?"

She darted her eyes toward the street and back again. "Reckon so."

"Wonder who that is with him?"

The interest in Miles' voice ignited a small fire in

291

the pit of Charly's stomach. "Don't know. Don't wanna know."

"Have you ever seen her before?"

She didn't want to look at the woman again. Didn't want to, but did. The blamed female was gorgeous and fragile-lookin', just the kind of woman *any* man would be crazy not to be attracted to. Even as the sun set, the woman was shading her porcelain-doll features and pale hair beneath a fancy pink parasol that matched a form-fitting pink coat which opened at the top to reveal the deep, square neckline of a tight pink bodice.

The lady in pink. Pink for girls. A very feminine color for a very feminine woman. And with every bounce of the wagon wheel, even Charly could see the tops of the woman's large breasts jiggle.

Charly looked quickly at Kent. The beast's eyes seemed to be locked at chest level on the witch. Goldurned . . . man!

All at once, as if he'd felt the lance of her eyes, Kent turned and looked directly into her eyes. Though she fought to keep her features blank, she felt the skin on her cheeks burn, felt the wrinkling sensation of the flesh between her brows.

Kent winked.

She gasped. The idjit. "Ooohhh!"

"Did you say something, my dear? I wonder what a lady like that is doing in a place like Tucson?"

Charly turned on Miles. "Swingin' a wider loop than she kin handle."

Chapter Eighteen

Charly cursed and flopped over, pulling the quilts off her feet. She mumbled and muttered and sat up to push the blankets over her frozen toes. She was darned tired of not being able to sleep.

But that night images of the Lady in Pink, of Kent, and Miles, too, following the woman with their tongues hanging out, haunted her dreams. She'd known it was too good to be true to think that two fascinating and handsome men could remain interested in a tomboy like *her*.

Sure, Miles had been polite and attentive during their meal together, but it was too late. His eyes had just glittered a mite too brightly and he hadn't been able to hide the envy in his voice when he saw the blond woman pawing Kent.

Burying her head beneath the covers, unmindful that she'd bared her feet and calves again, she wondered if anythin' more humiliatin' could ever happen to her than when Miles had walked her home and tried to kiss her good night. Goldang it, she'd seen him comin' an' had shrunk away. Started babblin' like a silly school girl. Finally, he'd put his hand over her mouth an' told her he couldn't understand a word she was sayin'.

Couldn't understand. 'Cause she talked like a

backwards hick, that's why. She'd been tryin' to do better. She really had. But whenever she got flustered an' excited, she couldn't seem to take the time to *think* before opening her mouth, like Nelly had told her to do.

Nelly? Nelly knew how to act and talk and dress like a lady. Maybe she could help turn a bumpkin like Charleen McAllister into another Lady in Pink.

Charly wrinkled her nose. Ugh! Did she really want to be like a highfalutin, prissy city woman? She flipped over and cold air crawled up her backside. Muttering more oaths, she flounced up and spread the quilts out one more time.

She bet the Lady in Pink never mussed a hair at night, less'n she was with . . . Charly scowled. She growled over Miles' reaction to the woman. Then she recalled Kent's big grin and the way he winked when the blond practically smothered him right there on the street in front of God an' ever'body.

The overgrown wolf. He'd enjoyed ever bit of the attention. An' she bet Miles would've sold his grand plantation to've been in Kent's place. Drat 'im.

If Charleen McAllister looked and acted like a fancy lady, would they ogle *her* the same way they'd done the Lady in Pink?

Charly yawned. Her eyes blinked heavily. First thing in the mornin', she'd go talk to Nelly. If bein' a lady was what it took to turn a man's head, then a *lady* she'd be.

At the other end of town, Kent Ashford stared up at the shadowed vigas in his room. He tried to blame his sleeplessness on the moon shining through a split in the worn, but clean, curtain. But he knew better.

The damned brat. What did he have to do to get the hoyden out of his system? Out of his mind? Worse yet, why didn't he really want to? No matter how often he told himself to stay away from her, every time he saw her he found, even made up, excuses to get near her.

That kiss Saturday night . . . Hell, his body still burned and ached with the desire he'd felt to take her right there on the street. And from the heat of her response, she probably would've let him.

So, what had happened to change things so drastically? When he'd driven the wagon past the station that evening, and he'd seen her leaving her home with the *gentleman,* one of her big, burly mules could've kicked him in the gut.

And then she'd hardly deigned to look at him. He'd smiled and given her a wink, kind of a secret acknowledgement that he was glad to see her, even if she had gotten all spruced up for the Southerner.

He stretched his long body as far as he could on the short mattress. Deep down, she couldn't be attracted to good ole Miles. She couldn't care for the man and then turn around and kiss *him* the way she'd done Saturday.

But tonight, when she'd glared at him and turned up that pert little nose, and then presented him with her back . . . Well, hell, he hadn't known *what* to think.

Women! The one he couldn't leach out of his blood, didn't want anything to do with him. And one that he didn't want anything to do with, wouldn't leave him alone.

A deep sigh deflated his broad chest. Christa Kelly. What was he going to do about that suffocating, clinging vine?

Charly entered Pederson's emporium around mid-morning the next day. Sarge Pederson was behind the counter, stacking canned goods on the shelf. Nelly didn't seem to be anywhere around.

"Morning, Miss Charleen. Anything I can do for you?"

"Well, no . . . Yeah. Is Nelly here?"

He nodded toward the storeroom. "She's in the back. Probably going through the new yard goods. Go on and roust her out."

"Thanks, Mr. Pederson." Sure enough, she found Nelly on her knees with bolts of material spread out over a large square of plain cotton.

"Look. Isn't this the prettiest calico print you ever saw?" Nelly said, when she spied Charleen.

Charly raised one brow. Yeah, she guessed, if ya liked bunches of dainty pink flowers. To her way of thinkin', it was kind of sissyish. But when she happened to see a roll of deep red grenadine, she sank down beside Nelly and sighed. "Isn't that the purtiest color?"

Nelly nodded. "It would make a lovely day dress."

"*Day* dress?"

"Sure. Something you could wear everyday."

"Oh. You mean not for dress-up."

Nelly smiled.

"Nelly . . . Ah . . ."

"Yes?"

"I been meanin' to ask you . . ."

Nelly folded her hands in her lap and waited, watching the changing expressions on Charleen's face.

"I'm a-wantin' to . . . uhmmm . . . learn to be a . . . lady." There. She'd said it. Charly kept her eyes averted, almost ready to duck, *anything* to avoid hearing or seeing Nelly's laughter.

"I see." Nelly studied Charleen's natural beauty, hidden too effectively beneath the thick layers of men's clothing.

Charly raised her head slowly. Her friend wasn't laughing. A very serious expression wrinkled her round features. Charly sighed. "Hopeless, aren't I?"

296

"Not at all."

"Huh?"

Nelly shook her head. "It's going to take time and practice. But you already have the most important things. You're pretty, and you have a natural grace that most women would love to have. All we need to do is get rid of those awful clothes and concentrate on your speech."

Charly looked stricken. "I can't drive a stage in no blamed dress."

"Of course you can't, goose." Nelly frowned. "But what about whenever you work in the office? Can't you wear a dress then?"

Charly chewed her lower lip. "Well, I reckon. But what about muckin' out the stalls?"

"Charleen! I told you the last time you were here. Let the men clean the stables. That's no job for a lady."

"I'd sure like to be a *lady*. But—"

"There are men around to do that chore, aren't there?"

"Well, yeah, but—"

"No *buts*. You don't have to do everything over at the station. Do you?"

Charly grudgingly admitted, "Don't guess, but . . ." It was just easier and she didn't have to rely on someone else to get the job done. And she wasn't always disappointed in her pa or brother or any of the other drivers.

"Ah, ah, Charleen. Remember. No 'buts.'" Nelly clapped her hands. "Now, let's get started on your speech. The wardrobe, we'll work on gradually."

Charly grinned. With Nelly's help, Charleen McAllister was going to be a *lady*.

Charly flipped open her watch and drummed her stubby fingernails on the Celerity's frame. Where was

297

the durned conductor? It was Wednesday. They were goin' to try to get the mail through.

Had he up'n quit? And here her pa thought he'd hired a real dependable, trustworthy soul. Ha! Men were all the same. Just a bunch of weak-minded . . .

"Oh-h-h, Mr. Ashford. I do declare, you say the cleverest things. I'll surely miss you while you're gone. Do you really have to ride on that bumpy ole thing?"

Mr. Ashford? Charly's head craned around like a hungry stork's. Her stomach muscles clenched at the sight of *the* Mr. Ashford and the Lady in Pink—oh, yes, she wore bright pink today—standing together at the rear of the stage. The witch was straightening his collar and fussing over him like a possessive mother hen.

"I do declare. You say the cleverest things," Charly mimicked. Hogwash! The man was having a good day if he managed to get through it without having his horse stolen.

She smiled briefly. She bet she was the only female the city dandy knew who'd made off with his prize stallion. If for no other reason, she'd always occupy a tiny space in the back of his mind.

Flipping the watch case open again, she reached for the bugle. With a mischievous tingle of excitement skittering down her spine, she tooted the brass horn.

Jed McAllister ran out the door. "What be keepin' ya, gal? Yore two minutes late."

She shouted sweetly, "I do declare. I'm waitin' on my dad bla . . . on my conductor. Why, Pa dear, I thought you hired someone *reliable.*" Charly glanced over at the coach door as her pa closed it on the empty interior. The Confederate scare was keeping many of the passengers away. Their first rider wouldn't board until the San Pedro Crossing.

Kent's pack landed barely a foot behind her as he

swung up beside her. His deep voice growled in her ear. "I'm right here, damn it. Why didn't you tell me you were ready to go?"

She glowered at him. "Ya . . . you seemed much too busy at the time."

Kent looked back over his shoulder and smiled indulgently at the little blond woman waving her handkerchief. "I was, wasn't I?" He cocked his head in order to see her face. Had he, perhaps, detected a hint of jealousy in those green eyes? God, he hoped so.

Charly felt his eyes on her and immediately cracked the whip. Kent didn't budge as the team strained in the harness and jerked the coach into motion. Durn it.

From the corner of her mouth, she muttered, "I didn't expect you'd show today."

Kent cocked his brow. "Why? I *am* the conductor."

He'd made the statement as if he was explaining to an ignorant child how to add two and two. "I was hopin' yore . . . your first exper . . . experi . . . trip would've been more than enough," she ground through her clenched teeth.

Kent's mustache twitched. He clucked his tongue. "Tsk. Tsk. Miss Charly, you disappoint me. I figured you'd be anxious for my company." And deep down, he admitted to feeling a little hurt that she hadn't seemed at all glad to see him. Surprised, maybe. Glad, definitely not.

She snapped the ribbons. "I thought when you . . . disappeared . . . the other day, you might've left Tucson fer good." She swallowed a lump of cotton, hoping he wasn't noticing her hesitancy and how slowly she chose her words. If she followed Nelly's advice, they'd be at the next station before she finished three sentences.

Kent noticed that there was *something* different about his Miss Charly, all right, but was too busy

299

drinking in her precious profile and enjoying the verbal sparring to wonder exactly *what* it was about her that had changed. Damn, but he'd missed her. "So, you noticed that I was gone, did you?"

"I noticed the *stallion* was gone. He always . . . nickers at me when I go . . . to . . . the stables."

He exhaled swiftly. He should've known she'd put the horse above him.

"How come . . . you came back?"

"To Tucson? Or to ride with you?"

She shrugged.

Kent certainly wasn't going to tell her that his plan to protect her, even if it was from herself, hadn't changed. "Have you forgotten? You said yourself that Jed gave me money in advance. Guess I should do something to earn it, huh?"

"Oh." Yes, she'd forgotten that he'd need to work out the money. No, she hadn't forgotten that he'd given her that beautiful skirt and the silver combs. But she had worked real hard to put it all out of her mind. Didn't like feelin' beholden to him.

They rode in silence for several miles. "I was beginnin' to think you weren't gonna be able to drag yourself away from that fancy lady." Oops! Charly's eyes widened. She shut her mouth so fast she bit her lip. Lordy, what'd gone and made her say that out loud?

Kent turned until he was facing her. "What did you say?"

"I . . . uhmmm . . . was wonderin' who the fancy . . . who your . . . friend . . . was."

He looked down at the cropped ear on one of the mules. He studied it very intently until he was able to control his twitching lips. By damn, Miss Charly was green in more places than just her eyes. She *was* jealous. She sure as hell was. Hallelujah!

Kent cleared his throat. "Her name is Christa Kelly."

"Oh?" C'mon. Surely he was gonna tell her more'n that.

The only sounds were the whirring of the wheels and the straining grunts from the mules.

"She from around . . . here?"

"Her brother owned the Santa Rita mine."

"Uh-huh. Owned?"

He mentally kicked himself. "Heard he just sold it."

A wheel bounced through a deep hole and Charly had to take a firmer grip on the ribbons. Instead of gabbin' so much, she'd best pay attention to her drivin', she scolded herself.

Kent sighed, grateful that she wasn't going to push the matter. "How's your friend, Gentleman Miles?"

"Huh? I mean, what?"

"Who," Kent corrected. "I saw you last evening with the new school marm. You and he hitting it off, are you?"

She bristled. "Whaddaya mean by that?" Then she winced. The dratted aggravatin' man. She couldn't concentrate on what she was gonna say an' put up with him at the same time.

"Just looks like you two are getting pretty friendly."

Her lids narrowed slyly. "Why'd ya—you say a thing like that?" He couldn't've taken his eyes off the Lady in Pink long enough to see who *she* was with.

He shrugged. "Seems like you've really dressed yourself up for him lately. Last night, especially."

"Oh, reckon that was when I saw *you*, with that *lady*." The inflection she gave the term should've warned him what she really thought of the witch. "An' if'n . . . ahem. And if I recall correctly, she was hangin' all over you, like a drape o' Spanish moss." Her chest constricted until she could hardly catch her breath when he glanced sharply at her from the corner of his eye.

301

Kent could barely contain his glee. She was turning green again. And here he'd thought Miss Charly had just been ignoring him.

Silence surrounded them as they both thought over the implications of their discoveries. The team dipped into a narrow wash. The coach lurched and the supports creaked ominously. Charly's pack jostled across the roof of the stage to settle behind her.

Kent grabbed hold of the bench. A bullet struck the wood beneath his hand, spraying splinters into his palm. Charly heard his curse but didn't realize what was happening until the rifle report echoed eerily in her ears.

From both sides of the narrow canyon, masked horsemen swarmed toward the stage. Charly snapped the whip and hollered at the struggling mules. Kent swung his rifle up and cursed when the stock drove a splinter deep into his smarting flesh.

He fired quickly, and felt somewhat vindicated for his own pain when the closest outlaw flung his arms wide and did a backward somersault off his mount.

Charly darted a glance over her shoulder. One of the riders caught her attention and her hands slackened on the reins. Darn, but somethin' about the man was familiar. But his heavy coat and the turned-up collar, along with the slanted tilt of his hat, blocked her view of his features.

One of the wheel team stumbled. The sudden jerk on the ribbons caught her by surprise. The reins leading to all three of the right-hand mules slipped from her fingers. Falling on her knees, she reached over the frame, trying to catch them. It was like watching snakes slither over uneven terrain until they landed to drag on the ground amidst the swirling dust.

Kent heard a string of oaths. He looked quickly in her direction. His heart skipped several beats as his first thought was that she'd been wounded. All he could see was the rounded thrust of her hips and bottom. The rest of her was dangling over the front of the box.

"Charly!" The cry tore from his lips. God, she was falling. Soon she'd be ground beneath flailing hooves or crushed by a wheel. In retaliation he snapped off a quick shot at an outlaw just reaching out to grab onto a swinging door. His bullet took the bandit square in the chest and a grim sense of satisfaction permeated Kent's being.

With the loss of another man, the outlaws pulled back. Kent set his rifle on the floorboards and hurriedly leaned over to help Charly. "Hang on, honey. I've got you."

A heavy hand settled on Charly's squirming shoulders, nearly catapulting her from her precarious position. Dust from six pairs of churning hooves clogged her nose and throat. She coughed and sneezed and batted back at the durned hand, falling further forward, hanging on only from the strength of her thighs braced against the coach.

Kent thought she was trying to grab for a handhold and clasped her fingers.

She jerked her arm, but couldn't free herself. "Let go of me, you oaf. You tryin' to get me killed?"

Kent blinked. Had he heard her correctly? Her voice was strong, if a little strangled. And she wasn't reacting at all like a person who'd been shot and was in danger of tumbling from the stage. Yet he refused to relinquish his hold on the struggling woman.

"Hang on, damn it. I'll keep you from falling on your fool hard head."

Since the reins were lost anyway, she let him go ahead and haul her up. As soon as she found her footing, she whirled and pointed behind them. "You got better things to do than bother me. Here they come."

The stage hit a rut and bounced three feet in the air.

Kent made a grab for the rifle and caught it in midair. Charly took a death grip on the remaining reins and wrapped them around the brake handle so they, too, wouldn't be lost.

She bided her time until Kent turned his back and was busy firing at the outlaws, then turned back toward the runaway team. Carefully climbing over the front lip of the dipping, diving coach, she balanced her right foot on a narrow, two-inch board just above the tongue that hitched the team to the stage. Her right hand steadied her body as the mules continued their all-out dash. The left half of her body swung out, reaching, waiting for the right moment to leap onto the braces between the wheel team.

The only way to regain control of the team was to go after the reins.

The road took an uphill curve. The team began to slow. Charly readied herself to jump. Pushing off with her right leg, she leaped into the air. An iron band caught her just below the ribs. Breath whooshed from her lungs. Pain crushed her chest. She couldn't get any air.

Kent's angry face loomed into her blurred vision. She felt herself being dumped onto the bench. His mouth opened and closed. Rage boiled from his eyes. But she couldn't hear a word over the buzzing in her ears.

A glance over her shoulder was all it took to see that the outlaws had stopped. But because of Kent's rash action, the team was still running wild.

All at once, she looked back at him, took a swing and walloped him on the cheek, very close to the jagged scar. He raised his hand. She flinched and ducked. But instead of hitting her, he grabbed her coat collar and shook her like a rag doll. ''What'd you do that for?''

The quick movement of her arm reminded her of her tender ribs. Holding her arm across her stomach, she regained her feet, and started forward, shouting, "Don't take much sense ta see what's gotta be done. Now, stand aside, city man."

Kent blocked her progress with his body. He placed his hands on her shoulders and shoved her back down, surprised at the little resistance she exerted. "Listen up, woman. You're the one that's going to sit right here and be a good little girl. When I get the reins, I'll hand them up to you. Understand?"

Her hand shot out and grabbed his sleeve. She pleaded, "Let me go. You'll get hurt."

"And you wouldn't!" he exploded. He took a deep breath, pointed at her and at the bench. "Stay."

In less than a heartbeat he lowered himself from the box and was poised in the same position as Charly'd been when he'd snatched her from the air.

The tired team began to slow down on their own and he only needed to wait until they reached a flat section of ground to make the jump. Finally he found the right moment and leaped. He landed with one foot on the swinging, jingling traces, the other dangled above the rocky ground.

Arms spread, he balanced himself on sweaty, lathered backs. After catching his breath and steadying his racing heartbeat, he slowly, foot by foot, maneuvered his way along the narrow strip of wood.

After reaching the wheel team's hitch, he ran out of a place to walk. A sinking sensation took his breath away. He would have to jump to the next brace.

His hands clenched in the pair of mules' manes, he was preparing himself for the move when the right mule flipped its head. Kent just happened to glance to that side and saw the loose rein hanging from a harness buckle.

Before it could be jarred loose again, he snatched at the long strap and caught it in his fist. Looking back over his shoulder toward Charly, he cursed when he

305

found her leaning out over the edge of the box. Damned brat! She minded worse than a three-month-old puppy.

But he flipped the rein out and back several times, judging the distance to the box. He signaled with a nod and gave the leather a hard snap. He sighed, relieved, as Charly made a mad dive, caught the rein, and managed to keep from falling on her noggin.

The hard wooden box dug into Charly's tender middle as she reached for the rein. Air again whooshed from her lungs. She had a heck of a hard time breathing it in, because as she watched, terrified, Kent leaped awkwardly up to the middle team. The brace rocked just as he landed. His foot slipped.

Charly tried to close her eyes, but couldn't. Instead of righting himself, he remained down in the traces fumbling with something. She held her breath. He was trying to untangle the rein from around the mule's foreleg.

Looking ahead, Charly's face paled. A series of low hills and narrow gullys was going to make it harder for Kent.

Suddenly the mule tripped. Charly yelped as Kent was the one who nearly went down. Stupid man. If he went and got himself killed a-doin' *her* job, she was gonna strangle him.

Soon, though, she was reaching out for that second rein. Only one more to go. She gnawed the ragged flesh on her lower lip and began to tug on the reins she already held. She cursed when all she received for her efforts were rolled eyeballs and another plunging dash forward by the frightened mules.

Charly shook her head. Although from the time she'd lost the reins to that very moment had probably been only five minutes, she was as exhausted as if it had been five hours. And it had all been so unnecessary.

Anger and frustration gripped her stomach. Damn

those outlaws. Why were they suddenly goin' after every coach? What did they want that was so durned important?

Drivin' for the Overland Company had always been dangerous. She was well aware that in just the first sixteen months of operation, Butterfield had buried twenty-two men. Very seldom had they needed to settle their one hundred and twenty-five dollars a month salary.

Yet things had gone from bad to worse. Why? Was it *all* connected to the threat of war and the approach of the Confederates? Confederates. Perhaps some of her own kin. And they had no more regard for life than . . .

A rein slapped her on the hand. Charly started, surprised to see a grinning Kent on the tongue, preparing to haul himself back aboard. She scowled. The durned man had enjoyed himself. Blamed if he hadn't.

She snatched the rein and wound the six straps through her fingers. "Whoa, now, ya consarned jackasses. Whoa!"

Several tugs and a constant stream of reassuring oaths slowed the heaving team. Charly gazed down at Kent and smiled. An expression of surprise, then . . . fear . . . registered on his face. Then he disappeared.

"Kent! My Lord, Kent. No!"

Chapter Nineteen

The stage continued rolling. Charly frantically fought the reins. If it weren't for the mail, she'd have jumped from the coach and let the team keep right on a-goin'. Her arms felt like they were being torn from their sockets. The muscles down her back burned almost as badly as her fingers. But at last she was able to bring the mules to a prancing walk and guided them off the road and around Spanish dagger and spiny yucca to turn the stage.

She searched the lane ahead. No one. A minute later the curving road straightened. There. Just ahead, she saw him. Her heart leaped into her throat. Nausea churned her stomach. Kent's long body was stretched face down in the rocks and dirt. That goldurned burnin' sensation pricked the backs of her eyes again. Her hands shook the reins and the excited team quickened their pace.

Taking a deep breath, she tamped down her mounting fear and deftly used her hands and voice to calm the mules. Setting the brake, she wrapped the reins around it and climbed from the box. She was in such a hurry that she tripped and fell over the side, but managed to land on her feet.

Then she was kneeling at Kent's side. Her hands hesitated over his still body only a second before gently rolling him to his back. Her eyes scanned him from the roots of his wavy brown hair to his boot-clad feet. The only injury she could see was scraped skin and a puffy knot on his right temple.

Immediately her hands followed the route her eyes had just taken. Her fingers sifted through his hair searching the back of his head and down his neck. She unbuttoned his shirt and spread the material wide enough to poke and prod down his rib cage. Several patches on his smooth skin were beginning to purple, but she could find nothing broken.

She ran her hands down his arms, then moved to his legs. Her fingers squeezed and massaged down his left thigh, knee, and calf. Nothing seemed amiss. She began working up his right calf, over the knee and spread her palms against his thigh. A muscle jerked beneath her probing fingers.

Her breath caught in her throat. She stopped immediately. He wouldn't have responded if he hadn't felt pain. Unconsciously, she chewed her lower lip. Lord, please don't let him be badly hurt.

Guilt ached through her chest. If she hadn't dropped the dadburned ribbons . . . If she hadn't let him go after them . . . It was her fault. All her fault. Something wet and warm trickled down her cheeks. She tilted her head and wiped her face on her shoulder.

Doggone the man. He'd been tryin' to protect her. Why hadn't he listened when she told him she didn't need his help? She'd never had a guardian angel before and didn't want one now. It was too much responsibility. Yet, she admitted, her blood flowed thicker and warmer through her veins to think he actually cared enough to look out for her.

Shaking her head, she gently pressed his thigh again. He groaned. Her blurry eyes shot to his face. Amidst the brown velvet, gold sparks flared back at her. He was conscious. He'd been watching her. His

310

dark, glittering pupils jolted her with spiraling heat.

Kent wasn't sure he believed what he saw when his eyes blinked open. Charly. Bent over him. Doing things to his body that a woman shouldn't do to a helpless man. And she was crying. Huge, crystalline tears traced a path down her dusty cheeks, one after the other, streaking her face and dropping in cold little pools on his bare belly.

He reached up and caught a droplet on the tip of his finger. He stared at it for a long time, until muffled hiccuping drew his awed gaze back to her face. "What's the matter, honey. Why're you crying?"

She sniffed and wiped her cheeks and her nose on the sleeve of her coat. "You mangy coyote. How long have you been awake an' eyein' me?"

He raised his head to the accompaniment of an aching throb in his right temple. Bringing his damp hand to his head, he touched the swelling and winced. But nothing so minor was going to sway him from his purpose. "I asked you first."

She wet her lips. His eyes darted to her mouth. She quickly drew in her tongue. He wanted to know why she'd been cryin'. Cryin'? If he hadn't mentioned it, she wouldn't've realized she'd been doin' it. A long time ago she'd learned that cryin' was only a waste of time and emotion. She hadn't shed tears since. Until today.

So why *was* she cryin' for Kent? The answer was too terrifying to think about. She might have to admit to feelings she never expected to have for a man—any man—especially some no-account drifter.

Her head cocked to one side as she studied the man who watched her in return. Lately, she'd come to be suspicious of Kent Ashford and his reason for bein' in Tucson. She'd always sensed there was more to him than just a man lookin' to earn enough money to buy his next meal. And her instincts were seldom wrong.

But then his hand touched her face again and she

311

nestled her cheek into his palm. She stared into his handsome features and delved into the dark brown eyes clear to the goodness of his soul.

No matter what she'd done to him—stealin' his horse, pesterin' him in jail, beggin' her pa not to hire him—he still thought it necessary to protect her.

And then the night they'd made love . . . The most precious night in her entire life. Suddenly, her eyes widened. Realization dawned on her. She wouldn't have let just any man touch her the way Kent Ashford had, no matter how wonderful he'd made her feel. She wouldn't have given herself to someone she didn't have feelings for—strong feelings—no matter what she'd tried to tell herself at the time to justify her unusual behavior.

Those *feelings* now emerged to grip her heart, to turn her stomach upside down, to flash behind her eyes like a bolt of lightning to illuminate what she'd been afraid to acknowledge. Sure she'd been able to admit that she liked him and that she cared about him—some. But the honest truth had remained hidden beneath layers and layers of doubt and denial.

She loved the durned man. She loved Mr. Kent-somethin'-Ashford. She'd cried because she'd been afraid she'd lost him. What would she have done if she'd never seen that gorgeous smile or that rakish tilt to his eyebrows again? Or—never felt again the tenderness in those large hands as they caressed her burning flesh.

Kent was lost in Charly's luminous eyes. And she still hadn't answered his question.

His muscles contracted as one of her hands unconsciously moved up his leg to lie palm down on his belly. He gulped and swallowed a groan as her fingers spread and slid into the narrow line of hair trailing down the lower half of his chest. Her nails grazed his flesh, plucked a wiry curl and . . . drove him *crazy*.

312

He'd awakened in the first place because of the heat her probing had generated in his groin. His whole body had quickened beneath her thorough ministrations. He inhaled sharply. If she wasn't going to respond to his question, he'd answer hers, just to take his mind off her wandering hand.

"Uhmm, you wanted to know how long I-I'd been awake. Not . . . not long." She smiled and his heart did a nose dive into the already excited portion of his lower body.

"Ya hadn't?"

He shook his head. Her other hand brushed his temple so gently that at first he thought he'd only imagined it. But her movement brought her upper body closer. She was hovering over his chest. Her eyes looked as deep as green shimmering pools reflecting a summer sun. She smelled fresh as morning dew.

Charly took a firm rein on her emotions. She'd slipped back into the *old* Charly's bad habits. If she wanted to make a lasting impression on Kent, she needed for him to see, hear, and know the *new* Charly . . . Charleen.

She cleared her throat. "Are you in pain? The only injury I've been able to find is that bump on yore . . . your hard head."

Kent was only paying attention to the warmth curling through his belly. Where she leaned over him, her body heated the chilled flesh on his chest. "I-I'm fine . . . I think. My head hurt. But it's b-better now." And he told the truth. The only throbbing taking place in his body was a long way from his head.

"You were mightly lucky, then. Must've . . . have fallen directly under the coach and away from hooves and wheels." While she spoke slowly, she couldn't resist running her hands over him, reassuring herself that he was truly all right.

313

"Yeah. Lucky." He stifled a groan.

She inched both hands up his rib cage, pausing over the bruises. "You sure you don't hurt here?"

"No." His voice grated as rough and deep as gravel.

Her fingers curled around his neck. Her breath fanned his dry lips. "Nothin' hurts here?"

"God, no," he whispered.

Lowering her arms, the backs of her knuckles traced down his chest and belly. She finally spread her hands over his hips. "And you're all right here?"

Hell! He ached and strained against the confines of his trousers. All right? She was a witch to tantalize him so. Didn't she know . . . His eyes lifted to catch the mischievous glitter in hers. The little tease! She'd known exactly what she was doing.

And he knew exactly what he was going to do to her.

He'd waited long days to give her what she wanted. Or from the determined set of her jaw—what she demanded. But just to be sure he hadn't misread her, he captured her wrists and pulled her down where he could study her face and eyes. "You know what's going to happen now, don't you?"

The tiny pink tip of her tongue darted out to moisten her mouth. She nodded and grinned. He moaned and thought he must've died and gone to heaven after all. Days and weeks of frustration, of pushing himself away, had brought him to this point. And he'd never felt so good or *right* about making love to a woman. His woman.

The sweet song of a meadowlark drifted on the breeze. Insects chirruped. The dust had finally settled and there was a freshness in the air that was all Charleen McAllister. He pulled her on top of him. She fit into his arms and against his body as if fate had saved her just for him.

The thought was a little disturbing, so he pushed it

314

aside. Later, he'd think about the ramifications of what fate might have in store for him. Right now, a warm and willing hoyden wanted to have her way with him. Damn right.

Once his lips fused with hers, the only thought in his mind was of Charly. Miss Charly.

Charly let herself succumb to the glorious passion of his lips, the deep probing of his tongue. She returned the kiss with every fiber of her being. Her bones melted to soft butter. Her flesh ignited to sizzling embers. She squirmed to get closer, but was hindered by too many layers of clothing.

All of a sudden, Kent lifted her away from him. He shifted his backside on the hard, rocky ground. Charly giggled at the pained expression on his face. His gut contracted at the musical sound of her laughter.

Together, they looked toward the stage. She laughed again at the stunned embarrassment darkening his precious features. She whispered, "Since you were late, you couldn't know. We're in luck. No passengers."

"Thank God." His eyes rolled heavenward.

She cupped his face in her palms. "What would you've done right now if there were a stage *full* of people?"

Rising from the ground with his woman still trapped in his arms, he growled, "I'd have opened the door, like so, and informed them that they could either stay and watch the show or get out and just listen. Either way," his lips nuzzled her earlobe and he nipped the sensitive flesh. "Either way, you would've been mine, honey. Right here. Right now."

The possessive huskiness in his voice sent shivers of desire down her spine. The knowledge that he meant every word he'd said fanned that desire to an unbelievably feverish pitch that Charly'd had no notion she'd be capable of reaching.

She wanted this man. Had to have him. Touching her, filling her—the way she needed air to breathe and food and water for nourishment. At this moment, he held her life in his hands. He was her everything. Her past. Her present. Her *forever*.

Kent lifted her into the Celerity, then followed her inside. Before he could remove his already unbuttoned coat and shirt, Charly had shucked off every stitch of her clothing and was spreading the layers atop a hard bench.

Her enthusiasm, her nakedness, her trust, expanded his chest until he thought it might burst. He could hardly catch his breath. He'd thought so before, but . . . God, what a woman!

His clothes were added to hers. His gaze raked down her gold-tinted flesh and long, long limbs. She had legs that wouldn't quit and he was forced to kneel down and run his hands over every satiny inch of her calves and thighs. His tongue moistened the backs of her knees and the smooth expanse of her inner thighs—tasting, testing, teasing.

Charly moaned and dug her fingers into his thick, wavy hair. Then she clutched at his shoulders for support as he spread her legs and tilted her backward until she sprawled on the padded seat.

She tensed and tried to push him away when his lips, and then his tongue, invaded her most private, feminine core.

"Sh-h, honey. Relax. Let me. Let me love you. Please?"

His *please* won her over. That, and the fact that she was turning the consistency of weak broth with the heat and pleasure he was bringing her body. Spasms of delight contracted her muscles, only to ease and leave her pliant and melting. And then she'd convulse again.

His name became a litany on her lips until he finally took her mouth with his. Her stomach knotted with a fierce desire to pleasure him as thoroughly.

She reached between their bodies and touched him. His manhood pulsed and stiffened in her palm.

Kent shuddered and stilled her fingers. "Easy, honey. Slow and easy. Are you ready for me? Do you want me inside you?"

In silent answer, her hips bucked upward. She wrapped her arms around his back. Her legs hugged his hips, pulling, urging him to enter her. "Now, Kent. Yes, I want you. Now."

He didn't hesitate to accept her invitation. He plunged inside her with the furor of a dehydrated man plunging into water. Damn, but he liked the sound of his name on her lips. Throaty and seductive, with just the faintest hint of her Mexican accent. The soft, slow word contrasted so wonderfully with the hot, wild thrust of her hips and the bite of her nails as she clutched at his back.

Greed. Needy greed. Hungry desire. Both urged Charly to take all of him. Deeper. Deeper. He filled her and she was consumed with an intense, overwhelming sense of being . . . home? She stiffened. Surely she was half-crazed by the long period of denial and now her acceptance of a strong emotional attachment to Kent.

Kent gazed down into green eyes glazed with arousal. Her body seemed determined to devour him. She'd wanted him. Had been ready for him. Even eager. He'd never been with a woman so passionate, so giving, so willing to share her love.

Love! Good God! Sure they were *making love,* but as he rocked above her, driving deeper with each thrust, it became something more than mere desire and want and need. He seemed to be delving into her soul. And she was reaching out to his.

She contracted about him. He closed his eyes and plunged again. Harder. Deeper. Into forever.

Charly cried out his name.

He arched his back and buried himself, glorying in the fiery heat licking at his insides.

The coach became a vehicle of light—exploding, erupting—then dimming—as, panting and exhausted, they cradled themselves together. The hard bench could've been made of granite or goose down for all they noticed or cared.

Charly snuggled her nose into the pulsing hollow at the base of his throat. He attempted to find the strength to hold his weight above her, but she urged him to her, wanting to feel every inch of his sweat-slicked body against her feverish skin.

He buried his face between the pillows of her breasts and inhaled the essence of her scent, his scent, as they mingled and became one.

A mule brayed. The coach rocked. Kent grabbed hold of the bench to keep them from falling to the floor. Charly grinned and Kent thought any light he'd seen before paled in comparison to the sweet brilliance reflected in her eyes.

"What?" he asked. "What are you smiling about?"

She licked a drop of salty perspiration from his shoulder and rejoiced in the shudder that rocked his virile frame. "You."

"Me? Why?" He ran his hand over her hip and up her rib cage to cup a full breast. A pert, alert nipple begged for his touch. He obliged.

"Ah-h-h, you're one tough character, ya know?"

He cocked his brow and immediately felt her fingers brushing across his forehead. "Tough?" And here he'd pretty well admitted to himself that he was little more than clay in her hands. "What makes you say that?"

She sighed. "Don't know any other man who could take a nose dive from a runaway stage and come up feelin' so . . . fine."

"Is that how I feel? Fine? I'm glad to hear it." He

318

shifted to slip out of her, then lay on his side and pulled her into the crook of his arm. "Didn't know that falling on my ass could be described as a 'nose dive,' but it sure sounds more dramatic and dangerous."

She reached around his hip and slapped his bottom. "Does it hurt there?"

He growled and smothered her in a bear hug.

The coach lurched. Harness jingled. Impatient hooves stamped the ground.

Charly and Kent groaned in unison. Kent rolled slowly to his feet, pinching and petting her in the most provocative places as she struggled into her clothes. Just when he was about to help her remove the concealing articles again, she snapped open her watch. "Hurry it up, Windy. We're way behind schedule."

He swatted her backside as she crawled past, but he didn't take long to dress.

While Kent was still inside the coach, Charly took the time to carefully inspect the team and harness. They'd been lucky. For all of the excitement, nothing had been damaged.

The mules had cooled down and pulled into the traces with only a minor display of temper when Charly flicked the reins. Riding to the San Pedro station, she and Kent were lost in silent thought. Charly was convinced that the outlaws were trying to stop the mail completely, and wondered how long they'd manage to dodge the bullets.

Kent kept watching Charly from the corner of his eye. He was determined to stop her from driving another stage. She was a woman, for God's sake. She wasn't meant to be involved in this kind of danger.

Charly eyed Kent. He'd been lucky today. If she had her way, this was the last trip he'd be making as conductor for the Overland Mail. For once, she was determined to protect *him*.

*   *   *

They rode horses back to Tucson. The westbound stage had failed to show, but even that tremendous disappointment failed to affect the new glow in Charly's world.

She took a deep breath of cool air, refusing to be disconcerted by the constant dust. They were riding into one of the most beautiful sunsets she'd ever seen, or at least paid attention to. A brilliant yellow and red sun had faded into the horizon a few moments earlier. Now all that remained was the deep purple outline of the earth, above which was a band of burnt orange layered by a lighter shade of yellow, then rose, and then a hazy dark blue that stretched up and up into the heavens.

No clouds disturbed the sky to reflect the color. A lone saguaro cactus, standing tall and stately, and a jagged ridge of mountains were the only silhouettes against the dark backdrop.

She glanced sideways and saw that Kent was also staring into the Western sky. As if sensing her eyes on him, he turned and smiled. Her heart did funny little skips and jumps and her lips quivered slightly as she returned the gesture.

They'd had no opportunity to repeat the afternoon of lovemaking, for they'd taken on passengers at each stop until reaching Dragoon Springs, and then the journey back had been spent avoiding Apaches and a group of several riders that appeared to be trailing them.

But she and Kent had worked together to cover their tracks. They made early camps, building small, smokeless fires from dried yucca stalks for their tea or coffee, and always extinguished the flames before dusk. They slept together for warmth, but because of the constant danger and the need to stay alert, they'd only shown their caring with a little touch here, or a

320

gentle caress there, or with a smile or long, heated look.

Her blood continued to sing through her veins whenever he cocked his brow in that roguish manner, or crossed his legs, molding his trousers to his muscular thighs. And it was still difficult to believe that someone like Kent would look at *her* like . . . that. Lordy, the smoldering embers in his eyes could start a prairie fire.

Kent had to look away or pounce on her like a mountain lion on a baby bunny. God, he couldn't believe what was happening to him. He wanted her. Right now. With an urgency that sent his body into spasms of pain and desire. He'd never been like this before. Never. He was in a constant state of agitation.

As the sparse lights of Tucson came into view, he jokingly plucked the bugle from the saddle horn and gave a wavering toot. Damn, if she'd just quit looking at him with those huge eyes that, in the twilight, seemed silvery and haunted. He'd said it before. She was a witch. She'd worked her magic and cast a spell over him. He was powerless to resist.

Charly glanced at Kent and winked, but her voice held a serious tone as she quipped, "Why, Windy, if you're not careful, we're gonna have to find a conductor with better lungs." Her words held a double meaning. Besides her wanting Kent to quit the job, a lot of the people in Tucson, especially Americans, were there because the dry air was good for a coughing disease from which they suffered. She'd brought a lot of them to town on the stage.

Kent shifted in the saddle and refused to respond to her banter. He decided that now was the time to take control. He was a determined man. She was his woman. She *would* listen to reason and use the brains God had given her.

He darted her a wary glance. His fingers tapped the

321

saddle horn. She looked over and offered a weak smile. All right, now was as good a time as any. "Charly?"

She cocked her head. "Yeah?"

He cleared his throat, but strengthened his resolve when he gazed into her beautiful face. "There's something I need to talk to you about."

"Yes?" she prodded. And in the back of her mind she prided herself on how much she'd done to correct her speech. Sure, she'd slipped a time or two, but she'd really concentrated most of the time. Then she frowned, 'cause the dratted man hadn't even seemed to notice. Or, maybe he had. She looked at him expectantly. Was that what he wanted to talk to her about?

"I don't want you to drive the stage again." There! Now she'd show how much she cared for and respected him by doing the right thing.

"Wh-what?" Of all the mule-headed things she'd ever heard come out of a human's mouth, that took the prize.

"I said, I don't want you driving anymore." He reached over and confidently placed his hand on her thigh. "It's just too risky. We've been lucky to ward off the holdup attempts, but that won't always be the case. Less than half of the stages are getting through as it is. The Company might as well give up trying to get the mail delivered along this route."

Charly swallowed. She blinked rapidly. Everything he said might be true, but—

"And driving a stage just isn't a suitable job for a woman, honey. It's hard and dirty and dangerous. Why, most men shy away from working for the Overland Company. So—"

"Ya blamed, two-faced polecat. Of all the simple-minded hogwash I ever did hear." She sputtered, unable to voice her irate confusion. "Jest who do ya think ya are, a-tellin' me—not askin', mind ya—but

322

demandin' that I quit a job I'm durned good at."

Kent leaned back, as if to avoid the sparks that crackled with every word. For a while, he'd given her credit for having sense. And didn't what they'd shared mean *anything* to her?

"Look, woman, I didn't want to argue about this. I figured you were smart enough to know when to give up. Do you have a death wish, or something?"

Her chin jutted out. "No. I just don't wanna be *told* what I can or can't do. Ain't right that you should say such things. Ya don't own me."

"I have every right. We've made—"

"That don't make no dif'rence. Ya ain't gotta say over my doin's just 'cause . . . Well, just 'cause." She could hear herself slippin', bad. It wasn't no use. She'd never be a lady, no how. 'Specially in *his* eyes. She was rough 'n' dirty 'n' . . ."

Kent snapped his mouth shut. Damn her! Let her get herself killed, if that was what she wanted. It'd be a cold day in July before he bothered to be concerned for her wellbeing again.

Charly kicked her horse into a lope. Dadburned interferin' sidewinder. How'd she ever come to *like* the highhanded city dandy? Let alone *love* him.

323

Chapter Twenty

Ed and the handlers were waiting with the new team when Charly and Kent rode up in front of the Overland station. He looked at his sister, then stepped further into the street and scanned the road behind them.

"What's goin' on here? Where's the stage?"

"Looks like the line's been cut back east somewhere. Nothin's gettin' through." Charly glared one last time at Kent and slid from the saddle. "Bandits tried to hold us up afore San Pedro Crossin', but we scared 'em . . . them off and at least got the mail as far as Dragoon Springs."

Rubbing her sore backside, she led her horse toward the stable. Inside the barn, she put the animal in a stall, curried off the salty sweat stains, and forked some hay. The entire time she forced herself to think of anything, anyone, but Kent Ashford.

The man had a lot of gall, tellin' her what to do. She loved this job, loved the challenge of gettin' the mail delivered on time, or even ahead of schedule. Wasn't no one gonna make her quit. But then she sighed, long and dejectedly. Drat it, the choice might not be left up to her. It didn't look like the mail would be comin' through Tucson much longer, if at all.

325

Closing the gate to the borrowed horse's stall, she turned and almost ran into her brother. "Oops. Sorry."

Ed handed the reins of the mules he was leading to another handler. He stuck his hands in his pockets and eyed his sister. "Ain't seen much of you lately."

She shrugged and absently brushed bits of hay from her trousers. "Nope. Been busy."

"Too busy ta check up on things around here?"

Charly took off her hat and rubbed the red crease in her forehead. "Why'd I wanna do that? I've got my own job." Or *had* a job, she thought to herself. "You're gettin' along without me, ain't . . . aren't you?" Dang it, she chastised herself. Watchin' her language and bein' a lady was hard work.

Suddenly she realized that Ed still stood in front of her, staring as if she'd just sprouted a third eye. "What? Did you mean that?"

She frowned. What'd she said? Her mind was so filled with thoughts of the mail and the durned city dandy's overbearin' ways that she was havin' a hard time concentratin' on *anything*. Imagine! Windy wanted her to quit drivin' just 'cause things were gettin' rough. An' mostly 'cause she was a "female." So? She was proud to say that there wasn't a man around who could do better.

"I'm wantin' to know if you really think I'm doin' a good job here." Ed scuffed his foot through a pile of straw, but only briefly took his eyes off his sister.

Charly blinked, trying hard to recall exactly what she'd said. Wasn't it that he was gettin' along without her just fine? She glanced around at the neatly staked hay bales, the manure piled in the aisle ready to be carted outside, and sniffed the permeating aroma of harness oil. By golly, she'd said it, and meant it.

326

"Yep . . . Yes. Everything looks great, little . . . Ed. Why?" She cocked her head and studied her brother. All of a sudden, he didn't seem like her "little" brother anymore. Something had changed. He had changed.

"No reason, don't guess. You just surprised me." He shook his head like he still couldn't believe what he'd heard. He stared at her mouth as if he doubted that praise could've passed through *her* lips.

"Surprised? That isn't the half of it," she muttered, quickly taking her leave. She had to get out of there before any other startling revelations rocked her usually solid foundation.

Brisk night air chafed her cheeks as she hurried along. She hunched her shoulders against the chill, although the bitterest cold seemed to clutch at her from within. How long had her brother and pa been holding up their ends of the chores without her even noticing?

Most importantly, *why* had she been so blind? Was she just too stubborn and hardheaded and set in her belief that everyone had to do things *her* way or not at all? Was she really the "bossy britches" Ed claimed her to be?

Or . . . did she keep such a sharp eye on things just to fool herself into believing she was needed—to make herself think she was important and that they couldn't get along without her?

Sure, her family of males had probably been at a loss when her mother died, wonderin' how to manage a ten-year-old girl. Had what she considered to be callous indifference just been a deep fear that they might do somethin' wrong? Just as she was now learning to be a woman and to love like a woman, yet was faced with the fear of being rejected by someone she cared too much for.

Did they know she loved them? Or know that she realized now they'd done their best? When was the

327

last time she'd told them she cared? She *had* told them that. Hadn't she?

Kent was as relieved as Charly to have a chance to catch his breath alone. His nerves had been worn to a frazzle. The hours they'd spent riding back to Tucson together, he'd been surrounded by her scent, had been so damned close to that curvaceous body . . . Yet all that time, he hadn't felt free to reach out and touch her.

Women! Who could figure them? He was concerned for her, that was all. Why couldn't she understand?

"Señor Ashford? Excuse me, señor Ashford."

Kent stopped in front of the post office. "Howdy, Manuel. Sorry, but I don't have any mail for you today."

"Sí, so I have heard. But there ees a message for you. A man, he drop eet off two days ago. I want for you to have it, seence you no come inside so very often."

"Thanks." Kent took the folded paper and carefully placed it in his coat pocket, then shook hands with the postmaster. Kent had made it a point to check with the office at least twice a week, but since he'd been riding the stage and was gone more often now, Manuel must have gotten worried. After the weeks of asking, it was Kent's first letter.

Manuel grinned. "The post office, she weel be a lonely place, no?"

"Looks that way, amigo."

Kent headed down the street toward his room and welcome thoughts of a change of clothes and a long nap. The first thing he did after closing the door behind him was take off his boots. The second was to read his message.

He reached up to trace the jagged line of his scar. A

328

hard knot formed in his stomach. His superiors were getting impatient. They wanted word of how his mission was progressing. Now.

He chuckled sardonically. Mission? What mission? For the past week he'd completely ignored his duty to follow after one Miss Charleen McAllister like a bull with a ring in its nose. And he'd been made to feel about as stupid as a steer that had been turned into a corral full of cows in heat.

According to Miss Charly, she'd been better off before he ever came along. She didn't *need* him to watch out for her. Fine. He had better things to do. Important work. Work that wouldn't allow him the time to worry over a headstrong female.

He sank into the only chair, stretched out his legs, and wriggled his toes. To take his mind off the hoyden, he thought back to the recent holdup attempts. Now that the chances of the mail getting through were almost nil, how was he going to send his missives? Since he and Charly had been followed from Dragoon Springs, the outlaws would probably be intercepting riders on horseback as well as stages. And what were they looking for? Whatever it was, they hadn't found it yet.

A shudder worked down his spine. He had a gut feeling that somehow he'd been found out. "Someone" knew he was here. Or at the very least, suspected a spy in the vicinity. But who was that "someone?" Had a trap already been laid?

If so, "someone" had better hope it worked soon. Kent Ashford had a plan.

Tuesday morning, Kent felt rather good as he left the post office. Tucson was buzzing with the news that an eastbound Overland stage had made it as far as Maricopa Wells. The regularly scheduled Wednesday stage would be running as usual, and his first message would be on it. Now all he had to do was wait and see if the outlaws took the bait.

"Kent. Oh, yoo hoo. Kent Ashford . . . I declare, I've looked all over Tucson for you."

A pink silk parasol preceded a pink-gloved hand that wrapped around his forearm. He flinched at the cloying odor of strong perfume and felt suddenly suffocated, like a tree trunk buried by poison ivy. But he politely tipped his hat. "Good morning, Miss Kelly. I'm surprised you're still in town." She fluttered her lashes and he nearly choked.

"I could hardly leave without saying my good-byes to you."

He cocked his brow. "Ahem, how nice. Any particular reason you were looking for me?" His stomach clenched as he awaited her answer. Females of his acquaintance lately were renowned for their dangerous and inventive requests. At least the one female who came immediately to mind.

"Why, yes," Christa giggled. "My brother sent a message that he has the papers ready to sign. The Santa Rita is almost yours."

He smiled. "That *is* good news." Which meant that soon he'd be reporting that an important part of his mission had been successfully completed. That should please his people back East.

"And . . ." She tightened her hold and pressed her plump breasts into his arm as they walked. He glanced warily up and down the street, hoping that no one was witnessing her embarrassing display. He'd always believed that the man should be the one to do the pursuing.

Suddenly his nervous gaze was captured by a pair of sparkling green eyes. His stride faltered. Charly! Standing in the shadows. Hands splayed on her slender hips. Glaring. And she was wearing the prettiest calico dress. A matching ribbon dangled from long sable hair that had been pulled back and

330

braided into a single coil. Beautiful.

"Kent? Are you all right, darling?"

He cringed and tried to unwrap the clinging woman from his body. Once the task was accomplished, he glanced quickly toward Charly. His heart plummeted to his knees. All he found were shadows and more shadows. In the blink of an eye, the lovely vision had disappeared.

In fact, as he continued to search, he began to wonder if he hadn't just imagined her. She'd been on his mind constantly. Perhaps . . . But his flesh still prickled. Damn!

"Who was that woman, darling?"

Ah, Christa had seen her, too. Charly was more than just his imagination. Kent pulled his arm from Christa's grasp—again. Then, when it looked like the woman was going to puddle up on him, he took her elbow and led her into an empty doorway. "Look, Miss Kelly, I'm nobody's *darling*. You're a pretty, sweet lady, but that's as far as my feelings go. I hope you understand—"

Christa jerked back as if he'd just stung her. "Then you've been leading me on? You don't have any feelings for me at all?"

"Christa . . . Miss Kelly," he sighed. "I never led you on about anything. You know that."

She patted a red curl into place. "Does this mean you won't take me with you when you go to the mine?"

Kent cocked his head. What had happened to the tears? The whiny little voice? The nervous fluttering of her hands? The childish pout? In front of him now stood a stern, very determined woman.

"Well, does it?" She tapped her foot on the packed earth.

He shrugged. "Since it seems I have to go there anyway, I see no harm in your riding along."

A smug smile creased her lips. Sweat trickled down

331

Kent's back. "How nice of you, darling. When will you pick me up?"

His wary glance encompassed the stage office, the impatient Christa, and the noon sun. "Tomorrow morning. Early."

Kent was leaving his room, on the way to eat supper that evening, when a young man delivered a sweet-smelling missive. He recognized the expensive, cloying scent immediately, and grudgingly handed the boy a coin. Damn. Couldn't the woman take a hint?

After reading the note, he sighed despairingly and pulled on his suit coat. Ever the gentleman, he had no choice but to honor the lady's request to accompany her to supper. She did have to eat, and it was quite unseemly for an unescorted woman to enter a public place.

If he had to take anyone to supper, he wished it could be Miss Charly. However, the hoyden had made it pretty clear that it would be a cold day in the Arizona desert before she wanted to see *him* again. The stubborn hardhead.

The note hadn't said, but Kent assumed Christa would be staying at the Butterfield station. It was the only decent place a woman could find a room. He also figured that Jed McAllister had seen the wealth dripping from the lady and was charging her a healthy price.

Hell, why not? A man had to make do for his family any way he could nowadays. Although from what Kent had seen, Jed didn't do much for his own daughter. With her damned abrasive personality, though . . . Aw, maybe he wasn't being completely fair.

"Why, there you are, darling. I've been waiting for you."

"Evidently." He gritted his teeth. Hell, he hadn't even gotten through the door.

"I'm ever so hungry. And it's so much more pleasant to dine when you have company. Don't you agree?"

"Yeah, sure."

As they entered the dining area, Christa clutched his arm and pointed, "Why, look, darling. Isn't that the . . . I guess it's a . . . woman, who was staring at us this morning. You never did tell me her name."

Kent hadn't heard a thing. Like his companion, his eyes had been glued to the corner table since entering the room.

Charly wasn't alone. The damned "gentleman" sat across from her, talking and gesturing as if she was rooted to his every word. And from the enraptured expression on her face, she damned well was. Gullible female.

Then before he realized what was happening, Christa was leading him toward that very same table. Dear God.

"And just when will you be taking the mail again, pretty lady?" Miles took hold of Charleen's hand and frowned at the callouses hardening her fingers and palm.

"Well . . ." His thumb sensuously caressed her palm. She tried to control the shiver that started down her spine. "I may be goin' sooner . . . Oh, how . . . hello."

Startled, Miles irritably glanced up at the two intruders. "Ashford. What a surprise," he drawled, intimating that he wasn't surprised at all, but was extremely annoyed.

Kent blessed Christa's little heart for deciding to interrupt the cozy twosome.

Christa tugged on Kent's arm. "Aren't you going to introduce me, darling?"

Kent did the honors and rolled his eyes when

333

Christa gasped out loud, "Oh, my God. *You* drive those ugly ole stages? I've never heard of a *woman* doin' such a thing."

Charly sent a glare at Kent, who shrugged and looked away. He wasn't going to say a word. Not tonight.

Miles smiled proudly toward Charleen. "Yes, she's quite something, isn't she?"

Christa fanned her face with the end of her neck scarf.

Kent sighed.

Charly beamed. Finally, she'd found someone who understood and wasn't bent on givin' her a hard time about her job. In fact, Miles seemed extraordinarily interested in everything she did, and when and why. He made her feel good and proud of her work. And he hadn't once acted like he'd rather be with the Lady in Pink.

A large hand suddenly clapped Kent on the back. He swung around, fists clenched, but stopped just as quickly.

"Howdy, Kent. Been a long time." A huge, beefy man kept that same hand held out.

"Damn, Ben, it sure has." Kent composed his features and offered his own hand.

The man named Ben turned his attention to the pair seated at the table. "And I'll be doggied. Lookit—"

Miles' chair scraped the packed earth as he jumped to his feet. "Miles Cavanaugh, sir. I didn't catch your name."

"Ben Matthews." Ben's bushy dark brows drew together.

Kent took a deep breath and stepped back. He hastily scanned the room, wondering if it was too late to make his escape. He couldn't afford to have Ben give him away. Not yet. But there stood the waitress, blocking the door and pointing to an empty table.

334

He darted another glance at Benjamin Matthews, vice president of Ashford & Co. Railroad. If it became common knowledge that Kent had connections to the railroad, and was snooping around southern Arizona, people—especially those with Confederate persuasions—might find a hasty, and very final, means to bring his mission to an end.

If the Overland Mail was stopped completely, another vehicle for transporting the mail would have to be found—quickly. And then, his experience would become invaluable to the Union. Kent would scout the best route to lay the tracks for a railroad.

Christa Kelly turned her attention from her pensive escort and batted her thick lashes at the well-dressed newcomer. Here at last was a man who looked as though he could keep a lady in style.

She sidled closer and crossed her arms under her generous bosom, displaying her flesh to its best advantage. Surreptitiously, she glanced back at Kent Ashford and fumed. The uncouth beast wasn't paying her any heed. Although he'd as good as told her he wasn't interested, she hadn't believed a word of it. She was pretty, well-schooled, and came from a fairly well-to-do family.

While Ben Matthews was busy with the little blond, Miles ran a finger beneath his collar and tried to stretch the constricting material enough to swallow. Of all the people to turn up in Tucson, it would have to be Ben Matthews, an influential man who was acquainted with Miles' railroad affiliations. The big man could ruin everything.

Charly frowned when Benjamin Matthews looked from the Lady in Pink to her. "Your name's sure familiar," she blurted, and then smothered a conspiratorial grin when the big man did some fancy footwork to avoid Christa.

"Well, ma'am, that's mighty flatterin'. I've been known to do a little railroadin' in my time."

The grin froze on Charly's face. Railroad? Oh, no! What was a railroad man doin' in Tucson? Was he deliverin' the final blow to the Overland Mail? Durn it. She'd been afraid of this ever since Butterfield lost the line.

It had been a constant naggin' ache in the small of her back. Things were changin', and she didn't want any part of it. She wouldn't consider movin' to another town, another job. Tucson was her home. Here she would stay.

Ben gradually became aware of the fact that the gorgeous dark-haired woman wasn't impressed with his credentials. Kent Ashford wouldn't even meet his eyes. Miles Cavanaugh was pretending not to know him. And the crazy lady in the pink dress wouldn't keep her hands to herself. It was time to retire to his room—alone.

He bowed to both ladies and favored the two men with a chagrined shake of his balding head. Maybe before he left Tucson, he'd find out what in the hell was going on.

"Well, it's been a real pleasure, folks, but I'd better call it a night. Kent, I'd sure like to see you again."

Kent didn't miss the pointed glance and nodded. Then he abruptly grabbed Christa's elbow, keeping her from following Ben from the room, and directed her rather forcefully to the only empty table before either Charly or the "gentleman" started asking questions.

"But, Kent, darling . . . You should have invited your friend to join us. Poor thing. He's probably going back to a cold, lonely ole room to—"

"Don't worry about Ben, Miss Kelly. Last I heard, he and his wife were expecting their eighth child. The man needs his rest."

The next morning, Kent and Christa Kelly were

getting a late start out of Tucson. He muttered harshly under his breath as Christa primly tucked her skirt about her ankles. Women. He'd yet to meet one that was ever on time. Except for one.

He flicked the reins, signaling the team of bays to jog. A clanging bell and the excited chatter of children drew his gaze toward a small adobe structure at the outskirts of town. Begrudgingly, he waved at the "gentleman" school teacher.

Damn, but just the sight of Miles Cavanaugh caused his gut to knot. What did Miss Charly find so fascinating about the sissified fellow? He was too smooth-talking, too good looking, and too ready with false smiles to suit Kent. Any man that flashed his teeth as often as the "gentleman," had something to hide.

Kent was determined to find out more about the southerner and then set Miss Charleen McAllister straight about her choice of friends, or "gentlemen" friends.

"Is the schoolteacher married to that person who drives the stage?"

Kent turned to stare fixedly at Christa Kelly. "No. Why'd you ask?"

She began to pull her gloves on slowly, smoothing the leather down her long fingers. "No reason. The few other times I've seen them, they've been together. And last night, when they left the dining room, they shared such intimate little glances, and all. I thought maybe they were newlyweds."

"Not hardly," he muttered, missing the smug tilt of her chin when he glowered over his shoulder at the grinning Miles. Damn the man for looking so happy and satisfied, for being in Charly's favor. But not Kent. Oh, no. The she-cat would barely spare him a glance.

Well, if that was what she wanted, some silly, citified dandy . . . He stopped in mid-thought and shook his head. Damned if he wasn't starting to think

337

like the little brat.

His gaze drifted over his companion's perfect profile, her perfectly coiffed hair, and perfectly elegant style of dress. Mentally he compared her to the seemingly less than perfect Miss Charly, and the "perfect" creature was the one who came up lacking. At that moment, he also came to one important conclusion. Women! Who needed the aggravation?

Charly walked into the stage depot, dusting her dirty hands on her worn leather britches. It felt good to be wearing her old clothes. The worst chore she'd had all week was tryin' to stay clean and pretty, all gussied up in that dress. She just wasn't meant to be no fancy lady.

And from the caliber of the fancy ladies she'd met lately, the world would survive without another one. She snorted. Last night at dinner, she thought she'd throw up if she heard one more sickenin' "dahlin'" or seen one more adoring little smile directed at that durned Kent Ashford.

Her stomach was still a little queasy this morning just thinkin' about the Lady in Pink, and she was relieved that Uncle John was taking the stage today.

After helping her pa load the mail sacks, she stood back as two brave passengers boarded. Their faces were pinched and wary-lookin', and it was easy to understand why. As dangerous and inconsistent as the stages had been lately, she didn't envy them their trip.

Rubbing her throbbing temples, she sighed, regretting the fact that her own respite wouldn't last long. Tomorrow, she'd be drivin' an unscheduled stage, carryin' packages that weren't usually accepted and important correspondence coming from California and goin' all the way to Washington. If she was guessin', she'd bet the messages had somethin' to do with the increasin' hostilities between the fellas

338

tryin' to convince California to secede from the Union and those who'd die before lettin' such a thing happen.

Men, she said to herself huffily, were so foolish. They couldn't sit down and try to work things out peacefully. Oh, no. They had to come to fisticuffs and eventually start a war.

As she looked down Tucson's main street, she wondered if there *was* a war, what would happen here. Most of the Americans she'd heard talkin' around town were leanin' on the side of the South. But there were a few, the quieter bunch, who believed in keepin' the nation together.

Far as she was concerned, both "sides" had their points, but to end up havin' Americans fightin' Americans? It would be a sacrilege.

Jed McAllister tapped her on the shoulder. Charly jumped. "Wake up, gal. 'Pears ya got comp'ny comin'."

She glanced down the street again and spied Miles Cavanaugh. He grinned and waved. Chewing at her lower lip, she wished her heart would turn somersaults and her pulse would race out of control every time she saw Miles a-comin' instead of just that goldurned Kent. But . . . That wasn't the way of it.

"Mornin', pretty lady. I was afraid I might've missed you."

All of a sudden, the bugle sounded and Uncle John whipped the team into motion. Miles started and stared from the big driver back to Charly. "I thought . . . I mean, you aren't . . ."

She smiled and shook her head. "Nope. I didn't have to drive today."

Miles fiddled with a button on his coat and darted a glance after the departing coach. He blinked. "Well, that's, uh, great. Maybe we can, uh, have dinner again. Tonight, or tomorrow night. Whichever's most convenient for you."

339

Sliding her fingers into her back pockets, she looked toward the stables. "It'll have to be tonight, I guess."

"Oh? Why?"

She hesitated. "'Cause I'll be outta town tomorrow. And probably a few more days."

"I see." When it became clear she wasn't going to tell him any more than that, he narrowed his eyes. "Then tonight it is. I always look forward to our time together."

Charly smiled weakly and sighed, "Yeah."

Chapter Twenty-One

"Let's go!" Charly McAllister cracked the whip. The six-mule team jerked into action just as the morning sun peeked over the eastern horizon. Vivid hues of pink and purple and orange battled for dominance, only to blend together and suffuse the dark sky with a brilliant sunrise that took Charly's breath away as she guided the stage directly toward the natural phenomenon.

"Damn it, why'd we have to leave so early? Could've at least waited 'til a man had his mornin' coffee an' a decent breakfast."

Charly rolled her eyes. Well, it *had* been a beautiful morning. She reached into her pack and withdrew some jerky. "Here, put this in your mouth an' shut up your dadblamed complainin'. I swear, you're worse than an old woman."

Ed McAllister grumbled deep in his throat and bit down hard on the dried venison. He gnawed and pulled and ground his teeth into the tough, stringy meat. At last he was rewarded with a loud snap and worked the small piece between his jaws until the pungent, smoked flavor seeped into his taste buds.

Charly shook her head at her brother's sigh of satisfaction. Jerky might be a staple in her diet, but that didn't mean she *liked* to eat the stuff. She'd get just as much pleasure and flavor from gnawing on a boot sole.

"Why'd I have ta come, anyway? What happened to that big guy that's been ridin' with ya lately?"

"I've told you a hundred times, Ed. The man wasn't nowhere to be found. Do you think I like havin' you along any better'n you like bein' here?" And did he know how embarrassin' it had been to have Miles accompany her all evening while she searched through the cantinas and the, ahem, *other* places a man might go to . . . Her cheeks flamed anew. Naturally, she'd refrained from asking Miles how he'd known where the *other* places were.

Ed flushed. "I'm sorry, sis. It's . . . Well, I had other things that needed doin'."

Grudgingly, she defended Kent. "I reckon he must've, too. But it ain't his fault. He didn't know I was takin' this stage."

"He shoulda checked with Pa 'fore he took out an' left, anyway."

Charly nodded. Secretly, she was also wondering where on earth he could've gone that no one knew his whereabouts. The only thing that kept her from goin' crazy with worry was that his landlady had said his clothes were still in his rented room.

She slapped the reins against a bobbing brown rump. "Tell you what, Ed. If it'll stop your whinin', I promise we'll both give the sonofagun a piece of our minds when we get back."

Later that afternoon, Kent rode his stallion into Tucson. He looked around at the one-story, flat-roofed, mud-colored houses. Some had one or two windows, others no windows at all. He gazed at the patches of tilled ground, brown with the remains of plants poking through the mounded rows, and wondered at the sameness of it all.

His eyes drifted past the building set aside for the schoolhouse and, a few seconds later, he pulled his horse to a sudden stop. He stared at the closed door and windows. There was no sign of inhabitants anywhere around the school. He pulled out his watch. Only one o'clock. It was the middle of the week, wasn't it? And school was out? Must be nice. He'd seldom been so lucky when *he* was a kid.

But he shrugged and rode on down to the stage depot. He was in a hurry to put the deed to the Santa Rita mine into his saddlebags and then back into the safe.

When he entered the Overland office, he spied Jed McAllister behind the desk and asked, "What's going on around here? There a holiday or something?"

Jed looked up from his papers and hooked his thumbs under his suspenders. "I was jest fixin' ta ask ya the same thing. That is, whenever ya reckoned ta show yore face agin."

"What?" Kent frowned.

"We'uns looked all over town fer ya last evenin'. An' I mean *all* over. Couldn't find hide nor hair of ya."

"I was . . . out of town. Just rode in. Why? Why were you looking for me?"

"Needed ya ta ride conductor on a stage this mornin'."

"*This* morning? Even if the stages were running on schedule, there wouldn't be one today."

Jed sat back and gave Kent a smug look that said the younger man didn't know nearly as much as he thought he did. "This'uns one that's not on any schedule. Reckoned ta throw them owlhoots off the cent a mite."

A tingle of apprehension ricocheted along Kent's spine. "Who drove today?"

"My Charly gal."

"And did she go without a conductor?" In the back

343

of his mind, he prayed the young gun hand, Orlando, had come around again. And he unconsciously registered the pride in Jed's voice when the man spoke about his daughter. Kent had never noticed it before when Jed mentioned Charly. Or vice versa.

"Nope. Ed t'were the onlyest one 'vailable."

Kent grimaced, knowing that she and her brother weren't on the best of terms. But maybe this was good. Maybe spending the time together would help them settle a few of their differences.

He asked Jed for his saddlebags, and while he placed the papers inside, remembered the reason they'd gotten started on the subject of his being out of town. "How come school's out today? Something special happening in Tucson?"

Jed scratched his belly. "Naw, don't reckon. Cain't think o' no reason, less'n the new schoolmarm turned 'em out a-purpose."

Kent chuckled, glad to know that someone else held the same opinion of Miles Cavanaugh. But he still had a funny feeling . . . "Seems strange to me. It was sure open yesterday."

Suddenly, a young Mexican boy ran into the office with a paper crunched in his hand. "Mr. McAllister! Mr. McAllister! Thee señor at thee telegram, hee theenk you should know. Thee wires, they are down somewhere east of town."

Kent's head snapped up. "Which way was Charly headed?"

"East. She'd be close ta Cienega de los Piños station by now."

"Good God. She could be headed into big trouble. We need to wire the station and see what's going on. They could warn her—"

"Calm down, son. There's nuthin' ta get riled 'bout. This ain't nuthin' unusual. Wire coulda gone down in a gust o' wind. Or maybe a pole fell over. Ain't got no call ta go off half-cocked."

344

Kent sucked in his breath. "But there could also be Apaches or outlaws out there, just waiting to trap her."

Jed laughed. "Yore shore a dramatic young fella. Nope. We'uns'll wait 'til we hear more, or that somethin's delayed the stage, afore we start worryin'. 'Sides, my Ed'll keep the gal safe. See if'n he won't."

Kent couldn't say that he'd been too impressed with young Ed, or his qualifications to guard either Charly's life or the mail. But Jed was right in one respect. There was no sense in expecting the worst. If only it wouldn't take so damned long to get word, especially with the telegraph down.

As soon as his saddlebags were returned to the safe, Kent left the stage depot and walked across the street to the cantina. Nursing a shot of *aguardiente*, he thought about his unnatural reactions to Miss Charly. What was this obsession he seemed to have for the brat?

He took a sip of the liquor and recalled the first time he'd ever seen the hoyden—clad in buckskins, dirt smudges on her nose. And the last time he'd seen her—all dressed up, the perfect lady—and impressing the hell out of Miles Cavanaugh.

He sighed and ran the tip of his finger around the rim of the glass. Charly was making an effort to better herself, and he admired her for it. But damned if he didn't think he liked her better in buckskins and her floppy hat. At least he could deal with *that* Charly. The new Miss Charleen had him stumped.

As far as Kent knew, no one had pushed her to change. The new clothes and fancy hair style must have been a conscious decision on her part to improve herself, and under conditions that had to be hard and even embarrassing in a small town of people who would see and hear and comment on her every action.

He cocked his brow and stared into the mirror

345

hanging behind the bar. Maybe that new Charly wasn't so different after all. She was still gutsy and feisty and willing to tackle anything or anybody.

He raised his glass to the bartender for a refill and rested both elbows on the bar's sticky wood surface. He took a drink. The liquid burned a fiery trail down his gullet, reminding him of the way his insides ignited whenever he held Charly's wild, supple body in his arms; and of the pain that knifed through his chest each time he saw her with the "gentleman."

Why? How had she managed to squirm her way into his soul? Of course, they'd made love, and it had been spectacular. But what he felt for her now was more than just a physical attraction. He'd lusted after a lot of women, but none of *them* had flounced in and taken control of his mind. *They* didn't appear at the most inopportune times to upset his world.

He smiled and downed the glass in one gulp. Unlike the other women, there was one thing that drew him to the hoyden like a kid to licorice—Miss Charly needed him. Whether she was willing to acknowledge it or not.

And . . . he *cared* for her. He did. Yet even that word would never adequately explain the tightness that gripped his chest at just the mention of her name.

God, wouldn't it be ironic if the city dandy had fallen in love with the knife-throwing, whip cracking brat?

He held the glass up for another refill, and then another . . .

A rounded sliver of moon was beginning to peek from behind a dark, billowy cloud as Kent made his way unsteadily to the stage station. The beam from a coal-oil lantern beckoned from the office, but when he shoved the door open, there was no one inside.

346

"Hello. Jed? Anyone around?"

A loud bang came from the mail room. The next thing he knew, a dark form rushed at him. Caught off guard, Kent was knocked into the desk as the lantern and loose papers fell to the floor. The odor of kerosene permeated the room just before flames ignited the soaked parchment.

Indecision tore through Kent. He should stay and put out the fire but, oh, how he wanted to go after the fellow whose footsteps he could still hear running across the baked surface of the street. Damn, he wanted that coyote!

Finally, he peeled off his jacket and began to beat at the burning papers. Smoke blurred his vision. He choked and held his free arm in front of his face, but it didn't help.

Through the crackling and hissing of the dying fire, a muffled curse caught his attention. Quickly, he smothered the last of the flames and hurried into the mail room. Jed McAllister lay on the floor, gagged and bound hand and foot.

Removing the cloth first, Kent immediately went to work on the ropes. Jed coughed and sputtered. "Thank the good Lord ya come when ya did."

Kent helped the older man to his feet and brushed a coating of dirt from his clothes. "What happened, Jed?"

"Caught that damned hombre a-sortin' through ever' piece o' mail in the place."

"Did he take anything?"

Jed rubbed his wrists and scanned the room and the upended mail sacks. "Not so's I kin tell. Ya come in 'fore he got started good. 'Sides, there warn't nuthin' left here but them old Butterfield flyers."

Kent shook his head. The outlaws, Confederates more than likely, were becoming pretty brazen when they had the gumption to break into a busy stage office.

347

His eyes narrowed. The safe! Had they found his saddlebags? He ran into the main room. A relieved sigh filled his shaken body when he saw that the door to the safe was still closed and locked.

Jed followed, rubbing his wrists. He sank into his chair. "Damn all the luck. If this ain't been a hell of a day."

"What else has happened? Have you heard anything about Charly?"

"Naw, but a rider come through sayin' the stage that went out the day afore hers was stopped."

Kent shuddered. "Anyone hurt?"

"Uncle John took a piece o' lead in the shoulder, but he's gonna be all right."

"Thank God." Kent knew how much the big man meant to Charly. "But no word on Charly, or what might've caused the break in the wire?"

"Nope. 'Ceptin' this rider, he said the weather's been good back the way he come. No storms an' hardly any wind."

Again the suspicious tingle wormed its way down Kent's spine. "Well, if you haven't heard anything by morning, I'm going after her. I'll find out for myself what's going on out there."

"If'n it warn't for some'un needin' ta stay in the office, I'd go with ya, son."

Kent stared down at the older man and read the concern in the rheumy eyes. Then he remembered the man's youngest son was out there too.

The next afternoon, Kent stopped on a grassy rise, removed his hat, and used his bandana to wipe the sweat from inside the headband. Here it was, the first of March, and it was already an unusually warm day, even for the desert. He uncapped his canteen, took a drink, and swirled the tepid water around in his mouth before swallowing.

He ran his hand down the stallion's sweaty neck, then looped a lead rope over the saddle horn and reached back to rub the mare's ears. The same mare Charly had ridden that day she'd found his stallion. By using the two horses, he'd been able to ride for twelve straight hours without wearing either to the ground, and had cut off a lot of miles by traveling across the country instead of following the road.

He scanned the area ahead. Still no sign of Charly or the Overland stage. She and Ed had reached the San Pedro station, and he'd heard there that they'd made it as far as Dragoon Springs, only to learn that the relief driver had been waylaid and was waiting at Apache Pass. No one had heard from or seen them since.

He replaced the canteen, dismounted, and transferred his saddle to the mare. A sense of urgency prodded his actions. Every instinct screamed, *Hurry! Charly's in danger.*

An hour later, at the sound of distant gunfire, Kent pulled the mare to a sliding stop. He cocked his head and listened. The shots seemed to be coming from his right, at the base of a steep-cliffed mesa. He let the lead rope out so the stallion could swing in behind the mare on the narrow trail between sharp-thorned mesquite and pointed yucca blades.

Whenever he reached an open area, he nudged the mare into a faster gait. But as the sporadic shots grew louder, he slowed the horse's pace, wanting an opportunity to scout the situation before charging in blind. Finally, he happened onto a short, narrow gully nearly hidden by the thick mesquite and grease wood. He tied the horses and left them concealed there.

Taking his rifle from the saddle boot, he levered a

shell into the empty chamber. He took an extra pistol from his bedroll and tucked it into his waistband. He was about to move out of the brush when he heard the clack! ping! of a rock rolling downhill.

Quickly he moved to the horses' heads, laid down the rifle, and covered their noses with his palms. Between the bare mesquite branches, he caught sight of a flash of red halfway up the hill. His eyes narrowed as he made out a bronzed back, high leather moccasins, and a red headband. Apache!

Sweat beaded his forehead and upper lip. The stallion stamped and fidgeted. Kent finally realized his palm had contracted on the animal's nose and he eased the pressure.

Once the Indian was out of sight, he released the horses, pulled his hat down tight, picked up the rifle, and started up the slope. He moved in a crouch, working his way steadily, using every bush or cactus he could find as a shield. He searched the ground for dry twigs or loose rocks before taking each step.

The top of the hill seemed to loom ever farther away. His leg muscles cramped and his lower back ached from the unfamiliar position, but he kept moving. Slowly. Surely. Upward. At last he topped the ridge. Kneeling behind a large boulder, he surveyed the downward slope and the narrow valley ahead.

Perspiration dotted his face and neck and spread to his palms. He felt suddenly chilled. There, at the base of the next hill, against a sheer cliff, lay an overturned Celerity coach. Two mules were down in the traces. The rest of the team stamped and brayed loud enough that he could hear them over the gunshots.

Even from his location atop the hill, Kent couldn't see the stage's defenders. And it was impossible to determine the number of Apaches, so well had they blended into the landscape.

Then directly in front of him, about fifty feet down the slope, an Apache arose and loosed an arrow toward the stage. At the same time, a puff of smoke rose from behind the Celerity's front axle, preceding the rifle report which reverberated between the twin rises.

Kent hunkered lower to the ground. For a moment there, he'd almost given himself away when he thought he'd seen the dented crown of a brown floppy hat. The sight was enough to give him hope and the courage to buck the odds. If Charly was down there, he'd get her out.

He carefully scanned the ridge and the slope leading down to the valley. Studying a boulder here, a scrub oak there, he picked out the areas where he would find protection as he began to work out a plan. Then as stealthily as possible in his heavy coat and thick-soled boots, he crawled to a multi-based mesquite and balanced the rifle barrel on a thick root. He continued on and took shelter behind a thick-trunked soap tree yucca.

Barely settling in place, he'd just drawn his revolver when five or six Apaches emerged from their concealment and let loose a barrage of arrows. One Indian, using an older model carbine, also stood and fired. Answering shots came from the coach, but they were slow and carefully aimed, as if the people there might be low on ammunition.

This time, instead of falling back, the Indians began to move forward. He watched closely and saw movement in various positions in a half circle near the Celerity. He guessed there were between fifteen and twenty savages.

A hollow ache ripped through his insides. Charly and Ed. Since it was a special stage, he doubted they carried passengers. The two of them against twenty Apaches, and no telling how long they'd been pinned down.

Kent's throat went dry. He prayed his plan would work, or soon they'd all three end up as meals for the buzzards.

His voice cracked and sounded gravelly as hell, but rang out loud and long. "Forward, troopers! Ready! Fire!" He snapped off several shots at the Indians below him on the hill. One dropped, but the rest of his bullets only sent up sprays of sand.

Reloading his pistol as he moved, he ended up behind the mesquite and grabbed for the rifle. Shouting and firing, he was rewarded with another grunt and a moan. With the start of his attack, the gunfire from the stage increased.

Kent lunged to another position behind a group of rocks and fired more rounds toward the startled, confused Apaches. "Aim carefully, men. Take your time. Make every shot count."

The Indians began to disappear one by one. Kent charged down the slope, firing at any target that presented himself. Reaching the valley floor, he ran toward the stage, shouting, "Don't shoot. I'm coming in."

He drew his knife and immediately set to work cutting the dead animals from the harness. In a heartbeat, Charly and Ed were beside him, helping to move the remaining mules.

Ed grinned. "Thanks, man. Where're the others?"

Kent cut through a thick leather strap. "I'm all there is." If there'd been time, he could've laughed at the stricken expression on the young man's face.

"You mean there ain't no cavalry?"

"Nope."

Charly was directly across from him, guiding the mules on her side away from the downed animals. "Well, Windy, I reckon we owe you our lives. Thanks." Then she dusted her hands together and stepped over to the coach. "If we can lift this thing and get it right side up, we might be able to clear out of here 'fore the 'Paches realize they've been tricked.''

All three of them went to the top side of the Celerity. Sliding their hands beneath the rim, they lifted. The coach rocked up several feet. Kent bent and put his shoulder into it, and it came up another foot. Ed was able to do the same.

"Bend your knees," Kent ordered. "On three, give it all you've got. One. Two. Threeeee!" The coach creaked and rose higher. It rocked on two wheels. Kent rushed forward and braced his arms against the side, tipping it the rest of the way over. The Celerity bounced on its supports. The canvas stretched and tightened. Finally, it settled, upright and as good as new except for a few protruding arrows.

Charly's eyes had been on the far slope. She grabbed up her rifle. "Hurry, Ed. Get up there and drive. Take the mail on and send us back some help."

Ed set his jaw. "No. I ain't goin' without you."

Before she could argue the point, Charly found herself kicking at thin air as a pair of strong hands encircled her waist and none too gently deposited her on the stage. Ed whipped up the team. Frantically, she looked down at Kent and held out her hand. "Come on."

He stepped back and shook his head. "Get out of here, Ed. I'll hold them off 'til you get a good start."

"No-o-o! You'll be killed." She could've strangled the idiot when he just shrugged. What'd he think he was? Some kind of dadblasted hero?

"I've got horses. When I can . . . I'll follow you out. Now you heard me, boy. Go on." He turned and headed back toward the slope he'd descended earlier.

As the stage jounced over rocks and brush, Charly looked to the west and saw the vague hint of shapes and almost imperceptible movements. She looked back at Kent, still standing where they'd left him, shading his eyes, watching as they worked their way across the uneven valley floor. Praying he'd be able to

353

see her, she pointed toward the thick brush, then cupped her hands around her mouth and shouted, "The Apaches. They're back."

Kent's gaze followed the direction of her arm. The sun glinted off something shiny on the side of the hill and he dove behind a large, flat rock just as a bullet whined overhead. Another bullet chipped fragments of rock and he shielded his face from the flying shards. Whoever once told him that Indians weren't good shots needed to be here with him now, Kent thought maliciously.

Crawling to the end of the boulder, he dug out a layer of dirt so he could see through a small space between the ground and the rock. Everywhere he looked, he could see shadows gliding through the brush, flitting behind the yucca and cactus as the Apaches steadily approached.

A state of calm settled over his nerves as the bolder Indians began to show themselves, taunting him, willing him to waste his valuable ammunition. Thank God, Charly was safe. At least for now. If he could just last long enough to give her and Ed a good start, they might just make it to the next station.

The sound of distant gunfire suddenly jarred him. Damn! He'd been afraid of that. Some of the Apaches had gone after the stage. But he'd seen Charly shoot. He had faith in her. More shots shattered his calm and sheer rage brought him out from behind the rock. He fired the rifle, took a step forward, and fired again. "Come on, you bastards. Come down here and get me."

Maybe, just maybe, if he made enough noise and presented a seemingly easy target, he could draw the Apaches back this direction, away from the stage.

An arrow thunked into the sand just a foot in front of him. Another bullet whined past his ear. He ducked down and crawled on his belly to a thick mesquite. Sand had piled up around the roots and

354

trunk, providing good protection, at least from the south.

He raised his head and peered through the branches. The scar near his left eye twitched unmercifully. God, it looked like all twenty warriors were rushing him at once.

Kent took a deep breath, thumbed more bullets into his pistol, and rose to his knees. Hell, there was no sense in waiting for them to come and get him. A grin slashed his mouth as a rush of energy charged through his body. If he had to die, he was damned sure going to take a few Apaches with him.

A rifle fired directly behind him. He ducked. An Indian arched his back and flung his arms wide as he fell to the ground. The rifle spit again and another Apache clutched his stomach. Kent regained his senses, aimed his pistol and fired, aimed and fired.

He heard rocks grind together to his right and he swung around to find himself facing Miss Charleen McAllister.

"Scoot over, Windy. Air don't do much good at deflectin' them arrows."

He stared into wide, excited green eyes and a flushed red face. She was enjoying the battle. She was going to get herself killed. The damned woman was having the time of her life.

"Goddamn!"

Chapter Twenty-Two

A rifle report echoed across the valley. Kent dragged Charly to the ground and threw himself on top of her as a bullet whizzed past where her head had been.

"What in God's name are you doin' here, woman?"

Charly reached up and patted his cheek, pouting somewhat because now she was only—*woman*. Not honey. Not Miss Charly. Or even plain Charly. Woman. Harrumph! "Thought you were a smart man, Windy. I'm here to help you."

His eyes widened. His lips went numb. He sputtered, "H-help me? M-me?" Hell, he'd gotten into this mess expressly for the purpose of saving *her* precious hide. And *she* thought *he* needed help? Lord.

Looking down into her large, shimmering green eyes, so filled with defiance and . . . fear . . . sent a shiver of terror crawling down his backbone like a slithering snake. He wasn't afraid for himself—he'd flirted with death many times. But he couldn't face the thought of Miss Charly's fiery spirit being snuffed out as quickly or easily as a candle flame.

She meant too much to him, no matter their misunderstandings and differences of opinion. She was a strong lady, with her own sense of what was fair and right. He'd been wrong in trying to impose his will on her. Very wrong.

An arrow thudded into the ground, spraying sand into his face. He shook his head and quickly sighted his pistol. Later he could try to make amends. Right now, the Apaches seemed hellishly determined to cut their lives short.

Charly grunted and squirmed from beneath Kent's body. She flipped onto her stomach and rested the barrel of her rifle on a sturdy branch. Picking her targets carefully, she began to fire.

The direness of the situation wasn't lost on her. She just couldn't go off and leave him alone. It hadn't been a matter of making a choice. Even if it meant her life, she'd *had* to come back.

Kent took a deep breath to calm his temper and stretched out beside her. Later—there were a lot of things they had to settle *later*. But the sight of nine or ten bronzed bodies glistening in the afternoon sun did little to keep his hope alive that a *later* would ever come about.

Suddenly, two Apaches broke into the clearing on Kent's left. He saw the movement and rolled to face the charge. His bullet took down one Indian, but the other was on top of him before he had a chance to fire again. A searing pain lanced his left side. Instinctively, he clamped his elbow down, pinning the Apache's hand, which still gripped a bloody knife.

He jabbed his right fist into the Indian's face and felt the crunch of bone against his knuckles. Drawing his arm back, he landed another powerful punch to the warrior's stomach. A heavy weight tugged against his left side, shooting another jolt of pain through his body. Unclenching his arm, he allowed the unconscious Indian to fall to the ground.

A blood-curdling yell echoed in the air behind Kent. He spun as an Indian leaped over the mesquite ree and hovered over Charly. The Apache hesitated a split second, as if stunned to find his adversary was a woman.

The fingers on Kent's left hand had gone numb. He tried to lift his arm, but couldn't. The Apache grinned and raised his war club. A helpless, sinking sensation prompted Kent to close his eyes, but he caught the glint of something in Charly's hand and held his breath when it disappeared into the Indian's chest. A gurgling groan was the Apache's last war cry.

Charly yanked the knife from the dead warrior and turned to face more attackers. Her eyes collided with Kent's for the barest moment, just long enough to read the regret . . . and something more . . . much more . . . shining there. Then he staggered over and they stood shoulder to shoulder to face the last charge. There were just more Apaches than the two of them could handle. Painted faces surrounded them, barely ten yards away. Yipping voices resounded down the valley.

"Bye, Windy."

"Charly, I—"

A ghostly sound blended with the war cries. Charly cocked her head, convinced she heard a bugle. A bugle? It couldn't be. Her wishful imagination was playing tricks on her.

Kent dropped the now useless pistol and with his right hand picked up a fallen warrior's war club. He swung, connecting the stone with a leaping Apache's face. The Indian's momentum propelled his body into Kent and they both went down.

Kent's fear for Charly, the unpalatable thought of leaving her alone, gave him the strength he needed to wield the club again and finish the job quickly.

But as he crawled wearily to his knees and focused on the remaining Apaches creeping relentlessly toward them, one thought rose uppermost in his mind: Charly. She mustn't be alive when they finished with him.

Nausea churned his stomach. Sweat burned his eyes. She was looking at him with such trust. She knew. She accepted. God, what a woman!

He raised his arm. A drop of blood fell from the club and soaked into the sand, leaving a small, round stain. The muscles in his arm shook violently. A shudder racked his body, and he saw that she trembled, too. He couldn't. He had to.

"Wait!" Charly's eyes opened wide. She pointed to their left.

Kent's head felt funny. He wondered if it was possible for his stomach to turn cartwheels. His arm wavered. Charly's face blurred in and out of focus. But he had to protect her. He couldn't fail her now. It would be quick. Clean. No pain.

"Kent, listen. Horses. Lots of horses. The Indians are leaving. Look, Kent. It's the cavalry." And this time the bugle rang out loud and clear. Another shudder rippled down her spine—a shudder of intense relief.

Kent staggered sideways. He blinked and wiped the sweat from his brow on his sleeve. Yes, now he could see. The flag unfurled and he saw . . . Damn! He grabbed Charly's hand and thought he'd started to run. But his legs felt like lead. Her hand slipped through his fingers. Dark. Why was it so dark?

Charly screamed when Kent began to fall. She tried to catch him, but his superior height and weight were too much for her and they both sagged to the ground. When she pulled her hands from around his waist, one came away sticky with blood. For the first time, she noticed the red stains on his shirt.

She gasped once, before panic gagged her. Moisture trickled down her cheeks. Lordy, she thought fleetingly, swiping at the tears, she'd cried more since meeting up with that scoundrel than she had in her

360

entire life.

The jangle of bits and clinking of sabers drew her worried gaze. Her mouth dropped open but, again, her throat refused to work. She'd been right. It was the cavalry. In gray uniforms. And there, in front of them all, staring intently down at her, wearing a long, dark duster, sat Miles Cavanaugh. Miles!

A groan from Kent wiped all thoughts of gray or blue, Confederate or Union, from her mind. She didn't care about any of that war stuff now. Kent was wounded and needed help. Her eyes beseeched the man she'd thought of as her good friend. "Help me, Miles. Please."

Miles signaled his men to dismount and handed his reins to the nearest soldier. Charly glanced briefly at the sergeant's familiar face. She frowned, but Kent moved and immediately commanded her attention.

Peeling soft, deerskin gloves from his hands, Miles asked, "What happened here, Charleen? When did you find Ashford? And how'd the two of you get caught out here with the Apaches, alone?"

The way he continued studying the valley, Charly got the impression that there was something else he wanted to ask, but that he had decided against it. Her mind worked furiously, trying to figure out just what she could, or should, say. Now that she'd seen Miles in a uniform, some of the questions he'd put to her before began to make sense.

She raised her chin and glared at him, wondering how he could stand there so calmly while she was falling apart. "This man saved my life, Mr. Cavanaugh. He could bleed to death before I finish answerin' all your durned questions."

Miles glanced over his shoulder. "Sergeant, send the doctor forward, immediately."

"Yes, sir." The red-haired man saluted, then sent Charly a wicked leer behind Miles' back. She shivered. What was it about that man . . . Where had

361

she seen him before?

Miles sighed. "Mr. Cavanaugh, now, is it?" His eyes wandered lazily over Kent's inert form. "My dear, I assure you, we want to keep that man alive every bit as much as you do."

Charly's brows puckered. What did he mean by that?

Miles slapped the folded gloves against his leg. "I had expected that you'd be with a stage. Where is it?"

The hair on the back of her neck prickled. Yes, he'd tried to help her find Kent the other night, so he knew she was taking out a stage, or planned to. But this Miles didn't act like the Miles she'd befriended. She suddenly didn't trust him with the truth.

Her mind whirled. Hadn't Kent mentioned something about having horses nearby? Maybe she could get away with a tiny lie. Well, all right, a granddaddy of a lie. "What stage? You know the mail line's nearly severed. Kent, ah, Mr. Ashford, 'n' I, decided to, ah, scout around fer . . . for . . . a better trail near Apache Pass, just in case the Overland Mail ever starts up again. But . . . As you can see, we ran into a mite o' trouble."

Miles looked around the valley and up the slopes to his right and left. Several Apache bodies lay sprawled like broken dolls. "Really? You were just scouting?"

A dozen questions of her own warred for answers. Who was Miles Cavanaugh? Was he really a teacher? Why was he wearing that uniform?

But she just gulped and nodded. The doctor arrived, and she leaned over his shoulder to watch as he unbuttoned Kent's shirt. Then she winced and pulled back at the sight of the long, bloody gash on Kent's ribs.

The doctor glanced up at her. "Don't worry none, ma'am. He's lost a lot of blood, but the wound looks worse than it really is."

She sighed and smiled at the nice man, whose deep

drawl reminded her of relatives she'd met back in Tennessee. A sudden tingle down the back of her neck caused her to turn her head. She stared into green eyes very much the color of her own.

Blinking and shaking her head, she took an unsteady step sideways. "Rigo? Lordy, Rigo."

A dark, mustachioed man in a crisp uniform with lieutenant's bars came toward her. A smile curved his thin lips and lit up his swarthy features. He held out his arms.

Charly rushed into his embrace, clutching frantically, afraid he'd disappear if she ever let him go.

"Yes, baby sister. I'm here. Really."

She sniffed and started to wipe her nose on the back of her sleeve before she caught herself and reached into a pocket for her handkerchief. All the while she held on to him with her other hand. "I can hardly believe it. You've been gone so long. Five years, Rigo. An' you never wrote, or let me know where or how you were. I reckoned you were dead."

Another rakish grin slashed his handsome face. "Not me. You know better than that."

After replacing her handkerchief, she stepped back and eyed him from the crown of his wide-brimmed hat down his gray-clad body to his shiny, black boots. "What're you doin' in that get-up?"

He swatted dust from his pant leg. "I've been secretly workin' for Major Cavanaugh, although I just met him in person this week."

"Workin'? You mean spyin', don't you?" Her eyes narrowed. She turned her cold, green gaze on an interested Miles. "You've been usin' me, haven't you? Bet you got a real kick outta takin' in a poor little bumpkin."

Miles held out his hands. "No, Charleen. That's not the way it was at all. I never even realized who you were until I met your brother. Remember? I thought your name sounded familiar. Now we know why."

She stepped back, out of reach of both Rigo and Miles, confused by the mixed emotions raging through her. Elation. Fear. A sense of betrayal. The tug of loyalty. Of all things—loyalty. But to whom? Her brother? Miles? The man lying injured at her feet? Whom could she trust? Or dare she trust anyone?

A large hand wrapped around her ankle. She nearly jumped out of her skin at the unexpected pressure. Her gaze shot down and she found herself peering into glazed brown eyes. Trembling knees sank out from under her and she slumped down beside Kent. "H-how are you?"

Kent swallowed. "All . . . right."

From his pallid color and intense expression, she sensed that even that small motion had been painful for him. "You sure?"

His chin tucked down in a slight nod. Without thinking, she cupped his stubbled jaw in her palm. The chill that had shaken her heart thawed when he moved one side of his mouth into a tired smile. She felt drawn to Kent Ashford more now than ever before. He was the one stable, dependable factor in her life.

Until she found out what the Confederate troop was up to, what Miles was doin' at the head of it, and why he was treatin' Kent like some dangerous prisoner, she was goin' to stick to the city dandy like a hen to a nest of eggs. She wasn't going to risk losin' him now.

She looked up at Rigo and Miles, her expression grim. Her brother and the major had a lot to answer for.

During the next hour, the Confederates fixed a *travois* for Kent and rounded up the stallion and the mare. Charly hastily explained away the one saddle by figuring that the Apaches must've taken it and that the troop's arrival probably scared them

364

away before they could strip the other one.

Of course, *she* knew that the Indians would've taken the horses first, especially one as handsome as the stallion, if they'd found them. But she prayed that maybe the soldiers, new to the Southwest and Apache customs, wouldn't be aware of that fact.

Her eyes locked with Rigo's. He was frowning and seemed about to speak. Finally, he shook his head and turned away. Relief was a long time coming, though, as she watched Miles and waited. A cold layer of perspiration slicked her body before he nodded his acceptance of her story.

Two guards rode at either side of Kent's conveyance, so Charly rode back toward Tucson beside her brother. She sat stiffly in the saddle, still hurting because he hadn't trusted his family enough all these years to get in touch with them. And she told him so.

"I'm sorry, sis, but I couldn't. Most of the time I wasn't anywhere that I could send word, anyway. Then when it looked like I was going to be coming back to Tucson, I had to be real careful. There's a Union spy in town, and no one knows for sure who he is. It was just too dangerous to contact you, or even Pa or Ed."

Her chest rose and fell heavily. "So, you think there's really gonna be a war, do you?" She flinched at the excitement in her brother's voice as he expounded, "I *know* there will. In fact, we're expectin' to hear any day now that New Mexico Territory, including Arizona, of course, will be declared part of the Confederate States of America. Isn't that great?"

Charly's throat constricted. She was sorry, but she couldn't think of anything "great" about Americans fightin' one another.

Miles reined in beside her and Rigo dropped back, ignoring the silent plea in her eyes with a resigned shrug. Miles saluted. "Thank you, Lieutenant. I just

365

wish to speak with your sister for a few minutes, then you can have her back." To Charleen, he added, "I know it must be nice to be able to visit with your brother and catch up on old times."

She glared at him and shrugged.

He sighed. "You're angry. I'm not surprised."

"Who are you, Mister—or Major Miles Cavanaugh? What are you? Are you really a schoolteacher? Or was that just a convenient disguise?"

"I was a teacher, once, a long time ago."

The sadness in his voice and expression didn't deter her. "But not now. Now you're a goldurned Southern spy usin' gullible women like me to get your precious information, any way you can."

"I never intended to hurt you, Charleen. You must believe that."

Oh, sure, she thought. He'd just flattered her, making a backward nobody feel pretty and special. Why, for a while there, she'd actually believed she might be able to make herself into a lady, to be *somebody* to someone who cared. Ha! It was like tryin' to turn a hen into an eagle.

She shivered. In a whisper that no one could hear, she announced, "But you did hurt me. You did." Then in a stronger voice, she asked, "Why're you wearin' that uniform now?"

Miles shifted and straightened in the saddle. "Because it's time. It's time for the people of Tucson and New Mexico Territory to know that the South has her soldiers ready and in position to defend her people when the war begins."

There was pride and determination in his words, and such vehemence in the way that he delivered them, that Charly was convinced as never before. If everyone felt as strongly in their beliefs as Miles, on whatever side, there would definitely be a war. And the realization saddened her.

A young corporal trotted up to Miles and saluted.

"Major, sir. The prisoner's causin' trouble. He wants to get up and ride into Tucson."

"Prisoner! Prisoner?" Her suspicions had just been proven accurate. "He's talkin' about Windy . . . Mr. Ashford, isn't he? Why? What's he supposed to have done?"

Miles took a deep breath. "Calm down, Charleen. We're taking him in for questioning."

"Why? Tell me, you scum-eatin' varmint." Her hands clenched into fists. The mare shied sideways when she unconsciously jerked the reins.

Afraid Charleen's anger might cause her to do something foolish, Miles sighed, "All right. We've known for some time that there's a Union spy in Tucson. Day before yesterday, we received a description that fits your Mr. Ashford. *Now* can you understand why we want to question him?"

She winced and glanced away. Kent Ashford? A spy? No! She wouldn't believe it. He was nothin' but a drifter. He wouldn't, couldn't, be a part of this *war* mess. But a tiny niggle of doubt wormed its way into her heart. She'd always thought there was somethin' about him . . .

Charly chewed her lower lip. *If* he was a spy . . . Wouldn't that mean *he'd* been usin' her all along, too? Oh, no. Please, no.

"Corporal, tell Mr. Ashford that he is to remain where he is. If he causes any more trouble, tie him to the *travois*."

"Yes, sir."

Once the soldier had turned his horse and left, Charly said accusingly, "I thought you weren't certain that he's your spy."

"I just want to make sure he's still with us when we reach Tucson. Remember when we went looking for him the other night?"

She nodded. How could she forget?

"Well, you might not be concerned, but *I* want to

367

know where he'd disappeared to. I'm curious as to why he didn't tell you or your father, his employers, when he'd be back, in case you needed him."

Charly sighed deeply. She'd wondered about that, too. But then again, since the stage line had almost quit runnin', Kent might've thought there wasn't any reason to check in at the office.

"Then I learned that he'd returned to Tucson, and suddenly left again. By that time I'd also received that description of the spy I'd been looking for. So, I decided to follow him. Admit it, Charleen. The man's actions *are* suspicious."

Charly's chest expanded until she felt lightheaded. Miles had just relieved her mind about *one* thing. If Kent was the only reason the soldiers had come in this direction, it meant that they didn't have any real *proof* that a stage or a shipment of mail was headed toward St. Louis. She glanced in that direction. Maybe, if their luck would only hold . . .

Miles cleared his throat. "I was wondering . . . Do you know someone named Chip Perkins?"

Her brows drew together. "No. Never heard of him. Why?"

"No reason. Just thought he might be someone you'd met. A passenger on the stage, or perhaps a newcomer in Tucson."

She cocked her head to the side and studied this strange, different Miles. The Confederate soldier. "Or perhaps he could be another spy? You don't give up easy, do you, Major?"

Reining her horse around, she rode back to check on Kent. Maybe she could do something to keep him from gettin' himself killed before they reached Tucson. But as she neared the rear of the column, shouts and curses turned the air blue. She spurred the mare into a lope. Just ahead, she saw the black stallion. Several soldiers stood with their guns drawn and aimed toward the *travois*.

She rode up even with the group and slid her horse to a stop so quickly its hind hooves cut two furrows into the grass and dirt. Leaping to the ground, she ran to Kent. Her heart skipped a beat when she saw the fresh blood soaking his bandage. She marched over, shoved two young soldiers out of her way, and plopped on Kent's chest, effectively stifling his struggles.

"Miss Ch . . . McAllister," he roared. "Get the hell off me."

She calmly shook her head, trying to keep her balance and her dignity intact as he bucked beneath her. "I'll gladly move once you start behavin' like an adult instead of a spoiled brat." She mentally patted herself on the back for soundin' so sophis . . . sophisti . . . uppity and auth . . . authori . . . bossy. It must've worked, 'cause he'd gone as still as a stump.

Kent quit fighting. The brat had a lot of nerve to call *him* a brat, of all things. But, damn it, he didn't like being trussed up like a Christmas goose and treated like a baby when he could be riding. He was fine. Just fine.

The hoyden touched a rib near his wound and he nearly jumped off the *travois*. Well, maybe he wasn't *real* fine. He swallowed and asked her in as calm a tone as he could muster, "Can you tell me what in the hell is going on? And isn't that your *gentleman* friend in that officer's uniform? Huh?"

Her lips twitched. Men. Both of them had declared the other as *hers*. Thank you, but right now she wasn't sure she *wanted* either of them. But she did explain that Miles truly was a major in the Confederate Army and that he'd used the teaching position as a ploy to keep an eye on Southern interests in Tucson.

All the while she spoke, her mouth felt chalky. A telltale heat suffused her cheeks. She'd been one heck of a fool to be taken in so completely.

369

"So why's he taking me in? I thought I heard one of those . . . *children* . . ." He nodded toward the two young soldiers. "One of them said something about my being a prisoner." A muscle near his scar jerked. He didn't look her in the eye. "Am I? Am I their prisoner?"

She waited for his gaze to focus back in her direction before nodding. "Miles says he was sent a description of a Union spy who's supposed to be in Tucson."

"So? What's that got to do with me?" He swallowed and looked up at a dark thunderhead.

"He says you fit that description." She wound her fingers together in her lap.

"That's what *he* says, huh?"

She nodded.

Kent almost chuckled at the prim expression on her cute little face. Poor kid, what had happened to all those smiles and giggles he'd vowed to extract from her? But, at the moment, he guessed there wasn't much for either of them to laugh about.

Events had occurred faster than anyone could've predicted. With just one twist of words, he could be thrown from the ant hill into the cactus patch.

He couldn't tell her the truth. She'd know right away that he'd started out using her, just like her so-called *gentleman*. And he'd lose her. Yet, she was a smart woman. He'd lose her even faster if she figured everything out on her own. But . . . maybe by buying a little time, he'd be able to come up with a plan.

He took one of her hands in his. "Do you believe him? Do you think I'm a spy?" Her shoulders lifted and lowered and bent into a protective shield. His heart ached at the sight.

"I don't know what to believe anymore."

"Nothing we've been through together means anything to you, then?"

Charly rose from her position on his chest, though

she was tempted to stay right there, as close as she could get, forever. Instead, she just shook her head. "I'm not sayin' that. Dadburn it, you've saved my hide more'n once, and I appreciate it."

"That's not what I'm talking about, and you know it."

She looked toward the front of the column, ignoring him as she walked and led the mare beside the *travois*.

Kent narrowed his eyes at the interested gazes of the nearby soldiers and lowered his voice. "If I was the villainous person your *friend* has made me out to be, could you have done . . . have responded . . . the way you have to me?"

She sighed. The coyote had sure made his point. Surely she wouldn't have fallen in love with a man whose only purpose was to break down her defenses and gather information for a stupid war.

But Miles' deceit had wounded her deeply. No matter how badly she wanted to shout a fervent *No!* to his question, it *was* possible that Kent was evading the truth.

Then from out of nowhere, confusing her even further, Kent said, "You sure have looked pretty lately, in your dresses and all. And I've noticed how much you've improved your speech. Was it all for . . . the *gentleman?*"

She gasped. Her eyes locked with his. Sparks set off little explosions along her nerve endings. "N-no. Not *all* of it."

Kent nodded and smiled. He yawned and laid his head back. She hadn't said she'd done it for *him*, either, but somehow he felt reassured. A little of his natural arrogance returned. "Then you'll come visit if they lock me up."

Charly frowned. "They wouldn't do that, would they?"

He cocked his brow and those dratted sparks set off

371

a prairie fire in her stomach. "I-I'll come visit."

"Good."

Although Kent had tried to prepare her, Charly still couldn't believe it when they rode into Tucson and Miles ordered his soldiers to take Kent to jail.

"No, Miles. You can't do that."

"Yes, my dear, I can." He slapped the dust from his hat, then brushed his lapel with the backs of his fingers.

"But he's not your spy. He isn't." She desperately tried to convince herself that Kent was innocent, that he wasn't the man Miles was seeking. And if Miles would only release Kent . . .

"Let's just say that I'm going to keep your friend where I can find him in a hurry." He patted the white-knuckled fingers gripping his arm. "He'll be where the doctor can check his wound regularly, and he'll get plenty of rest."

"Well, I guess that wouldn't be so bad." She knew there'd be little chance of keeping a man like Kent down long enough for his wound to heal properly. But jail? An uneasy feeling settled into the pit of her stomach. Something wasn't quite right.

Finally, she looked into Miles' alert gray eyes and nodded. Heading toward the stage station, she tried to put Kent out of her mind for a while. She was anxious to speak with her pa and see if he'd heard anything about Ed and if he'd gotten the mail as far as Apache Pass.

And wait until she told her pa about Rigo! He'd be so surprised.

Jed McAllister was sitting behind his desk, heels propped on the dusty surface, arms raised and folded behind his head. Soft gurgles and snorts drifted across the room. Charly grinned. Things in the office were back to normal.

A brisk wind sucked the door closed with a loud bang. Jed's feet thudded to the floor. He looked up at her and Charly noticed the clear whites of his eyes. He was sober. "Howdy, Pa."

"Was wonderin' when ya was gonna get back, gal. Glad ya made it safe and sound."

She blinked. "You are?"

"'Course I am. Yore my daughter, ain't ya?"

"Yeah." She plunged her hands into her back pockets. Before she got all misty-eyed, she changed the subject. "What about Ed? Heard from him?"

Jed nodded. "Yep. Got the telegraph workin' yestiddy. Yore brother's on his way back now. Says he don't know how far it'll get, but the mail's on its way."

"That's great." Excitement bubbled through her veins. It might be the last mail to get through to the East, and she'd had a part in it.

"Reckon there's gotta be somethin' good happenin'."

She caught the despondency in his voice. She'd been about to tell him about Rigo, but decided to wait. "What, Pa? What's happened since I've been gone?"

He took a folded paper from his desk and handed it to her. She opened it and began to read. Her eyes grew wider with each word. At last, she sank onto the desktop. "No."

Jed shoved his chair away from the desk. "'Fraid it's true. I checked with some o' the other stations. The Butterfield contract's done been annulled."

Chapter Twenty-Three

Charly scowled. "Annulled? What's that?"

Jed hooked his thumbs in his suspenders. "It means they done cancelled the contract. The Overland Mail ain't gonna be operatin' no more."

Her shoulders slumped. Surely someone had made a mistake. She'd . . . they'd all worked so hard. And she loved her job. Just 'cause they'd run into a few hard times, didn't mean the durned Confederates were goin' to stop the line completely. *They* needed mail, too.

Her chin jutted out. "Someone's got a little antsy, is all, Pa. The mail's gonna run again, soon's the . . ." Her voice faded as her pa kept shaking his head.

"Ain't no way in hell, gal. This southern route already be a thousand miles longer than it oughta. Nobody's makin' any money on the deal. An' over in Texas, the Confederates are confiscatin' livestock and cartin' off equipment. The Butterfield Overland Mail ain't never gonna be no more."

She closed her eyes and rubbed her aching forehead.

"If'n we ain't keerful, gal, they's gonna do the same thin' here. We got lots of good stock jus' standin' in them corrals, an' a couple stages that're

375

bet'r'n new."

Suddenly, Charly slid off the desk. Spit and fire and defiance tensed every muscle in her body. "They dadgum better not try it, or—"

The door opened and Rigo McAllister stepped inside the room, a sheepish expression on his handsome features. Yet Charly noted the hint of a smile crinkling his eyes and the corner of his lips when he saw her and their pa.

Jed stared at the uniformed soldier. Then he blinked and took a step forward. The next moment he had his oldest son wrapped in a bear hug strong enough to crack ribs. "By God, son, I like ta didn't know ya."

Rigo slapped his father on the back and strode over to grab up his baby sister. "There. I couldn't do that out on the trail, so I've gotta make up for lost time."

Charly grinned and kissed his cheek. Her lips brushed the tip of his long mustache. "Since when did ya . . . you start growin' hair on your face?" Some of her happiness faded as she thought of Kent and the bushy hair growing on *his* upper lip—and remembered how much she liked the feel of it on her bare flesh when . . .

Rigo just shrugged as an answer to her question and was quickly maneuvered aside as Jed stepped forward to glare at his daughter. "Ya knowed yore brother was in Tucson an' ya didn't tell yore old man? What's the matter with ya, gal?"

"I was goin' to, Pa, but we got to talkin' 'bout other things." She spun to face Rigo with her legs braced wide apart. "You soldiers aren't gonna take over our livestock and stuff, are you?"

Rigo shook his head. "To be honest, I don't know what the major has in mind." He chucked her under the chin, the way he used to do when she was just a little thing. Bright red color flushed her cheeks and he grinned. "But I'll see what I can do."

She threw herself into his arms again.

He chuckled. "I didn't make any promises. Remember that."

"Yeah." But this was her older brother. Her hero. He could do anything. Maybe even . . . "Rigo?"

"Yes?"

"How's Windy . . . I mean, Mr. Ashford? Are they treatin' him all right? Is his wound real bad? Is—"

"Whoa. Hold on a minute." Rigo took a firm grip on her shoulders and held her so that he could see her face. "Why are you so concerned about that man? Just who is he? And what's he got on you?"

"Got on me? Nothin'." Her brows grew together, furrowing her forehead. "Pa gave him the job as my conductor, is all. I just don't like seein' him hurt or mistreated."

"Uh-huh."

She stuck out her chin. "What do you mean, *uh-huh?*"

"Just, uh-huh."

"Pa, tell him he ain't . . . doesn't have any call to act so smug an' uppity. Tell him *you* hired Windy, and that . . . that . . ." But her pa was giving her the same considering look as her brother.

"Don't know, gal. Ain't never seen ya so het up over a fella a'fore. 'Specially no hired hand."

Her jaws worked, but nothing seemed to come past the lump in her throat. She backed toward the door. All of a sudden the walls were closing in on her. Her family's grinning faces mocked her feelings. "Go on and grin. Make fun of me. But you're gonna eat them foolish words when he leaves town—alone."

She turned and rushed through the door.

Rigo called after her. "Go on over and see how he is for yourself. Bet he could stand to see a friendly, adoring face about now."

Charly covered her ears and ran toward the barn. But when she stepped inside, the welcoming warmth she always found there seemed to have evaporated. Since the stages had all but quit running, most of the drivers had drifted on to other towns and other jobs. The lantern in the back swung in the slight breeze her entrance had created, dark and forbidding. Bales of hay and straw were stacked neatly atop one another. And no matter how hard she listened, she couldn't hear the sounds of good-natured joshing or the soft shuffling of cards.

Walking over to one of the many empty stalls, she slid down the support beam to sit in a pile of fresh, fragrant straw. Sharp stalks bit into the seat of her pants and she squirmed to find a comfortable spot.

Thoughts of Kent and Miles and her family and the mail line flooded into her mind, nearly overwhelming her. Miles, her friend, had deceived her. Her beloved brother had returned, but as a soldier in the Confederate Army. And Windy—Kent—was in jail accused of being a Union spy.

She sighed. Truth be told, she didn't quite know what to think of Kent, what to believe. Yet her heart was connected to him. He would always be a part of her life, no matter where he went, or what he did, or why he did it.

Slowly she pushed to her feet. Yes, maybe she should go see him, just to find out how he was. Just to let her eyes feast on his handsome features one more time.

Kent stood at the tiny jail window, gazing through the bars, remembering the first time he'd been locked in that same cell. Things had been a lot different then. Charly had been on the other side, and then in here—with him. He'd almost enjoyed himself.

But not this time. Two soldiers sat at the desk with the constable, playing cards and grumbling about having been left on duty while the rest of the troop had the run of the town. Kent grimaced, thinking of all the mischief the soldiers could cause.

And he wondered what the *gentleman* was up to, if the major was having any luck making amends to Miss Charly. A brief flicker of his lips was as close to a smile as he could come as he recalled Charly's reaction to being duped by the Southerner. Getting back into her good graces wasn't going to be easy for Miles. That thought increased his urge to smile.

He watched as Constable Ortega stood up and stretched and then lit the lantern. His gaze switched toward the window again and he realized that while he'd been standing there, staring at nothing, the sun had set. Dark clouds blotted the remaining brilliant rays of the sun. He shuddered. The night was going to be as cold and dark as sin.

Rubbing at the tight bandage across his ribs, he wished he could take a deep breath. The damned thing itched like hell, and he'd have given the rest of the money in his saddlebags to have had a bath before being wrapped up.

The constable approached Kent's cell. He heard the thud of boots and turned to face Roberto Ortega.

"Good evening, señor. Why you have come back so soon?"

Kent shrugged. "You have such a cozy place here, I just couldn't stay away."

"Ah, you make thee joke, no?" Constable Ortega looked out at the black night. "Thee streets I must wrap up. Soon, your *comida*—supper—weel come. You weel like, no?"

Remembering the last meal he'd had in the jail, Kent agreed with the constable. "No." But he nodded and twitched his lips in a slight grin as Roberto turned to leave.

The constable hadn't been gone five minutes when a light tap sounded on the closed door. One of the soldiers cursed and reluctantly put his cards face down on the table. Even as he walked toward the door, the young Confederate kept a close watch over his shoulder.

Kent sat down on his cot, thinking it was hell when a man couldn't trust his comrade not to cheat when his back was turned.

The door swung open to admit the same little round, pleasant-faced woman who'd brought his meal over six weeks ago. She carried a large tray that suddenly rattled and then began to dip. The soldier quickly recovered it and placed it on the desk.

The aroma filtering across the room caused Kent's stomach to grumble. He grimaced. It appeared the meal would be a repeat.

After the woman took her leave, the soldier who'd taken the tray stared at the three bowls of watery beans and the plate of tortillas. "Damn, but I'm hungrier than a starved hound. Think anyone'd know or care if we keep the spy's portion?"

The other soldier cleared away the cards, making more room for the food. "None of that kind of talk, Beau. You know what the lieutenant said. The major wants this'n taken real good care of."

"Yeah, well, still—"

"Feed the man, 'fore you do somethin' stupid that'll get us both in trouble. If you hadn't gone and got us locked up in that last little burg we went through, we'd probably be out there havin' a good time tonight. Now give him the food."

The man called Beau muttered all the way over to the cell, balancing the bowl in one hand, fumbling the keys in the other.

Kent licked his lips. His muscles tensed, causing him to grimace, but he remained alert, watching the other soldier whose back was turned while he set the bowls on the desk. Scooting to the edge of his cot, Kent studied the situation and calculated his odds. Neither soldier seemed too concerned that a hungry, wounded prisoner might try to leave their charming company, especially before enjoying the "wonderful" meal.

Well, maybe they'd understand what he was going to do once they tasted the stuff.

"Come 'n' get it." Beau stood in the cracked doorway.

Kent attempted to stand, groaned, and sank back down. He tried again. His breath came in harsh gasps. "Can't. Hurts."

"I ain't a damned slave, ya know," the soldier mumbled as he walked to the cot.

Kent lifted his arm. His hand trembled as he took the bowl. "Gee, thanks."

The soldier turned and started back to the open door. Kent carefully set the bowl on the floor. Stealthily, he rose to his feet. His feet slid noiselessly over the floor.

Beau hesitated and started to turn. Kent's right arm snaked around the man's narrow chest and up so that his palm covered the soldier's mouth. Kent's left hand groped for the Confederate's gun. At last his fingers curled around the butt. Withdrawing it from the holster, he raised the barrel and brought it down in a swift chop to the side of the soldier's head. There was a muffled grunt. Kent held his breath as he lowered the unconscious man to the ground.

"Hey, Beau, hurry it up, will you? This looks good."

The second soldier laid the tray to one side. Then his eyes grew wide when the tray lifted, as if with a life of its own, and crashed into his face. He fell to his knees, then toppled onto his side.

Kent took both soldiers' guns and grabbed his coat from the peg. Throwing open the door, he raced outside.

"Ouch. Dadblame it, watch where you're goin'."

"Hell!"

Charly was caught by surprise when the door came

381

swinging open and a huge figure lunged out at her. She went down in a tangle of arms and legs.

"Ooofff." Air gushed from her lungs as the person landed squarely on top of her.

"Hellfire, woman. Let me up."

Charly's arms had instinctively closed around the solid set of shoulders in a desperate gesture to save herself. Kent's muscles rippled beneath her fingers, but she immediately dropped her arms at his barked command.

"Goldurn, Windy. I gotta have some help. It's kinda hard to keep my feet when a steam engine rolls over me."

Kent managed to crawl to his feet, nursing his tender side. He tripped over one of Charly's feet. Suddenly, his arms were taken in a very hard, very rough masculine grip. He felt the guns being lifted from his waistband.

He looked back to see the bloodied features of the soldier whom he'd cold-decked with the tray. But the man holding him up was none other than the *gentleman* himself.

"Well, Mr. Ashford. Is there some particular reason you were so anxious to turn down our hospitality?"

"Yeah. I don't much care for your cooking. It's enough to make a man run for his life."

Charly scrambled unsteadily to her feet, feeling as if every inch of her body had been squashed by a ton of lead. Yet every bit of her tingled and throbbed from the brief contact with Kent's muscular body.

She dusted off the seat of her britches and looked up to see him being held between Miles and another worse-for-wear soldier. Her eyes registered shock as she realized Kent was out of jail.

Kent glowered at her. Heat climbed up her neck and over her cheeks. "Wh-what happened?"

Miles smiled. "Looks as though you just foiled an escape attempt, my dear. We're very grateful to you."

"But I—"

"Private, take this man back inside. It appears he's even more clever and dangerous than I suspected. Tie him to his cot if you have to, but make sure nothing like this happens again. Lucky for you, Miss McAllister came along at the right time."

"Yes, sir." The private saluted, then grabbed Kent and shoved him back into the jail.

Charly was speechless. Miles made it sound like she'd purposely stopped Kent from escaping. She blanched as she sought his eyes one last time. He was looking back over his shoulder. She cringed at the accusation in his cold brown eyes. Surely he didn't believe . . .

Miles took her elbow, but she yanked her arm away. "Don't. Don't touch me, you yellow-bellied . . . Confederate."

"Please, give me a chance to show my appreciation, pretty lady. You may have saved us all considerable grief by stopping that man. After what he tried just now, I'm certain he's our spy."

Miles reached out and captured a long strand of hair that had worked its way from under her hat. He rubbed the fine end between his fingers. "You know I never meant to hurt you, Charleen. I care for you very much, and I've enjoyed our evenings together, more than I ever imagined I could. If only you would find it in your heart to forgive me . . . During times of war, a man sometimes has to do . . . things. Things that—"

"I haven't heard that war's been declared yet, have you?" She stared at him unblinkingly.

He had the grace to blush and she felt somewhat mollified.

"No, not yet. But it will be. Soon."

"That's just dandy. Must make you real happy."

"No. Not at all." He humbly shook his head, then walked over to stand in the jail's doorway. He looked at her, his eyes filled with regret. "I *am* sorry, Charleen. Truly, I am."

Charly sat behind her pa's desk in the Overland office. She'd lost track of time, but figured she'd been there several hours. It didn't much matter, there wasn't anythin' else to do—except think. And she'd been thinkin' so hard her head hurt.

Another fantasy had been destroyed that evening. By trying to escape, Kent might as well have written "SPY" on his forehead for everyone to see. Miles was certain Kent was the man he'd been searching for, and so was she. Now.

His actions had also confirmed her suspicions that—like the low-down cur, Miles—Kent had only been using her. And she'd never felt so devastated. So alone. So lonely. Her heart ached so that she thought she might be sick.

It was bad enough, bein' betrayed by a friend, but when the man you loved took your heart and soul, chewed them up and spit them back at you . . . Well, she couldn't think of words terrible enough to describe her feelings.

The door squeaked open. She blinked and scrubbed her cheeks with the sleeve of her coat.

"Sis? What's going on?" Rigo rubbed his hands up and down his arms. "It's freezing in here. How come you haven't built a fire?"

She shook her head.

He sauntered over and sat down on the edge of the desk. "It's that Ashford fella, isn't it?"

She shrugged.

"I heard what happened this evening."

Charly plucked at a thread hanging from the end of her sleeve.

"Well, his days of causing you, or anyone else, misery are over. Pretty soon, he'll be out of your life for good." He cocked his head and shrewdly watched her carefully blank features crack like the surface of a dry pond.

She gulped. A muscle in her cheek jerked. "Wh-what? What do you . . . mean?"

He pursed his lips. "Oh, I just heard somethin'. But you wouldn't be interested. Kent Ashford doesn't mean anything to you. Right?"

"Right. He's nothin' but a no-account . . . spy." She cleared her throat.

Rigo drew out his knife and began to whittle on a block of wood Jed kept on his desk for a paper-weight.

Although the familiar sight brought back wonderful memories of the many animals and toys he'd carved for her over the years, she was too intent on thinkin' of ways to find out what her brother knew about Kent to watch the slow, suddenly annoying, process. Finally she decided just to ask him straight out. "Wh-what've you heard? What're they gonna do with him?"

All sorts of horrible punishments were taking form in her mind. After all, Kent *had* tried to escape. But he was hurt. His wound hadn't begun to heal. They couldn't . . .

"I guess the major thinks your Mr. Ashford is a dangerous criminal. Says he's going to send the spy to a Confederate prison in Texas."

Charly jumped to her feet. The chair skittered out behind her. "The dadblamed idjit! Why, I'll squash him like the blood-suckin' skeeter he is."

"Who? The no-account spy or the dadblamed idjit?" He pressed his lips tightly together.

Exasperated that Rigo could be so hard-headed, she shot a fist under his nose. "Your damned major, that's who. He's walkin' on thin ice, that'n is."

Charly stormed to the door, then turned and smiled at her brother. She had a notion that his

385

appearance in the office hadn't been accidental. "Thanks, Rigo. I owe you."

Charly ducked into the nearest alleyway and stopped long enough to catch her breath and gather her scattered wits. She stood as still as a granite boulder, her feet too leaden to budge. Her teeth ground together until her temples throbbed. So, Miles was going to send Windy to a Confederate jail in Texas, was he?

The bottom dropped out of her heart. Kent would be leaving Tucson, all right. But not because he wanted to.

Then anger stiffened her spine and hardened her jaw. Anger at Miles. At Kent. At herself.

Spy or no, she couldn't let the man she loved rot in that prison. Cold chills ran up and down her spine at the thought of what they might do to him there.

Why she even cared anymore was beyond her understanding, but no matter her hurt and disillusionment, she'd never be able to live with the knowledge that *she'd* been responsible for his capture.

The choice had been taken from her; it was now up to her to set him free.

Late that night, unable to sleep for worrying about Kent, Charly was in the barn sorting stacks of tack. She was bending over a large wooden box, one foot barely balanced on the ground, when someone tapped her on the bottom. She reared up so fast that she banged her head on the heavy lid.

Behind her, a male voice chuckled, "Didn't mean ta scare you."

Her fuzzy vision cleared enough to find her brother, Ed. Her pulse began to beat again. "Dangnab it,

Ed, you took ten years off my life." She hid the rapid pounding of her heart beneath her spread palm.

"I saw a light an' thought that someone must be up to no good. What're you doin' in here, anyway?"

She cocked one brow. Ed? Worried about somethin'? Usually, once he left work, the animals or the tack or the other equipment never seemed to cross his mind again until the next day.

"Guess with all the Confederates around, I was just worried."

"Hmmm." He narrowed his eyes. There was something about Charleen that wasn't right. She was too tense. Too evasive. "You still haven't told me what you're doin'."

"Just lookin' around. Decided to repair some of the tack and keep an eye on the place tonight." She darted her eyes to Ed, to a wall peg, then toward the barn door.

Ed sat down on a stack of straw and folded his arms. "I'm not goin' til you tell me the right of it."

She gave him a long, considering look, then sighed. "All right. I'm lookin' for somethin' to use to help me break a man out of jail." Maybe he'd think she was jokin' and go on about his business.

"What?" Ed was on his feet, standing nose to nose with her in less time than it took for a frog to fall off a lily pad.

She jutted out her chin. "You heard me."

"Yeah, I sure did. I just can't *believe* what I heard. What fool shenanigans are you up to?"

"It isn't a joke, Ed. I'm gonna bust Windy, my conductor outta that jail."

"Why, for God's sake?"

She rubbed the back of her neck and began to pace. "'Cause Miles is gonna send him to a Texas prison. An 'cause I can't let that happen."

"You love the man that much, do ya?"

She stopped and stood perfectly still. Her fingers

387

wound together. She whispered, "Yes."

Ed nodded. "Then what's your plan?"

"P-plan?"

"Yeah. What're ya lookin' for in there?" He tilted his head toward the box. "How're you goin' ta pull it off?"

"Well, don't reckon I know for sure . . . yet."

"How long've we got?"

"We?"

"Ya don't think I'm goin' to let my little sister have all the fun, do ya?"

She swallowed a lump as hard and sticky as a prickly pear cactus. It hurt so badly goin' down that her eyes misted. "Rigo seemed to think . . . a couple of days. But don't you go blabbin' about this to anyone. We could get Rigo in a mess of trouble."

Worry furrowed her brows. Rigo had taken a big risk to let her know about Miles' plans for Kent. And she wouldn't do anything to put his life in danger.

She grimaced and kicked at a dried mound of manure. Until now she'd thought everyone was just giving her a hard time about the city dandy. Dang it, were her feelings for the man really *that* easy to read? Her gaze shifted to Ed. Well, it was pretty obvious that if *he* was aware of the depth of her emotions, anyone could figure out she loved the man.

Ed was spellbound, watching the changes in his sister's expressions and body motions. Finally, he realized she was staring at him. "You don't need to remind me about Rigo. He's my brother, too, ya know. Ahem, guess we better get busy and think of somethin' fast."

She nodded as Ed put his arm around her shoulder and started walking her toward the door. Gradually, her arm crept around his waist.

A little over twenty-four hours after Charly and Ed

had had their conversation, Kent was dozing fitfully in his cell. He had just turned over and was scratching groggily at his scar when a loud commotion in the street snapped his eyes open.

Constable Ortega, muttering several Spanish words that Kent was certain he didn't want to know the meaning of, stomped into his boots before rising from the bunk in the next empty cell where he'd been resting.

A different shift of soldiers left their card game to stand at the window, trying to see what was happening. The older of the two, a red-headed, stockily built man, cursed. "Little early for the boys ta be cuttin' the wolf loose, ain't it?"

"Not for me, it ain't," said the freckle-faced, blond-haired boy. "Watchin' a sick, helpless prisoner in a dirty little cell ain't 'xactly my idea of havin' a good time. Wish we was out there with 'em."

Loud, boisterous voices drifted into the jail through the cracks in the door.

"Hey, Jimmy. Slow down, will ya?"

"Shore, Vicente, but why?"

"'Cause I heard there be a couple o' them there 'Federate boys lazin' 'round in the jail."

"Yeah? I heerd that, too. Hic. Whatcha reckon they's doin' in there tonight, Ed?"

Kent sat up. He shrugged his shoulder muscles, trying to ease the strain on his arms. His hands had been tied behind his back, except to eat, since he'd tried to make his escape. Despite the stinging pull on his joints, he tried to see out of the window, too.

He'd heard the deliberate use of the name *Ed*. But if it *was* Charly's brother, he was probably just out sewing a few wild oats and raising a ruckus for the hell of it.

The soldiers looked at each other and shuffled restlessly.

Again the voices filtered into the small room.

389

"Reckon they's sittin' on their soft asses, like they do all day on them big ole plantations, sippin' their lemonade an' watchin' other folks do their work."

"Haw! Haw! Ya think that's what them sissies is a-doin'? Settin' in there on their fat asses?"

By now the revelers had come even with the window. Kent counted four of them, staggering, their arms thrown over each other's shoulders. Then they moved on, out of his line of vision.

Constable Ortega had come up to stand in the doorway, and he blocked the exit as the soldiers, who looked to be only poor farmers affronted at being compared to high-class gentry, tried to push past him. "The horses you hold, no? Thees business, I weel handle."

The red-haired soldier cursed and replaced his gun in his holster. Both of the southerners muttered and looked at Kent, but they remained inside. Kent favored them with a wide smile the next time they scowled in his direction, which set off a round of colorful oaths.

Kent stared at the redhead. Every time the man had been on duty, Kent had studied him. There was something about him . . . something dangerous and sinister. And something familiar about the way he held his crippled hand—that disturbed Kent.

After the room had quieted, he cocked his head and caught snatches of fading conversation between the constable and the revelers. Suddenly, it sounded like one of the drunks had run back to the jail, for his voice came from just outside the window. "What'd I tell ya, boys? Them soldiers sent one poor Mex out ta do their work. Yeah, they's sissies, all right. Stayin' inside, keepin' them fancy uniforms all clean an' pretty."

The door to the jail slammed open as the redhead fell over the blond soldier on his way outside. Kent heard the solid thwack! of a fist hitting flesh and winced.

Eyes glued to the door, Kent was hardly surprised when a slight, dark figure slipped into the opening. The tall, slender person hesitated until someone, who appeared to be one of the revelers, ran up and dropped something that jingled like keys into an outstretched hand. Then the second person disappeared amidst the sounds of scuffles and grunts, leaving only the dark form silhouetted against the night.

Then the person came closer. From the graceful, swaying walk, Kent figured it damned sure wasn't young Ed. He just set his jaw when Charly stopped in front of his cell and pushed back the brim of her hat.

"What in hell are you doing here, woman?"

Charly shrugged and began trying keys. She sighed. It didn't look like things had changed much. She was still *wo-man*. He was grouchier than ever. Finally, relief flooded through her as the lock clicked and the door swung open.

Kent was on his feet instantly and turned his back to her. Charly gasped when she saw his hands were tied. Even in the dim light, she detected black smudges around his bindings. Blood. Her stomach knotted. How long had they kept him like this?

She slipped her knife from her boot and cut the rope. Once he was free, Kent hurried over and found his gun in the bottom drawer of the desk, then grabbed his hat and coat from a wall peg. As a last precaution, he blew out the lantern.

Guiding Charly toward the door, he stepped in front of her when she would have darted outside, and carefully checked both ends of the street. A lot of people filed past, most of them heading toward the fight, which now encompassed at least twenty brawlers. No one paid particular attention to the jail.

Kent took Charly's hand. He slipped out the door and put his free arm around her shoulders, hurrying, but pretending they were just another couple

391

wondering what was going on. At the corner, he hesitated.

Charly stepped out of his grasp and moved into the dark shadows ahead of him. She tugged insistently on his hand. "Quit watchin' the durned fight. We gotta hurry. The horses are down this way."

They had just rounded the back corner when a shout rang out. "Thee prisoner. He ees escaped."

Uh-oh, Charly thought. Constable Ortega had gotten free of the melee sooner than they'd expected. And they still had a wide, open space to cross before reaching the trees where she'd hidden their horses.

They'd barely stepped away from the building when a bullet whined past, kicking up dust in front of her feet. She tried to duck, but Kent burst past, picking up speed as he dragged her behind him.

After they safely reached the trees, she gasped for air and tugged on his hand to get his attention. She pointed to their left. "Over there."

Kent quickly looked in the direction she indicated and found his stallion and her sorrel mare. The horses were saddled, with bulky bedrolls tied behind the cantles. But before he mounted, he grabbed Charly, shaking her harder than he'd intended, but determined to get his point through her thick skull. "If you come with me, you'll be a fugitive. You won't be able to come back."

She jerked free of his grasp and glared at him before turning and stalking to her mare. "If you hurry and get on that four-legged piece of crow bait and we get outta here now, before they catch up with us, no one'll suspect that I'm the one who turned you loose."

He grabbed the horn and swung into the saddle without using the stirrup. Hating to be the one to disavow her naive way of thinking, he hollered, "If you're waitin' on me, woman, you're foolin' around."

Chapter Twenty-Four

Kent Ashford and Charleen McAllister rode away from Tucson, the Confederate Army, and an irate Constable Ortega.

Charly headed east for several miles, then pulled the mare down to an easy jog and cut back south.

Kent followed, glad that she was too busy for conversation. Between moments of helping the stallion pick his way over the rocky terrain, he was battling his conscience. Without Charly, he never would have gotten out of Tucson a free man. He would be eternally grateful for her assistance.

On the other hand, he suffered terrible pangs of annoyance that not only had a *female* masterminded his escape, but that she was also the one familiar enough with the country to lead him to safety. His pride was all but shattered.

After a quick glance over his shoulder to check their back trail, he urged the stallion up beside Charly and the mare. "Where are we going?"

Charly shot him a superior look and said huskily, "Just set back an' watch. You'll see soon enough."

He ground his teeth, but managed to keep a tight rein on his temper. Arrogant brat. Yet since the moon had cleared the clouds and was almost full, he did begin to recognize the rough, hilly countryside.

Though they were approaching from a different direction than before, he knew exactly where she was headed.

The valley. The cave. Where they'd first held each other . . . and warmed their naked bodies. He glanced toward Charly and caught her peeking at him. She quickly looked away. The chill in his bones from the freezing, whipping wind became gradually less noticeable, replaced by a deep, inner warmth spreading from his lower body. Was she, too, recalling that night and the storm of unfulfilled passion they had created there?

If the night sky had suddenly opened into a violent display of jagged lightning or reverberating thunder, Charly couldn't have been any more aware of the man riding at her side and their intended destination.

Beneath the fringe of her dark lashes, she cast him another shy glance. Heat spiraled down her spine and leapt back to throb in her chest. He was looking at her—in that odd way he had of cocking his brow and quirking the left corner of his mouth toward the thin line of his scar.

Was he also thinking of that wild night when she'd been so cold and terrified as she lay in his arms and he'd warmed her—body and soul. Did he sense the depth of her feelings? Was he trying to figure a way to let her down gracefully, without causing a scene? Would coming to the valley just make it more difficult—for both of them?

No matter what he was thinking or feeling, she'd done what she had to do. And it had just occurred to her that since he was a wanted man, nothing awaited him in Tucson now but danger. All she'd done was speed up his departure.

She took a shaky breath and knew that she wouldn't have done anything differently. Sooner or later, Miles would've taken Windy from her. At least now she could be content, as if she would ever feel that emotion again, knowing he was free.

And then a little spark warmed her heart. Maybe every once in a while he'd remember that she'd been the one who helped him get away from Miles and his soldiers. Maybe he'd remember her with fondness, if nothing more . . .

Yep, her life would go on. She didn't need Mr. Kent Ashford. Charleen McAllister didn't need anyone.

Kent looked everywhere but at Miss Charly. His conscience was giving him fits again as he thought of all she'd sacrificed for him. Ever since their first encounter, she'd gone to great lengths to set things right. She'd given him her innocence. And now she'd given up her life.

Whether she wanted to face it or not, she'd now be an outcast in Tucson. With the Confederate Army in control, Southern sympathizers would feel free to declare their loyalties.

Oh, yes, Miss Charleen McAllister was some special lady. A stirring combination of a hoyden and a tomboy, a daredevil and a stunningly feminine beauty. The thought of never seeing her again pained him like a gaping wound in his chest.

And most importantly, how would she manage to keep from breaking her pretty neck, or getting trampled by a mule team or, maybe, even getting shot, without him around to look after her?

She needed him.

Descending the rocky slope into the valley, the riders were bathed in the eerie light of the moon. A sense of *déja vu* settled over the pair as they silently rode past the hidden cave and up to the shimmering pool. They dismounted and the horses greedily buried their noses in the cool water, sucking the liquid around their bits and splashing with their lower lips.

The mare stomped her front feet and took several

mincing steps forward until she was ankle deep in the pool. The horse would've gone farther if Charly hadn't backed her out. "Oh, no, you don't. You aren't gonna go for a swim tonight, especially with my saddle an' supplies strapped to your back."

Kent grinned when the mare tossed her head and mane in an obvious display of temper. "What about you, Miss Charly? *You* aren't carrying a bedroll. Want to go for a midnight dip?"

Charly broke out in chill bumps at the image she conjured in her mind of Kent and she, naked, their bodies slicing through the rippling, silvery surface of the pool. Their wet bodies would come together, all slippery and soft. Even now she could feel the pressure building—the heat . . . the . . . love.

"Miss Charly?"

She started. "Wh-what?" He was so close, his warm breath fanned her ear. How'd he been able to sneak up on her like that?

"You remember, too, don't you?"

She gulped. "Remember? Remember what?"

He traced his index finger along the downy curve of her cheek. "You know . . . what."

His deep, husky voice rasped seductively across every nerve ending in her body. She shivered. "We . . . we better strip the horses and hobble 'em outta . . . out of sight. Just in case."

Kent gazed thoughtfully over the still, empty valley, then turned his attention back to Charly. "You know what I'd rather strip, don't you?" He raised his brows and smoothed the tip of his mustache.

Looking into the smoky depths of his eyes, how could she not? "Quit askin' all those idjit questions I can't answer, would you?" She stared longingly at his lips, caught herself and quickly turned to unsaddle the mare. After rubbing the horse down, she led it behind a thick copse of scrub oak and down into a sheltered gully.

Kent followed and hobbled the stallion next to the mare. The two animals snuffled and sidled up to each other. Charly stood transfixed. Her hands shook as she ran her fingers through her hair. The sight of the goldurned horses greeting each other like long-lost lovers was enough to set her insides aflame.

"Seems like the horses have the right idea about how to spend the rest of the night, don't you think?"

Shivers raced up and down her spine as Kent's breath blew wisps of loose hair against the sensitive skin on her neck. She turned and scolded, "I said to quit askin' . . ." But her movement carried her closer to him. She felt the heat radiating from his large, masculine body; saw the short, stubby whiskers shading the lower half of his face, lending him a hard, desperado-like countenance.

And it was that thread of danger she always sensed lurking beneath the surface of his general goodness that excited and tantalized her, that lured her gaze to his. He reached out and touched her. She shuddered as his hands soothed up and down the sleeves of her coat.

Kent felt the strength of her response and took her into his arms. "Thanks, honey, for getting me out of that cell."

She nodded and leaned into him.

"I'm just sorry that you're the one who'll have to suffer the consequences of my actions."

"No," she insisted again. "No one knows—"

His fingers dug into her upper arms as he suddenly held her away. His eyes bored into hers. "Listen to me, Charleen McAllister, and listen good. I saw your brother and the other Wells Fargo stable hands start the fight with those soldiers. And now, suddenly you've left town. Just how stupid would a person have to be not to put two and two together?"

Charly gulped. Constable Ortega might do things

397

a little slower than some, but he was anything but dumb.

Lordy! All at once, Kent's warnings began to sink in. What if someone *had* recognized her at the jail? What *would* happen when she returned to Tucson?

She turned pleading eyes to Kent. "B-but . . . what could they do? There's no way anyone can *prove* it was me. An' all I did was—"

"Break a spy out of jail."

Silence hung heavy between them until she asked weakly, "Are you a spy?" Her heart thundered in her breast. Her ears buzzed. She held her breath, waiting for his answer.

"Yes."

Her lips parted slightly. She'd almost said the word aloud with him. Yet, if his grip hadn't tightened, she would have fallen when her knees buckled. "But, I thought . . . I mean, I didn't think . . ."

"I haven't made contact with my superiors, or sent out damaging information. But I would suppose I'm the man your *gentleman* friend's been looking for."

She took a deep breath and her legs felt steadier. "You're a Union soldier then?"

"No. Guess you could call me a troubleshooter. I can't tell you *what* I do, but I'm not enlisted."

Charly blinked at the darned burning sensation in her eyes. His admission wasn't much consolation, but it helped. It didn't sound like he'd been sneakin' around and snoopin' into everyone's business, and then tattlin' back to some high-rankin' general.

Yet beneath her sense of relief flowed a deep hurt.

No matter how he said it, or how hard she tried to convince herself otherwise, he'd used her.

"I didn't. Not really."

Her head snapped up. "What?" Surely the blasted man hadn't read her mind.

"I never used you. Although I might have, had the

398

need arisen."

Yep, he'd read her mind. The city dandy never ceased to surprise her.

"I wouldn't hurt you, honey. Not for anything. You do believe that, don't you?"

She nodded. Sure she believed him. She had to. Because she still loved him—more than she ever dreamed possible. And she was dying inside. Because of his work for the Union, he'd be leaving. Leaving—not running. He was too much of a man to let a few Confederate soldiers and the threat of jail scare him away. It was the pride shining in his eyes and the determination in his voice that gave proof of where his loyalties lay, forever and always.

Kent lifted her chin and stared into her liquid green eyes. Moonlight reflected from their dark depths, and he thought of sparkling jewels, diamonds in the rough, tomboys and ladies. Powerless to resist the complexities of her allure, he lowered his head and found her soft, parted lips.

He tasted and sipped, drinking in her essence as surely, and as unsurely, as a thirsty man would dive head-first into a pool of water. Crushing her to him, he kissed her in a way that he'd never kissed another woman—with all of the passion and soul stirring . . . love . . . at his command.

God, he had to have her. Now. Here. Forever. And he knew at that moment he'd never be able to leave her. When he departed Tucson, Miss Charleen McAllister would be with him, willing or not, or his name wasn't Kent Leland Snake Galoot City Dandy Ashford.

Charly really tried to remain immune to his charms, but once he kissed her, as if she were the most important and fragile person on earth . . . Well, she was lost. She couldn't summon the will to stop him or resist him. It was as if fate had decreed they should have this last time together.

At last Kent broke the kiss, but he took hold of her hand and kept her near while he started a small fire. Together, they unpacked the bedrolls and erected a makeshift shelter with one of the tarps.

Charly caught her breath as the fire flickered to life. Light and shadow danced across his features, highlighting his chiseled cheekbones and his strong, square jaw. Lordy, but he was the most handsome man she'd ever seen. And tonight, he was hers. Only hers.

Kent spread the blankets beneath the tarp. He cocked his brow and threw Charly a mischievous glance. "At least there'll be more room here than in the cave."

She cupped her flushed cheeks in her chilled palms. "Yeah. But the cave wasn't so bad, was it?"

"No . . ." He pulled her into his arms and collapsed back onto the pallet. "Come to think of it, it was pretty nice." He nibbled the tip of her nose, her cheeks and chin, then whispered, "But tonight will be so much more . . . comfortable."

A giggle burst from her lips. "What's the matter, Windy? You not as limber as you were then?" She grinned at the memory of some of the awkward positions they'd been scrunched into that night. And he'd been such a gentleman, and so-o-o cold, as she had been.

He'd ended up warming more than her body that night. He'd crept into her heart and created a wildfire that only he could quench.

She ran her hands beneath his coat. Her trembling fingers pulled his shirttail from his waistband, then fluttered over his bare rib cage, avoiding his wound, absorbing the feel of his muscles and sleek flesh. Her mouth went as dry as a sandy arroyo and she licked her lips.

Kent was mesmerized by the sensuous route of her tongue as it left a moist sheen on her lower lip. His body responded so intensely that he groaned and quickly began to divest her of her clothing.

Charly enthusiastically dove into the project, helping him off with his. In less time than it took to draw and cock a pistol, they lay naked together, staring into each other's eyes. And were suddenly hesitant.

As anxious as they'd been to begin their lovemaking, something more important was going on in each of their minds. Kent and Charly seemed to recognize that there was something special about their joining, but were each afraid to speak of their feelings.

Doubt hovered beneath the surface of their passion. Anxiety warred with desire. Slowly, they began to explore each other's bodies, cherishing those tender, vulnerable places that brought back wonderful, exciting memories. Their breaths quickened as their bodies began to glow with each tender caress.

Charly was overcome by her emotions and the need to become a part of Kent. To know everything about him, if not his mind or thoughts or feelings, then his body, until the feel of him was ingrained in her heart and soul forever.

He was the man she could take as her own. A man who could take her as she was—understand her actions and reactions, her strengths and weaknesses, and not be scared away. He was stronger than she, yet didn't feel the need to prove his mastery. Lord, but she loved him, and wished he could love her in return.

Kent stared into her eyes. His heart stilled, then began to beat erratically. He'd seen something in those emerald depths he'd never seen in a woman's eyes before—something that set his body aflame. He felt as if he were being consumed.

Feelings of urgency and need spurred their actions, replacing any remaining hesitancy.

Charly pressed against Kent's long, hard body, igniting the core of her femininity into a cauldron of bubbling liquid. Her skin drew taut and the sensation of flesh against flesh was almost painful.

Kent suffered his own kind of pleasurable hell. He couldn't seem to get enough of her. He fondled and kissed and caressed and laved her silken skin until his muscles and flesh melted. His body felt as hot as a June sun at high noon, but immense tenderness guided his every touch.

He gently spread her thighs and levered himself between long, long legs that deftly cradled his narrow hips. Her fingers enfolded the pulsing length of his manhood. A low groan hissed through his teeth.

She held his strength, his soul, his love in her hand. As she guided him into her honeyed sheath, the sensation that he was hers to command caused him to shudder. The thought didn't make him feel any less a man. Rather, the power in his movements allowed him to understand that by possessing this woman, he had the ability to conquer the world.

He surged into her, joining them as one.

Charly felt Kent's muscles contract, sensed the tension flowing inside him as he entered her. Then as he began to relax with each rhythmic movement, pressure swelled within her, rolling, driving until she quivered with need. A need for him. For what he did to her body, to her mind, and to her soul.

Suddenly, her nails gouged his back. She stiffened and bucked feverishly as he carried her over the edge of rational thought and down a path laden with shock after shock of an explosion so high and intense that she felt she might never return to earth. Yet the encompassing power of his arms, holding her tightly, reassured her that she was indeed a part of the world—his world.

All of the love in her being centered in the depths of her womanhood, making her feel special and very fortunate to have been loved by a man like Kent.

Lordy! She would cherish every moment they had spent together, whether the memory was of a quiet moment, fighting and arguing, or making wild, passionate love. He inspired her to greater things than just being Charleen McAllister, stagecoach driver.

Her arms wrapped about him. She wanted to hold him close for as long as possible, to absorb his strength and his warmth.

Kent smoothed his hands down her sweat-slickened body. She was lean and firm, yet soft and supple beneath his roving fingers. How he loved the feel of her, and his mind kept wandering to images of her trim figure growing round with child—his child.

Then her hands gripped his buttocks, squeezing, fondling, teasing until he couldn't think anymore.

The sky was just beginning to lighten when Charly blinked open an eye and glanced outside. Frost twinkled on the tips of the yucca stalks. She shivered and snuggled her nose into the warmth of Kent's chest. He felt so good. It was easy to dream that she might awaken like this every morning. Wouldn't it be heavenly?

Gazing at his face with all the love she possessed, Charly traced her finger along the scratchy bristles of the whiskers darkening his jaw. She shifted and felt the tingle in her breasts where those whiskers had nuzzled her sensitive flesh just a little while earlier.

"So, you're awake, are you?"

A slow smile curved her lips. "Yep."

He tweaked a pebbled nipple. "Bet you feel like you were rode hard and put up wet."

She laughed at his quote of one of her favorite sayin's. "I'm a mite sore." She wriggled her hips. A grimace contorted his features and she giggled. Her heart soared with the knowledge that even now she

403

could arouse him.

"What was it in particular that woke you, Miss Charly?"

She yawned. "Just been thinkin'."

"Oh." He couldn't hide the disappointment in his voice. "About what?"

Charly was hesitant to bring up the subject at all. She didn't want that moment, the whole wonderful night, to end. She loved the feeling of closeness, of comfortable sharing they were experiencing. But . . . after what he'd said about not sending messages as a spy, she needed to ask him a question.

"Windy, have you ever met a man by the name of Perkins?"

Kent stiffened. "Perkins?" Good God, what kind of coincidence was this? How had she heard that name?

"Yeah . . . yes. Chip Perkins, I think."

He cleared his throat. One hand slid down to her bottom and held on tightly. "Can't say I have. Why?"

She sighed. Thank the Lord. "Oh, Miles has been askin' around for the fella."

Kent sucked in his breath. Hell, now he knew who'd been attacking the stages, and why. And he hoped Charly's friend, Uncle John, hadn't been hurt.

What would Charly think if she found out her *gentleman* was behind all of the holdups? How good a "friend" was the man?

"Ouch!"

"What?"

"You're pinchin' my behind."

He tried to relax his grip and smile. "Sorry."

Charly frowned. All of a sudden, there was something different about Kent. That name must've meant more than he'd been willing to admit. But why?

She ran her hand over his shoulder and down his arm. He was as tightly coiled as a startled sidewinder.

404

"You're lyin'."

"Ahem. What?"

"You recognized that monik . . . name."

He took a deep breath. "All right. Yes. I know it."

She felt as if all the warm blood suddenly drained from her body through an enormous gash. The fingers she'd wound in the wiry hairs on his chest clenched into a fist.

Kent winced, but didn't remove her hand.

"You *are* a danged spy."

"I've already admitted to that, in a way."

She waited, wishing he'd denied it. The pedestal holding up her world tilted precariously.

"Chip Perkins isn't real. He's just a name I made up." He hesitated, wishing he didn't have to continue. She was drawing away from him. Although he didn't want to, he understood. She'd think he was just another man who'd betrayed her trust. And because of their intimacy, what he'd done would be unforgivable.

Now he had to compound her hurt. "I sent a decoy message to Washington on the last stage and signed the name Chip Perkins."

Charly closed her eyes. Nausea churned her stomach. Damn! "So, the only way Miles could've known that name . . . was if *he*'d stopped . . . gone through . . . the mail." It was a statement of dire fact, not a naive question.

"That's right."

"Lordy!" The one word exclamation said it all. It told of her utter disillusionment. The stage holdups, the men needlessly killed or injured, could mostly all be traced back to one man—Miles Cavanaugh. And Miles had been determined to intercept messages from one spy—Kent Ashford. Both of the men in her life, or so she had let herself imagine at one time, were responsible for the misery she had suffered for months.

Kent tried to ease the tension from her body by caressing the knotted muscles in her shoulders.

Charly jerked away and grabbed a blanket to shield her nakedness. "I'll fix us somethin' to eat." Although food was the farthest thing from her mind, it would get her away from him and give her something to do. She didn't want to think just then—about Miles—about Kent—about the pain gripping her heart.

Kent covered his eyes with his forearm, not bothering to pull the covers back over his chilled body. "Damn!" Damn his mission. Damn Miles Cavanaugh. Damn everyone to hell.

Chapter Twenty-Five

Charly glanced up from the coals she'd been prodding, left over from their noon meal. Kent walked toward her, leading the black stallion. Silence reverberated in the chill breeze of the gray, overcast day. He began to saddle the big horse. She began to fidget.

Finally, unable to stand the strained quiet or her own idleness, she threw down the charred stick and rose to her feet. Sauntering casually in Kent's direction, she had to clear her throat twice before asking, "Where're you goin'?"

With a sardonic glance, he continued to tighten the latigo. "Got a little unfinished business to take care of."

"You can't mean you're goin' back to Tucson?" Fool man. "They're bound to still be lookin' for you."

"Maybe." He shrugged stiff shoulders, hating the wall that had come between them. He didn't want to leave her like this, with all the uncertainty and hard feelings. But, perhaps for the time being, it was best.

She stepped between Kent and the horse. "You ain't goin'. I went to too much trouble, savin' your durned hide, to let you go an' get it all shot up again."

His features hardened. "This is something I have to do."

"Then I'm a-comin' with you." Someone had to watch after the ignorant man. Things were too dangerous for him to handle on his own.

He tried to step around her, but she wouldn't budge. So he glared into her brilliant green eyes and shook his finger under her nose. "That's what you think, young woman. You're going to stay right here and look after the camp. The constable or some of the townsmen are more likely to stumble upon us than they are a lone rider." And the more he thought about that, the more he wished he didn't have to go back to Tucson, or that he could take her with him. But, no, she would be safer here.

Charly's chin tilted stubbornly. "I'm a-goin'."

The stallion shifted its weight, bringing its big body into sudden contact with Charly. She stumbled forward and wound up in the circle of Kent's arms. Fighting the tremendous surge of desire that blazed through his insides at her mere touch, he grabbed hold of her shoulders and shook her.

"You're going to stay if I have to hogtie you to the nearest tree," he commanded. It took almost more will power than he could summon to keep from hugging her to him and kissing the hurt from her gorgeous face.

She wet her lips and glanced apprehensively toward the woods. His fingers dug into her tender flesh. It was about time she began to take him seriously, but her vulnerability and innocence were wreaking more havoc than his body could handle.

"Do you understand?" His voice was deep, stern.

Silence.

"You are not going to follow me, either." He shook her again, to keep himself from kissing the pout from her lips and soothing the frown from between her brows. "Understand?"

She gulped and finally nodded. She understood what he wanted just fine. But he hadn't made her promise.

Kent waited outside Tucson until well after midnight. The activity in town had dwindled and only a few lights illuminated the street. The cantina was still busy. A lantern burned in the Wells, Fargo office and he kept a close watch. Before he left Tucson that night, he'd have to get inside and retrieve his saddlebags.

But first, he had a man to see.

Tethering his stallion behind a deserted adobe, he crept stealthily toward the portion of the big Butterfield hacienda reserved for folks wanting to stay overnight.

He was just about to cross over to the doorway when a group of soldiers pushed through the cantina's swinging doors and staggered into the street. Breathing a sigh of relief when they turned and went off in the opposite direction, Kent ducked low and hurried through the open space between himself and the building.

A few minutes later, he stood at the end of a long hallway, his ear to a closed door. He checked the corridor, then, satisfied that he was alone, rapped sharply three times.

Almost as if the occupant had been standing on the other side waiting, the door was pulled open. Dark, bushy brows lifted questioningly, then furrowed, as Ben Matthews directed Kent to enter. "Good God, man, what's kept you? I've been going crazy in here for three damn days."

Kent eyed the ill-kempt room. The bed was unmade. A suit coat draped haphazardly over the back of the room's only chair. Papers were either stacked neatly on the top of a scarred chest of drawers

409

or were strewn in crumpled confusion across the floor.

"Sorry, Ben. Didn't mean to worry you."

"Well, you did more than worry me, son. I've been near frantic all cooped up like this. You know I gotta have fresh air beatin' my face ever' day."

Kent sighed. "I said I was sorry, Ben. Damn it, I've been a little busy the last couple of days."

Ben took his coat off the chair and threw it onto the bed. The springs squealed when he plunked down next to it on the mussed blankets. "Sit. I heard about some of your troubles."

Kent lowered his aching body into the vacated chair. "Just what did you hear?"

"That some spy had been locked up for his own safekeeping, but was busted out."

"Anybody know *who* broke me out?"

The big man shook his head. "Been a lot of speculation but, so far, no one's in jail for it."

"Thank God." Maybe it would be safe for Charly to come back after all.

"Then again, I've heard that the gal over at the stage station's been missing."

Kent clenched his fingers and stretched out his long legs. "But no one's said they actually think . . ."

"No one," Ben added quickly, taking pity on the younger, desperate-looking man. All at once, he got up and walked over to take a packet of papers from the chest of drawers. He handed them to Kent.

"My orders."

Ben nodded.

Kent unfolded the papers. He read them through once, then a second time. When he looked up, his eyes felt so tired and scratchy that he could hardly blink. "When do I have to leave?"

"They didn't say?"

"No."

"Then, I imagine, as quickly as possible." Ben

walked around the room, stepping over wadded paper and a loose sock. "They want to get started on a railroad across the plains as soon as you map out a route."

Kent just nodded. Damn! He'd hoped to stay in the area a while, at least long enough to straighten out the situation with Charly.

"How long have you known the Cavanaugh boy?" Ben leaned an elbow on the chest and stared intently at Kent.

Kent's head jerked around. How did Ben know the *gentleman?* "Just met him. Why?"

Ben frowned. "But I thought . . . When I saw you folks the other evening, I assumed . . ."

"What, Ben? What did you think?"

The older man spread his arms wide, palms up, and shrugged. "That you'd known each other for a long time. You two have a lot in common. Can't believe you haven't met before now."

Kent thought of Charly. Yep, he and Miles did share *one* common interest.

Ben scratched his chin. "At first, I thought the two of you might've merged and been going to work together."

"Me? And Miles Cavanaugh? Now why would we want to do that? What're you talking about, Ben?"

"Oh, I know better now. Especially since I seen the Cavanaugh boy in them Confederate grays. But it would've been good had the two of you joined—"

"Ben! What on earth gave you the idea that I'd ever want to work with that country gentleman on anything?"

"You really don't know him, do you?"

"No." Kent left the chair and began to pace off his frustration. Sometimes Ben reminded him a lot of Miss Charly with her very effective evasiveness. "Well, are you going to tell me, or just keep me

411

guessing about whether you've lost your mind or not?"

Ben grinned. "Thought surely you'd at least recognize the name. Miles Cavanaugh is from a railroad family, same as you. Just figured he was out here, like you, scouting a route to start laying rails."

Kent stared at Ben. Cavanaugh. Cavanaugh? Of course. Now he knew why he'd disliked Miles on sight. The Cavanaughs had beaten his family out of a fortune over the past few years, besting the Ashfords' figures on the cost of putting down rails in nearly every part of the South.

"So now my superiors want me to go North and just leave the Southern route wide open for the Confederates?"

"Don't fret so much. The South needs a good rail line, all right, and they're doing their best to get it. But I have a feelin' all hell's goin' to break out soon and the boy's goin' to be too busy to think about a railroad."

Kent stood plastered against the adobe wall of the stage office. Just to his right was the one window. A lantern still burned inside, spilling a muted, yellow light onto the walkway that reminded him of the color of leaves just after the first frost.

A shiver raked down his spine as he took off his hat and leaned over to peer through the dirty glass. The front room appeared empty, but the mail room door was closed. Jed, or one of the other employees, *could* be in there working late.

Taking a deep breath, he ducked under the window and stepped softly to the door. Cooked dry by years of intense heat and wind and arid cold, the hinge squealed loudly. Kent hesitated, but when no one challenged him, continued inside. The soles of his boots thudded on the packed earth. He picked up the lantern and carried it behind the counter. Flickering beams of light shone onto the safe.

The heavy padlock was prominently in place, but Kent only smiled. Though Jed carried the key with him, Kent had seen Charly reach under the desk to find a spare once when a passenger needed something and Jed wasn't around. He began his search under the middle drawer. A splinter jabbed his finger. He cursed. There! It was hidden in a crack between two slats.

With the key located, he walked over to the mail room door, cocked his head, and listened. Not a sound. But just to be sure, he pushed the door open and looked inside. Empty. Good.

Quickly, he returned to the safe and inserted the key. The heavy lock swung open. Taking out the saddlebags, he upended freight vouchers, small packages, and a few personal valuables.

He relocked the safe and was turning to replace the key when he heard the hinge on the front door squeal. Ducking behind the counter, he crab-walked to the far end. But with the lantern on the floor at his back, all he could see in the room were dark, eerie shadows.

Carefully, he eased the saddlebags from his shoulder and tried to set them on a nearby shelf. Leather scraped against wood. He held his breath. The hinge stopped making the telltale noise. A slight shuffling sound reached his ears. Someone was approaching the counter.

He drew his gun and waited, melting into the hard wood as far as he could, hoping the lantern would momentarily blind whoever was about to round the end of the counter.

A boot toe came into his line of vision. Then the whole boot. Then two legs. He rose like an avenging soldier, grabbing a heavy wool collar. Jamming the barrel of his pistol into a lean belly, he ordered,

"That's far enough, mister."

The intruder doubled up in pain as a familiar womanly scent filled his nostrils. Immediately, he returned the Colt Navy pistol to his holster and reached to support Charly.

"Damn it, woman. What in the hell are you doing here? I thought I told you to stay at the camp."

Red-faced and gasping for breath, Charly clung to Kent's arm. When she was able to drag in healing gulps of air once again, she righted herself and turned to spit, "You dadblamed scalawag. You're gonna be the death of me yet."

The way things were going, Kent was afraid she might be right. But he still grinned.

The blaze of white teeth infuriated Charly. She'd sat back at the camp, an inferno of emotions, debating about what she should do—let him go to town alone and land his mangy hide in jail again, maybe even get himself killed—or put her grievances aside and come rescue the idjit.

Once he'd left and she'd had time to think, it had been easy to realize that no matter *what* he'd done, she still cared enough to make sure he didn't get into even more trouble. And sure enough, just look where she'd found him.

Her fist struck him in the gut, just below his rib cage. He gasped for air and she nodded at a job well done. "What in tarnation are you doin' hidin' back here?" she demanded.

Weakly pulling the saddlebags from their place of concealment, he held them up for her to see.

She kicked his shin. "Why didn't you tell me what you were goin' to do? I could've made it a lot simpler for you." Then she watched him lean down like he was going to grab his leg, but instead put away the hidden key. She scowled. "Why, you—"

From the shadows, another voice interrupted, "Come out from behind the counter. Now. With your hands in the air. This here's a scatter gun, an' I got a mighty itchy trigger finger."

Charly and Kent froze. For several seconds, the only sounds in the room came from ragged breathing. Finally, Charly found her voice. "Don't shoot, Pa. It's me, Charly, an' the danged city dandy you've taken such a shine to."

"Come on out here where's I kin see ya." Jed McAllister stepped further into the room. "An' bring the damned lantern. I cain't see a blessed thing in these shadows."

Kent shouldered the saddlebags and bent to retrieve the lantern at the same time Charly did. They bumped heads, cursed, and then straightened to look into each other's eyes. Charly rubbed her temple and giggled. Kent resettled his hat and chuckled. Jed boomed, "You'uns best do as I say an' c'mon out. Sumpthin's goin' on, ain't it, gal? I smell a polecat sure as shootin'."

Kent rolled his eyes and muttered something about "saving the world from old men." He snatched up the lantern and led the way from behind the counter as Jed lowered the shotgun.

"Well, now, ain't that all cozy an' nice. What was the two o' you'uns up to back there?"

Jed pointed toward the counter with the barrel of the gun. Kent grabbed Charly and pulled her behind him, just in case her father had been bending his elbow at the cantina all evening.

"Pa," Charly began, but then hesitated. She didn't want to tell him that Windy had broken into the safe and put who-knew-how-many valuables at risk. She didn't want to explain her relationship with the city dandy. Her pa wouldn't understand. And neither did she, really.

Chewing her lower lip, she glowered at Kent. There were a lot of things he had to answer for.

"Never mind, gal. I'm jest proud to've run inta ya

tonight. We'uns got work ta do."

Charly scowled. "Work? Now? But there hasn't been a stage . . ." Excitement suddenly tensed her nerves. "What happened, Pa?" She glanced toward the mail room. "We gonna try to get the mail that's piled up through, again? Bet I can find a way—"

"Here now, gal. Settle down. Ain't no such thin' gonna be happenin' any time soon, sorry ta say."

Charly's shoulders slumped. Kent could almost feel her dejection, and he understood her feelings perfectly. He'd felt the same sense of frustration every time a train route was delayed, or construction of a railroad was held up for reasons beyond his control. He knew the helplessness she was experiencing.

"Then what work are you talkin' about, Pa?" She watched with guarded wariness as her pa's normally rheumy eyes began to take on a new sparkle.

"We'uns is gonna move the whole damned station tomorry. Ever'thin', down to the last horseshoe. Them Rebs gonna be in fer a big surprise if'n they come confiscatin' 'roun' here."

"Yore leavin'?" Charly shivered. A chill colder than any blue norther skittered through her stiff body. She wrapped her arms around her waist, but she couldn't shake the hovering premonition of disaster.

Her family was goin' to pack up an' move again. And they seemed to expect her to go with them. Thought she'd pull up stakes an' leave her only friends and the home she'd worked so hard to create.

The door creaked. Charly jumped. Kent spun, his hand grasping for his pistol. Jed raised the barrel of his shotgun, only to lower it with a wide grin splitting his weathered features.

Charly heaved a great sigh and also started to grin, until she noticed the hard glint of her brother's eyes as he gazed directly to her right. Windy. Rigo, the Confederate officer. Had he come for the escaped prisoner?

Before she had time even to think about her actions, she moved in front of Kent, holding her arms out and away from her sides in a motion calculated to keep Kent in place and to stop Rigo from advancing.

Rigo continued to stare at the man his sister had chosen. "My God, sis, I thought I recognized that mare tied behind the stable. But I'd hoped to hell I was wrong. Tried to convince myself that you were smarter than to show yourself around town when folks are still so riled."

He took off his hat and ran his fingers through waves of black hair. "But no, here you are, and with *him*." Rigo held up his left hand and pointed to Kent. "Neither one of you has the brains God gave an ass for showin' up in Tucson again."

Kent watched the Confederate—evidently another brother of Charly's who had crawled out of the wood-work. He never took his hand from his pistol, wondering how many more family members she had stashed away just waiting to give him grief.

But he consoled himself with the thought that if the soldier had intended to do something stupid, he probably would've issued a challenge the moment he came through the door. But Kent wasn't about to take any chances. He moved back and stepped away from Charly.

Sensing Kent's movement, Charly sidestepped with him, continuing to act as his shield. "What're you goin' to do, Rigo?" She winced as her voice quavered slightly, and hoped no one noticed her weakness at a time when she really needed to show her strength.

Rigo swatted his hat against his thigh. When his gaze shifted up to Charly, it was rife with indecision. "I have to take him in. You know that."

Charly retreated until her back was pressed to Kent's chest. "No. Please, Rigo. I'm beggin' you. Let him go. We were just leavin'. An' he won't come back to Tucson." She turned her head and pleaded, "Tell him, Windy."

Kent blinked and took his gaze from Charly's brother for the first time since the man had entered the room. He was stunned by the shimmering intensity in her dark green eyes and the firm set to her usually soft, pouty lips.

The woman was begging—for him, She was sacrificing her pride—for him. He was humbled, at a loss to describe the feelings that rioted through him as he realized the extent of her love—for him. No one had ever acted so unselfishly and with emotions dredged from the depths of their soul—for him.

Rigo also sensed his sister's deep feelings. Once again, he riffled his fingers through his hair. "I'm sworn to duty, Charleen. I've got responsibilities . . ."

Jed McAllister turned the barrel of his shotgun in the direction of his older son. "Reckon ya know this ain't easy fer me, son, but I got respons'bilities, too." He tilted his graying head toward Charly. "Go on, gal. Git. Git yore man out'n here."

During a long pause, while Charly tried to come to grips with what her pa was doing, Jed looked directly into Kent's eyes. "Me'n the gal . . . we'uns ain't always seen eye ta eye on thin's. Mebbe this'll even us up a mite. But ya better take good keer o' 'er, ya hear?"

Kent could hardly swallow, let alone move. Besides just learning that the woman he loved, loved him in return, her father had entrusted him with her safe-keeping. Finally, he nodded, took Charly's elbow and escorted her limp, unresisting form past a glowering Rigo.

But Charly stopped. She stared back at her pa, then at Kent, who released his hold on her so she could go over and give the old man a kiss on the cheek.

Jed grumbled and tilted his head to wipe his cheek

against his shoulder. Then he gave his daughter a lopsided grin.

Charly turned to her brother and flung herself against Rigo's chest, holding on as if she'd never let him go.

Rigo slid his arms around her slender shoulders. Suddenly he held her away and tipped her chin until he could see into her eyes. "Take care, little sister. We'll meet up again. Real soon."

Charly gave him a watery smile. "I know."

Over Charly's shoulder, Rigo scowled at Kent. "I hope you know what a lucky bastard you are."

Kent just nodded.

"If you don't treat her right—"

"Rigo," Charly scolded, a pained expression on her face. "You don't understand. Uh, Windy'n I . . . we . . . aren't—"

"Jed, give us ten minutes, if you will. Then it won't matter if they turn all the dogs loose." Kent quickly escorted Charly from the depot, then grabbed her hand and pulled her around to the side of the building and into the shadows. "Where's your horse?"

"But, I can't leave. They think that you . . . 'n me . . . are . . . Well—"

"Hush up, woman. Let them think anything they want. We have to get out of here before your brother sets the entire Confederate cavalry on our trail." Besides, he argued with himself, he didn't mind the impression Charly had given her family. As soon as possible, he intended to make that *impression* a reality.

"But . . ." At Kent's stern expression and the tightening of his fingers on her wrist, she decided it wasn't wise to continue the argument. He was much too strong and forceful when he was upset—and she loved it. "The mare's behind the stable, close to your stallion."

419

"Then what're we waiting for? It's a long way back to camp."

They kept to the shadows until they reached the horses, and rode out of Tucson as slowly as Kent's nerves would allow to keep from attracting undue attention. On the outskirts of town, he kicked the stallion into a ground-eating lope, and reveled at the sight of Miss Charly, cheeks glowing in the moonlight, riding at his side.

However, her eyes were dark and troubled, and he could tell the news that her father and the stage station were all moving North had upset her.

He had decided to keep his own orders a secret until they reached camp, but perhaps it would make her feel better if he told her now. "You were right, back there in the office."

His words drifted across the space separating the horses, carried on the cool wind. "'Course I was right. Thought you'd learned that by now."

He smiled and shook his head.

Finally, she prodded, "Right about what?"

"I'm leaving."

Charly grinned. "Silly. I know you're leavin', an' I'm goin' with you. An' when we get back to camp, I'll rustle us up somethin' to eat. My ribs're beatin' against my backbone."

He sighed. "No, really leaving. I've gotten my orders. I'm heading North tomorrow."

She turned her face away. That dire premonition settled in her stiff spine. Her heart ached unbearably and her throat constricted until she couldn't have spoken if she'd wanted to. The moment she'd been waiting for had come at last. Yet, lately, she'd let herself hope . . . even believe . . .

"And I want you to go with me, Miss Charly." He reached over and took her cold hand. "What do you say? Will you come?"

Chapter Twenty-Six

Charly froze. The mare pranced nervously as her hands grew heavy on the reins. Go? Leave Tucson with Windy? She was stunned—thrilled—devastated.

But Tucson was home. She felt like she belonged.

The moonlight accented her sickly gray features. Concern sharpened Kent's voice. "Charly? Are you all right? You're not ill, are you?"

She swallowed a throat full of bile. All right? No. Ill? Yes. She was sick at heart for what might have been. Slowly, numbly, she shook her head, then remembered his question. "I'm fine."

"The hell you are." Kent frowned. "What's the matter?" She'd *been* fine, just a minute ago. Then he'd asked her to go . . . Kent's body stiffened reflexively, causing his legs to squeeze the stallion's sides. The horse snorted and tensed, ready to bolt.

"Easy, boy," Kent soothed. But his eyes continued to bore into Charly's strained features. "Was I that mistaken? I thought you lo . . . cared for me, that we could make a life together."

Pain knifed through Charly's insides. Care? Heck, she loved him more than she'd ever loved anyone in her life. But she needed more. She needed the sense of security and peace that went with having a stable home. She couldn't see herself trailing after Kent forever, wandering from place to place, like her pa'd led her family for so many unhappy years.

But if she tried to tell Kent her feelings, he'd think she was foolish, stubborn, or too sentimental. He'd never be able to understand how she could love him and still refuse to follow him.

"I-I care for you."

Kent pulled his horse to a stop. The mare followed suit, as if sensing that its rider had ceased giving it directions. "Then what's the problem? Why do I get the feeling that you're going to turn down my offer?"

His deep, gravelly voice indicated how much her answer could hurt him. She flinched and kicked the mare into a fast walk. "I just can't go, is all. Sure, I have feelings for you, strong feelings. But Tucson is my home. I got friends and family there." Well, her immediate family was leaving, but she could always get in touch with her grandparents. They'd like that. "No, I won't leave."

Besides, the more she thought about the way he'd asked her to go, never mentioning love or marriage, the more she wondered what had prompted him to behave so impulsively. For all she knew, he might take her to hell and gone and then run off and desert her.

The scar near Kent's eye rippled along with the jerking motion of a muscle in his jaw. "You *won't* go. No matter what?" All he concentrated on was her overstated rejection. He chose to ignore the quaver in her voice, the pain and regret in her eyes.

"I can't," she whispered.

"If that's what you want." He let the stallion have its head to pick its way over a particularly rough section of ground. Then he shrugged, as if the gesture ridded him of the burden of her unpleasant words. "Good thing we'll reach camp soon. I'm hungrier than a grizzly coming out of hibernation."

He kicked the stallion into a lope, hoping the

action would take his mind off Charly and the dreary thought of living the rest of his life without her.

The moonlit landscape was icy and still, devoid of warmth and life. God, he hurt. Like he'd never hurt before.

After returning to camp, they both hardly picked at their food. They just sat, stiff as boards, contemplating the pallet they'd shared so joyously the night before. Now, all of a sudden, neither of them wanted to approach the beckoning blankets.

Charly shivered and added more sticks to the fire. She wasn't a bit sleepy. Maybe she'd just sit up all night.

Kent hid a yawn behind his hand as he pretended to scratch his nose. Why didn't the fool woman go to bed instead of sitting there nodding, barely able to hold her eyes open? As far as he was concerned, she was welcome to those cold, empty blankets.

Another quarter of an hour elapsed. Charly and Kent took turns slumping, shaking their heads and straightening, then slumping again. They made a move toward the pallet at the same time, saw what the other intended, and sat back down.

Kent cleared his throat. "It'll be light soon. I think we could both share the same blanket without losing control of ourselves, don't you?"

Charly blinked and lifted her chin. "Sh . . . sho . . . Yes. Of course. I know *I* can." She yawned and stretched exaggeratedly. "Why, I'll be asleep soon's my head hits the ground."

"Me, too."

They walked to the pallet. Kent shook out the blankets to be sure no crawly creatures had decided to take a claim to the covers, then she helped spread them back again.

But once she was under the blanket, with every

stitch of clothing but her boots intact, and separated from his warm, wonderful body by mere inches, her eyes refused to close. Her body tingled. Her arms ached to hold him. Her fingers clenched in an effort to keep from reaching for him. Goldurn it, how was she ever goin' to make it through the next twenty years alone, without her city dandy? Were her home and friends worth sacrificing her one, true love?

Memories of the years of frustration and the hard work she'd put into the station flickered like wildfire through her mind. She dredged up every reminder she could on how she'd planned and fought for everything she had. She couldn't turn her back on it all now. She couldn't.

"Aw, hell!' Kent turned toward her, pulling and bunching two layers of blankets as he did so. His hand caressed her cheek. "I'm not nearly as strong as I thought I was, honey. I can't lie here beside you and not touch you. God, I want to kiss you. Need to kiss you. So badly that I ache all over with wanting you."

Tentatively, she reached out to trace the white line of his scar. "I-I feel the same."

A growl tore from his throat. "Come here, then, woman. Time's a-wastin'."

She pushed against his chest. "Wait. I've been wonderin', for a long time . . . How'd you get the scar?" She tenderly touched the slightly puckered flesh, willing away the pain he must've suffered, thanking the Lord that the wound hadn't done worse damage.

He laughed shortly and started to turn onto his back. Charly grabbed his hand and held his palm firmly against her cheek. Finally, he sighed and pulled her into his arms. "It was stupid, really. I got into a fight . . . with my best friend . . . over—"

"A woman," she supplied.

He nodded and pulled her shirt collar open until he could nuzzle his lips into the silken flesh at the base of her throat.

She gasped but kept her attention focused. "And . . . did you love her?"

He groaned. "I thought so, I guess, at the time."

"But?"

"Damn, but you're a persistent little minx, aren't you?"

She couldn't answer because he'd taken her lips with his. He tasted and explored, driving her wild with desire and need. But she found enough willpower, though it was dwindling quickly, to push him back. "Tell me, please."

"Oh, all right," he grumped. "No, I didn't love her. I think I was only interested because my best friend wanted her. Anyway, we ended up fighting over her, neither of us realizing that she was a selfish little bitch, just after money and prestige. There, I told you it was stupid. Since then, I've avoided entanglements with women. They're not worth the pain or the effort."

Charly shivered. Money? Pres . . . prestige? Who was the real Kent "Windy" Ashford? Union spy? Drifter?

And if he were truly of the notion that women weren't worth his time and trouble, why *had* he asked her to go North with him? Her heart tumbled over itself. He must think she was just a little special.

She kissed the scar. "And your friend? What happened to him?" The way he tensed beneath her caused her to think that maybe she should've left well enough alone.

"Oh, he came out of the fight with a scar, too. From a gash on the arm." He chuckled. "Then he married the woman and they had five kids. I've thought many a time that I was a damned lucky man to have gotten the worst of that fight."

He grinned and Charly smiled. "You know, I've never loved a man . . ." Suddenly, she clamped her mouth shut. Consarn it, she hadn't meant to say that out loud. And she'd almost gone so far as to finish the rest of what she'd been thinkin'—"But you."

Kent's heart stopped. For a moment, he'd begun to hope that she'd changed her mind. Especially when she'd responded so willingly to his kisses. But how could he keep fighting someone who wasn't ready to trust him? Who couldn't believe that he'd care for and provide for her?

Hell, he'd fetch her the moon if she'd just ask. She'd come to mean more to him than anything—or anyone—in the world.

But now he had his answer. It wasn't just the home and friends keeping her in Tucson. She had no reason to want to leave. She didn't love him.

He set her away and rolled over, turning his back, willing his body to relax. But the empty ache pervading his gut would be there for a long, long time.

Charly turned on her back, staring blankly into a sky just beginning to lighten in the East. What had she said? Tonight was the closest she'd ever come to admitting her deepest, innermost feelings and he'd just pushed her away. Hurt cracked her voice. "'Night, Windy."

Kent hissed, "Good night, Miss Charly. Sleep tight."

Charly had just doused the breakfast fire and was morosely watching Kent saddle the stallion when the sound of hoofbeats caused her to drop the dripping frying pan. Her eyes searched the meadow as she ran toward her saddle and carbine. All she could think of was that Miles or the constable had found their camp.

The next thing she knew, however, was the shock of being grabbed around the waist and hauled behind a sycamore trunk.

"Damn you, woman. What're you trying to do?

426

Get yourself killed?"

Charly swung her elbows and was rewarded with a muffled "Ooomph!"

"Dangnab it, let go a me, you durned bully. Get on that cayuse of yours an' hightail it outta here."

Kent whispered in her ear, "Careful, honey. Your language is fouling the air again."

She sputtered and fumed and was about to give him a deserved tongue-lashing when he placed his palm over her mouth and pointed toward an approaching rider. "You must not think I'm much of a man to believe I'd go off and leave you to face a posse alone." His softly growled words sent a shiver racing down her spine.

Whipping her head around, she opened her mouth to explain that she'd just been trying to help, that she'd never met a better man. But his accusing glare froze the words in her throat. She gulped. No, she'd learned that lesson well during the past few months. Kent Ashford never abandoned a woman in danger.

Satisfied from her flabbergasted expression that Miss Charly had at last been put in her place, Kent turned his full attention to the meadow. The rider was still coming, slowly, bending low in the saddle every now and then as if searching the ground.

Damn, Kent reprimanded himself. He'd been so distracted last night by a beautiful, hardheaded woman, that they'd probably left a trail a drunk miner could follow.

Her startled gasp, and then her warm breath against his cheek, drew his gaze immediately back to Charly. An elbow to his belly caught him off guard, and the next thing he knew, she was on her feet and running.

"Damn it, come back here." The foolish brat! What if there were more men behind that one, just waiting to . . . He drew his pistol and dashed after her.

"Ed! Ed, over here." Charly raised her arm over her head and waved.

Kent stopped several feet behind her, squinting into the bright morning sun. Thank God, she was right. But unsure of where her brother's loyalties lay, he kept the gun out where the boy would be sure to notice it.

A few minutes later, Ed McAllister dismounted and regarded his sister and the dangerous-looking ex-conductor with sly consideration. "Well, well. Looky here. Thought two hunted fugitives would have the sense to hide their trail. Hell, a jackrabbit in new snow couldn't've left bigger tracks."

Kent felt the skin on his neck warm considerably. Damned obnoxious know-it-all. Just because he was right, didn't mean the kid could scold them like two-year-olds. "What is it you want, McAllister? Or did you ride all the way out here just to exercise your jaws?"

Charly was surprised by the amused glitter in Ed's eyes as her brother splayed his legs and stood up before the taller, menacing Kent Ashford. Ed stuck out his chin and glowered right back at the city dandy. Pride swelled her chest.

"I'm here to talk to my sister. Don't reckon that I gotta answer to you, no how."

"Listen, pup—"

Charly stepped between the two men, her back toward Kent. Over her shoulder, she cast him a warning glare, then asked, "What *are* you doin' here? Thought Pa had big plans for today."

Ed pointedly removed his gaze from Kent. "Ned, uhmm, Rigo," he amended when Charly frowned, "stopped me in the street this mornin' with damn near the whole Confederate army at his back. Said he was takin' his men after the escaped prisoner." He glanced meaningfully at Kent, who was now standing close beside his sister.

428

"Anyhow, he says someone'd come to the major late last night after spottin' the spy and some suspicious-like, curvy-figured boy." Ed unbuttoned his coat and scratched his chest. "Figured you'd wanna know."

Charly nodded, then began to pace along a narrow path in the grass.

Ed hunkered down in front of his gelding and plucked a long, thin reed from the ground which he promptly poked between his teeth. "Me an' Pa figured he stopped me a-purpose. We decided that if we was plannin' ta leave town, it'd be a good time while most of the troop was out combin' the cactus."

Charly's stomach churned. For just a minute, she'd hoped that maybe they'd changed their minds. Yet, her estimation of her pa suddenly increased. He was taking his responsibility seriously. "So, you're really leavin' Tucson?" She just needed to hear it again.

"Yep. Soon's we get back." Ed suddenly frowned and shoved his hat back farther. "Say, what do ya mean, are *you* leavin'? Ain'tcha comin', too? That's mostly the reason I'm here. Ta get you."

She dug her boot toe into a clump of dry roots, unable to meet her brother's questioning gaze. "I-I ain't goin', Ed."

"'Course ya are. What foolishness has gotten inta ya?"

Kent decided he'd held his peace long enough. "She's been spouting the same nonsense to me for the past twelve hours. Just sticks her little chin out and closes her ears to reason."

Charly crossed her arms over her chest and glowered, making sure to keep her chin tucked in. Somehow, it was easier standing up to the *two* of them. Alone, Windy was far more dangerous and intimidating.

Ed looked intently into Charly's furious eyes. "You're sure that's what you want ta do."

429

"Yep." But inside, she was quaking like a leaf. She wasn't sure about anythin'. She was confused and frightened and already lonely.

Moving closer to his sister, Ed said softly, "Well, then, I'll not try to change your mind. You can be an awesomely stubborn woman, Charleen McAllister."

She sniffed, took a step forward, and awkwardly hugged her brother. "You take care of yourself, an' Pa, you hear, big brother?"

Ed stepped back and grinned as he resettled his hat. He mounted his horse, spun it around, and shouted back over his shoulder, "You, too, little sis." He then urged his horse into a gallop, showering Kent and Charly with clumps of sod and dried grass.

Kent cleared his throat. "I'd best be going, too. Maybe I can catch up with your family on the other side of town. They'll probably need all the help they can get moving the horses and mules." He glanced toward the waiting stallion, wishing he could leave her as jauntily as Ed.

"Besides, it looks like we're all headed in the same direction . . ." Damn it, he hated this feeling of being reduced to a blabbering, spineless idiot nearly on the verge of tears.

Charly nodded and bit the inside of her lip. She needed to be strong now, to let him ride away without breaking into a thousand weeping pieces. She wanted him to remember her as a woman who stood proudly by her convictions—a woman who had set her goals and would see them through to the end. The bitter, awful end.

She tucked a wayward strand of hair behind her ear, but just as quickly, Kent stood in front of her, pulling it out again. He gently rubbed the lock between his fingers and she sucked in her breath, what she could get of it.

"You have the softest hair I've ever felt. I liked it when you wore it hanging loose down your back."

430

His gut constricted as he remembered that the only times she'd purposely worn it down, she'd been with Miles Cavanaugh.

He roughly tugged her hat from her head and let it drop to the ground. He loosened each pin, one by one, trailing his fingers down the long, rich length of her sable tresses. When her hair was finally freed, he placed his hands on either side of her temples.

His breath wafted through the loose tendrils. Charly's knees trembled. She inhaled the male essence of him and would have swayed against him except for the pressure of his hold.

Then, very slowly, his head dipped. She focused on his lips, waiting, anticipating his kiss, longing for the feel of his tongue mating with hers, the crush of his chest against her breasts. But all she felt was their butterfly swiftness as they brushed the tip of her nose. Disappointment stiffened her body.

"'Bye, Miss Charly. I . . . love you." But he'd already turned away. Charly blinked, imagining he'd finally said the words she'd been praying to hear. *I love you.* But whatever he said had been spoken so softly that she figured she must've just dreamed them.

And she was too determined to remain proud and in control to make an ass of herself by runnin' after him, beggin' him to repeat what he'd said.

What difference would it make, anyway? He was leavin'. She was stayin'.

Kent mounted, then couldn't resist riding over to take one last look at her pale, upturned features. "You'd best be leaving soon, too. The Confederates could happen on this valley any time."

She gulped and nodded.

"Well . . ." Quit stalling, Ashford, he scolded himself. With a brief flick of his hand and a dreadful ache in his gut, he spurred the stallion in the direction Ed McAllister had ridden.

431

Charly stood as still as a cottonwood branch on a windless day, watching until he was only a dot on the horizon. When he finally disappeared over a distant ridge, she collapsed like a felled tree trunk, more bereft than she'd ever been in her life.

Peering through puffy eyes into the clear blue sky, she cried, "Oh, Lordy. What have I done?"

Chapter Twenty-Seven

Late the next morning, Kent pulled his stallion to a stop atop a high rise. Before him, spread out in a long, winding line, was a sight that made his heart sad. A cavalcade of mules and horses and a train of dust-covered coaches trekked its way North.

The drivers, Uncle John in particular, whom Kent could easily pick out even at a distance, were grim-faced and very aware of the difference in today's sneaky departure from Tucson and their arrival three years earlier to shouts of welcome, gun salutes, and waving flags.

Although Kent had only heard of those gala events, he sympathized and felt the dejection of all of those connected with the Butterfield Overland Mail during its heyday. Now, Wells, Fargo would either stand on their own merits or go down with John Butterfield.

He sat his horse, thinking of the men who'd lost their lives, and the strength and courage of those now wending their way toward a new and unfamiliar route. As usual, his thoughts were not too far away from one woman who'd excelled in a man's profession, earning the respect and love of her peers.

Love. Yes, she'd also managed to acquire *his* love and admiration through her grit and determination and her refusal to admit defeat. And she'd done it all, unconsciously keeping her femininity intact.

The further he'd ridden from Tucson and the more he'd thought about her actions during the past few days, the more he realized that she'd behaved just like a woman in love. A woman who'd put the life of her lover ahead of her own. A woman who'd unselfishly let him ride away . . .

Suddenly, a huge grin curved his lips. He patted the stallion's sleek neck and reined the horse back toward Tucson. With a nudge from his knees and a loud whoop, he sent the animal down the hill.

Charly waited until dusk to enter Tucson, just in case everyone considered her a "wanted" woman. She just couldn't resist coming back to the home she'd given up so much to possess.

But there was something different about the town that night. The streets seemed too quiet, too oppressive. No lights, no signs of life were visible from the stage station. A wave of sadness overwhelmed her when she looked into the darkened office and her pa wasn't there, standing behind the counter with his tousled hair, his thumbs hooked in his suspenders as she scolded him for some imagined neglect.

Through the chill of the evening crept a secret warmth, the realization that she'd misunderstood her family. All along it had been her own personal drive to do more and more, to take over for her mother, to make herself responsible for everyone's lives, that had pushed them into the dependent roles they'd adapted to so well.

Thank the Lord she'd recognized her own guilt and repaired some of the damage before the whole outfit had been ordered North. She sighed and turned away, already missing the excitement of the move, the challenges that would be faced once they reached that central route across the nation.

The barn door creaked when she pulled it open. The mare snorted and shied back on the reins when Charly led it inside. Cocking her head, Charly listened. Her eyes scanned the shadows. It was too quiet. Loneliness and emptiness surrounded her. Gone were the welcoming snuffles of the horses and the impatient stomping of the mules' hooves. Even the smell of hay was just a lingering scent.

No shuffle and whir of cards. No laughing voices of drivers arguing over who'd be more attractive to the ladies at the cantina that night.

Nowhere was the warm, cozy feeling of "home."

She put the mare in a stall, rubbed it down, and fed it a few flakes of hay that'd been left in the rear corner of the barn. All the while she worked, she stole glances through the small opening she'd left in the door out to the main street.

There were so many new buildings. She hadn't noticed that before. Where had all the people come from? When had everything begun to change?

She wandered up to her home and pushed open the door. The lantern was still on the table, so she lifted the top and lit the wick. Everything was so bare. The living room. The kitchen. Her eyes puddled. She chewed on her knuckles to keep from sobbing.

Her pa's jacket wasn't on the floor in the corner by the door. Ed's dirty shirts weren't draped over the backs of the chairs. She walked over to one of the straight-backed, hard, uncomfortable seats and slumped into it. This wasn't "home."

Surging to her feet again, she searched the cupboards and found a few supplies her pa and Ed had left for her. In no mood to light a fire in the cook stove, she gnawed on a strip of jerky, then washed it down with a swig from a crock jug that'd been overlooked behind a muslin curtain she'd made to conceal and add a little color to the plank shelves.

The liquid burned its way into her stomach. She gasped. The jug thumped onto the table. Soon, though, a welcome warmth spread throughout her insides—the first warmth she'd experienced in months, it seemed. She took another tentative swallow of the shine, felt the added glow, and smiled.

Another tilt of the jug helped her decide to return to the barn. At least the horse would be more company than these empty rooms.

When she'd left the barn earlier, she'd closed the large double door. Now, feeling a little giddy and unsteady, she avoided the heavy portals and entered by a smaller side door.

Humming to herself, she whirled and kicked through the loose straw covering the floor. Swaying to the rhythm of an imaginary tune, her toe connected with something hidden beneath the straw and she stumbled. She giggled and then hiccuped. Stopping abruptly, she stared around her at the dark, eerie shadows.

"Durn it." She patted her pockets, looking for a match to light the lantern.

The sound of a muffled scrape penetrated her foggy brain. She stopped fumbling through her coat. Cocking her head, she waited. She didn't hear anything else, but she *felt* . . . something. "Wh-who's there?" Swaggering boldly forward, she warned, "I'm not scared. C'mon out an' show yourself. Hic!"

The mare snorted. Hooves rustled the straw. Charly released the breath she'd been holding. Walking over to pat the horse's neck, she continued to peer into the shadows. An uneasy feeling made her cautious.

The mare's looming presence reassured her and she again patted her pockets. "Aha! There you are." Wobbling slightly, because her legs just couldn't

436

seem to go where she willed them, she reached for the lantern. Using the seam on her trouser leg, she slashed the tip of the match downward. When the taper sparked and ignited, she grinned proudly.

Lifting the globe, she stuck the flame to the wick and then replaced the glass. Charly was about to blow out the match when she happened to glance down the aisle. She froze, her lips still puckered.

"Wh-who . . . Wh-who . . ." Gulping she cursed her weak owl imitation. "Who are you?"

A dark figure moved toward her. She warily backed up a step. "Whadda you want?"

The match flame burned down to her fingertips. She cursed softly and dropped it into the straw. By the time she'd ground out the sparks, the stranger had walked into the dim circle of light.

"Miles? Hic." She pursed her lips, silently regretting drinking so much of her pa's shine. The strong liquor had addled her brain and slowed her reflexes. She should've realized sooner that she wasn't alone in the barn.

"Hello, pretty lady. I was beginnin' to think I wouldn't ever see you again."

Since his tone was relaxed and friendly, Charly's nervousness eased a little. "What made you think that? I live here, ya know. Hic!"

Miles came closer and grasped her chin. Tilting her face up, he stared down into her glassy eyes. In his finest Southern drawl, he admonished, "Why, Charleen McAllister, I do believe you're tipsy."

She tried to shake her head, but his grip wouldn't permit it. So she just grinned. "Nope. Not me. I know how to hold my . . . Hic! . . . lic . . . lick . . . whhhhissky."

He chuckled. "Then you're a better man than I am, sometimes." He looked at her meaningfully, realized she wouldn't understand, and shrugged. The woman had no way of knowing that he had spent the last two nights at the cantina, drinking like a fish that had been caught out of water. "Where have you been the past two days?"

She blinked. "Wh-what?"

"Where've you been? I've looked all over town for you."

"Well, ah . . ." She lowered her eyes, though he continued to grip her chin. She had to think of somethin' quick and couldn't do it when he looked at her like that—so intense—as if he already knew and was testin' her.

Miles tilted her head until she had no choice but to look into his eyes. "Where is he, Charleen?"

She gulped. "Wh-where's wh-who?"

Another voice vibrated from the shadows. "Let me question the *little lady,* Major. I'll get your answers. All the answers you want." A red-headed soldier loomed into the light.

Charly rolled her eyes in the direction of the venomous voice. She gasped. That face. Now she recognized the man from the card game in Mesilla. And here he was, in Tucson, wearing a gray uniform. How could she have been so preoccupied that she didn't remember him right away?

"Stay out of this, Sergeant." Exasperated, Miles tightened his fingers until Charly winced. "You know *who.* And I know you were the one who released Kent Ashford. Make this easy on yourself, Charleen. Tell us where he is."

Charly couldn't believe this was the same Miles Cavanaugh she thought she'd come to know. Where was the sweet, mild-mannered teacher? The soft-spoken Southern gentleman? This man was tough, and he meant business.

And Red had stalked close enough that she could see the evil menace in his beady eyes.

Lowering her own eyes, she pretended to be contrite and on the verge of confessing. Instead,

438

though, she drew back her foot and kicked Miles on the shin with the sharp toe of her boot. At the same time, she raised her hands and gouged the wrist holding her chin, clawing and digging in her nails until he yelped and released her.

"Damn it, Charleen, I didn't want to hurt you." Miles groaned and bent double, limping as he clamped his wrist to his chest.

She'd already started running, the threat in his voice lending wings to her feet. However, she realized she'd made a grievous mistake the minute she came up against the redhead's barrel chest.

"I got 'er, Major." Red twisted her arm behind her back, bringing her hand up between her shoulder blades.

Charly felt sure her arm was being torn from its socket, but refused to utter a sound that would let the leering beast know he was hurting her.

Turning her head to the side, she found Miles not two steps away. The suddenness of his recovery and appearance, besides the horror of Red's threats, broke her resistance. She screamed. And the strangeness of her reaction scared her even more. "Kent! Kent! Help me! Pleeease!"

Kent had almost come to the conclusion that if Charly had returned to Tucson, she must have gone to a friend's house. There was a light on in the McAllister living room, but he'd checked inside and the place was deserted. Even the barn was closed up tight with the doors barred from the outside.

He mounted the stallion and reined the horse around, but just happened to take one last glance toward the barn. He was looking just right to catch the flicker of a light between two cracks in the door. The flicker became a steady lantern glow.

How do you do. *Someone* was inside.

Then he heard the woman scream.

* * *

Charly tried to twist and turn, but Red's grip was too painful.

Miles came to stand in front of them, wincing as he wrapped his wrist in a handkerchief. "Quit fighting, Charleen. We won't hurt you. Just answer my questions." He was as close to begging as he'd ever come. He truly didn't want to see Charleen come to harm. He liked and respected her.

For that matter, he didn't hold anything personal against the Ashford fellow. He seemed a nice enough sort. It was the damned threat of war, and he had his orders.

He'd been sent to rout out a spy in Tucson and deliver that spy to a Texas prison. No matter his own feelings, he had to follow through.

But when he looked into Charleen's features and saw the real pain reflected there and the almost gleeful expression on his sergeant's face, Miles forgot about his own wounds and ordered, "Release her, Sergeant. Now!"

Red shook his head. "She knows where that bastard is. And she's damned sure gonna tell us." He levered her arm higher.

Charly rose on her tiptoes and moaned.

Miles didn't hesitate a second. He drew his gun and held the barrel to the soldier's temple. "I said, *now*." His voice was deceptively calm and smooth.

Red's face drained of color, but he didn't release his hold. "But, sir, she's no better than a friggin' spy herself. She's one of the enemy." The pistol gouged the skin above his ear. He dropped the woman and stepped back, retreating from the pure rage in his commanding officer's pale eyes.

"She's still a lady, Sergeant. You never treat a lady with violence. As far as her being an 'enemy,' it has been pointed out to me before that war hasn't been

440

declared, yet." Miles narrowed his eyes at the soldier. "And now that I've seen you in action, I have a few questions for *you* concerning the number of drivers that just happened to turn up dead after you stopped their stages. I'd given you strict orders that there would be no killing."

Red backed up another step. "But they was shootin' at us, Major. There weren't no choice."

"You always have a *choice*, Sergeant."

"Yes, sir, but them two, that bitch an' the spy, they're gonna get what they deserve fer doin' this ta me. Yessir." Red held his mangled hand out for Charly to see, as if he was reminding her *why* he was after his revenge. And with his left hand, he went for his gun.

Miles' fist shot out. He clipped Red on the tip of his chin. The older man staggered and then dropped like a chunk of lead.

Charly gritted her teeth as she moved her aching shoulder and couldn't stifle a moan.

Miles came to her and took her other arm. "I'm really sorry for that. But, please, honey . . . If you'll just tell me where our friend is, I'll let you go."

Charly stiffened. Please? For once she ignored the entreaty. And *honey?* How dare Miles call her that—Kent's special name. Just the thought of the way Kent sometimes said *"honey,"* all low and husky-like, caused shivers to race up and down her spine . . .

All at once, with her mind focused on Kent, a feeling of awe shuddered through her. Faced with a situation she couldn't control, *she'd called out his name.* For the first time in a *long* time, she'd realized that she couldn't always handle every situation alone.

She needed Kent. And she freely admitted she needed him *now.* Yet, her stomach rolled over at the thought that if he were there, his life would be in jeopardy. "Kent."

441

Miles nodded. "Yes, Kent. The spy. Where is he?"

One side of the double door was suddenly flung open. A tall, dark figure was silhouetted by the moonlight. "I'm right here, Major Cavanaugh. Now let the woman go and find someone more your size to pick on." His eyes sizzled over Charly, quickly and expertly. Seeing that she was all right, he felt his shoulders lift, as if a ton of weight had just been removed. When he'd heard her scream, he'd been afraid—so afraid.

Miles set Charleen aside. He spread his legs and held his arms out away from his sides. He didn't blame Ashford for looking like the hounds of hell coming to defend the woman. Miles felt ashamed himself for the roughhousing she'd had to endure. But as attested to by the pain in his wrist and shin, she'd done an admirable job of defending herself.

At least now he'd be able to vindicate himself and take the prisoner back into custody. "I'm glad you decided to show up, Ashford. You're the one I was wanting, anyway. There's a nice, cozy jail cell that's missed you lately."

Kent took off his hat and set it gingerly on a pile of clean straw. "So, we're going to do this the 'gentlemen's' way, are we?" If Miles had been going to use his gun, he would've done so by now, Kent figured. And he was more than pleased to settle this the good old fashioned way, with their fists.

His coat followed his hat. Then he waited, watching while Miles did the same. Simultaneously, warily, they both unbuckled their gunbelts.

Miles had been assessing the bigger, heavier Kent Ashford, and when Kent looked down for a place to lay his gun, Miles flicked the end of his belt. The heavy buckle caught his opponent square on the cheek.

Kent staggered backwards. When he regained his balance, he eyed the *gentleman* with a little more

442

respect. Ducking quickly beneath a roundhouse left, he jabbed a hard right into Miles' stomach, then smashed his left fist into his opponent's nose.

Miles side-stepped the next blow and with his fists held in front of his face, began to dance to one side and then the other, keeping the larger man off guard.

Charly stood still just long enough to shake her head at the spectacle the two men were making of themselves, grunting and groaning, pounding each other's flesh to a pulp. Of all the foolish, simple-minded . . . She calmly drew her pistol. Her opportunity came soon enough, when Kent slammed two fast blows into Miles' ribs, driving the Southerner backwards and almost into her.

She raised the pistol and brought the butt down sharply. A grimace captured her lips at Miles' cry of surprise and the sound of the dull thud when the handle bounced off his head. Her heart contracted when the Confederate officer crumpled at her feet. She dared to glance down at his unconscious form and whispered, "I'm sorry, too."

Kent, his breath coming in harsh rasps as he wiped blood from the cut on his cheek, tried to scowl, but the attempt hurt too much. "What did you do that for? I was just about to finish him off."

Staring at Kent's puffy left eye, which seemed to grow worse with each breath he took, she finally shrugged. "Sure you were. I just didn't want you to hurt poor Miles any more."

Kent wiped his palms together, then bent to straighten Miles' contorted body. Taking a rope from the next stall, he was about to bind the officer's hands and feet when something stopped him. He stood looking down at the man for several seconds and then threw the rope to one side. Shaking his head, he turned and came face to face with Miss Charly.

Kent stood in front of her, hands splayed across his

lean hips, head thrown back with challenge still glittering from his dark eyes. Charly thought she'd never seen a more magnificent male. "Why'd you come back?"

Kent was momentarily speechless. All the way back to Tucson, he'd planned what he was going to say, rehearsed a reply for her every argument. But suddenly, his mind was a blank. Why had he come back?

He felt his back pocket for a handkerchief while he tried to think. When he started to dab at his cheek and winced, Charly took the cloth and began to gently soak up the blood, which had slowed to a tiny trickle. She frowned. "Well?"

Kent decided to forget the planned speech and just tell her the truth. Charly was the kind of woman who would appreciate his coming straight to the point— might even look upon him more favorably.

"I had to come back." He cleared his throat. "I caught up with your family and was about to join them when . . . I couldn't go another mile . . . without you."

He moved closer to her and put his hands on her shoulders. "You love me, you little hardhead, whether you know it or not. And one way or the other, when I leave here tonight, you're coming with me." His head dipped in a sharp nod. He was satisfied that she would obey him, even if he had to hogtie her.

"All right."

"Now I know what you've said before, that Tucson is your home and that you'll never leave. But I—"

"All right. I'll go with you."

Suspicion flared in his eyes. "You will?"

She nodded, trying to hide the twitch at the corner of her mouth.

"Why?"

"Why?" She blinked innocently.

"Yes. Why? Why now, all of a sudden, are you so agreeable?"

Charly sighed. "Because I love you. And because I realized tonight just how much I need you."

Kent's fingers tightened on her arms. My God! His Miss Charly actually admitted that she *needed* him? The thought was almost frightening. And she loved him. He grinned and felt his cheeks flush.

"Now why'd *you* come back?" She wrapped her arms around his neck, pressing her body tightly to his.

He swallowed. "I just told you."

"No," she whispered, "you didn't. I want the truth." Her lips teased his with a feather-light brush. He bent his head to kiss her more deeply, but she avoided his mouth. "C'mon, city dandy. I want to know. Right now." Her hips moved suggestively.

Kent lifted a hand to swipe at the perspiration suddenly dotting his brow. Damn it, he hated this female honesty stuff. "Hell, I guess I love you, too. Though why I ever got myself involved with a gun-toting, swearing, hardhead like you . . . I'll never know."

She levered her body up and down his in slow, tantalizing motions. She felt his arousal swell into the indention of her thighs. "I know how rough it's been on you, poor thing."

Her voice was so throaty and seductive that Kent groaned and lifted her in his arms. He searched for the nearest stack of straw or hay, or anything remotely soft to lay her on.

A gunshot spun him around. Charly squealed. Another shot echoed eerily behind the other throughout the empty barn. He dropped her legs and steadied her, then lunged for his gun.

By the time he'd drawn the Colt from the holster, everything had quieted again. He stared in stunned disbelief at Miles, who sat in the middle of the aisle,

445

rubbing the back of his head with one hand, while holding a still-smoking pistol in the other.

A few yards away sprawled the body of the redheaded sergeant, whose lifeless fingers curled around the butt of a revolver. A fine cloud of smoke hung over the still form.

Charly stood almost paralyzed. Tarnation! She'd completely forgotten about the low-life sergeant, and even Miles. It was just another unnecessary indication of how besotted she really was with Kent and how much he'd come to mean to her.

Kent quickly stopped Charly when she headed toward Miles. "I'm not sure what happened here, but I think we owe you our lives," he grudgingly admitted to the blurry-eyed officer.

Miles smiled, then grimaced. "Hey, I needed something to take my mind off your loving display. But if you two criminals don't get out of here, you'll be spending your honeymoon in that jail cell after all."

Kent glared at the *gentleman*, but cocked his head when Charly's fingers dug into his arm. He, too, heard the jingle of bits and spurs and a sharp-spoken command. The major's troop was back in town, probably drawn even more quickly by the gunfire.

He whispered in Charly's ear. "He's right, honey. We've got to hurry." But he grabbed her hand when she would've passed him to saddle the mare. He cupped her cheek in his palm and searched her eyes. "You're sure? You really want to go with me?"

She smiled. "Yep."

He grinned and turned to heft her saddle from where she'd left it in front of the mare's stall. Charly looked into the barn's rafters and silently thanked God and her pa for leaving that jug of whiskey behind.

If the liquid hadn't weakened her stubborn pride a tad, she probably never would've called out for Kent, never would've realized that even *she* needed some-

446

one sometime. Yet, as she watched him quickly ready the horse, a deep warmth washed through her. Her heart throbbed until she could hardly catch her breath.

No, she hadn't needed the jug to make this decision. From now on, she would always need someone—and that someone would always be Kent. Wherever he was, she would always be at "home" in the comforting circle of his arms.

Suddenly, she ran over to Miles and knelt beside him. She kissed the tip of her index finger and held it to the bump on his head. With a wink and a grin, she rose and whispered, "Thank you, my friend."

Kent led the mare over to Charly and helped her mount. He opened the side door and held it for her to pass through. The *gentleman* called out, "Name your first boy after me," and Kent scowled.

Reining the mare into the deep shadows, Charly pouted and sighed, "I haven't even a husband yet. How can I promise to name a child?"

"The hell you haven't," Kent growled as he stalked toward the stallion. "We're getting married in the very first town we come to. You're not getting away from me again, woman. You got that? You're mine."

She just smiled and leaned down to run her fingers through his thick, dark hair before he covered it with his hat. Yes, she was his. And he was hers. She was even beginning to like the idea of having a big, forceful man to take care of her. Beginning to like it a *lot*.

Kent glanced up just in time to see the brief gleam of her teeth. She was smiling. Glory hallelujah! By damn, he was going to keep her purring like a contented kitten the rest of her life.

"Windy?"

He frowned at the weak question in her voice. "Yeah?"

"What am I gonna do? Reckon we'll be anywhere

447

near the new stage line?''

Sudden, frightening images of a grinning Charly at the throttle of a careening engine flashed through his mind. Yet he had to smile. "Honey, you can do anything you want to do."

Their eyes locked. He exhaled sharply. Damn. Her expression read trouble. Big trouble.